STRATHARD

Face to Face

JEAN BISBEY

authorHOUSE®

AuthorHouse™ UK
1663 Liberty Drive
Bloomington, IN 47403 USA
www.authorhouse.co.uk
Phone: 0800.197.4150

Published by AuthorHouse 06/30/2017

ISBN: 978-1-5246-6711-5 (sc)
ISBN: 978-1-5246-6712-2 (hc)
ISBN: 978-1-5246-6710-8 (e)

CHAPTER 1

Stevenson Bruce watched the two little tugs pull the 26,000 ton ocean liner into the St Lawrence River. Around him passengers waved excitedly to the crowd of well-wishers left standing on Pier Number eight. The ship's musicians were playing 'Now Is The Hour'. A spontaneous burst of singing was joined by a blast from the ship's horn while the tugs whistled their own response to the glamorous occasion.

It was an emotional farewell with laughter and tears while the sun burned in a cloudless sky. As the gigantic hull of the liner cut her passage through the river, the Montreal skyline of skyscrapers, like some gigantic three-dimensional block graph, gradually receded into the distance.

Stevenson Bruce, or Steve, as he was more commonly called, took no part in the general excitement. Feeling like a villain in one of his own detective thrillers, he backed from the ship's rail, jostling passengers and porters as he hurried to reach his stateroom on the Empress Deck. He had a mission to perform.

Gaining the sanctuary of his veranda suite, he locked the door, knowing that his self-appointed minder, last seen singing his head off and chatting up a bird, would soon be hot on his trail. What needed to be done must be done and done quickly before he was forced to reconsider.

He extracted a monogrammed black leather valise from his luggage which had been delivered earlier by the cabin steward. He placed it on the chesterfield which lined one wall of the cabin while fumbling in his trouser pocket for the key. With trembling hands he inserted this into the lock. Throwing back the lid, he delved into its contents of shirts, socks and underwear until he found the object of his desperation. He stood for a moment, eyes closed, caressing the unearthed treasure with a far from steady hand, feeling its smooth outline and visualising its contents. His forefinger and thumb crooked stealthily round its neck. His body screamed its demand. A sigh between triumph and torture escaped him as he opened the bottle, avoiding his image in the cabinet mirror above the washbasin in the bathroom, found a glass and filled it. His nostrils quivered with ambrosial temptation and, in one final masochistic act, he succumbed to what was impossible to resist. Only when he'd emptied the glass and had begun counting the five long minutes till the alcohol should reach his brain, did he have the courage to face his mirror image.

He looked the same as usual. His eyes were self-deprecating as they inspected the smudges of shadow beneath their blue depth, the faint network of lines, the unruly, thick, corn-coloured hair, but at least his bone structure was regular and well defined. All in all, he considered, it was a physiognomy worthy of an upright, honest, twentieth-century Canadian.

He straightened his six-foot frame, released the tension in his broad shoulders while muttering on a long breath, 'By God! I needed that!'

It was going to be a hot afternoon. He unpacked then changed into cotton shorts and shirt. He slipped the bottle into the bathroom cabinet before crossing the cabin to the door leading to a small veranda. Opening it, he stepped on to his balcony, sniffing the promise of the beckoning sea. Alcohol on target, he began relishing his renewed vigour and was ready for his adversary.

Talking of the devil! He heard the infuriating knock, a light rhythmic drumming, tauntingly left unresolved. Steve now resolved it with a heavy-fisted crotchet thump on his side of the door.

'Go away!' he yelled.

'Can't. I'm stuck,' was the reply, delivered in recitative. 'I've thrown away the key!' yelled Steve.

More recitative.

'I'll get another from the steward.'

But Steve was already unlocking the cabin door. Buddy Regan sauntered in, humming a phrase from Faust. His name was Benjamin but he was known as Buddy.

'Hey man,' he now queried in his Canadian drawl. 'Hardly a warm welcome. Eh?'

2

'Who says you're welcome?'

Steve watched his friend and agent, chauffeur and mm-der sniffing like a bloodhound through his hooked nose.

His supple bulk padded round the cabin then into the adjoining bathroom. He opened the cabinet above the washbasin smiling with satisfaction as he reached for the offending bottle.

Steve, with as much nonchalance as his growing resentment would allow, leaned casually against the doorjamb. 'Lost something? Eh?' he goaded while searching his pockets for his cigarette case.

'My cool!' snapped Buddy, brandishing the bottle at Steve. 'You bloody, bloody fool!'

'Ah!' said Steve on a long sigh, then inclining his head towards the bottle. 'Have one on me.'

Buddy glared at him.

'Yeah! I think I will.'

He unscrewed the cap then very slowly and deliberately poured the remaining vodka down the plug hole.

Steve's smile hardened but he kept his voice light. 'That makes you feel good? Eh?'

'Nope!'

'Too bad.' Steve extracted a cigarette from a gold-plated case. 'I feel great.'

He offered Buddy a cigarette which was refused. They returned to the cabin. Steve lit up, threw himself on the chesterfield and lay on his back aiming smoke rings at the ceiling.

Buddy, running a hand over his balding head, heaved his bulky frame into one of the two deep armchairs. The ship gave another blast of her horn answered by cheerful whistles from the tugs still on convoy.

'You're not going to lecture me, I hope,' said Steve, smiling, eyes narrowed on his smoke rings. 'You know it won't do any good.'

Buddy didn't answer. Steve swung on to his feet and again offered a cigarette. This time Buddy took one and accepted the light Steve held towards him. He inhaled deeply then lay back in the chair eyeing Steve's guarded defiance with composure.

'You know the score,' he said, 'and as your agent, I am going to remind you that the publishers are pressing for your next book. I'm having a hell of a time stalling them with lies I never knew my imagination was capable of inventing.'

He drew hard on his cigarette.

'Maybe you should be writing the book,' said Steve, again supine on the couch, intent on more smoke rings.

Buddy was not for parleying.

'Unpack your portable and get cracking, for God's sake. We've six days on this barge, enough time to get a skeleton story on type. You can put the meat on when we get to England.'

'Why on earth - I've been meaning to ask you - are we going to England?' queried the laconic Steve.

'That's where the ship's going - to Liverpool. We can think again when we get there - after you've finished a skeleton draft.'

Steve, swinging his legs from the chesterfield, stubbed his cigarette on a maple leaf ashtray.

'Whose idea was it anyway?' he grumbled.

'Yours! You wanted to get away from your troubles, remember,' Buddy grunted.

'Oh yes. I remember,' said Steve, his wide blue eyes feigning a look of sudden discovery. 'My wife left me for another man - a toyboy in a sari with a guitar dangling round his neck. I do indeed remember. The same man - correction, toyboy, took my wife and son out of Canada and into America to join a stupid protest march from Semla to Montgomery. Oh yes! I remember.'

'I only wish they'd done it sooner,' said Buddy.

Steve cursed softly.

'Hell! I forgot. At least my boy's still alive.'

'And mine was one of the yellow ribbons on the stupid protest march to Montgomery.'

Buddy rose, stubbed his cigarette and walked to the balcony.

Steve followed.

'All right?' he asked awkwardly.

Buddy turned on him.

'I'm all right. You're the one we have to worry about. Just remember this. It wasn't the toy boy who took your wife and son from you. It was your drinking and abuse that drove them away.'

Steve bridled.

'I have never abused my wife and son.'

'You can abuse someone without laying a hand on them - neglect, humiliation, derision. I could go on but that's something your wife couldn't do - to go on living with you in the state you got yourself into so she left for something worthy of the salt in her tears - a stupid protest march!'

Hearing a knock, they returned to the cabin. It was the steward to enquire of possible needs.

'Coffee,' said Buddy, returning to his armchair. 'Very black.'

'And cake,' said Steve, seating himself more decorously on the chesterfield.

'No cake,' said Buddy.

The steward looked bemusedly from one to the other. Steve, about to protest, shrugged.

'Just coffee.'

'It's time we talked business,' said Buddy leaning across the coffee table to accept another cigarette from Steve.

'Money business or nanny business?' asked Steve, clicking his gold-plated lighter.

'Money business. I'm serious about your next book,' said Buddy.

'Why?'

'The more books you write the more I can afford a first-class passage to Europe on a first-class liner. I'd hate to travel steerage.'

'Nobody travels steerage nowadays. They call it tourist.' 'Whatever. But it's not just the book,' Buddy added, exhaling slowly.

'Here comes the nanny talk,' sighed Steve raising his eyes to the ceiling. 'You know I won't thank you for it.'

The steward returned with the coffee. When he'd gone Buddy poured while Steve, nursing his annoyance, began treading the carpet.

'Sit down and start thinking,' ordered Buddy. He waited until Steve had settled again and accepted the cup of coffee. 'A repetition of today will soon screw you up again. Is that what you want?'

'I don't know why you're so worried. I can't remember my last drink.'

'I can.' Buddy snarled. 'Two days ago. I had to rescue you from a fight, remember.'

'I've only your word for it,' said Steve. 'Frankly I think you're making a fuss about nothing.'

'Steve, You're not an alcohol abuser. You're addicted!'

'So you keep saying - you and the so-called experts!' he said running his fingers through his thick blond hair. Buddy made another attempt to reason.

'They know what they're talking about. Haven't you listened, man? Don't you know the difference?'

'Stop bullying,' grumbled Steve.

'Haven't you counted the cost?' Buddy persisted.

'That's the problem. The cost's more than I can afford. I drink and I function. How do you think I've written thirty books and fattened your wallet? If I don't drink, I don't function.'

With a struggle, Buddy reverted to his normal gentle manner of speaking.

'You've got to find a way off the fast track to self-destruction.'

'Melodrama!' scoffed Steve.

'Get real,' snapped Buddy. 'You've stopped writing. You've estranged most of your friends. You have health problems and worst of all, you've lost your marriage. The next thing to go will be your self-respect.'

'One Southern Comfort and I'm invincible.'

'And you don't think straight. You can't see what's happening. You do things that in your sober moments you'd never believe possible.'

'And do you think your boring lectures are going to make any difference?'

'Probably not, but it's the best I can do,' said Buddy with a sigh.

'If I want to drink myself to death that's my choice,' said Steve grimly.

Buddy leaned forward, speaking slowly, measuring his words.

'You're not even drinking yourself to death, man. You're drinking to survive, at least that's your illusion. You drink and you feel good and you think that's all right. You won't admit that you drank to feel good before then, and before then, and before then. You've to keep drinking more to feel good a little less. It doesn't ever make you feel as good as you'd like and you damned well know it. You're in a death trap, man. The longer you wait the worse it will be. Just remember that every time you raise your elbow you're losing time you won't be able to claw back.'

There was a lengthy silence before Steve spoke.

'Why should you care?'

Buddy gave a hollow laugh.

'I need the money and there's nobody who pays as much as you do.'

'Is that why you put up with me and my misery? For the money?'

Buddy ignored the plea for reassurance and returned the conversation to safer ground.

'You're in the perfect place for the perfect plot,' he cajoled. 'You only need to promenade the decks and look around you to find your characters. You'll have all sorts to pick and choose from. There are plenty of villainous types around. There will be gorgeous women draped all over the ship just waiting to be conned and murdered and there's the convenience of the sea to receive their severed limbs, all in your usual vulgar style.'

'You're ridiculing my plots,' said Steve, taking his cue.

He knew only too well his books could in no way be described as literature. They were savage but well structured. They were butchery but brilliant. They were yellow penny dreadful stuff but they paid well. They allowed him to buy what he wanted, go where he wanted, do what he wanted to do. If only! He changed tack.

'Talking about gorgeous women, who was that long-legged filly you were ogling on take off?'

'Now *you're* ridiculing *me*,' said Buddy.

'I think she's half your age, twice your height, too much hair and not enough skirt.'

'But you should hear her voice,' enthused Buddy: 'She sings like a linnet.'

'When did you ever hear a linnet sing?'

'I read poetry,' said Buddy. 'But back to your book. I suggest we look around the ship for some background material.'

'I suggest that you fall overboard and leave me alone,' sighed Steve.

'You're not fit to be left alone and since it's costing you an arm and a leg, we might as well make the most of it. So let's promenade.'

Buddy had the adjoining suite to which he now returned to follow Steve's example of changing into something more suited to the heatwave.

In contrast to the air-conditioned stateroom, promenading on deck was like walking naked into a furnace. Passengers, still flushed with excitement, were frantically determined to relax. An assortment of hats and sunglasses protected heads and shielded eyes from a merciless sun. Scantily clad bodies on deckchairs were being doctored in oils. They were the dedicated must-have-a-marvellous-tan brigade. Not a minute to be lost. The ship's rails were still surprisingly crowded. Some passengers were listening to the slapping water on the ship's hull. Others were more interested in the sea craft making their own ripples on the water at a safe distance.

It was all too busy for Buddy. More familiar with the ship's layout than Steve, he led the way to the St Lawrence Club.

'Let's look in here for a minute,' he suggested.

'Is this such a good idea?' asked Steve.

'You might as well get used to bars if you're going to learn to ignore them.' He ordered two tomato juices. 'They look like Bloody Marys,' he consoled as they took their glasses to a table which offered a wide view of the surroundings.

Steve's genial expression was masking inner torment. He resented Buddy's well-meant tactics but knew that without his friend he'd be as useless as an eye out of its socket. He maybe didn't agree with his friend's prognosis but his own company, which was all that was on offer these days, was not enough. His writer's eye took in the details of his sumptuous surroundings.

The French connection was everywhere. A deep-blue carpet was suggestive of the river. Coats of arms of French families associated with the St Lawrence decorated the wall behind the bar. There was a large mural of a brig sailing up river in the early days, in stark contrast to another mural showing the commercial development along the river banks since.

Passengers were arriving for pre-lunch aperitifs, gesticulating and talking volubly in French. The bar was soon crowded. Steve, sipping his 'Bloody Mary', watched the excited gatherings become steadily merrier and louder. These were the seasoned voyagers, already tanned and well oiled. For them no unseemly rush to the deckchairs to bare their etiolated limbs, but rather to herd in the bars, the women with plunging cleavages and fluttering eyelashes, the men behind giant cigars. They smoked, flirted, guffawed and gibbered volubly.

Steve listened to the background of excited chatter and watched men who looked as if they'd just left cattle ranches throw back their drinks.

His irritation, never far below the surface, rose to choke him. Given the chance, he could drink them all under the table. He'd still be walking a straight line when they were flat on their back with their boots on. He didn't understand what Buddy was so afraid of. He could hold his drink. He'd always been able to hold it and could never understand when the quacks told him that it was his extreme tolerance of alcohol that was his undoing. He'd only had a swig of vodka, for heaven's sake. Was he any the worse for it? He was a damned sight better. He knew that he was in control, in spite of the pessimistic predictions of those who'd no idea of what they were talking about. Surely he could allow himself the occasional snifter. They had to say something to justify their fat fees.

'Are we to suffer that foreign gibberish for six days?' he groaned as the hubbub increased.

'What do you expect in the French Club with passengers embarking in Montreal? But the atmosphere's good, eh? Just right for your story?'

'I reckon,' Steve replied. 'Now pick me a mademoiselle I can murder.'

'You need no help from me.'

They left the club. The deck seemed less crowded but the heat more intense. Buddy pointed out the splendid edifice of Chateau Frontenac dominating the shoreline

'It's not my idea of a castle,' mused Steve. 'My kind of castle has turrets and a moat, a drawbridge with a hole above the entrance where boiling oil can be poured on unwelcome visitors. There would be knights in armour riding magnificent chargers and maybe an odd cannon or two.'

'That sounds a good setting for your next victim. Eh? Boiling oil. That's rich,' laughed Buddy.

'I've always dreamed of buying a castle one day but not a pseudo one like the Chateau Frontenac.'

'It might look like a castle,' said Buddy but it's only a Canadian Pacific hotel. Nothing exciting in that, I agree.'

Watching the Chateau Frontenac through his tinted glasses, Steve remembered those dreams when he would own a real castle somewhere in the European heartland. And all those other dreams. What had happened to them? What was happening to him?

They left the rail against which they had been leaning and continued to promenade, filling the time till the scheduled call to deck stations and after that, there would be lunch. Buddy was humming some operatic aria, seeming gently amused and content with his lot. Steve was still brooding on castles and knights and recollecting story times with Sam, the toddler, when they had both inhabited a fairy tale land generously endowed with castles and knights on chargers. He was remembering the cuts and thrusts of their imaginary swords and his angel-faced son, astride the arm of the chair, urging his steed to the rescue of a damsel in distress. Sometimes Susan had joined in the high jinks and they had it all - fun, beauty and love, lashings of love.

Abruptly he changed the film and began concocting a murder at sea. The trouble was, he mused, as he sidestepped a young couple in a clinch, he couldn't seem to summon the enthusiasm for another trash novel. It never ceased to amaze him that some people were fanatic about his trash and couldn't get enough of it. He was beginning to feel on the brink of admitting that he'd now had more than enough. It had lost its punch. It bored him. He couldn't be bothered and there seemed nothing to put in its place.

He became aware that Buddy was transferring his attention from the blue horizon to something or someone nearer at hand. He followed his friend's gaze and saw a young woman leaning against the ship's funnel. She was tall, had long legs, topped by a margin of skirt and a cotton top which revealed more than it concealed. Her curves were in all the right places. Her eyes were brown, shining like a conker newly bursting from its spiky case. Her hair, too, was richly brown and abundant, framing a pretty face.

All this Steve absorbed in a practised glance. She struck him as an interesting victim for his next story. What type of man could he create who would wish to dismember those shapely limbs or cut the heart from such a ravishing breast? What twist of fate would make this warm-blooded creature a victim of such a man?

'It's the linnet,' whispered Buddy.

The woman looked up, startled, as Buddy hailed her.

'Hi there,' he called. 'You're settling in then, eh?'

Steve detected a flutter of concern and an instinctive tendency to flee. She glanced around as if to make certain the greeting was for her although, at that moment, no one else was visible. She recovered quickly returning Buddy's greeting.

'I'm sorry, I don't know your name,' said Buddy as he began an introduction.

She hesitated before replying in a broad American accent.

'Miranda Morrison.'

'I'm Buddy Regan. This is Steve Bruce.'

She turned to Steve and he thought how well the round brown eyes married with the abundance of chestnut brown hair. Her mouth was good, lips curved. Her teeth were even and white, nose straight, skin flawless but there seemed something wrong with her smile. It ill-matched the message of the short skirt and very low cut blouse through which two well-endowed breasts were asserting themselves.

Steve, accustomed to admiring glances from the opposite sex, was slightly discomfited by the close-range scrutiny to which he was now being subjected. Although happy to admire her feminine assets, his interest stopped short of closer acquaintance.

'You sing too. Eh?' she was asking him.

Steve raised his eyebrows.

'Like an old crow,' he replied.

'Your friend - Buddy,' she added hurriedly, 'has a wonderful voice.'

'I was telling Steve how beautifully you sing,' said Buddy avoiding Steve's eyes.

'Like a linnet,' said Steve, grinning.

Her eyes never left his face.

'I could have been an opera singer,' she sighed. Then with a pout of her pretty lips and a shrug of resignation, concluded. 'Itjust wasn't meant to be. Unfortunately recurring throat problems put paid to that.' Her eyes encompassed the sky, the sea and what remained to them of the earth. 'Just think,' she added, a sweep of her arm encompassing them all, 'I might have been singing in all the grand opera houses in the world by now if I hadn't been so unlucky.'

Before either of them could respond, they were interrupted by the signals for Boat Muster and found themselves drawn into the general confusion of passengers attempting to find their deck stations. Buddy had done his homework and knew exactly where they should be. Miranda Morrison tagged along with them. There followed a great deal of light-hearted bantering among the passengers until the ship's officers eventually quietened them to attention. After brief instructions and some elementary demonstrations for life survival, Buddy informed them that, according to the ship's itinerary, lunch was being served informally on the first day.

'Perhaps you'd care to join us?' he asked Miranda.

'Sure,' Miranda Morrison drawled. 'I guess that would be swell.'

'Steve?'

Steve shrugged and reluctantly followed the others to the Mayfair Club which was as English as the St Lawrence Club had been French. It was decorated with madroño wood panelling and ice-blue curtains. One wall featured a large bough of may blossom, executed in metal.

A buffet lunch was laid out on tables along one side of the room. It was already congesting and Buddy asked Miranda to stay at the table he chose while Steve and he fetched some food.

As Steve jostled his way past the surging and highly excited passengers his irritation surfaced. He experienced one of his emergency inspirational inputs, as he called his practised ability to extricate himself quickly from awkward situations. Here was the perfect opportunity to ditch Buddy long enough to buy a replacement bottle. Besides, he had no interest in this woman and Buddy could hardly withdraw the invitation just given and desert Miranda.

'Look Bud. As you have already so aptly pointed out, I have a top priority job to tackle. I think I'll skip the goodies, unpack my portable and start clicking.' He didn't give Buddy time to argue. 'Give my apologies to Miranda. I'm sure you'll have a lovely time together and,' he couldn't resist adding, 'you have so much in common.'

He fled before Buddy could retaliate. He remembered having seen a ship's boutique and set about finding it. He bought a large bottle of vodka. His only concern, as he hurried to his cabin, was where he could conceal it. Thinking of Buddy, he chuckled. Buddy was smitten. He'd been captivated by a songbird. Buddy was no mean singer, forever humming and strumming and occasionally giving full voice to some operatic aria. Great! The more smitten he was, the more time he'd spend with the linnet and the less with himself. He must lend the liaison his full cooperation.

As he hurried to his cabin his mind raced ahead of him. Perhaps one small glass to celebrate? It would also get him started on his outline and after that, maybe a small topping would dull the yearning that never left him. He felt excited at the prospect.

CHAPTER 2

On entering his cabin, Steve saw a buff-coloured envelope on the coffee table. It was addressed to him in his son's handwriting. He placed the bottle on the table, took the envelope in his hands, turning it over, holding it to the light and examining the postmark. It must have been brought on board at Montreal. But where had it been posted? The postmark was too blurred to identify. Could Sam have been in Montreal? Surely not. Montreal was a long way from Vancouver. He felt crushed with a mixture of fear and agonising hope but that was no excuse for postponlng the inevitable. He needed a drink. He half rose in h is chair then sat down again. Would he need it more p read Sam's letter? Better wait.

How had Sam learned of his whereabouts? It could only have ben Buddy. He'd always taken his godfather responsibilities seriously. Bless Buddy! Curse Buddy! God, it was hot. He looked longingly at the bottle on the table as he slit open the envelope with his thumb.

There were two pages of small cramped writing and the first few words told him what he wanted to believe. His son was missing him. That gave him heart to read on. The march to Montgomery was a thing of the past. They had sung protest songs and worn wreaths of flowers round their neck. Now they were home again. Steve supposed that 'they' meant Sam, his mother and her toy boy. He scowled.

"I've been dropped from the team, Dad. Coach said I missed too many practices. Maybe if I try hard, he said, I might get back in. My grades have dropped a bit but I'll soon catch up. Mama says that what I learned on the marches is more important than silly artificial grades or competitive games that can only bring out the worst in me. You know Mama, she can make you feel real good and bad at the same time, but I think more good than bad. Don't you think so Dad?"

My God! What were they doing to his son? Telling him good grades were not important; killing the will to compete; bedecking him with flowers and having him sing protest songs. If anyone had grounds for protest it was the boy's father. He cursed his wife aloud but the sound of her name conjured images that constantly haunted him. He could only see Susan one way, the way he'd seen her when they'd first met. There had been no glamour, no hair crimping or face painting, no fashion-plate dressing. She had no need of artifice. She was nature's choicest bloom. He remembered the heady perfume from her golden hair which fell in soft natural waves to her shoulders, turning into her face, providing a curtain of silk behind which she sometimes chose to hide. She was so perfectly formed, so sweet and gentle, her skin as smooth as a rose petal. He had cherished the delicacy of this prize bloom and vowed to protect it with his life.

He ran his hand through his hair as he tried to remember when the bloom had begun to fade. It had been a gradual wilting. Although her hair still shone and her skin never lost its faint blush, those large violet eyes had stopped receiving him. Instead of melting at his touch or firing with his passion they had hardened like cold steel. She stopped communicating. She had nothing to say any more. Susan never wasted words in futility. She left him with all the explaining to do and he'd made a botch of it.

He grabbed the bottle. As he rose from the chesterfield he stepped on Sam's letter which had dropped to the floor. Replacing the vodka bottle on the table, he stepped on to his balcony and watched gulls diving for the ship's garbage. A few smaller ships had stayed with them, their frothy wake trailing their passage through the water. There was a burst of merriment from below. He was unaware of his knuckles whitening on the rail or his teeth clenching against his consuming anger.

His anger was not against Susan. He had never stopped loving Susan. There had been no other woman after her. He'd worked long and hard to churn out the books in order to give his family wealth and security. And it had busted! They said it had been the bottle. Of course, he'd emptied a few but drink had fuelled his driving power. But it seemed he'd choked his engine and now he was stalled. He wasn't angry with Susan. He was angry with himself.

He needed a drink now, this minute. But first, he must find a hiding place. If he were to be incarcerated for six days he had to know it was within reach. As he gazed at the bottle Sam's face got in the way, halting his move. He remembered his tousle-headed, wide-eyed-with-wonder boy, Sam. No more laughing or ball punching together. There was only the memory of the final painful goodbye. Steve closed his eyes knowing that he must surely close his mind to his own misery.

Maybe Buddy was right. He should fix a new book. He gave a hollow laugh, thinking that fixing was exactly what his writing had consisted of for so long. He fixed plots within the easy framework of a tried and tested formula. His books were more a manufacturing process than the outpourings of creative energy but, he consoled himself, they brought home the money. He grabbed the bottle then decided that he'd postpone that drink. First, where to conceal? The cabin suite didn't offer many options.

At one end of the chesterfield there was a shelf holding a large-based reading lamp. To his relief, the base of the lamp was hollow and wide enough to receive the bottle. Next he set up a make-shift working station and resolutely began an outline of a mystery-horror plot. This came easy to him. He'd once vowed, when quality writing had been high on his priority list, that profanity was out. He had two reasons. He had, in his youthful writing aspirations deemed that a constant use of foul-mouthing was an indication of a limited vocabulary and cramped style. The other reason was more profound. He'd been reared in an atmosphere of alcoholic abuse where curses and clouts were the cannon of domestic warfare. Instead of wasting copy on repetitive four-letter words he'd invested his characters with ingenuity to target, trap and dispose ruthlessly of their victims, all designed to keep the reader gasping in horror rather than relishing wicked execrations. It had worked and now formed the backbone of his plot formulae.

Realising his hunger, he rang for the cabin steward and ordered sandwiches and ate them as he began fashioning the outline of a plot. It worked as Buddy had predicted. He forgot his emotional clamours and stopped mentally abusing himself, transferring his energies into devising what would be his cleverest and seediest murder operation yet.

By the time he heard Buddy's typical drumbeat on the door, he'd restored some normality to his feelings.

'You've got started then?'

'Satisfied?'

'It's what I wanted to see.'

'And what I needed to do. Go on, say it.'

'Don't have to apparently.'

The interruption had broken Steve's concentration. Lying back on his chair, arms raised, clasped hands behind his head, he asked after the linnet.

'She only wanted to talk about you. It seems the more offensive you are, the more attractive you are to women.'

'It's my magnetic attraction. Can be embarrassing.'

'She told me she was born in a Scottish castle where her father was the Laird till he was gored to death by a stag called by the ridiculous name of Monarch of the Glen.'

'You told her, of course, that I am a direct descendant of Kubla Khan. He had twenty-five sons, you know. There are a lot of us hanging around.'

'Her mother then shot herself,' continued Buddy ignoring the interruption, 'and Miranda was shipped off to a rich uncle in California.'

'By the way,' said Steve, 'I've made her my victim.'

'You can't do that. Linnets are an endangered species.' 'She's sure endangered because you're going to stalk her constantly before you dismember her and throw her entrails to the sea.'

'Why me?'

'Because she has something you want and will kill for.'

'Oh?'

'Her voice. It holds you spellbound and you want it. You must have it. For yourself.'

'I'm not likely to have it if I kill her.'

'Ah! But you don't mean to kill her. You only want to imprison her - keep her in a cage and save her all for yourself.'

'And how am I going to find a cage in this tub?'

'Haven't worked out the details yet.'

'I've arranged for her to be on our table.'

Steve smacked his thigh.

'Just what I thought. You are smitten.'

'I feel sorry for her.'

'She's phoney. I can't put my finger on it but she's not what she seems. I've an uncanny intuition when it comes to sizing up strangers.'

'Give your imagination a rest. You're not writing now. She's a poor little rich girl. That's all.'

'Rich. Eh?'

'Apparently. It's a heavy cross to bear, she says. Never knows if people like her for herself or for her money.'

'Married?'

'No, but not for the want of being asked.'

'Waiting for Mr Right. Eh?'

'She kept on about you. Asked if you were married.'

'And what did you say?'

'Never discuss clients with strangers.'

'You'll have one client fewer if you do. Discussion of my personal life is strictly taboo, remember.'

'I told her you wrote books.'

'That's all right.'

'She wanted to read one so I gave her a copy of Bones in the Bag.'

'That should keep her awake at nights.'

'I warned her about possible side effects.'

'Scared her. Eh?'

'I think she's a tougher cookie than she looks,' said Buddy with a smile.

'Where's she heading?'

'To find her roots in Scotland which, I believe, gives you something in common. Your father was a Scot. Eh?'

'Did you tell her that and did you tell her that my father, far from being rich and famous, was a Glasgow drunkard who escaped to Canada for a better life?'

Buddy stopped responding.

'Did you tell her that the one thing he couldn't escape from was the bottle. He had the magnetic charm too and magnetised my mother from a respectable God-fearing prairie family to the Gaz town of Vancouver where the life was slowly and painfully squeezed out of her. Did you tell your precious linnet that I heard him cursing her, watched him beating her, and saw him finally hold a gun to her head?'

'Make him your villain,' Buddy suggested.

'I've never had an alcoholic villain.'

'Maybe it's time you did.'

Steve hurled a book to the floor.

Jesus! I need a drink and don't say anything - not a word! I want none of your smarmy advice, none of your smarmy concern, none of you. Get out and let me be.'

'Your tantrums don't bother me.'

'Is that what you think this is - a tantrum?'

'I never said it would be easy.'

'Look, Bud, I know you mean well but you're getting too damned interfering. You wondered where you'd find a cage in this ship. This ship's the cage and my prison. No cell with iron bars could be more so.'

'Save your melodrama for your book. You're not the first man to have problems.'

'Get out!'

Another book went flying, missing Buddy's head by inches. A third dislodged a picture from the wall.

'Get damned well out!'

'Glad to. Go on. Smash up the place. You can well afford to pay for the damages. And smash yourself if that's what you want to do but just remember those damages will be irreparable.'

After Buddy left, closing the door quietly behind him, Steve made straight for the table lamp, grabbed the bottle, walked to the bathroom and filled a glass.

'To Hell and Damnation!' he toasted his mirror image before emptying the glass.

It was always the same when he thought of his father. Fury. Frustration. Hate. He had dug that groove for so long, he had buried himself in it. The man damaged him more when dead than he had ever done when alive. The more he struggled to escape his father, the tighter he felt his grip. He stood gasping, waiting for the green light when the alcohol should hit its target. It seemed to take forever. Smothering a rising panic, he refilled his glass, raising it to his lips with a trembling hand and gulping it in one.

'That's better,' he gasped.

Afraid to let go of bottle and glass he carried them to his cabin lounge and dropped into a chair blaming Buddy for putting the heeby-jeebies on him and vowing to damn well keep him in his place from now on.

'He's only my agent,' he said aloud. 'That's all. My agent. Not my keeper.'

Slowly his confidence was restored. He went to his portable and pulled the sheet of foolscap from the carriage and read the outline of his first chapter. He was going off the idea of having Buddy as the villain. He was too spineless and anyone who could sing 'Caro Mio Ben' to melt the unsuspecting heart was not cut out to be a villain. He could do a betterjob himself. He sure felt vile enough.

'It's not such a bad idea,' he said aloud. 'I'll be the villain. I'll stalk that filly till I know her every whinny. But it's not her voice I'm after. I want her secret. She is playing with one and I'll squeeze it out of her before I make her walk the plank.'

That made him think of setting the story at sea after all.

Spurred with the idea, he rolled a fresh foolscap on to the platen of his typewriter, flexed his fingers then began to type. Only when he'd finished did his hand reach for the bottle. Then he had a better idea. He'd have a look at the lounge he'd passed on his way from the shop, the one with the splendid bar. The Banff Club it was called.

On his way he stopped on deck to look at the sea. They'd almost lost the sight of land. All that was left was a jagged silhouette against a red sky. Now the water dominated the senses. A few seabirds were all that remained of the convoy.

There was the sound of water lapping against the ship's stern, the faint heart beat of the engine room. Somewhere a string quintet was playing Schubert's Trout. The air was cooler and Steve felt sufficiently confident to have another celebratory drink. But I'm damned if I know what's to celebrate, he thought, as he stepped inside the Banff Club.

He barely glanced at the timbered walls and ceiling as he made straight for the bar. Perched on a stool, he ordered a Southern Comfort and while waiting, inspected a carved mural of totem poles and animals of the West which was mounted behind the bar. Covering the entire front of the bar was a specially treated rawhide burned with famous cattle brands.

His drink arrived. After the first gulp he swivelled on his stool and studied the various groups at the tables. The couple in the corner still carried confetti in their hair. The cruising family of four hadn't quite calmed their boarding excitement but it was the group nearest, spreading across three small tables and one gigantic sofa, that gripped his attention. It seemed to be dominated by a large vociferous Texan with close-cropped hair and well-manicured hands. He was dressed for dinner in tuxedo and black tie. The ladies in the party were heavily jewelled. The Frenchman - only a Frenchman could talk so eloquently with his body - sat with an arm behind the shoulders of his mistress. Only a mistress could be 30 years younger than an elderly monsieur. Steve's eyes recorded the details automatically while his ears strained to catch the conversation. Many of his best stories had been sparked by eavesdropping.

The Texan was bewailing President Johnson's increased surcharge to help finance the Vietnam war. He was allowing no opposition although the Frenchman made a gesticulative attempt to stem the flow and reminded him of the bombing of Haiphong. The American rounded on him, telling him to keep his criticism for his own president who had recently been encouraging French separatism. The Frenchman retaliated by lifting his shoulders, spreading his hands and declaring in the words of his general 'Vive le Quebec libre'.

'Bollocks!' breathed Steve into his drink.

He was feeling good again. He had a mind to join the battle but a ship's officer had entered the lounge and was approaching the lively party. Whether by accident or design, the conversation took a turn to a question and answer on the ship's machinery. The officer talked about double-reduction geared turbines and turbo generators and diesel generators and 26,000 cubic ft of insulated storage space. He certainly knew how to quieten the rowdy passengers. They were in no position to argue with him.

Steve ordered another drink and while the barman turned to replenish his glass, he re-examined the mural and could have sworn that the totem poles had stretched and the buffalo had moved. The officer was telling his apparently spell-bound audience that Marconi radio telephone equipment had been installed which meant passengers could, if they wished, talk to any part of the world.

Steve carefully replaced his glass on the counter. That's good, he thought. That's devilish good. He turned on his stool. The officer had finished talking and was walking his way. Steve beckoned him over.

'Mr Bruce?' queried the officer. 'Mr Stevenson Bruce?'

'You know me?' asked Steve, enunciating his words slowly and with extreme care.

'I'm one of your fans,' said the officer with a smile.

Steve recognised something familiar about the officer's voice.

'I've read all your books, sir, and I've never been able to identify the murderer. You're a wizard with plots.'

'Are you Scottish?' asked Steve, peering at the officer through a gathering haze and pointing an accusing finger. 'I am, sir, and might I say proud of it.' 'Are all the damned people on thish sip Shcots?'

'I wouldn't say that, sir. Mostly French and Canadian with a few American. We're probably the only Scots.'

'I'm not Scottish,' protested Steve with a vehemence which surprised the officer.

'With a name like Stevenson Bruce there must be some connection,' he cajoled but that was a road Steve didn't want to travel.

'You were talking to them about a telephone. Eh?' Steve asked, nodding to the nearby company.

The officer nodded.

'Can anyone use it? Can a-a-a-I ushe it?'

'Sure, whenever you like, sir.'

'Good,' said Steve. 'That's devilish good.'

He offered to buy him a drink but the officer declined, saluted and left. The others were making signs of leaving and Steve decided to do likewise.

It took him longer than he bargained for to return to his cabin and change for dinner. By the time he found the Salle Frontenac the restaurant was full. A waiter who seemed to know who he was directed him to his table where he found Buddy anxiously watching his approach. It was a table for eight. Steve exchanged a keen glance with his agent. He knew the questions in his friend's eyes and he answered them with a sardonic smile.

'Ah, my little songbird,' he greeted Miranda as he took the vacant seat beside her. Her smile was interested but wary before returning her attention to her bowl of Consommé Mimosa.

'Shut up,' hissed Buddy.

The waiter handed him a menu which Steve pretended to study.

'The Crème Marie Stuart is particularly delicious,' the waiter prompted.

Steve sniggered.

'Is she here too?' then in answer to the waiter's raised brows, 'Marie Stuart?'

'Stupid name for a soup,' boomed a voice opposite from the other end of the table.

Slowly Steve raised his eyes and focused them on the speaker. It was the Texan who was forking some jumbo shrimps into his mouth.

'Would you rather it was called Crème General de Gaulle?' he asked.

'I would not.'

Steve eyed the Texan as he downed a glass of wine. 'Haven't we met before?' he taunted.

'I hardly think so.'

The Texan's remaining shrimps disappeared into the swim. He called for more wine and ignored Steve. Steve was in no mood to be ignored. First there was Buddy who was apparently keeping his distance and Miss Mystery who was eyeing him suspiciously and making no attempt to conceal her curiosity. The Texan's wife - only a wife could be so long-suffering - kept her eyes downcast while spreading her pâté de foie gras on her brown bread. Replacing her knife on the plate, she pulled a silk handkerchief from her sleeve, wiped her fingers and delicately patted the corners of her mouth.

Steve leaned towards her, quoting with what lucidity he could manage.

And she would wipe her upper lip so clean
That not a trace of grease was to be seen.

The lady blushed and everyone else fell silent in amazement. Steve beamed vacuously while Buddy cursed under his breath.

Next to the Texan couple was the face of an elderly lady rising from a froth of lace. It bore an expression of lively interest.

'I think you were the man on the bar stool,' she said to Steve.

Buddy dropped one of his melon balls.

'You probably saw my brother then,' she suggested with a note of triumph. 'I saw you looking at us.'

'For my rudeness I apologise,' said Steve with exaggerated humility.

'Oh no please, I wasn't - I did not mean...'

Her colour crept from froth to forehead.

'Eat your avocado,' ordered the Texan, throwing a murderous look at Steve.

The embarrassed lady was on the verge of tears.

'She was all sentiment and tender heart,' fell unbidden from Steve's tongue.

Miranda stifled a giggle.

There was the sound of an orchestra tuning up and microphones being tested.

'It's a dinner dance and cabaret tonight,' the new bride delightedly exclaimed.

'You know I don't dance,' moaned the new husband.

'You promised you'd try. You know I love dancing.'

The waiter arrived with the Texan's fish course of Digby Scallops and his wife's Vol au Vent Toulousaine. Steve was again handed the menu while the honeymoon couple's whispered argument continued.

The waiter, anticipating trouble, suggested turbot and looked relieved when Steve agreed. Steve was showing more interest in the newly weds. He was really enjoying himself. He leaned across the table, waving an accusing finger.

"Didn't you promish to love, honour an' obey?' he asked the bride who tossed her head and shook the confetti from her hair.

Some of it landed on the Digby scallops. The Texan's face sickened beneath his healthy tan while to all and sundry, and to Steve in particular, he announced that cruises were not what they used to be.

'Whas that? Steve asked Miranda as her fish course was set before her.

'Vichysoisse en Tasse,' she replied primly.

'It looks shick.'

Miranda bristled and Buddy intervened before she could retort.

'You're disgusting,' he hissed.

But Steve was beyond insult and grinned idiotically to prove it. The honeymoon couple was stonewalling. The Texan's elderly ladies had donned an air of detachment. Grinning fatuously, Steve continued to enjoy himself. He raised his carafe of iced water, summoned a waiter and ordered him to turn it intowine. The Texan, annoyed beyond endurance, expressed his disapproval.

'Young man, you are offensive. I don't travel first class to suffer such insolent remarks as you have chosen to make in this company. You are forcing me to request another table as far removed from this one as possible.'

Steve staggered to his feet, knocking his chair to the floor.

'Sho shorry,' was as much as he could maage.

'That's it!' the Texan bellowed. Steward!' he yelled and a steward arrived from the wings. Insist on being moved to another table,' he thundered.

Buddy half rose from his chair but Steve who had remained slightly swaying on his feet waved his arms for calm.

'Nobody move,' he slurred. 'I know when I'm not wanted. I'll bid you, bid you…'`

Buddy signed to the Chief Steward.

'Remove your hands,' Steve ordered the latter as he felt his arm gripped, 'or I'll shue you for ashault."

He now had a room full of diners as audience. The musicians, ignoring, or perhaps attempting to detract attention from the fracas, struck up 'Alexander's Ragtime Band'.

Struggling for an impossible dignity, Steve repeated that he knew when he wasn't wanted. As Buddy restrained himself with difficulty Steve staggered from the table and, hardly aware of it, was gently guided to the exit by the diplomatic steward. He put on a show as he staggered out of the restaurant, commenting loudly on the sip's roll and the risen storm. Throwing off all proffered assistance, he staggered on deck, amazed to find a sea as stormy as a dewdrop on a rose. He leaned over the rail, enraptured by the gentle slapping of water on the ship's hull. It looked invitingly cool and deciding to have a swim, he lifted a leg to bestride the rail.

'It's colder down there than you think,' said a soft Scottish voice.

Steve studied the white-clad officer who appeared at his side util recognition dawned.

'Ah – the telephone engineer,' he exclaimed. 'I want to make a phone call,' he lisped. 'You said anytime…'

'Of course, sir. Come with me. There is a telephone very near your cabin. I'll take you there.'

Happily, Steve complied but when they reached the small booth at the end of his cabin deck he stopped and, swaying unsteadily, told the Chief Engineer it was a very private call, a secret call.

'It will be completely private, sir. The system is supplied with speech inverters for that very reason.'

'That's good,' lisped Steve. 'That's devilish good.'

He beamed.

Left in the booth he searched his mind for the number he wanted. He dialled and, after some minutes, he was connected.

'Is that you, son?' he stuttered.

A woman's voice replied, 'This is Sam's mother. What do you want?'

'I want Sam. I want to speak to my boy.'

'You're drunk.'

'Why do you always shay I'm drunk?' he asked plaintively.

'Because you generally are.'

'I want Sam. Let me shpeak to my son.'

He could hear murmuring at the other end before another voice spoke.

'Hi Dad.'

'Sam, son.'

'Where are you?'

'I'm in prison, son. I'm in a prison and I can't get out.' He heard a gasp then the woman's voice again.

'Please phone again when you're sober.'

'Let me speak to my son.'

'Dad?'

'What are they doing to you, son?'

'Nothing, Dad. I'm fine. I must go now. Ring again some time when...'

His voice trailed off and there was a click.

Steve put down the telephone as the booth door opened. Buddy helped him to his feet.

'I've spoken to Sam,' Steve told him. 'Isn't that wonderful? I've spoken to my son.'

Grimly Buddy led him to his cabin, directed him towards his bed, then left.

'I've spoken to Sam,' Steve kept telling himself.

He slid to his knees, lowered his head and wondered why he was sobbing his socks off.

CHAPTER 3

'Drink this!" ordered Buddy. Steve, tears spent, dragged himself to his feet then sat on the edge of the bed.

'Stop feeling so damned sorry for yourself,' said Buddy. 'You should know the score by now.'

'I'm trying to remember what happened.'

'Nothing to be proud of, I can tell you.'

'Oh God! It's coming back. That awful man. I want to be sick.'

He staggered to the bathroom. When he moaned his way back, the glass was on the table. He emptied it quickly. His face contorted in disgust and, with a shaky hand, he returned the glass to the table. Having rid himself of Marie Stuart and the turbot, the hammering in his head eased. He sat, clasped hands dangling between his knees.

'It will help,' said Buddy.

'Nothing will...'

'Shut up!'

Steve, elbows on knees, dropped his head between his hands.

'What have I done?'

'Only alienated yourself from everyone in the dining room and probably blighted your copybook with the crew.'

'That bad. Eh?'

'Worse.' Buddy retrieved the glass. 'You'd better get into bed and sleep it off. I'll fill you in with the details in the morning.'

He slept badly, tormented by demonic dreams. With morning came consciousness and the feeling that something had gone badly wrong. His head still hurt and his mouth was like a bag of sawdust. He heard the key turn in the lock and Buddy entered, carrying a tray which he placed on the coffee table.'

'Don't think you're having this in bed.' he said. 'Get up and make yourself respectable.'

His early morning clinical cleanliness offended Steve,

'I don't want anything,' he said with a dismissive gesture.

The steward's prepared this specially – scrambled egg, brown bread and butter and tea. It's an order.'

Rather than argue, Steve sat up, trying not to groan, and shuffled his way to the bathroom. He stuck his face under a running tap, dried it briskly, donned his dressing gown, ran a comb through his hair, rinsed his mouth and returned to the cabin lounge. Buddy was pouring two cups of tea.

'Might as well stay and make sure you eat this,' he said.

'I'm poor company.'

'Then try to be pleasant for a change.'

Steve attempted a sardonic smile saying he had his reputation to consider. He took an experimental sip of tea, felt better, finished it in a long gulp then held out his cup for a refill.

'Eat,' ordered Buddy.

Steve forked some egg then bit unenthusiastically on his brown bread and butter.

'Your reputation is in shreds,' said Buddy.

'Okay! Okay!'

Steve swallowed more egg, more bread, seemed to approve and lifting his knife, tucked in with enthusiasm. Buddy refilled his cup.

'What time is it?' he asked Buddy between gulps of the hot liquid.

'It's 11.10 in the morning and I've just left Cocktail Music in the Banff Club. Schubert and Brahms. Most enjoyable.'

'I suppose the linnet was with you.'

'No, and isn't it about time you stopped calling her the linnet. Her name's Miranda.

Steve pushed away his empty plate, reached for a cigarette and accepted a light from Buddy who had anticipated his need.

'I'll skip lunch,' said Steve.

'Scared to show your face?'

'It's the Texan's face I'm worried about. I want to punch it.'

'No need to worry about the Texan. I've changed our table arrangements.'

'No Texan?'

'A table for three. It will make things easier all round.'

You changed to suit yourself, Steve accused. 'You really *are* smitten. That bird's sure got you in her beak.'

'Rubbish!' said Buddy unconvincingly. 'Have you any idea how appallingly you behaved?'

'Can't remember.'

'That's always been your trouble. You say you never remember.'

'I don't, most of the time.'

'How much did you drink?' asked Steve.

'For Christ's sake, Bud, leave me alone.'

'Is that what you want – to be left alone – for the rest of your life –no family, no friends?'

'You don't understand.'

'No, I guess I don't. I don't understand why you can allow yourself to become such a self-pitying disaster.'

'It's not my fault that...'

'Oh no. It's your father's fault. I've heard all that before.'

'You head what the shrink said – predestination, genetic tendencies.'

'I heard and I know it makes it harder but you're you. You're not your father.'

'Nor his father before him?'

'If you believe what you're saying you're condemning your son to addiction.'

'Don't you think I know that?'

'Then break the chain.'

Don't you think I want too?'

'Then prove it. Resist.'

Steve crushed his butt on the ashtray. Buddy began stacking the tray.

''Do it for Sam,' he said gently, arranging crockery with care.

I phoned him last night,' said Steve.

Buddy swiped a crumb from the table then went on stacking.

'He knew I was drunk. His mother wouldn't let me speak to him. Told me to ring again when I was sober.

'Why don't you make a pact with yourself that before you disembark you'll speak to him again – stone, cold, sober.'

Buddy rose, lifted the tray and moved towards the door.

'How much longer in this prison?' sighed Steve.

One hand balancing the tray and the other on the door handle Buddy considered.

'Let me see. This is Wednesday. We'll be in Greenock on Monday, Liverpool Tuesday – six more nights. Think of Greenock and phoning Sam from there. Do you think you can stay sober until Monday?'

Steve raised his head and saw what he took to be a challenge in Buddy's eyes.

'You're on!'

'You mean it?'

'Yep'

'Then where have you hidden it?'

Steve's face closed like a trap.

'Steve!' cautioned Buddy as he steadied the tray.

What makes you think I've hidden anything?'

I don't think. I *know*. I'm not budging from here till you tell me.'

With the body language of someone about to offer himself to the scaffold, Steve walked to the table lamp and raised it aloft.

Buddy stared in disbelief.

'You cunning bastard,' then, lifting the bottle, he manoeuvred it on to the tray.

Steve looked at him in mute appeal.

'There is a time to every purpose under heaven,' quoted Buddy, adding 'except to relent. The answer, my friend, is no.'

So saying, he left.

Alone, Steve lit another cigarette. Monday at Greenock. Could he keep in control till then? Six days was a long time. He thought of Sam and struggled against a surge of longing. Agitated, he stubbed out his half-smoked cigarette. Why the hell was he worrying? He was in control, wasn't he? If he wanted to do without a drink for six days he could. He was damned if he'd let Bud put the fear of doom on him. He'd do it for Sam. He'd reassure his son that it wasn't all bad. Monday at Greenock!

He went out on his balcony. Today's heat was no less intense than that of yesterday. There was nothing now but sea and sky. The land was left behind. The convoy of ships and birds had been left behind. The ship seemed to move along on glass. This had got to be a record heatwave. Thank God for money and the comfort of air-conditioned first-class cabins. Surrendering to the sea's hypnotic attraction, he thought again of Greenock.

The word Greenock was no stranger to him. He'd first seen it on his father's birth certificate when going through his mother's papers after her death. When he had seen it on the ship's itinerary he dismissed it as coincidence. He turned into the cabin and stretched himself on the chesterfield. In minutes he was asleep. He slept through lunch, through the afternoon and when Buddy later roused him it was time to dress for dinner. He showered, dressed and feeling refreshed, filled himself with good intention.

When they entered the restaurant Miranda was already seated at the table laid for three. Although she smiled warmly at Buddy, her expression became guarded as she turned to Steve who gave a half bow before sitting opposite. He was feeling quite good. His sleep and starvation had given him an appetite and he was warming to a new confidence. This was generally the case after a heavy binge when it was easy to say never again! He meant to do justice to the food and, with Buddy's clever manoeuvring he could forget about drink. With only the three of them at table, there need be no loss of face.

After they had each given their orders he turned to Miranda.

'I owe you an apology,' he began.

She gave a small flick of the hand.

'That's okay.'

'No, it isn't okay. I behaved abominably by all accounts.'

'It's okay,' she emphasised with a slight lift of her shoulders but she didn't sound comfortable.

'I'd like to make it up to you'

'She said it's okay,' said Buddy, irritated.

'Tell you what. There's a cabaret in the Canada room after dinner. Let's go and you can give us your opinion of the singers.' Remembering that she was supposed to be the victim in his next story, he thought some closer acquaintance might not be a bad idea. 'What's your favourite aria?'

'Pardon.'

She looked blsank.

'Aria, you know – as in opera.'

'Oera?'

'Yes. Did't youell us that if it hadn't been for illness you would hae been a famous opera star?'

'Oh yes, of course.'

'Well then, what's our favourite aria?'

'O like them all.'

'But...'

Buddy intervened.

'I was telling Miranda that you are a famous novelist.'

Miranda brightened.

'I wrote a book once.'

Surprised. Steve looked into those large, nutty brown eyes. They were the eyes of innocence. He was intrigued.

'Was it published?'

'Unfortunately it was lost in a fire.'

The eyes were lowered, their innocence hidden.

Steve tried to catch Buddy's eye but that stalward was examinig the large mural on the wall, portraying the period of change from French to English Upper Canada. Steve looked back at Miranda who was concentrating on her meal.

'What was its title?' he asked, leaning towards her. 'Your novel,' he added to her uncomprehending gaze.

'Oh, I've forgotten the title. It was such a long time ago.'

She turned her attention to the Beef Empress which the waiter set before her.

'Haven't you written since?' asked Steve.

'You're worse than a Spanish inquisitor,' said Buddy, leaning back in his chair to allow the waiter to remove his empty plate.

'I'm interested,' said Steve.

He was more curious than interested. He had a nose for mysteries and he felt he was on the trail of one here. His earlier feeling that Miranda Morrison was not all she seemed was growing and he welcomed any distraction in what he feared would otherwise be a tedious journey.

After dinner they went on deck. The moon now rode the sky. In contrast to the sun's fiery rays, her cool beams shimmered on the water. What could be more romantic than moonlight on water, Schubert in the background and a beautiful, mysterious woman by your side thought Steve? He suggested a moonlight promenade. To the strains of The Trout Quintet, they sauntered off to enjoy the ship's delights. To his surprise Buddy, after a few minutes, said he would prefer an early night. 'Damn,' said Steve under his breath. Before leaving, Buddy reminded them to advance their watches one hour.

'It's nice, just the two of us,' whispered Miranda.

'Damn,' Steve repeated, but this time to himself.

They were not the only passengers enjoying a moonlight promenade. Some romantically disposed were gazing at stars seeming close enough to pluck from the sky. Others were engaged in spotting the occasional surfacing fish. In the shadows couples were embracing. Miranda strolled from his side to lean on the rail. Steve watched her. Any moment now, he guessed, she will raise her eyes to the moon and sigh. He guessed right.

'A penny for them,' he said, hoping it would be a penny well spent.

She turned to him.

'I've never been alone in the moonlight with a man before,' she whispered.

Her polished brown eyes, raised so eloquently to his, reminded Steve of Sam's spaniel, Lucky, when begging attention.

'You're joking. An attractive woman like you should have men falling over themselves for a date.'

'There were plenty of men,' she said, 'but I have a problem. I am a very rich woman and believe me, it's no fun being so rich. I have to be constantly on my guard, never knowing if the man is interested in me or my money.'

'And are you on your guard now?' he asked, intrigued in spite of himself.

'Oh no,' she hastily assured him. 'You're different. I feel safe with you.'

How right you are, Steve thought.

'It must be a lonely life for you.'

He felt he was reading a line from a script.

She turned her back to the sea and, elbows on the sip's rail, arranged the rest of her body invitingly. That was not the distraction which Steve had in mind. She may have the right curves in the right places but he was not interested.

'You have your singing. You like to sing. Eh?'

He smiled disarmingly.

'I love to sing. There was a time when my diary was full of engagements.'

Steve's nose twitched.

'That's good.'

She took a step towards him, presenting her body from another tempting angle.

'I'm sure enjoying your book,' she said, speaking in her exaggerated American drawl. This irritated Steve. He didn't know why. He He had no quarrel with the American accent normally. He frowned.

'My books are pretty gruesome.'

'Buddy told me you've sold millions worldwide. They can't be that bad.'

'There are a lot of blood thirsty folk out there.'

'You're exaggerating,' she said, trying to close the gap between them.

'Believe me, I'm not. They are full of murder and mayhem.'

'But you enjoy writing then. Eh?'

Again Steve frowned, puzzled. He took his gold cigarette case from his breast pocket, flicked it open and offered it to Miranda. She shook her head.

'I've never smoked.'

'You've denied yourself one of life's little pleasures.'

I have to consider my voice.'

'Of course.'

He inhaled deeply looking at the beautiful profile she was presenting as she again turned her concentration on the moon.

'And I've never drunk alcohol,' she said.

'Very sensible.'

She turned again towards him.

'I was once attacked in the street by an alcoholic.'

Steve was getting used to her surprising admissions and was tempted to lay some ridiculous counter claims of his own but it seemed hardly worth the effort.

'What about your family, Miranda? Buddy told me the tragic story about your father and mother. Do you still live with your aunt?'

'I live alone.'

'I'm sorry,' he offered in well-intentioned sympathy

'By choice,' she hastened to add. 'I've had dozens of proposals. Some men were madly in love with me. In fact one committed suicide because I refused his hand in marriage but as I told you, I couldn't trust ay of them.'

'I find that very sad,' mused Steve, wondering how best to bring this meeting to an end.

There was the distant sound of a Viennese waltz.

'Do you dance?' she asked him.

'Not often now but I used to enjoy it.'

'I love dancing,' she said.

'Don't tell me,' he said, 'that you would have been a great ballerina if you hadn't been so tall.'

The irony was lost on her.

'I haven't had a dancing lesson in my life,' she said.

'Perhaps we could dance in the shi['s ballroom some time,' he suggested.

'That would be swell,' she drawled, her eyes fired with enthusiasm.

Why not? thouthe Steve. It will help pass the time.

Aloud, he said, 'It's a date.'

They continued their moonlight promenade. When he later delivered her to her cabin door, she beamed on him.

'It will be wonderful to dance with you.'

'I shall look forward to it,' he lied.

She didn't see his grimace as he turned away.

Later, relaxing his muscles as he prepared for sleep, Steve chided himself for letting himself in for something he might regret. Then in self-defence, told himself he should be grateful. He realised that he hadn't thought of his own problems all night. Better to feel so sorry for her than for himself. That would get him nowhere.

CHAPTER 4

Steve felt that he was between the devil and the deep sea, the former being Miranda in her many guises and the deep sea a morass of self-pity always waiting to engulf him.

Miranda was tireless in her desire for entertainment. Steve resigned himself to activities which he generally scorned and Buddy seemed happy to leave them to it. Steve wondered if this was deliberate on Buddy's part. Did he guess that by giving him carte blanche with Miranda she would provide a convenient distraction for him? How much of a sacrifice was this on Buddy's part? How did he really feel about his little linnet?

With Miranda's insistence, Steve played table tennis, all the deck sports, even bingo. They danced wherever there was music to dance to. They saw Divorce American Style in the cinema and judged a children's fancy dress competition.

Miranda, whether in shorts and skimpy tops, printed cotton afternoon dresses or evening glamour wear, was childlike in her unabated enthusiasms. Steve was thankful to have his days filled and his lonely nights shortened. The only thing that kept him from rebelling was the knowledge i that if he wasn't doing this he'd be making a strong casej for another visit to the Banff Club. Not that he shouldl worry. He knew he was in control.

Tempted as he was to squeeze into the little phone booth; each night on the way to his cabin, he stuck to his guns and determined to wait. He'd set his timepiece for Monday in Greenock when, stone cold sober, he would talk to Sam and, with luck, perhaps have a gainful chat with Susan.

He generally rose early and made a brave attempt at his novel but it wasn't going anywhere. Was he having a writer's block after all these years of prolific output or was it a growing belief that his writing was no longer providing the right source of satisfaction? He'd always suspected, but never admitted, that it was trash but before his problems began it had always provided a bit of fun. Now it meant nothing to him. As a meaningful component of his life it was going the way of everything else he valued. He dared not consider how little was left. There was Buddy, of course, and now Miranda.

The name Greenock was becoming symbolic in his mind. It both cheered and haunted. It meant speaking to Sam and proving to the unbelievers that when he made up his mind to abstain he could abstain. It would be what he wanted and not what they dictated. Hatred of his father had resurfaced and become the largest contributory factor to his present lamentable condition. Perhaps when he laid eyes on the town it might exorcise those fears. Perhaps if he came face to face with his father's early environment it might help him to understand. Then again, perhaps it might be wiser to keep Greenock at arm's length and shut himself in his cabin with the curtains drawn when they anchored there.

In the meantime, the more he pandered to Miranda the less time he had to think about himself. Not only did she claim to have been trained as an opera singer whose career was ruined by a serious throat condition, but she had also written a book which had never been published. She had driven one of her countless suitors to suicide and apparently she had also just missed being chosen for the Olympic swimming team. Steve referred to her as Miss Might-Have Been-Famous. There was, however, one claim which, when put to the test, proved surprisingly true.

The heatwave which had begun on boarding ship at Montreal persisted. Every deck was overlaid with deckchairs on which lay comatose bodies basted in oils and shielded by canopies and eye-shades. Miranda scorned such laxity and, abetted by Steve, succeeded in wheedling Buddy from the library to the swimming pool.

'We can discover if Miss Might-Have-Been-An-Olympic. Swimmer, is as good as she claims,' Steve said to Buddy when Miranda was out of earshot.

'Don't be too hard on her,' admonished Buddy.

'What's it to us anyway?' replied Steve with a shrug. 'We'll never see her again after Monday.'

The Coral Pool, as it was named, was illuminated under, water, from both sides, and the surrounding walls were covered with mosaics depicting coral and exotic fish. But the sea creature who commanded both men's attention as they prepared to dive into the water was an underwater swimmer who was shooting from one end of the pool to the other with long graceful arm strokes. She was hatless, he hair riding the water like exotic seaweed. Both men were' watching in admiration when she surfaced and momentarily, cupped her wet and shining face with her hands. Mirand, spotted them and called them into the pool before slippin' effortlessly underwater again.

'Well, well,' said Steve. 'That girl's full of surprises.'

But Buddy was already alongside Miranda. Her swimming was, without question, superb. Her love of the water obviou to anyone watching and Buddy and he had not been th only admiring spectators. Buddy was a powerful swimme but she held her own. There was nothing gauche about tht water baby thought Steve who, for a moment, considere; reinstating her as victim. This is where the deed could ye dramatically be executed. He visualised a killing by a crocodile or maybe a lurking shark, waiting to rip apart those long lovely legs and arching arms. He visualised the body decapitated and the chlorinated water diffused with the Victim's blood. How his readers would love that.

He was no mean swimmer himself but knew that he was no match for Buddy or Miranda. Long neglect had slackened his muscles. He had the beginnings of a paunch and his body had the unattractive pallor of an indoor cabbage. For years he had neglected even the most elementary fitness schedule and it had taken Miranda's lithe body and water skills and Buddy's superb physical fitness to make him realise this. He felt an increasingly familiar creeping Of self-disgust, warning him of the slippery slope he was on and his need to grab anything that would keep him from tumbling into a black hole. His main support he knew was alcohol. He wanted it. He needed it and sometimes had felt he'd kill for it.

He dived into the water, ignored by the others who were performing some sort of water dance, and swam around half-heartedly wondering how it would feel to be ripped apart by a crocodile. Would it be any worse, he wondered, than being ripped apart by alcohol addiction?

It was Saturday night. Three more nights on board, thought Steve, allowing himself a pat on the back. 'Sober for Sam' bad become his mantra which he repeated to himself when a dark mood threatened his resolve.

Buddy and he had found a quiet corner of the deck Where they settled to enjoy an after-dinner cigarette and a spectacular sunset. The sun was leaving the celestial stage in a blaze of extravagant colour. Even before she sank into the sea, the moon was peeping from the wings. In the distance a solo cellist was performing a mournful melody, as solo cellists are wont to do, and Buddy was unashamedly wallowing.

Steve, comfortable in the evening cool, glanced speculatively at Buddy. He hoped to have a word with him. This seemed as good a time as any to probe his friend's feelings about Miranda before he spoke his mind.

Miranda, it seemed to him, was demonstrating a possessiveness out of all proportion to their superficial relationship. He couldn't take it seriously but should it go too far he'd have no compunction about bursting any romantic bubble her wishful thinking might be blowing. She was beautiful, having all the necessary components - well-modelled bone structure, flawless skin, good colouring and a curvaceous figure - but it did nothing for him. He knew he was using her. He constantly hedged her insatiable curiosity, about himself. He was aware of what lay behind it. Are you available? The last thing he wanted to do was to bare his soul to a mixed-up woman still trapped in the naivety of childhood who, come Monday, wasn't likely to figure in his life again. She would be taking the high road to Scotland while Buddy and he would take the low road to Liverpool. He became adept at the art of fobbing off. He encouraged her other demands as a diversion from his own concerns. She'd helped to subdue his cravings for alcohol. She might be beautiful but she was immature. She didn't ring true. Although Buddy had been happy enough to leave thenf together most of the time, he'd seen the way his friend had looked at Miranda. Her music was a great attraction tó Buddy, of course, but was that all? Could it be that his friend's interest went beyond music?

It was so easy to forget about Buddy's personal suffering A man who had lost his wife to cancer and a son to war within months of each other must surely show the ravages of the experiences. Not so Buddy. Unlike himself, he seemed devoid of any personal fight with fate. Why was it, Steve wondered, that setbacks in his own life were overwhelming him with anger and hatred while Buddy, on the other hand, had managed to withstand such negative forces? He had none of his own confusion or hostility to life.

Steve knew that in Buddy's cabin was his son's guitar. Buddy went nowhere without it. It was all he had left of Em in the physical world and with it the constant reminder of the joy it had once expressed of his son's love of niusic. After Em's death Buddy had gradually learned to sing and dance again and listen to his beloved operas but one thing he had never been able to bring himself to do was play his son's guitar. He carried it with him only as a visible symbol of remembrance but he had never tried to make it sing. That was a secret which Steve had always respected.

'You love to dance, Bud. Eh?' he now asked his friend. The cellist had ceased his mournful lament and Strauss was now on the air waves.

'Why do you ask?' queried Buddy, sitting up and looking enquiringly at Steve.

'If you think Miranda can sing, you should see her dance. She's terrific.'

'She's a terrific girl,' said Buddy, relaxing back in his chair again.

'Why don't you take her to the ball tomorrow night? It's special event for those leaving the ship at Greenock,' Steve suggested.

'I'm sure she'd much prefer your company.'

'I've monopolised her so far. I'm trying to do the decent thing.'

'You've enjoyed monopolising her. Eh?'

'Let's say I've found her useful. Forgive my modesty, but I think she may be falling for me.'

Buddy snorted, 'I could always tell her you're a married man.'

'I'll kill you if you do. That's nobody's business but mine.' 'Then don't send her wrong signals.'

'Haven't you any signals you'd like to send her?' Steve didn't get the answer he'd expected.

'If I knew the right signals I'd want to signal that she should believe in herself more. I honestly don't think she's aware of the potential of her talents. Incredible, I know, but I think it's true.'

'What do you really think of Miranda?' he now asked Buddy. 'Apart from her talents, of course.'

Buddy crushed his cigarette butt with finger and thumb then pitched it overboard.

'I think she is confused and lonely and unhappy.'

'I think that she's as bogus as a baby on stilts,' said Steve, and as American as a Zulu warrior. I figured that from the start.'

'You think so. Eh?' asked Buddy in surprise.

'How many Americans turn a statement into a question as you've just illustrated? "You think so. Eh?" was what you said. That little word eh is a dead giveaway. Eh? It's uniquely Canadian and she uses it liberally. I think your little linnet is a Canadian posing as an American and I think she has a big problem.'

'And what might that be, I wonder?' said Buddy. 'Here she comes,' said Steve. 'Let's ask her.'

Miranda was wearing a strapless evening dress in shimmering gold. It was moulded to her body accentuating her slender waist. She was lavishly bejewelled and her long hair. was brushed back and piled on top of her head, secured by gold combs.

She sat between the two men and began laying out he*j wares to their full advantage: dress, jewels, legs, cleavag and curves. Beneath her sophisticated spread Steve sense., a lack of confidence. He was puzzled. Why, when she was beautiful, talented and rich was she so unsure of herself?

Her mood was ecstatic. A mention of the sunset had her recalling her own previous efforts at oils on canvas to achieve just such glorious effect. How near she had been to capturing the colour tones and hues when they had all too quickly dispersed leaving her thwarted. Buddy listened indulgently, one foot tapping in rhythm to the distant strains of a Viennese waltz. Steve could only marvel at her extraordinary claims and decided to tease some more information from her.

'Where are you heading, Miranda?'

'To Scotland, of course.'

'To find your roots?' he prompted.

'That's right.'

He watched her carefully, conscious of guards rising. 'How do you know where to look?'

'I have my birth certificate. I was born in a castle in Strathard, a small village in the Scottish Highlands.'

'Do you know if the castle is still intact and not now perhaps a crumbled ruin?'

'I know for a fact it's still intact even if it's.

She broke off. Buddy's foot stopped tapping. He was giving his full attention to the conversation.

'If it's?' Steve prompted.

'Even if it's a queer set-up nowadays.'

'That sounds interesting.'

'It sounds awful from what I hear.'

'Go on.'

'I'm a bit scared to go back. There seem to be some queer people roaming around Strathard nowadays. I just wish you two were coming with me.'

'We're going to Liverpool,' said Steve firmly.

'And then where?' she asked.

'Haven't made up our minds. The world's our oyster.'

Buddy was eyeing Miranda thoughtfully.

'You'll be all right. After all, you planned the trip knowing you'd be all right on your own.'

'I thought I was all right till I met both of you. Now I know what all right really means and when you are no longer around I know I won't be all right.'

She was answering Buddy but looking at Steve.

'Why are you pretending to be an American?' Steve asked.

Miranda's head drooped. She began toying with an escaped tendril of hair. The sophisticated façade was turning gauche. Then in one swift movement she raised her head and beamed.

'I'm a good mimic,' she said. 'I used to have the kids in school convulsing when I mimicked the staff. I just thought it might be fun, that's all.'

'I guess that's not the real reason,' harassed Steve.

Miranda's response was to drop her lashes, heave her bosom and sigh. There was a long silence broken by her quivering voice.

'No, I guess it isn't.'

'And I guess Miranda isn't your real name,' Steve persisted.

'I guess not.'

To Steve, Miranda's voice was too stage whispered, her gestures too deliberate, her dramatic pauses too perfectly paced. Miss Might-Have-Been-Famous-Actress, thought Steve, amused.

Above, the moon too was centre staged, spilling her j magic earthwards. Miranda offered her loveliness to its flattery. In her golden sheath, she lay back in her chair in the pose of a Roman goddess but try as she might to offer a sophisticated image to her audience, there was something lacking. Steve guessed it was experience and self-confi dence. It was all one big charade. This was no woman of the world, much as she would like them to think so. She was rich, beautiful and talented but she was stymied. Her world was a fantasy world. Steve found himself inexplicably touched by her vulnerability. Could it be her vulnerability that attracted the protective Buddy? In her own way she was a lame duck and Buddy seemed drawn to lame ducks.

They sat in companionable silence for some time. The music had stopped. The soft sound of the sea lulled Steve enough for him to forego further investigation of mysterious Miranda but, to his surprise, he heard Buddy do a little probing of his own.

'Steve's always had a thing about castles, Miranda. What do you think he'd like about yours?'

'I was a baby when they sent me away,' she said. 'I only know what my aunt has told me.'

'And what was that?' asked Buddy.

Miranda shrugged, somewhat at a loss how to begin. 'Does it have a moat?' asked Steve.

'I don't think so.'

'A dungeon? Surely it has a dungeon.'

'It has a ballroom.'

'The ship has a ballroom. A hotel has a ballroom. Does it have a drawbridge and portcullis then?' asked Steve, knowing he was annoying her.

Buddy intervened.

'Perhaps you can tell us who owns it now.'

'An awful woman. She used to be a nothing but inherited a fortune and bought our castle. My aunt told me that it bad been a gracious home. Lords and ladies and important people like bishops and admirals were my father's guests. Now it's full of foreigners. There are Indians and Japanese and a queer mix of people you wouldn't be seen dead with.'

'How do you know all this?' asked Steve.

'I've read about it. Only a few months ago there was a screed about it in a magazine. A friend who was visiting Scotland sent it to me.'

'Do you still have the magazine?' asked Steve.

'Oh yes. I kept it.'

'May we see it?'

Miranda shrugged.

'What's the point. You're going to Liverpool. You're not really interested. When I leave the ship at Greenock I'll never see you again.'

Her voice had again dropped to a whisper.

'I'll be alone.'

Steve decided that if it was not real then she was a damned good actress after all. In spite of himself he was intrigued. Her boasts about swimming had proved true. Buddy vouched for her singing and he himself had thrilled to her dancing. She had taken to the dance floor like a duck to water. Where did truth and fiction begin and end? The detective in him was mildly engaged but he couldn't overcome a natural antipathy to Miranda Morrison. He wouldn't trust her with a button off his shirt.

'What is your real name?'

'I'd rather not say.'

'Fair enough, but you are Canadian. Eh?'

'Yes'

In the ensuing silence Steve was aware that the music had stopped. On impulse he asked Miranda if she would sing for them.

'I have no accompaniment.'

Steve felt a creeping thrill of sweet malevolence as he looked at Buddy.

'I'm sure Buddy will be glad to accompany you - if you ask him nicely. He plays the guitar and I know he has one1 in his cabin.'

Buddy returned his stare, his expression saying it all. 'You bastard!'

Was he being cruel, seeking revenge for Buddy's relentless campaign against his drinking? Or was he perhaps giving Buddy the catharsis he needed? At least his friend's response would give some indication of how far he was prepared to go to please this woman. He had a moment's compunction while awaiting Buddy's decision.

Miranda turned to Buddy and Steve listened to her coquettish persuasion until Buddy capitulated.

'Give me ten minutes,' Buddy mumbled, leaving them alone.

Steve didn't know whether to be glad or sorry. The lengths one went to on the prompt of a whim, he thought. When Buddy had gone Miranda moved her chair closer to Steve.

'I don't know what I shall do when I don't have you around.'

'You'll survive.'

'I've never met a man like you before, Steve.'

Steve rose and strolled across the deck to lean on the ship's rail. There was a subtle change in the water. It was more disturbed, lapping with greater insistence on the hull. The air temperature, although comfortable, was lowering. Miranda joined him, her arm on the rail touching his. Observing Miranda's naïve attempts to attract him turned his irritation to pity. He was now seeing Miranda, the coquette, on centre stage.

'I wish you would come to Strathard with me,' she wheedled.'

No chance.'

'But what will you do in Liverpool?'

'Write my next book.'

'You'd get more inspiration in Strathard,' she insisted.

He needed more than inspiration if his darkening mood was anything to go by but he reminded himself that this woman had the power to keep his own problems at bay, something Buddy hadn't managed to do with his alternate bullying and encouraging. Even his writing had lost its power to do it. Indeed his puerile attempts at that only added to his problem. But involvement with this crazy mixed-up woman seemed to do the trick.

'Tell you what Miranda,' he said. 'Let's do a deal. Show me that magazine with the feature on your castle and I'll promise to think about it.'

Even just saying the words brought a measure of relief. It set him thinking again of Sam and how they'd shared an interest in castles and knights and folk legends - all a far cry from his totally predictable modern day villains.

She seemed reluctant.

'The magazine is in the bottom of my trunk.'

'No magazine, no trip to Strathard.'

Buddy had returned and was to be heard tuning his guitar.

'You'd better join him,' Steve said.

'Aren't you coming too?'

'I'll hear you just as well from here.'

'You won't go away. Eh?'

'I won't go away.'

'I'll sing specially for you,' said Miranda and for a moment Steve thought she was going to kiss him.

He turned quickly to catch the sight of a flying fish which. had been spotted. He kept his eyes on the gently heaving water.

Buddy was twanging a lazy blues rhythm but Miranda joined him he concluded with a definitive which was like the stamp of a full stop after a long (cated passage of prose.

Steve watched the ship's lights play on the dark He seemed unable to stop his restless thoughts playing on his mind. He had no stomach for a continued life of struggles. He'd had enough. He must find a solution to his problems. He resented his loss of direction, not to mention his loss of wife and son, and couldn't understand how it had all come about. Was it asking too much to expect his wife to be faithful? Matters must be sorted out between them. They owed it to the boy. Maybe he could arrange to have Sam join him somewhere in Europe. Before he got excited by the idea, he decided it was hardly fair. Strong as his good intentions may be, he didn't underestimate the strength of his sleeping tigers. They would awake soon enough. They always did.

His thoughts had blanked his surroundings and suspended his physical senses until he felt his scalp tingle and a long finger of power tap him on the shoulder.

"As from the power of sacred lays The spheres began to move,
And sung the great Creator's praise To all the Blest above,"

He held his breath while he heard, 'Trembling notes ascend the sky and heavenly joys inspire.'

Miranda was singing Schubert's 'Ave Maria' accompanied by Buddy's skilfully executed running arpeggios on the guitar. He turned round slowly, afraid of breaking the spell. A small audience had gathered, They too had apparently been ensnared by the inexplicable power of music. Miranda, like a golden angel standing at the prow of the ship, her back to the dark waters, held everyone there in the palm of her hand. When the last pure note had died, Steve, almost grudgingly admitted that he was moved. This surprised him. Cynic turned sentimentalist? Surely not! But, he had to admit, she had a damned good voice.

What a strange woman. He wondered again what her problem might be for he was convinced that she had a problem. But then, haven't we all? he thought with a wry smile.

There was an outburst of applause. When Steve saw Miranda look in his direction, he raised his clapping palms above his head that she might see. Then she turned to Buddy, and after an exchange of words, she sang again and this time Buddy joined in harmony. The audience gradually added their voices and Steve, once more, beheld the muse demonstrating her powers in another direction. She was unashamedly manipulating emotions from raising aspirations to the gods to dragging them down in protest at the obscenities of war.

Steve found his own spirits plummeting and, like the words of the song, his thoughts were *blowin' in the wind*.

"How many seas must a white dove sail before she sleeps in the sand?" sang Buddy and Steve asked himself, 'How many times must fate knock me down before I can no longer stand?'

He turned away, feeling dejected by his change of mood. He strolled the deck, his thoughts turning again to Sam, comforted by the fact that very soon now he would be talking to him. He mustn't botch it this time. What would, he tell him? Perhaps talking about a Scottish castle would break any ice that might freeze their conversation. Suppose. he were to tell him that he was on his way to visit one and would write and tell him all about it. But would that be fair? He wasn't sure himself yet and he didn't want to make any promise which he couldn't keep. He didn't trust Miranda. She lived in a make-believe world most of the time and the Scottish castle might well be part of that. But why on earth should she dream up such a story without some reason? It was intriguing. He wondered if he should return and offer his congratulations but there would be time enough for that. In the meantime he had a better idea.

He was approaching the Banff Club. He glanced in as he passed, attracted by the bright colours and gay voices, the music and the excitement of people at play. He walked on, his steps dragging. He hesitated then turned back and entered the Club. Weaving his way among his fellow passengers he headed straight for the bar and ordered a large bottle of vodka for taking out. It was the greatest challenge he could give himself and the greatest commitment to Sam.

Smiling, and ignoring other temptations, he carried it back to his cabin. This was not for drinking. On the contrary, it was to make sure that he would not drink. He was upping his temptation so that he could up his determination. If he could just look at it and see it for the devil it was and tell it to go to hell then he would have passed the third degree and be well on his way to initiation into the noble rank of total abstainers. Surely that was something to sim for. You must help yourself, the shrink had said. Right. This was his way of helping himself.

Back in his cabin he looked around, decided against the table lamp and the cistern and pushed the bottle under his pillow.

With a new strength of mind he was happier than he'd en since boarding. Was the power of music still working ri his psyche or was it the thought of Greenock, two days tead? Whatever! He felt battle empowered.

And thrice he routed all his foes, and thrice he slew the slain!"

More hopeful than he'd been for a long time, he lay on the chesterfield with a cigarette. He was almost glad to hear Buddy's familiar knock. So glad in fact, that without thinking he replied in recitative. Buddy entered with such a comical look of amazement that Steve let rip with laughter.

'Well I'll be damned!' Buddy exclaimed.

'You see before you a reformed man,' said Steve. 'You see before you a reformed man,' said Steve 'I think you can thank your linnet's singing for the transformation.'

'You think she's good. Eh?' said Buddy.

'Surprisingly good.'

'She sent you this,' he said throwing a magazine on the coffee table.

'So there is one.'

'A most impressive article on Strathard castle. Read it.'

'I intend to.'

'We'll talk about it in the morning,' said Buddy then, to Steve's surprise, abruptly left.

Idly, Steve flipped to the castle feature. He saw a two page spread of a baronial style castle set against a background of moor. There was an impressive entrance classical style, turrets, and circular lawn with statue. He turned the page and saw the image of a woman with a mass of red

We are here. We are letting it be known that we are here. Not everyone will be, or indeed can possibly be interested but those who identify with our thinking and feel we could satisfy a need will, we believe, find us.

Interviewer:

Do you really think this little remote community can possibly do any good for humanity?

Jenny Fraser:

Good, like most things capable of growth, has to begin somewhere. Quality is vital.

Interviewer:

How do your visitors react when you tell them this?

Jenny Fraser:

We don't tell them. Individuals cannot be told how to think. They must find out and decide for themselves but they also must have the information of a variety of ways to do so. Our service is to find and furnish this information. It is then up to the individual to make his own choice. If the information on offer is quality information there is more likely to be quality choices made and that, in the end, must be good for humanity.

Interviewer:

What you are really doing is fighting prejudice. Am I right?

Jenny Fraser:

You could say that but I prefer the word *counteracting*.

He flipped back a page and looked again at the pictures of the extensive horticultural fields, surrounding forestry, farm animals, stables and an impressive looking library.

Laying aside the magazine he lit another cigarette, inhaled and thought about what he had just read. Although he was intrigued he didn't pretend to understand it. It all sounded a bit weird and unrealistic. Was it worth a change of plan? Miranda was not all that importantto them. They had no need to feel obliged to dance to her tune. But what was the alternative?

Liverpool? Another town, another hotel room, another prison? Then where? At least Strathard offered a castle, an unconventional communal experience – useful for a writer – and that face of exceptional radiance.

nterviewer: What you are really doing is fighting prejudice. Am I right?

Jenny Fraser: You could say that but I prefer the word counteracting.

He flipped back a page and looked again at the pictures the extensive horticultural fields, surrounding forestry, n animals, stables and an impressive looking library.

Laying aside the magazine he lit another cigarette, inhaled and thought about what he had just read. Although he was intrigued he didn't pretend to understand it. It all sounded a bit weird and unrealistic. Was it worth a change of plan. Miranda was not all that important to them. They had no need to feel obliged to dance to her tune. But what was the alternative? Liverpool? Another town, another hotel room, another prison? Then where? At least Strathard offered a castle, an unconventional communal experience – useful for a writer - and that face of exceptional radiance.

Stubbing out his cigarette, he went to his typewriter and the next hour pounded the keys and gave his imagination free rein. When he'd finished he was flushed with satisfaction. It maybe wasn't quality, he mused, but the quantity should be enough to satisfy the bloodhound Buddy. He stretched himself then walked confidently to his bed, pulled back the covers and unearthed the bottle of vodka from beneath his pillow. Smiling, he turned it slowly in his hands. He was admiring its beauty and telling it that it had lost its power over him when Buddy, after the most peremptory of knocks, burst in.

'God almighty!' he said. 'Is there no stopping you?'

'Steady on,' said Steve, showing no sign of contrition. 'You've the intelligence of a toad and seem to think you have the constitution of an elephant.'

'I can handle it,' said Steve without rancour. 'This is guarantee that I won't let a drop pass my lips.'

'Balderdash! You're a sneaking, conniving imbecile, thinking of nobody but yourself. You're not worth a rat's tail!'

'My, my! Toad, elephant, rat. What next, I wonder.'

'You're a Judas.'

'At least I'm in human form now.'

'You're sub-human.' But Buddy's assault was weakening. 'I don't get you Steve. I really don't.'

'That's something we agree on. I think you've be paying too much attention to the shrinks.'

'More than you have, apparently.'

There was an audible weariness in Buddy's attack now.

'Come here,' said Steve beckoning. 'Let me show you something.' He walked towards his work station lifting his bundle of A4 sheets and placing them in Buddy's hands.

'That makes you happy. Eh?'

'What is it?'

'The completed skeleton outline and first three chapters of what you've been crying out loud for since we board this floating prison.'

'You *have* been drinking,' accused Buddy unable to restrain an exploratory sniff.

'Wrong. Alcohol had no part in it. I've found other incentives.'

'Like what?'

'Never mind that. Aren't you happy for me? I've quit.'

'Where have I heard that before?'

'Your confidence in me is touching.'

'Steve mate, I *fear* for you.'

'Back off!' Steve's rush of irritation surprised himself but he did nothing to curb it. 'Mind your own bloody business. If I say I've quit then you better believe me. I've quit. Got it,' said Buddy grimly.

He turned and left the room.

Steve sat for a long time on the verge of misery. What was the matter with him? Why did his view of the world change everytime he lost his temper. Was his sense of proportion going the way of everything else? He couldn't afford to ostracise Buddy. He needed him. He was an okay guy and if he wasn't careful one of these days he would try him a step too far. He rose, swayed slightly as the ship adjusted itself to the outside storm and made his way to Buddy's cabin. He'd got to put things right. Hands poised to knock, I waited, listening.

Where have all the young men gone, long time passing.'

It sounded for all the world like a dirge.

Where have all the young men gone, they are all in uniform.'
Should he? Shouldn't he?

'Where have all the soldiers gone, long time passing.
Where have all the soldiers gone, gone to graveyards every one.'

He'd had enough! After a peremptory knock, he opened the doorr.
Buddy was sitting on his chesterfield, guitar on his knee, a glass of whisky
on the table beside an ashtray over-spilling its mess. He barely raised his
eyes when Steve sat opposite but went on singing in mournful voice.

'Where have all the graveyards gone, covered with flowers every one.'

-Steve let him finish, empty his glass, light a cigarette, accept one on
offer before speaking.

'I guess this is my fault,' he said. 'I've opened wounds, I'm sorry.'

'It had to come some time,' said Buddy, disentangling the instrument's
strap from his neck. 'It's been a long time passing, I suppose.'

'Damned war,' sympathised Steve, thinking it a safe response. 'What's
it all about, Bud?'

'Political stupidity,' said Buddy. 'That's what it's all about. Damned,
bloody, political stupidity. It's a war that never should have happened.'

Steve felt awkward. He wasn't much good at plunging into discussions
with any depth. He'd given up trying to make sense out of existence a long
time ago. When you were raised in violence and had no adequate defence
against it, the last thing you got to expect was reason. It was only when he met
Susan that he had found a reason for existence and the nearest he'd come to
contemplating it divine was when he first held his son in his arms. There had
been a tip of the sea-saw then. A working balance had been restored and for
the first time he thought he knew what it was all about. Now he wasn't so sure.

'I guess I haven't been much good to you lately,' he sai with misgiving.
'I've been nothing but a bloody nuisance.'

'For God's sake, don't get maudlin,' said Buddy, 'and take your soulful
eyes off that tumbler. I wasn't expecting you.'

'I'm not in the least tempted,' said Steve, astonished to discover that,
for the moment at least, he was not.

'No?'

'No!'

'Why are you here? It's not like you to make social calls on the
neighbours.'

Carefully Buddy returned the guitar to its case. His actions were slow and, to the watching Steve, seemed almost reverential.

'I've read the magazine article about Strathard Castle.'

'And?'

Imprssive stuff, but a bit over the top, I thought.'

'Is the concept of quality too much for your imagination to handle?' asked Buddy with the faintest of uncharacteristic sneers.

'It's an impossible ideal,' replied Steve, ignoring the nuance. 'People are only human...' he began.

'What profundity,' scorned Buddy, making no attempt to conceal the accompanying sneer.

'You know what I mean?' stumbled Steve.

'I don't know what you mean and for someone who makes a living from his pen you lack lucidity.' Buddy looked at Steve. 'I take it you're not interested in visiting this quality castle. Eh?'

'That's why I'm here. I'll give it a go if you will.'

Buddy brightened.

'Mind you,' said Steve. 'I'm not sure how I'll cope with Miranda. She's heavy going.'

'I'm afraid you will have to bear the brunt a little longer. I want you to take her to the ball tomorrow. No, hold on and listen to me. I've letters to write for posting when we embark. They're important. I'll also drop a line to the publishers and reassure them that we're in business again. I'll have to spend the rest of the day making alternative arrangements for disembarking.'

'Just a minute,' began Steve.

'No arguing. Do as you're told and give the girl a night to remember.'

Steve groaned. Buddy wished him goodnight and there was nothing for it but to return to his own suite and go to bed. Before switching off his light Steve looked again at the magazine, at the pictures of the castle, the extensive horticultural fields, forestry, stables, farming and the magnificent library. Then he turned once more to the picture of Jenny Fraser.

He fell asleep, unaware of the rain now lashing the decks and he dreamed that he was with Sam and that they were dressed as Knights of St John, carrying shields and riding horses. They saw a castle before them and Susan leaning out of a turret window, beckoning them but when drew rein beneath the turret they saw that Susan had red hair.

CHAPTER 5

It was Sunday morning, one day before the ship was due to anchor off Greenock. The weather had changed dramatically. After breakfast, when Steve went on deck, there were few passengers to be seen. Those he did see were covered in plastic macs and unsteady on their feet.

In spite of the ship's bulbous bow designed to reduce pitching and in spite of the stabilisers designed to reduce roll Steve had a struggle keeping his own balance - in spite of being sober!

Buddy and Miranda were singing hymns together at e Service in the Canada Room. Their change of plan had been discussed at breakfast. Miranda was ecstatic that they were to be with her in Strathard and expressed a desire to give thanks to the Lord, another of her personality facets, thought Steve who had declined her invitation to join her. Buddy, as always, had succumbed to her persuasive powers.

He'd welcomed the bracing wind after an hour's concentrated effort at his typewriter. He was feeling good. He'd weathered his doldrums and hoped for better days ahead. Why was he feeling so high spirited? Was it the breaking of writer's block? Was it the ear prospect of speaking to Sam? Oe perhaps it was because he'd lost the temptation to drink. There might be another reason, he mused. It could be beause of his dream where, as a knight of chivalry, he'd ridden horseback with Sam and seen the lovely Susan – with red hair!

Whatever the reason, Steve felt grateful. He lifted his face to enjoy the feel of rain on his skin and the taste of it on his tongue. He wasn't singing hymns but he was, in gratitude, experiencing a divine service of his own. As he stood between two lifeboats, grabbing the ship's rail, he leaned into the storm. Was he ever going to beat the curse? One thing was for sure. As long as he tolerated a burning resentment of his father, he didn't have a cat's chance in hell. Just thinking about him now threatened his feel good factor. He smiled grimly because in spite of all that, he was about to set foot in the place where his father had been born. He must think of Sam. The kid was missing him. That's what he'd said.

'Good day to you, Mr Bruce.'

Lost in his thoughts, Steve hadn't seen the ship's offlcer approach. It was the Chief Engineer.

'A bit rough,' said Steve.

'Ach! That's nothing. A wee bit rain never did anyone any harm.'

'I'm rather enjoying it,' said Steve, surprised at how receptive to the other man's company he felt.

'I hear you've had a change of plans.'

'That's right. How did you know?'

'Your friend, Mr Regan, has been making all the necessary arrangements. He was asking about Greenock and what to expect when we drop anchor there.'

'And what did you tell him?'

'More rain! This wee drizzle is just to break you in.'

'Is that a joke?'

'Indeed no. It will be raining when we drop anchor. You can bet your bottom dollar on that - as they say in your country.'

I'm Canadian, not American,' said Steve.

'Ach! I should have known better. You don't like people ng you up. Just like some folks calling us Scots English. It doesn't half get our danders up.' Then in answer to Steve's puzzlement, 'Raise our hackles. Ye ken.' He chuckled. 'I myself was born in the town of the green oak, other famous folk I could mention. James Watt, for instance.' He laughed at his own joke. 'Now there's someone Greenock can be proud of. You've heard of James Watt, I take it?'

Not a word.'

cottish engineer, inventor, chemist, to mention but a of what he did. Great man. If you haven't heard of him so far, they won't let you forget him in Greenock. Greenock is proud of James Watt. Watt institution, Watt scientific library, Watt memorial school of engineering and of course,

James Watt harbour. Aye. He was a great man,' concluded the engineer, a soft secret smile on his face.

Is it a pretty town?' asked Steve.

I wouldn't call it pretty. Indeed no. Not pretty. I'd say it was more interesting than pretty.'

'And what about the people - apart from the famous ones, like yourself'

'And James Watt?' Steve asked, smiling.

'The same as everywhere else, lad. There's the good, the bad and the waverers. They're the sons and daughters of steelmen, Clyde shipbuilders and navigators, hard working and hard drinking, you might say.'

Steve, still gripping the rail, swayed in sync to the ship's motion.

'Is drink a problem in Greenock?' he asked.

'Drink laddie, is a problem everywhere. There's an old proverb which says "When drink's in, wit's out. Never touch the stuff myself.'

Fortunately the engineer got off the subject of drink.

'Stevenson Bruce,' he was chanting softly. 'Aye, a Scottish name. Robert Louis Stevenson and King Robert Bruce, the saviour of the Scots.'

'Say that again,' asked Steve.

It was not that he hadn't heard. He wanted to hear those r's rolling round the engineer's Scottish tongue. 'Robert the Bruce.'

'He was the one with the spider. Eh?'

The officer edged closer, talking above a sudden gust.

'Don't let that fool you,' he shouted. 'It wasn't the spider who tried and tried and tried again that won the battle of Bannockburn.'

'No?'

'Oh no,' laughed the officer. 'It was the Knig Templar.'

The ship rolled after a bigger than usual sea swell. Water dripped from both men's jackets. Steve's hair was plaster to his scalp and his eyes screwed against the sheeting rain. It was invigorating stuff after the recent heatwave but bc men had had enough. By silent consent they fought their way below deck where the quiet seemed startling after the raging storm above.

'You'd better get out of these wet rags,' grinned the seaman who was sensibly protected.

Anxious as he was to shower and change, there was one word still ringing in Steve's ears which he wanted explaiñ 'You said Knights. Eh?'

'The crusaders. The Knights Templar, made quite a name for themselves. Got rich. Had to flee the continent or be tortured to death. Inquisition. Took to the ships with their treasure. Some found refuge in Scotland. Grateful. Good timing. Robert the Bruce heavily outnumbered by the English. Knights joined in the fray but,' warned the officer with finger to lip, 'for heaven's sake don't tell the English. Let them think it was the spider.' He grinned. 'There's a wee book in the library will tell you all about them. It's called Encyclopaedia.'

With that he strode off, calling over his shoulder, 'Don't advance your watch tonight. We're in British Summer Time now.

'Some weather!' called Steve before making his way towards the joy of a hot shower and the comfort of dry clothes.

In no mood for Miranda's possible religious fervour after morning service, he decided to skip lunch and have e and sandwiches brought to the cabin. He felt remarkably fit. After he'd chewed his last crust of bread and gulped his last dregs of his coffee, he sat at his typewriter and sketched the outline of a mini-saga about knights on the high seas fleeing the horrors of the Inquisition. He could write this story for Sam. He typed fast, skipping detailed descriptions for later, after he'd read the wee book in the library. For the moment he let his imagination milk the horrors of the knights' escape. He was good on horrors. Normally they were clinical passages in his writing but he felt more passionately involved in this one. He was thinking of the feelings of these fleeing knights, tossed in their little ships going to God knows where because of God knows what.

His keys rattled without stop and he felt a mounting high that brought only good feelings. His eyes never strayed from the page, missing the visible signs of the grey, damp world outside. When he'd finished, he decided there was no better time than now to visit the library and seek out the details to add flesh to the bones of the story and give it authenticity.

He met few people on his journey. Those he did were looking ill at ease which only added to his exultation at his freedom from sickness. The library was hushed and it didn't take long to find the encyclopaedia and extract some relevant detail. Knights of Jesus Christ and the temple of Solomon. Founded 1118 along Cistercian lines hence cloak and red cross. Pilgrimages, travel, banking organisations, holy wars and crusades. A pretty distinctive band of men, he thought. Age of chivalry. Ideal and perfect knights trained and destined to become incorruptible civilising power. Up against the political and the pious pope. Their power resented and envied. 1307 slaughter of Templar order. Ah, there it was. "Templars fought at Bannokburn. It is a fact of life that the Templar suppression ordered everywhere in Europe with the exception of Portugal and Scotland where no order for suppression was issued."

By the time he left the library his mind was buzzing knights, chivalry, the overcoming of obstacles and of all barriers of faith and fortitude. Wouldn't Sam love this stuff he thought. I'll make it live for him. If I don't write another junk book it doesn't matter. I'll write for Sam and then it's got to be good.

Passing the cinema he saw that *Triple Gross* was billed so went in and whiled away a couple of hours, time enough to face the oncoming ordeal of the evening, The ball Miranda! Thank God this was the last night on board.

The Carleton restaurant (tourist class) was named Sir Guy Carleton, the first Governor General of Upper Canada. They had previously decided to dine in tourist on their last evening, guessing it might be jollier. At least Buddy and Miranda had decided. When Steve arrived for dinner he felt an air of festivity among the ship's passengers and crew. The earlier isolated groups of strangers unsurprisingly, after five days and nights of communal experience, merged into an over-all pattern of belonging together. He wove his way among the high-spirited diners to the table where Miranda and Buddy were seated, deep in conversation.

It was the last dinner on board which many of the passengers would enjoy and they were making the most of it. Streamers draped the two giant murals, balloons were tied to the balcony and flowers coloured the damask linen on every table. Amidst the general hum of conversation and descant of laughter could be heard the popping of champagne corks.

When Steve looked at Miranda his heart sank. She was a vision of Marquise Pompadour with elaborate hair-style and low, revealing bodice. Her make-up was theatrical and her dress flamboyant. She was like a hothouse orchid and totally out of sync with the other female revellers. Was he expected to circuit the dance floor with this disastrous female in his arms? However, he hadn't been reading about Chivalry to no avail. He managed an easy smile and glib complement. He glanced at Buddy who was studying the menu and discussing roast milk-fed chicken with the waiter. When his own turn came he settled on the first familiar item he saw and ordered quarters of lamb, roasted with hot mint sauce. Buddy had spared him the embarrassment of refusing wine. A bottle of some innocuous red dye was already on the table. Miranda, the coquette, was on stage now. Buddy was forgotten and her wiles were totally directed at Steve.

He was reminded of his High School days when lanky teenagers followed him around the campus vying with each other for his attention. His favours had been bestowed as casually then as they were now. He found himself glibly complimenting and seeing how much it would take to throw her into confusion. He was misleading her and he knew it but then again, she was providing him with an antidote to his own discomfort. His attempts at chivalry had dissipated. So be it.

Buddy's non intervention seemed to give his seal of approval. He didn't deceive Steve who recognised that straight lip line, the slightly glazed eyes and fixed smile.

Miranda was aware only of the flattering attention She was receiving. She had eyes only for Steve. There was only one person there for her and he was, without her knowing, quite intentionally roping her in to the full. In his Hiigh School days he would have said he was making a catch. He forgot she irritated and annoyed him. He was remember a taste of his old power to conquer. He was simulating courting rituals almost forgotten, remembering the peacock feathers long since shed.

They had finished coffee when Buddy surprised them with a small neatly wrapped parcel he'd produced from his pocket.

'This is from Steve and me,' he told Miranda passing her the packet. 'A small gift to commemorate our crossing the Atlantic together. Steve's idea,' he added.

'Oh Steve! That's swell of you.'

Steve cringed.

'Buddy's too modest. He's the one with the inspiration'

'Thank you both. May I open it now?'

'Sure,' said Buddy while Steve looked on in amuseme Trust Buddy to spring the odd surprise. Slowly and with great many girlish gasps of rapture Miranda undid t wrapping, revealing a bottle of perfume.

She exclaimed in delight while Steve stared in sudden anguish. Damn Buddy, he thought as he watched Miranda remove the stopper and sniff, eyes closed, lips parted before saying in a whisper, 'Coco Chanel. It's my favourite How did you know?'

Buddy knew, thought Steve grimly. Buddy knew it was Susan's perfume. Miranda upturned the bottle on forefinger then transferred it to the hollow of her throat.

She continued to perfume her wrists and behind her ears all the time ejaculating little gasps of pleasure and delight.

Steve wasn't prepared for the full impact of the perfume on his senses. A yearning for Susan threatened to overwhelm. He wanted her. He needed her. He loved her. If he'd imagined he could do without her, how wrong he'd been.

He couldn't go on with this farce, he decided, but a look at Miranda's face, bright with expectancy, cautioned him. At the end of the feast Buddy said, 'Isn't it time you two went tripping the light fantastic?'

Miranda, after pushing perfume and paper wrapping into her small sequinned evening bag turned to Steve.

Shall we?' she asked with the slightest hint of uncertainty Steve sensed rather than witnessed.

He rose from his chair and bowed gallantly. He crooked an arm which Miranda readily accepted and together they left the dining room. Buddy was ignored.

The ball was scheduled for the Canada Room. They made their way up the curved staircase to the Empress Deck. The storm outside was still raging. Miranda took a tighter grip on his arm as the deck rolled slightly beneath them. They stood together inside the ballroom, Miranda still clutching Steve's arm which she had refused to relinquish.

There was a dome 20 feet above the dance floor, decorated with the moon and stars. A balcony ran round three sides of the room. Pale willow-wood panels were contrasted with dark-green curtains. The carpet which was specially woven had a golden background and incorporated the ten flower emblems of Canada - the Alberta rose, dogwood for British Columbia, Manitoba crocus and so on. To add to the effect Canadian leaf motifs were etched on glass screens.

Steve absorbed the scene as if from a great distance. He was well conditioned to note detail and while the New Brunswick violet and Prince Edward Island's lady's slipper received his automatic attention his heart was in Vancouver in a condominium where Susan and he first set up a home together. When married to Susan, with every day that passed, his father had faded to a bad dream. Only the good memories of his mother were retained. All the hatred and loneliness of his early days were buried and forgotten wi Susan came into his life. He adored her. They adored each other. Together they brought Sam into the world. He was the seal upon their happiness. They made friends. They partied, loved and laughed a lot.

He'd never been trained for a profession. His skills were limited, his income low and then he discovered he had the notion to write. He wrote and sold his first ever story to the local rag. Susan and he were over the moon. They were happy. He was going to write novels that would move the earth and make them rich. For a year he sold nothing else. They were still happy. Susan found a job in a craft shop in the Mall while he baby minded and began building a mountain of empty beer cans and cigarette butts. He wanted to produce quality writing but after that first story - about, joys of fatherhood - his work wasn't wanted. He despaired and when despair came in through the door, quality went out through the window. The stagnant pool of childhood, memories, long since buried under the construction of new life, seeped to the surface, mingling with the beer and butts, and he began to write trash. It sold and went on selling. He worked to make it quality trash but it was still trash for all that. They had money. again. They partied a lot and they still managed to be happy.

'Steve! You're not listening!' Miranda was saying.

'Sorry. I was miles away. What were you saying?'

'I was saying that I'd like to dance.'

He felt suddenly swamped in misery. He wanted Susan and he wanted her now. He needed her. The scent of her perfume, worn by this silly woman, was torturing him. He managed what he hoped was a smile and led her over the Iris of Quebec and the Saskatchewan lily on to the maple, and mahogany floor. The moon and stars shone down from the dome and the orchestra delivered the final blow by playing 'Embracable You' - their tune, the tune that Susan and he had danced to, cheek to cheek, their bodies moulded together as one, her perfume intoxicating his senses. God help him!

'I'm so happy,' whispered Miranda, 'and when I'm happy I can do anything I want.'

Steve looked at her, noting that beneath the layers of powder and paint a different Miranda was beginning to emerge. For one brief moment he mentally stripped her then immediately closed the shutters. Remembering Susan and being knocked off balance by her perfume, was doing funny things to him.

Miranda stepped closer and he was forced to draw her inside his arms. She was humming the melody. Her humming was rich, like the warm, rounded notes of a viola, and he felt his edginess smoothed down. Perhaps, he thought, if I don't look at her but think of Susan it will be better. He drew her closer so that he need not see her face or meet her eyes. He let the perfume evoke more memories and thought of his wife. When Miranda's cheek met his and merged with his memories he didn't move away.

She must have felt something of his mood. There was no chattering, no verbal intrusion on his thoughts. He filled his head with her perfume and induced feelings which, had they not been in a public ballroom, might easily have got out of control. The dance finished but another began. Now they were playing 'People Will Say We're In Love'. And so it went on. With every dance Miranda seemed to find inspiration. She a natural, thought Steve. The more relaxed she became the better they danced together.

The storm was having its effect on some of the dancers. As the evening wore on fewer couples took to the floor Miranda seemed to thrive on it and when a tango was announced she was on her feet instantly.

'I've never danced the tango,' warned Steve.

'Neither have I but it doesn't matter. We can make it up has we go along.'

And they did. Miranda led the way and Steve followed. Her inventiveness knew no bounds. They had the floor to themselves and in spite of his misery Steve felt exhillerated by the experience. He forgot his antipathy to the woman appreciating the unexpected talent emerging. In her more creative steps Miranda had shed her hairpins as a striptease artiste might scatter her clothing attire. Her chestnut curls escaped to her shoulders and bounced and bobbed to the rhythm of the dance. Her excitement became infectious. The orchestra rose - literally - to the occasion. The few onlookers left, clapped and whistled. Steve, unabashed by her wild abandon, matched her step for step, ensnared in a magic spell by those nutty brown eyes which were like pools of intoxicating liquor inviting him to drown. He twirled her, bent her, tossed her and she was like a feather plucked from some exotic bird. At the final chord she lay, panting in his arms, as reluctant to leave as he was to relinquished.

They were the only couple on the floor for the last waltz which was like the lull after the storm.

With surprising charm she thanked the orchestra with a noiseless handclap and regal curtsey. When she joined him she grasped his arm with both hands.

'This is the most wonderful night of my life. Let's promenade in the moonlight.'

Steve led her from the ballroom. I'm afraid there's no moon tonight. Probably a force 8 gale and more water above than below.'

'How disappointing. I don't want this night ever to end.'

'It's already ended. This is tomorrow and we disembark early today, if you get what I mean.' He led her towards her cabin. 'Soon we'll be in Greenock and it's going to be a hectic day. We'd better try to get some sleep.'

They had now reached her cabin door. She leaned towards him. He drank in Susan's perfume. His eyes fell on her low cut bodice, the rift of shadow between her breasts rousing him. He pulled her roughly towards him, crushing her mouth with his. She responded immediately. One hand crept to her bodice, his fingers caressing the shadow between her breasts. He fantasised, feeling no longer with Miranda. He was with Susan. He kissed her hair, her closed eyes, the hollow at her throat. His hand slipped inside her bolice. He heard her gasp of pleasure and edged her to the door. Her arms went round his neck. His desire became imperative.

So long,' he mumbled, drunk with rising passion. 'It's been so long.'

Then she spoke in his ear. Not a whisper. Not a merging of moods but a crashing discord on his fantasies which could not have been more out of tune with his feelings. It jarred his sensitivity and killed his desires. It jerked him back to reality.

I love you. Oh my darling Steve. I love you! Love you! Love you! You are wonderful! You are the man of my dreams.'

He felt like a plank of wood. He wanted quit of her. He clasped her hands behind his head and firmly distanced her. He knew immediately that he'd made a mistake. She may have been all woman in the ballroom. Now she had the reaction of a child. A hurt child who wanted to hit back. I'm sorry, Miranda.'

'For what? Making a fool of me? Taking advantage? Making me think you loved me? Kissing me? Holding and touching me?' Then, after holding a dramatic pause, fondling me? Is that why you're sorry or perhaps I haven't come up to your expectations. Is that it?'

Her body was taut. Her eyes reflected her fury and dismay.

'You're a swine,' she hissed and with the extraordinary strength that anger can induce, she slapped his face.

He didn't flinch and this seemed to madden her more/ As she fumbled for her key in her little sequinned bag she couldn't hold back her tears of rage.

'You'll pay for this,' she threatened as she unlocked her cabin door. 'There's nothing more certain than that. You'll pay for this.'

The door slammed in his face and, for a moment, he stood looking at it. Then he turned on his heel.

'Hell. That's all I need,' he mumbled and returned to his cabin.

Buddy was sprawled on the chesterfield when he went in.

'What the hell are you doing here?' Steve asked him.

'Waiting for you.'

'Why for Christ's sake?'

Buddy didn't answer directly but began a resumé of the disembarking schedule.

'I spoke to a couple who know the journey well. It seems we take a short train ride from Greenock to Glasgow. We can stay there overnight and fly to Inverness in the morning. It means we'll have the whole afternoon in Greenock. They recommended a hotel for lunch then, if the weather hasn't improved, we could do a matinee, have something called high tea, alias knife and fork meal, then on our way, What do you think?'

'Whatever you say but count me out for the matinee Maybe we could rent a room for the day in the hotel.'

I could do another chapter. It's your turn for Miranda and I think she might need a warm comforter after her experience of a cold douche.' When Buddy raised an eyebrow he added, 'Can I help it if they fall for me?'

It was meant as a light-hearted remark but fell flat. What did you do to her?' asked Buddy.

'Let's just say I gave her a night to remember!'

Buddy looked at him speculatively, then said, 'You swine.'

Steve was too weary to argue and when Buddy left he thought of the bottle under his pillow. Then he thought of Sam. He hadn't come this far to spoil it now. In a few hours he'd be speaking to Sam and he wasn't going to let that hitch spoil things. She was just a kid. Sure, he wasn't proud himself. He'd used her but she was young, good looking, and talented. A few emotional knocks wouldn't do her harm. They were part of life. She wasn't going to be speding the rest of her life pining for him. She could put it down to experience.

He was determined he wasn't going to spend the rest of life regretting the loss of an opportunity of getting his son back. He loved that kid and if keeping sober meant keeping Sam, then he'd drink water for the rest of his life. He felt better. He'd try to make it up to Miranda somehow. She wasn't such a bad kid.

He turned his thoughts to Sam again, deciding that he would ring from the hotel. He'd already calculated the time difference. He'd be tempted to ring him now but with eight hours between them Sam would still be at school. About 4 o'clock British summer time, when the others were at the cinema and he would be in the hotel, Sam would be getting ready to go to school. That would be a good time. Susan would be in the kitchen preparing his breakfast. Maybe he could have a word with her. He'd be stone cold sober and she could hardly refuse to talk to him. The more he dwelt on the idea the more his spirits rose. What would she say, he wondered, if he told her he had quit drinking and was coming back home? He'd tell her that he realised what he'd lost and it was too much to sacrifice for a thirst, no matter how compelling. He'd tell her that he wanted their life back together and now that he'd quit there was nothing to stop them trying again.

He held the bottle of vodka in his hands.

'It's good. It's devilish good,' he said aloud. 'I can look at you and leave you alone. You've lost your power. You can't compete with Sam and Susan.'

He placed the bottle on the coffee table, began ripping off his tie and preparing for bed. Miranda's magazine was lying where he'd left it. He opened it, turned the pages till he found again that face which had had such an incredible effect on him. There she was, Jenny Fraser and it wasn't, he thought with a smile, a mistake that he thought she was speaking to him. What was she saying?

'Life is good. Life is for living.'

That was it. He'd show them. He'd show them all. On that thought, he fell asleep.

CHAPTER 6

He woke with one thought in his mind. Today he'd be seaking to his son - and his wife. His mind was made up. He was going back at the first opportunity if they'd have him. Somehow or other he must convince them that it was for real this time. It had taken a painful separation from his family to bring him to his senses. He knew Sam missed him and needed him around and by now Susan should have her protest marches out of her system. As he dressed and shaved he felt cheerful. It was only when on his way to breakfast that he remembered Miranda and how he'd used her. He wasn't proud of himself but at least he'd stopped himself in time. No harm had been done. The incident irritated rather than worried him. He'd have to watch his step. He'd lost all desire to travel north now. All he wanted was a plane back home. He wouldn't ask Buddy. He'd tell him. The passengers due to disembark at Greenock were being served an early breakfast. When Steve entered the dining room it was unusually subdued, its occupants sobered by thought of a good thing coming to an end. There was an ominous silence hovering over his own table when he sat down. Buddy was pouring maple syrup on his pancake while Miranda, after a withering glance, continued buttering her toast. Steve poured himself coffee while trying to assess the situation. It was Buddy who broke the silence. 'I've been putting Miranda in the picture about our plans.' There was no response from either Steve or Miranda. The latter was obviously in a sulk. Steve had conveniently filled his mouth with food and couldn't speak. There was an awkward silence until Buddy chipped in. I've told Miranda that since you have another chapter your book to write you won't be coming with us to the matinee.' Buddy swallowed his last sliver of orange, wiped his fingers on his table napkin and pushed back his chair.

'I'm going to leave you two now while I check some immigration details and see to luggage arrangements. I suggest we meet up at immigration. It's in the Canada Room at eleven.'

Left alone with Miranda, Steve was silent, in the belief that saying nothing was preferable to saying the wrong thing. Miranda gave up any pretence of eating and turned accusing eyes on him.

'Call yourself a gentleman! Only a cad would try to take advantage of a woman. Thank God I stopped you in time.'

What sounded like a dry sob seemed lodged in her throat.

Steve looked at her, mesmerised by the sight of one dew drop tear travelling over her rounded cheekbone, past 1 chin before losing itself in the collar of her blouse. For life of him he couldn't decide how much was real and how much put on for his benefit. He decided to give her the benefit of the doubt.

'I apologise for my behaviour last night,' he said, hoping he sounded as sincere as he actually felt.

'So you think an apology will make it all right. Last night you made me the happiest woman on earth until you spoiled it all by trying to rape me.'

'Hey girl, steady on,' warned Steve, alarmed. 'It wasn't like that.'

'Your word against mine.'

Steve noticed that she had dropped her American accent which seemed to indicate this may be the real Miranda speaking, after all.

'I trusted you but all along you have been pretending an interest in me. I fell for it. I thought you were different from other men but you're all the same. Like all the others, you had only one thing on your mind. Thank Cod I stopped you in time.'

'I'm sorry if I've upset you.'

'You've devastated me.'

'It certainly wasn't my intention to kiss you, Miranda, but you looked so lovely I couldn't stop myself.'

He saw a flicker of interest in her eyes. Playing on her susceptibility to flattery he continued.

'With your hair falling loose about your face you looked so lovely,' he finished lamely.

'You think I looked lovely. Eh?'

'Beautiful,' he said.

However he was not to get off as lightly as he'd hoped. He was getting irksome. He knew he wasn't dealing with any ordinary woman here. She seemed neither girl nor woman. In some ways he pitied her. She was like a lost soul. Was that how Buddy felt? Was that why he was taking such pains to protect her? He decided to come clean.

'I'm a married man, Miranda. Perhaps I should have told you.'

'Then you're a bigger cad than I thought you were. Cheating on your wife. I was warned about men like you,' she said, attempting to look sophisticated but, had she known it, stirring in Steve, an unexpected pang of pity for her. 'To think I trusted you.'

He made no attempt to stop her, only wishing the tiresome meeting would come to an end. He was more than ever determined to fly home on the first available flight. He could certainly do without this high drama.

'Do you know what you remind me of?'

He shook his head, pouring himself more coffee. 'A horrible creepy-crawly spider.'

He had to restrain himself from smiling. The creepy-crawly was a give away. She's a kid who probably screams her head off when she sees a spider in her bath.

'I'll tell you something else,' she said as if reading his mind. 'When I find a spider I don't like, I go for it. I kill it.'

He looked at her and with a poor attempt at lightening the conversation put a scared expression on his face and a wobble in his voice as he said, 'Are you trying to frighten me?'

'You may well ask,' she hissed, 'but I won't forget what you've done to me, Stevenson Bruce, and believe me you'll pay for it!'

He heaved a sigh half of relief, half of exasperation as watched her haughty exit from the dining room. That walk, he decided, belonged every inch to the actress.

He returned to his cabin to collect his personal baggage. He took the bottle of vodka in his hands and looked at it marvelling again that it held no temptation for him. He considered leaving it behind but he'd already convincd himself that it was his safeguard. Buddy knew he had it and why he had it, so there was no need to hide it. He slipped it into his valise between his pyjamas and his sweater before leaving his cabin for immigration. The others were already queuing in the Canada Room by the time he arrived. Miranda had decided to ignore him.

The immigration officers who had boarded early were working steadily and efficiently. Finally they were cleared and instructed to make for the deck and the tender. Where once the passengers had sauntered and frolicked in shorts and bikinis they were now unrecognisable under wrappings of raincoats and hats, heads bent in futile defence against the relentless rain.

Further conversation was impossible when they boarded the tender Waverley which transported them to the Greenok wharf where, unfortunately, poor visibility denied them the natural beauty of the coastal scenery.

They landed on Princes Pier. Most of the passengers trundled towards a waiting train but Buddy began his search for a cab.

Miranda seemed unperturbed by the rain which was running off her plastic raincoat and down her bare legs. She wore a flimsy scarf on her head and her hair fell in long wet tendrils over her face. She continued to ignore Steve and kept watching for Buddy's return. When he did return she continued her sulks while Buddy, Steve and the cab driver organised the luggage.

There was no let-up on the rain and by the time luggage id been piled into the cab and they squeezed in after, the short journey to the recommended hotel was made in silence. A gloom had settled on the trio. It was a far cry from the sunshine of the Empress Deck or the pleasures of the Coral Pool. Miranda was the first to speak as the cab drew to a halt at the entrance to an unpretentious hotel.

'It's so small,' she drawled. 'Supposing they're fully booked for lunch.'

'No room at the inn, eh?' laughed Steve.

She looked through him.

'We'll cross that bridge when we come to it,' said Buddy. They needn't have worried. It seemed they were the only visitors. When they walked into the hotel no one was around. The reception hail was small and smelling musty. A wooden counter served as a desk, on the top of which was a round brass bell. Beside it, a tea-stained label said Please ring. Buddy thumped it with the palm of his hand while Miranda wrinkled her nose in disgust. The floor was bare of carpet. The walls and stairwell were painted a dark green, relieved by some framed photographs of what might conceivably be views of the town and, to add to their pessimism, they seemed to have brought the dismal weather with them.

After another thump on the bell a woman appeared, listened to their requests, assured them they could have lunch and since it was such a dreadful day, she'd light the fires in the dining room and lounge. Grateful, they piled the luggage in a corner of the hall where she said it would be perfectly safe and would steak and kidney pudding suit them? They said anything at all would be great.

'What a God-forsaken place,' moaned Miranda.

They were shown the washrooms then Mrs Grant, as she introduced herself, disappeared to order their lunch, promising to come straight back and take Steve to the room he wanted to hire for the afternoon.

'It's a bit wee,' she told him, panting with the exertion of climbing three flights of stairs.

The room had a single bed, a wardrobe, a washbasin, one chair and small table by the window. The panes we streaming with rain and he could just discern church steeples in the greyness outside. There was also a fireplace in the corner but no fire, only poker and tongs and a lidded trash bin.

If Miranda thought downstairs was God forsaken, I wonder what she'd think of this? thought Steve. At least was it was dry, if dank. He left his typewriter on the table and his personal valise on the bed, before going to join the others. From the top of the third flight of stairs to the hall he met no one. It was like a ghost hotel. He took note of a public telephone on the first landing then nosed his way to the dining room where a welcoming fire blazed in the hearth.

The soup was thick, hot and very satisfying. The steak and kidney pudding a novelty which escaped criticism and trifle to follow was as much as they were able for. Buddy had already ordered the evening meal which was to be ready at 6 o'clock. Apparently, he informed them, there would be a train to Glasgow departing some time around 9o'clock. In Glasgow they would find a hotel for the night and the next morning make arrangements to fly to Inverness.

Steve had already dismissed this journey from his mind. The only flight arrangement interesting him would be one to Canada. But this thought he kept to himself. After eating they veered towards the lounge where another fire of burning coals welcomed them.

The lunch had been eaten almost in total silence when even Buddy retreated into himself rather than attempt to hack at the wall of ice which had built up between the others. Now, with hunger satisfied and comfort restored, the atmosphere began to thaw.

Steve welcomed a direct look from Miranda, the first since breakfast. He welcomed any distraction which would keep his mind otherwise engaged until it was time to lift the phone and dial Vancouver.

They had the lounge to themselves. Buddy and he settled in comfortable armchairs on either side of the roaring fire and lit their cigarettes. Miranda sat between them. Steve met that ice-cold stare of Miranda's and determined to defreeze it, to tears if necessary. He waited until Mrs Grant arrived with coffee which she left on a side table then, breaking in on Buddy's recapitulation of plans for the rest the day, he spoke directly to Miranda.

'Are we talking again?'

She shrugged, leaning with outstretched hands towards the fire.

'Are you cold?' asked Buddy in concern, offering Miranda coffee which he'd risen to dispense.

She accepted the coffee with mumbled thanks and paused before replying.

'Not physically.'

'What's that supposed to mean?' asked Steve, amused.

'What it says.'

Nothing more seemed to be forthcoming.

'Why are you disguised as an American?' he persisted. Miranda frowned, relaxing back into the depth of her chair.

'I told you. I'm a natural mimic. I thought it would 1 fun.'

'Okay, but surely the fun's over. You're a Canadian. We're Canadians. There's no need for the pretence now surely?'

'I want to maintain the role,' she said, trying to convey a sophistication which somehow sat uncomfortably on her.

'It's important I am thought of as an American when I am in Strathard. I don't want my true identity revealed and I am hoping you will both remember that.'

'You will be lying and cheating,' said Steve.

'That's my business.'

'But you are expecting Bud and me to aid and abet you.

'Come on, Steve,' began Buddy.

'No, Bud. If Miranda needs our support that much we are to be her accomplices then we are entitled to know why. Who knows! She might be a drug trafficker.'

'Don't be ridiculous,' said Miranda.

'Then tell us the truth,' said Steve, 'because,' he added, altering his pace of delivery, 'unless you do, we will think twice about coming with you.'

Miranda looked helplessly at Buddy.

To Steve's surprise Buddy supported him.

'Steve has a point, Miranda. Perhaps we might even be able to help if you feel threatened in any way.'

'Why should I feel threatened?'

'I don't know why you're worried about being recognised' said Steve. 'You left when you were a baby, so you keep telling us, so no one's likely to recognise you.'

'You don't understand,' whined Miranda, the child.

'No, I'm, afraid we don't,' said Steve, 'and that's why we want you to tell us.'

Miranda now cowered back in her chair. Mrs Grant returned to ask if they would like more coffee. They declined.

'Come on,' said Steve, after the landlady withdrew. 'Spill beans.'

'I'm afraid of being disappointed in Strathard, I suppose,' said Miranda.

'Going by the magazine feature,' said Steve, 'it sounds to me ike a modern Shangri La.'

'That woman has ruined everything,' said Miranda.

'I think you know more about that woman than you care to admit,' said Buddy gently.

Steve held his tongue. He was remembering the face of 'that woman' and wasn't prepared to discuss the effect it had had on him. Also, he guessed that Buddy, in his gentle manner, was more likely to get Miranda talking than any bulldozing he might be prepared to employ.

'Before I tell you anything I must have a sworn promise from both of you that you will keep it to yourself and not go shouting your mouth off as soon as we get there.'

If we get there, thought Steve but added his assurance to that of Buddy. Mum would be the word. After all, whatever was between Miranda and 'that woman' was none of their business. He lit another cigarette and waited.

'Jenny Fraser is my sister.'

Steve shot up in his chair but whatever he was about to say was stifled by a glare from Buddy which said keep out of it. Miranda, elbows on knees and face cupped between her hands, was gazing into the fire as if now unaware of their presence.

'I was born in Strathard but not actually in the castle. My father was not the Laird of Strathard. He was the Laird's chauffeur and is still alive. We lived on the estate near the castle. My mother died giving birth to me and Jenny Fraser has never forgiven me for killing her. She hated me and has gone on hating me ever since. She disowned me then and still disowns me. I know this because my aunt told me as soon as I was old enough to be informed and she has gone on telling me all my life. She hates Jenny Fraser and has never stopped telling me that she committed a great act of mercy by taking me away from her and bringing me to Canada. At least that's what she says when she isn't telling me I was pushed into her arms and she was forced to bring me to Canada and that she's been bearing that cross ever since and I've never shown an ounce of gratitude for her sacrifice.'

She rose and walked slowly towards the fireplace. Laying one arm carefully on the mantelpiece, she continued with her story. Miranda the actress, thought Steve. She's on stage and is making the most of it.

'She is a hating woman is Aunt Sheena. She hates her neighbours. She hates the dogs and cats that belong to her neighbours. She hates their children and she hates me. But give her her due, she loves God. Oh yes, she loves God.'

Dramatic pause, observed Steve. A change of pose. Only her hand on the mantelpiece now, to highlight deliclous curve of breasts.

'I think she even hated Uncle Peter, her husband, even though he was the sweetest, kindest man on God's earth and when he died I wanted to die with him.'

She moved away from the fireplace and returned to her chair. I helped him run his factory after I left high school. I was good with figures and quite efficient on the typewriter but most of all, I wanted to be near him. He was the only person in the world who loved me and understood me.'

Her voice trembled for an instant.

When he died he left me all his money and it is a lot of of money. He left Aunt Sheena the house and a modest income but I got everything else including his sweetie factory which I sold straight away and got even more money. Dear Uncle Peter. Not only did he give me money, he gave me freedom to tell, at long last, my bitchy aunt exactly what I thought of her.'

Now she looked and sounded exultant. She jumped again to her feet, took a few agitated steps then sat down again. Steve felt he dared not move in case he stopped this revelatory outpour but into the sudden silence Buddy's voice gave a gentle prompt.

'Your father?'

Miranda responded with a dismissive gesture of her hand. 'Oh him. She hated him too. He came to Canada just before he war to help Uncle Peter in his business which was very new then. At first it was fine but I got to feel that he wasn't the least bit interested in me. He could hardly bear to be in the same room as Aunt Sheena and as soon as he got an offer of a job in Toronto he was off, leaving me with her. He had all the usual excuses - would be best for me in my best interests - and all that malarkey. To tell you the truth, I was fed up listening to his paeans of praise other daughter, his darling, wonderful Jenny who could do no wrong. So he kept telling me.'

She had jumped to her feet again, looking from one to the other of her audience as she tabled her father's utterances.

Jenny said this, Jenny said that, she did this and that, she was clever and wise and willing and able. He sanctified her.'

What a soliloquy, thought Steve uncharitably as she down again to emphasise the terrible effects this had had on her upbringing.

'Aunt Sheena hated father when he spoke like this and I got less fond of him myself. He couldn't care less that I wanted dancing lessons or a piano or that I wanted to go to parties and have dates and bring friends home to tea, all of which was taboo to Aunt Sheena. I was dragged to church twice on Sundays and very often weekdays and he'd watch me go off crying my eyes out. Uncle Peter was hardly at home at this time, working every hour God gave him at his factory. Uncle Peter would as soon cut off his tongue than utter a harsh word about anyone. At the first suspicion of a quarrel he'd scuttle off and go to ground. I never had him to myself until I worked with him and by that time Father didn't matter any more. I learned to fight my own battles with my aunt.' She turned her pleading eyes on each them. 'Have you any idea what it feels like to wear gymslips at school while every other girl is wearing the latest fashions? Have you any idea what it's like to go straight home after school, when you're fifteen years old, sometimes even to be collected at the school gates by a frumpy old woman when everyone else is messing around and enjoying themselves?'

Why had he no sympathy for this poor girl? wondei Steve. Was it because, sincere as her grievances may be, she insists on seeing herself as a drama queen?

'Of course, I rebelled, time and again, but that just made matters worse. I was never allowed out with friends. In fact eventually I had no friends. I spent my time dreaming about a castle in Scotland which my father and my brother praised to high heaven. Like them I'd been born there but, unlike them, I had no memory of it. I felt excluded. I felt I'd been robbed of my rights. But the wonderful Jenny and Callum had lived and enjoyed a freedom I'd been denied.'

Again Steve was struck by that same mixture of child and woman. She looked woman, dressed woman, sang and danced woman but her attitude was that of a rebellious child. She was, he reminded himself, a crazy mixed-up kid. He looked at the drooping shoulders, the flimsy handkerchief she twisted between her long expressive fingers. Was she about to burst into tears? But no, she was off on another tack, about another brother.

'I had another brother,' she whispered. His name was Graham. He was *not all* there as Aunt Sheena enjoyed telling me. Here she raised a forefinger to the side of her head. 'You know what I mean, *a loose screw* - Aunt Sheena's words, not mine. And do you know what,' she added, leaning forward, 'Do you know what the wonderful Jenny did? She put him in a

about relationships, especially with his father and he was dead. How could a dead man determine day-to-day thinking?

He felt restless. He rose from his chair and wandered over to some framed photographs on the opposite wall. They were a series of views of old Greenock. The Victoria Tower of the Municipal Buildings, he read on the label beneath, all of 245 ft high towering above the spire of the Mid Parish Church built in 1761. Had his father worshipped there? His eyes moved to a picture of the Old Harbour with a cluster of fishing boats and a background of stone and brick buildings with once again, the dominating Victoria Tower in the background. Was that where his father first put to sea? In contrast to the harbour buildings the Greenock Academy was a handsome Gothic structure finely situated in a spacious part of the town. Was that where his father went to school? And there was Princes Pier where they had disgorged from the tender only that morning. Strange, he mused. I didn't exist when my father left the pier but the day I arrive he is everywhere and yet he's dead.

He glanced at his watch again. Ten minutes since looked the last time. God! What was he going to do till 4 o'clock? He threw his cigarette butt in the fire, lifted the brass poker and squeezed it through the burning coalsjust for the hell of it, watching the flames spring back to life and listening, with a curious pleasure, to the hissing and spitting.

All right father, he thought. Let's walk in the rain together and have it out. I must be quit of you. .1 owe you nothing. He sure couldn't sit on his backside for another hour and burn his nerve ends just thinking about Sam and Susan. He wanted to reach them clear headed.

CHAPTER 7

Although it had stopped raining, the gutters were full and dark clouds warned of more rain to come. Steve, hatless, and wearing a short raincoat inadequate against the cold and damp, shrugged off a distaste for his surroundings. It was only August, for God's sake, and shouldn't be as cold and miserable as this. Perhaps he was a fool to leave the comfortable fireside. Even his attic room would be better than this. His feelings were confirmed when a passing car, driving too close to the curb, sent a spray of dirty water over him, soaking his trousers.

'Damn you!' he bellowed to the disappearing car, causing a passer-by to nod in commiseration.

'I expect he's laughing his head off,' said Steve to the passer-by who was already out of earshot.

Let's make for the bloody tower! Victoria Tower wasn't hard to find. For the next half hour he wandered the streets of Greenock reading names like Brisbane, Brougham, Nelson, Fox and Union, commemorations of Britain and her empire. He looked at churches and steeples and spires and pubs. He noticed the people, intent, unhurried, uncomplaining, and the road puddles like mirrors in the dim street lights.

Leaving the built-up environment he found himself on a sweep of esplanade. Did you play here when you were a kid, Dad? Did you swim on these rollers, sail along this coastline before you left it for good? Although his vision was denied the coastal beauty, he paused for a few moments, lifting his face to the wind and rain and filling his lungs with deep breaths of clean air. If he went on feeling like he did now, he might even consider giving up tobacco, he thought.

He made his way back to Greenock's many harbours, the Albert and Victoria and, of course, the James Watt Dock, so proudly acclaimed by the Chief Engineer. Now why couldn't you have been famous, like James Watt, father, and achieved something worthwhile for later generations, or even for your son?

He kept his walk at a brisk pace, trying to ignore the discomfort of his wet trousers against his skin but it only increased his general misery and, try as he would, he could not shake off the constant presence of his father. He craved revenge. He wanted his revenge. He had every right to be angry but, in the words of Francis Bacon, written hundreds of years ago, 'Why should I be angry with him for loving himself better than me?' In the matter of revenge, it would appear that human nature never changed.

No. The best option was to see his father in perspective. He'd sent himself to hell. Why should he follow? It was time to look after himself. Wasn't that what he was already doing? Hadn't he proved he could do without alcohol if he put his mind to it? From now on he was teetotal. Perhaps too, Miranda had helped. Her anger and lust for revenge looked pathetic to him. Did he look pathetic to others? He supposed he did. Well, that was all going to stop. He was a different man now. He was his own man, not his father's shadow. Sod his father.

He'd let Sam know that things were different. He'd tell Susan he was coming home as soon as a flight could be arranged. He had no wish to spend the rest of his life hating a dead man. He had a vision of his home. Susan would be in the kitchen in her robe and flimsy negligee, her pink toes peeping from her slippers as she padded around in the early morning kitchen ritual, her hair falling over her cheeks, flushed from slumber, her body still warm. He saw the nape of her slender neck as she bent over Sam's lunchbox and felt an overwhelming desire to closet her in his arms. His steps quickened as he hurried back to the hotel, when a glance at his watch showed him that there were still 30 minutes to fill. He'd have a shower, a change of clothing and by then the time would be right.

The hail was dim and gloomy and as silent as a morgue. He met no one as he climbed the three flights of stairs to his attic room. After he'd showered and changed, he walked down to the telephone on the first floor landing with no one around to worry him. His hand trembled as he dialled the number. He was ten minutes early but his patience was spent. He heard the ringing tone and waited like a love-sick maiden for her lover's voice. He felt a smile playing on his lips when the dialling stopped and he was connected. When he heard his home number announced in ajaunty voice his mentally scripted greeting was killed stone dead.

'Who's speaking?' his voice, which he hardly recognised, demanded to know.

'It's Joey, man. What do yau want?'

'And who the hell are you?' and without waiting for an answer said, 'Is Susan there?'

'Sorry man. She ain't here.'

'What are you doing in my house at this time in the morning?'

'Right this minute I'm drinking coffee, man. I live here.'

'Get Susan. I want to speak to her.'

'Can't mate. She ain't here.'

'Where the hell is she?'

'At the dentist with Sammy boy - an early appointment.'

Steve let rip.

'Steady on man,' cautioned the jaunty voice, 'I guess I know who you are.'

'Too right you do. I want to know why you're in my house at eight o'clock in the morning.'

'D'ya want me to spell it out to you mate? I don't think that's such a good idea.'

Steve slammed the phone on its cradle and sat there, sick and anguished. Both hands were shaking now and he was sweating like a pig, suffocated by misery. Somehow he reached the privacy of the tatty little room in the attic. Like a caged animal, he pounded its mean dimensions. He expelled his wrath in a volume of curses. He sat at his typewriter, already paper-loaded, and with a demented fury transferred his endless string of abuse on to the keys. 'When angry, count a hundred; when very angry, swear,' was what Mark Twain had advised. Well, he was very, very angry.

With every curse he pounded, he made matters worse. He ravaged the curses from scripture and the gods, from the sexual act and the body functions. He uttered words he'd never known he possessed. He dredged a hitherto unknown cesspool from the subconscious and when his paper was covered in black profanity and he swept it from the roller of his machine, there was no satisfaction to appease his anger. He was still caged and he wasn't just an animal caged. He was a wounded animal and it hurt like hell.

He had no remedy for the dissolution of the spirit, except one. He found a glass, fetched the vodka and began to drink it neat, slowly and systematically until the fire was douched, until the words he spewed from the cesspool of his mind were transformed into poetry, until his cage dropped its bars and became a launching pad. His room was now womb, warm and life sustaining. Incredible colours vibrated around him, solids dissolved to the touch. By the time he'd shaken the last dregs from the bottle he felt the happiest man on earth endowed with infallibility. He could be what he chose. He was a knight again, in shining armour. He must ride to his castle. He grasped the lid of the trash bucket for his shield and the poker for his sword.

He stood, swayed, tottered then fell. He picked himself up then with admirable concentration he zigzagged to the door, the landing then the stairs. Lowering one foot after the other was a problem, only solved when he stopped trying and let his body roll to the next landing. This cheered him and he continued on the second flight of stairs sliding on his bottom. Incredibly he knew the need for silence and, as if surrounded by a rowdy crowd, gestured with finger to lips, that they must be very, very quiet. By careful and clever negotiation he succeeded in reaching the main door and being rewarded by a burst of confidence, found the pavement and the road to victory.

Where was his charger, his trusty steed? Unabashed by ogle-eyed spectators he tottered in search, calling for his horse. Then he spotted it. It didn't matter that it had two wheels where there should be four legs or a handlebar where there should be reins. He made a valiant effort to mount but the charger refused to co-operate. Excited by the growing band of spectators, he made a sport of it and, like a toreador in the bull ring, teased his animal to respond.

'Hey you!' a voice cried from the throng. 'That's my bike. What do you think you're doing? Gie's ma bike or I'll get the polis on ye.'

Battle, thought the knight. Danger! Defend! He raised his shield and readied his sword. He watched the approach of the enemy and prepared himself. The enemy threatened to unseat him. He responded in full measure. He used his sword like a sledgehammer and after a mighty blow his opponent fell to the ground, stunned into unconsciousness.

Someone yelled, 'Get the polis! Get the polis!'

He was hemmed in by the crowd and imprisoned until authority arrived and confronted.

'Stand back now, stand weel back,' ordered the police constable in an effort to restrain the onlookers.

The police sergeant was supporting the warrior knight who was trying, with difficulty, to stand straight and to look menacing.

'I wanna punch you,' said the knight staring up under the policeman's helmet.

'I don't think that's such a good idea,' said the sergeant. 'Don't you think you've done enough damage as it is?' nodding to the fallen victim who was by now on his knees.

His fellow constable extracted his walkie-talkie from a breast pocket and rang for an ambulance.

'Now sir,' the sergeant said to Steve. 'I'd like some particulars from you. Now stay where you are or I'll clap the cuffs on,' he quickly cautioned as Steve lurched towards him. 'What's your name?'

Steve, still hopeful that he'd eventually reach the perpendicular, began to oblige, taking pains with his enunciation. 'My name sir, officer of the law, member of...'

'Never mind that, laddie. Just tell me your name.'

'My name ish - isss' He was having trouble with his sibilants. Then concluding triumphantly declared 'My name ish R-R-Robert the Br-r-ruce!'

'And mine is William Wallace,' the officer humoured. The onlookers laughed in derision.

At the same moment a light flashed in his face and Robert the Bruce stumbled into the sergeant's arms. A siren wailed, heralding the approach of the ambulance. While the paramedics took care of the bike owner, the bike owner's friend rescued the bike. By the time the siren wailed in departure, both policemen had conducted the offender to the police car.

'The station for you, my lad.' said one.

'Now clear off, the rest of you,' said the other. 'The show's over.'

Steve put up no resistance in the short ride to the station, nor on his arrival, nor on further interrogation because by now he was barely conscious and having difficulty dragging one foot after the other.

'Maybe we should have put him in the ambulance,' said the constable.

'Oh my God, my God,' he moaned, wrapping himself in a comforting blanket of self-pity. 'What have I done? Why am I here, locked up like a criminal?'

He was in no state to pursue this investigation. His head hurt, his stomach gripped him in spasms of agony. He stumbled his way to the bucket in the corner and relieved himself. The effort sapped what little strength he'd mustered. He wanted to be sick but he hurt too much to retch. Returning to the cot he stumbled over his shoes. He was considering which shoe went on which foot when the constable returned, ordered him to zip his flies and, as a great act of mercy, he told him, he'd help him tie his shoelaces.

This done, he led Steve, unwashed, uncombed and unwilling along a stark corridor into a small room where a grim faced, walrus moustached inspector of police sat behind a large desk. He didn't see the other occupant of the room. He was painfully concentrating on trying to make sense of what the inspector was trying to tell him which was what he already knew, that he was in no fit state at the moment for a sensible conversation but that everything had been explained to his servant. The words barely registered. It was only when the so-mentioned servant materialised from the corner of the room and moved forward to confront him that he recognised his friend Buddy. A shaft of sunlight momentarily lit the room and some of his burden dropped from Steve's shoulders.

It seemed that Buddy had done an excellent sales job with the constabulary. He'd sold them his employer's renowned and respectable Canadian background, his prestigious output as a writer of detective fiction, his present domestic problems which were at the moment rocking his otherwise safe-sailing boat. With consymmate skill he'd already visited and confronted the victim whoseemed, happily, none the worse for his ordeal and, confessed the servant, he had, in the name of his master, compensatedthe victim with staggering generosity.

Although unable to work everything out yet, Steve could feel a measure of relief lighten the weight of his worry. He submitted himself to the inspector's charges, agreed on their seriousness, and took heed of what might, but for the grace of God and the constitution of his victim, have had tragic consequences. His growing relief enabled him to voice his contrition in acceptable language and on the strength of this he was, after due and careful consideration on the inspector's part, relieved of prosecution. He was allowed to leave the building and even wished good luck and God speed. Silently Steve blessed Buddy. What would he do without his new-found servant? God only knows.

His new-found servant maintained this role, feeling it suitable for the occasion. He'd hired a car to which he now led his employer, bundled him in, told him to shut his trap and drove silently to a bigger, busier hotel where he had already booked two rooms.

He conducted Steve to his room, ran him a hot bath, turned down his bed, laid out his pyjamas, drew the curtains, mixed him a concoction, developed and improved with much practice and told him to sleep till he woke up refreshed in mind. Then they would administer to the body with appropriate food and then, and then only, he said grimly, they would talk.

With a mocking bow and a servile, 'Will tht be all, sir?' he left a cowed and crestfallen Steve.

When he woke, after long, deep sleep, he hadn't the will to break free. He wanted to escape into sleep again but, but try as he might, it was impossible. He lay in his bed, stretched flat, eyes closed self-pitying and self-loathing. Why was he here in this God-forsaking place, weighed down with discomfiting distress? The will to conquer seemed out of reach. He'd been unlucky again. The die had not been falling in his favour He felt he was out of the game.

When Buddy arrived he lay still as if he hadn't noticed his entry into the room. No help was offered. Only instrucions to rise, dress, pack and meet in the hotel restaurant where Buddy would order their meal. By degrees he summoned enough energy to rise, dress, pack and make his uncertain way to the hotel restaurant. Buddy was waiting for him. The instructions were drink, eat, and try to look interested. They had a plane to catch and planes waited for no one, not even millionaire detective-thriller-horror writers.

Buddy explained that when he'd found him missing, then discovered where he was, he'd packed Miranda off on the train to Glasgow with instructions to stay overnight and fly to Inverness the next day. She was to book in at the Station Hotel and stay until they arrived when they would set off together for Strathard. He'd phoned Strathard to make sure their accommodation was still available. He'd arranged to keep the hired car

'You weren't drunk.'

'Cold sober.'

'Well then you haven't botched. You can still speak to Sam.'

There was a long silence while they watched a river cruiser head into the landing pier. Steve finished one cigarette and lit another.

'But I did get drunk, didn't I?'

'Very drunk.'

'Why?'

Buddy sighed and said, 'I don't know.'

He lit his own cigarette and inhaled deeply.

'I thought I could handle it. I was certain I'd stopped. I *felt* I'd stopped.'

'Sure.'

Steve exhaled a spiral of smoke then continued.

'It's like smoking, I suppose. Old habits die hard. I've been so used to drinking when I'm rattled. It was just an old habit reasserting itself. It'll take time.'

'Sure.'

'Never again!' said Steve.

'Sure.'

Steve suddenly threw his half-smoked cigarette to the ground and, rising, heeled it hard.

'Christ! I was so sure I'd quit.'

'You still can,' said Buddy.

'For one thing I don't care a cuss about my father any more. He just seems pathetic now.'

'Sure.'

Steve, now enlivened by his rage, rounded on his friend. 'Is that all you can bloody well say?'

'I say,' said Buddy, rising, 'that we'd better get on our way to Glasgow Airport if we want to get to Inverness tonight. Miranda will be waiting for us there.'

'Hell!' growled Steve.

'She has her own problems, remember.'

'She's pathetic.'

They had reached the car which Buddy unlocked.

'Get in,' he ordered. 'I'll show you something pathetic.' Taking his seat behind the wheel he took a folded newspaper from the glove compartment which he unfolded and thrust into Steve's hands.

Look at that,' he said. 'Don't you think that's pathetic?'

THE CHARGE OF KING ROBERT THE BRUCE was headlined on the front page and beneath it an account of the fracas in town the previous night. There was a picture of Steve, legs astride, poker in one hand and trash bin lid in the other while looking down on his adversary lying sprawled at his feet. It was reported humorously but was also scathing in comment.

'I don't remember it. They've rigged it. I have absolutely no recollection.'

'Sure.'

The comment went unchallenged. Steve read the article again and as if the concern belonged to someone other than himself said, matter-of-factly, 'He could have been killed.'

'He was a lucky man - and so were you.'

Steve looked at his friend.

'How do you make that out?'

'If you'd killed him you'd have been arrested for murder.'

'I'm no murderer. I don't even like squashing flies.'

'Not when you're sound in mind. You were very drunk, Steve. Stop kidding yourself. You know what you're like when you're drunk.'

'That's where you're wrong. I don't know what I'm like when I'm drunk but I damned well know what I'm like when I need a drink.'

'Can't you see where it's all getting you? It's happened before. You're irresponsible when you're drunk.'

'So everyone says.'

'But you refuse to believe them. There's still time for you to change your mind. If you want to go to Canada I'll do nothing to stop you but if you decide to go to Inverness I don't want to hear a wrong word about Miranda. If you are tempted to think that she's pathetic, remember this.'

He took the newspaper from Steve's hands, folded it carefully and returned it to the glove compartment.

'And by the way,' said Buddy as he turned the ignition key. 'I've destroyed your suicide note. It's not something you want to leave lying around.'

CHAPTER 9

The journey from Inverness to Strathard was for Steve, a journey through which he was propelled against his will. As the hired car, with Buddy at the wheel, covered miles of ever changing scenery Buddy and Miranda were forging for themselves a dynamic duo while Steve sat humped in the back seat, ignored.

The duo was commenting constantly on everything they saw. The day was warm and bright with a dazzling blue sky. The unbroken sun's rays intensified their delight, capturing for them the occasional flashing silver of a waterfall, the mountain slopes, purpled with heather, affording them astonishing satisfaction. To the ecstatic Miranda, every village they drove through was so cute, every church perched on a hill with no visible path of approach was enchanting, every cow that raised her head to give them a curious stare from soulful eyes was adorable. The pièce de résistance came when Miranda made Buddy stop the car to admire shaggy headed Highland cattle, standing in a shallow creek which Miranda said was called a wee burn.

As the car followed the rise and fall of narrow twisting roads, every corner they turned revealed something unexpected. Steve suffered a series of running commentaries on the Scottish landscape.

He was directing his own mind on images of mile upon mile of straight roads and limitless horizons of prairie land for which he now longed. The car was too small and the rivers too timid. He missed the redwoods and the maples and would gladly have sold his soul to have the power to change the cute little cottages into Vancouver condominiums.

They stopped for a break. While Buddy tracked down some peaty spring water and Miranda spread herself sensually on a bed of heather, Steve sat on a boulder and watched the darting flights of birds. He swatted an army of tiny insects which Miranda said were called midges. Strange, he thought, they didn't seem to be bothering her.

The ever-practical Buddy had arranged for a packed lunch and this he produced from the trunk with a triumphant flourish and accompanying 'Tantantara Tzing Boom!'

He fetched them paper cups of clear, cool water from the spring he had found. Steve envied Buddy's capacity for joy. He was seeing a new Buddy and found it unsettling. He makes life seem so simple, he thought. Always smelling the rose and tasting the water. He sees what he wants to see and he wants to see happiness. Miranda and he were enjoying a camaraderie which excluded himself.

Since Steve had lost his licence, Buddy did all the driving and, after consulting his map, he took the wheel for the last leg of the journey and Steve again settled into the back seat while the other two sang hymns. Miranda was first to spot the sign to Strathard Castle The entrance was between two stone pillars and was guarded by a small stone lodge.

'Don't go in yet,' said Miranda to Buddy.

Surprised, Buddy drove the car into a lay-by a few yards beyond the entrance.

'Let's leave the car here,' said Miranda, 'and walk to the castle. We can come back for the car after we've done a recce.'

Buddy readily agreed. Steve wanted to protest but decided against it. Crossing swords with Miranda would only make him feel worse than he already felt and that was bad enough. Besides, he could do with some fresh air.

Buddy waited until Steve slouched out of the car then checked windows and locked all the doors. Miranda was already across the road and stepping between the large pillars. They passed the lodge unchallenged and began their journey down a long drive.

Steve held back, in no mood for conversation. He would have given his eye teeth to be on a plane back home. He'd lost interest in castles. Miranda irritated him. He lagged behind, watching Buddy take in every stick and stone, branch and twig of the journey along the winding drive.

Jenny Fraser was the first to speak.

'An atom of delight!' she declared as she raised her arms to the sky.

Steve, feasting his eyes on her face and thinking how all its various features merged into perfection, heard himself saying, 'What a perfect description.'

'Not mine,' said Jenny, as they all rose to their feet. 'It is the title of a book by a favourite Scottish author. But let me introduce myself. I'm Jenny Fraser and I welcome you all warmly to Strathard Castle.'

'Buddy Regan,' said Buddy offering his hand. 'We've spoken on the telephone.'

'I could never foret the voice.' She replied.

'Steve Bruce,' said Steve, offering his hand, which was accepted, accompanied by a warm smile.

'And this must be Miranda.'

'Morrison,' added Buddy, repeating slowly, 'Miranda Morrison.'

'Welcome to Strathard Castle, Miranda. I hope your visit will be a happy one.'

The outstretched hand was skilfully ignored by Miranda but this did nothing to chill the older woman's warmth. In place of the nymph-like creature, exulting unselfconsciously in the magic of dance, she now pulled on her armour of suspicion, marked with offhandedness, bordering on the rude.

'Come and meet the musicians,' Jenny Fraser said, leading the way to the portico.

When Steve stepped inside the castle it was neither the architecture nor the furnishings which captured his attention. It was the motley groups of people populating the entrance hall. He felt he could be in the travel lounge of an international airport or the foyer of an international concert hall. Then again it could be the mingling of delegates at an international conference.

There was no sense of crowding, no stridency, no haste. Groups formed, separated, regrouped, and although a semblance of purpose was evident, it was devoid of urgency.

The air was buoyant with expectancy. A fork-bearded musician, carrying violin and bow, emerged through a doorway followed by men and women in quiet but animated conversation.

from the Royal Society of Astronomers. Another, she blance of purpose
was evident, it was devoid of urgency. explained, was skilled in carpentry,
one in animal hus-

bandry and all seemingly under the same conditions of unwritten
contract as themselves.

'Generally,' said Jenny, 'people enjoy lending a hand. There is such a
variety of assistance needed. It's all voluntary, of course.'

What on earth, wondered Steve, had the queer mixture of Jews,
Hindus, Buddhists and no doubt atheists like himself and Christians like
Buddy do here for the good of humanity? Crazy! And so was this galloping
fascination for Jenny Fraser crazy. He felt like a small boy finding a bag of
candies and wanting to swallow them all in one go.

'Ah Father O'Doyle,' she called to an approaching priest wearing a
crucifix round his neck.

'Jenny, me darlin',' he replied. 'What is it I can be doing for you?'

'Come and meet our latest residents, Father. This is Steve Bruce, a
Canadian from Vancouver and Miranda Morrison, an American from -
where did you say in America, Miranda?'

'I didn't say,' Miranda replied.

'Ah then be sayin' it now, me darlin',' said Father O'Doyle.

'New York,' offered Steve and received a glare from Miranda.

'Ah! New York is it. Now isn't that grand. I'll be swearin' that one day,
with the blessing of St Christopher, the patron saint of travellers, that I'll
be parading in New York on St Patrick's Day. Tell me, me darlin', have
you walked with the saint in New York?'

'I am not a Catholic,' said Miranda.

'Ah, the shame of it. A darlin' lass like you outside the flock. You have
such a pretty face but I'll be swearin' I've never seen such toffee-coloured
curls and chocolate eyes together, have I not. Indeed I haven't.'

'Now stop your teasing, Father,' said Jenny. 'Can't you see you're
embarrassing Miranda.'

Father O'Doyle, she explained, had a chapel on the West Coast
but volunteered his services in Strathard from time to time. Besides
ministering to visiting Catholics, he lectured and held seminars on his
faith. Fortunately he would be with them for some time yet. They would
be sure to meet again.

The priest crossed himself, winked at Miranda, blessed them all and moved on. His place was taken by a young woman called Flora whom Jenny introduced as the housekeeper and official guardian of all castle comforts. She would take them to their rooms.

Buddy rejoined them to report that the car was now on the drive and their luggage was being taken care of. Reluctantly Steve watched Jenny walk away. Already he felt the loss. A voice hissed in his ear. It was Miranda offering him a poisoned chalice.

'She's married!'

He turned and looked at her, wanting to swipe the sneer from her face.

'You needn't get ideas,' she said. 'I saw the way you were looking at her. She's not for the taking.'

He wondered if this really could be Jenny Fraser's sister. He could recognise slight physical similarities but otherwise they couldn't be more different.

Buddy rejoined them and sensing the antagonism, suggested they all needed a breather and a shower.

'What I need is a stiff drink,' said Steve when Buddy and he arrived at their accommodation.

Buddy laid a warning hand on his friend's arm. 'Steady on, chum. It's not worth it.'

'That's your opinion.'

'Remember Greenock.'

About to say more he shrugged, sighed and entered his room.

Steve found his room large, well proportioned and uncluttered. The window offered a view of extensive gardens and glass houses.

'Good lord,' he muttered, dropping his suitcase and moving nearer to the window.

At the same moment Buddy burst into the room.

'I've the same view next door,' he explained. 'Have you ever seen anything like it?' His eyes were wide in amazement. 'There must be enough food growing there to feed all Scotland. I've always wanted to grow fruit and vegetables. Mary preferred flowers.'

This was the first time Steve had heard Buddy say his late wife's name. Never having stopped whingeing about his own misfortunes, he must have assumed that Buddy's cheerfulness, his singing and joking, his helpfulness to others meant everything was okay with him. Now, sensing a wistful note in his friend's voice, he wondered.

When Buddy turned to leave, Steve couldn't resist another whinge.

'Do you think you could get Miranda off my back?' he asked.

'She still fancies you,' said Buddy.

'I'm beginning to find her an embarrassment.'

'She's a mixed-up kid who'll sort herself out eventually.' 'Not without a push in the right direction.'

'Tell you what,' said Buddy. 'I'll persuade her to join me in some music making and I'll introduce her to the quintet. I see possibilities there. In fact, this could be a wonderful opportunity for her. I'd hate her talent to go to waste. She has so much.'

Alone again, Steve's mind flew back to Jenny Fraser where it now wanted to stay. When would he see her again?

Would she be dining with them? Would he have the chance to talk to her alone?

Smiling, he began discarding his clothing. He was still smiling when he stepped under the shower. There was something quite exciting about the whole set-up. There was enough material here for a dozen books, he thought as he soaped his hair, feeling an unaccustomed urge to write something of significance. He rinsed his hair, soaped himself and, holding his head back, enjoyed the stimulating force of the water on his body. When his thoughts became too highly concentrated on the face and figure of Jenny Fraser he adjusted the shower to cold, martyred himself for a few moments before stepping out and wrapping himself in a bath towel.

As he dressed he began taking in his surroundings in greater detail, the parquet floor, Persian rugs, the large four-poster bed covered in pristine white bedspread and matching curtains. The large wardrobe, chest of drawers and dressing table were highly polished and the general appearance of loving care was heightened by a bowl of autumn crocuses adorning the bedside cabinet in whose drawers he found stationery and a Bible. There was a small marble fireplace and on its hearth was a brass scuttle. This was indeed a residence of quality. His spirits rose. His luggage had been delivered.

When he unpacked he found his bottle of vodka. I can handle you, he thought, but felt reluctant to put it down. One small sip would make all the difference. It need only be one. He wanted to be fully functioning when he met her again. He felt an urgent need to impress. It was beyond rhyme or reason but the truth was he badly wanted this woman's approval.

He glanced at the door. Dared he? I've come to a sorry pass, he thought, as he looked again at the bottle in his hands, when I feel so threatened by my best mate. I must take control. I can do it. Only me. I know I can do it. The whole situation has been blown out of proportion. Too many meddlers in my life. Things must change.

Conscious of his racing pulse and the rising excitement in his groin, he uncapped the bottle and raised it to his lips. He only wanted to wet his tongue.

CHAPTER 10

He was lucky. Jenny Fraser arrived in the dining room when they had just begun their meal. Steve willed her to come to their table which she did. She offered more explanation of the castle organisation. The estate was completely self-sufficient, helped out considerably by volunteers. Some volunteers were happy to serve meals and help with kitchen chores. There were two permanent members of staff, called Flora, the housekeeper whom they had already met and Aggie, who was the cook. They were always on hand.

Volunteers were assured of quality living, ranging from quality produce, high standard living quarters, staggeringly beautiful environment, to participation in cultural activities which were contributed by volunteers from near and far. For a variety of reasons such volunteers found it worthwhile to share their talents or contribute their labour to life at Strathard castle.

'Is this what is supposed to be for the good of humanity?' asked Miranda cynically.

'It is more complex than that,' said Jenny, smiling. 'But it's true that part of the way we see it is that sharing talents and serving others can only benefit humanity.'

Miranda again! 'What's the religion here?'

'All religions and no religion,' said jenny.

'That's a contradiction if ever there was one.'

Buddy made some remark about wanting to make his contribution while Steve secretly wondered about the whereabouts of the missing husband. She had so far made no mention of him. She always used the royal we and now, for the first time, he took note of her wedding ring. He listened, enthralled, to her voice as she answered Buddy's questions about the garden.

'There's always a need for extra hands there. We don't use pesticides or any quick, easy gimmicks for plant control. Quality produce demands a lot of work.'

The royal we again, thought Steve. Who are they? Where are they?

'I'll offer my services in the garden,' decided Buddy, sounding more than satisfied.

'You seem to lay great stress on quality,' said Miranda. 'Does that apply to everything you do?'

'That's the idea,' said jenny.

'I mean personally,' pressed Miranda, to Steve's discomfiture.

'Personally, everyone is responsible for themselves,' said jenny.

'Quality is becoming less and less a considered option in our society,' said Buddy. 'Don't you agree, Steve?'

Steve, jolted out of his musings, focused on Buddy's remark with difficulty.

'Yes,' he said. 'Didn't someone say that "quality is never an accident; it is always the result of high intention, sincere effort, intelligent direction and skilful execution; it represents the wise choice of many alternatives?'

He was rewarded by a dazzling smile which, he hoped, was in admiration of his sagacity and felt heartily thankful for his excellent memory recall.

'Of course,' said Jenny. 'William A. Foster. A man after my own heart.'

'Me, or William A. Foster?' asked Steve.

'I'm sure you are both men of quality,' she said and his smile widened as he wondered at this miracle of happiness. Till Miranda put the damper on!

'You must let Jenny read one of your quality books,' she suggested with a sly look.

Steve cringed for both of them. Damn Miranda!

'Perhaps after dinner I can give you all a tour of the library,' offered Jenny.

'Miranda and I have been offered a session with some of the musicians,' said Buddy.

'A quality session,' Miranda smirked.

What a silly bitch she is, thought Steve.

'Miranda sings,' Buddy informed Jenny, surprising Steve with the evident pride in his voice.

'Like a linnet,' Steve said, his smirk as bad as Miranda's.

'Another time then,' said Jenny.

'I'd love to see it,' said Steve striving to hide his eagerness.

'Fine,' she said. 'There's something I must attend to first,' she explained, 'but I'll be in the library in about an hour, Steve, if you can find your way there. Anyone will tell you.'

Buddy and he rose to their feet as Jenny excused herself. 'I'll be there,' he said.

'I'll bet you will,' sneered Miranda, forking her cheese with unnecessary vigour.

'Must you be so ill-mannered?' Steve asked her.

'Must you be so cow-eyed? I told you she's married.'

'And so am I,' said Steve, hoping that was the end of the matter.

'You'd do well to remember that. You forgot before, remember?'

Buddy looked from one to the other, shaking his head.

'Have you forgotten about quality?' he asked them. 'Don't you think that, like charity, it should begin at home?'

'High-minded nonsense,' said Miranda. 'She's so high and mighty. I detest her.'

Buddy took one of Miranda's small hands in his, saying gently, 'There's one thing I'd like you to think about.' His voice was cajoling but, to the attentive Steve, seemed to disguise a deeper appeal. 'Quality singing. You have a wonderful gift, Miranda, which needs the best you can give it.'

Steve was surprised to see that Miranda's eyes were bright with unshed tears and this, together with her frown of nervous irritation, was betraying an underlying stress he was perhaps underestimating. He felt a momentary pang of guilt.

'Let's go and make music,' Buddy said.

Steve saw the reassuring pressure of his hand on hers which made him wonder anew at the kindness of this gentle giant. Was it just kindness or had this mixed-up kid really got to him?

He followed them from the dining room then made his solitary way to the reception hall. He wanted to absorb everything about this place, find out who all those people were, where they had come from, why they were here.

This time, with fewer people in the hall, Steve had more opportunity to note the sofas and deep armchairs, the coffee tables and potted plants. There was an abundance of fresh flowers. On the sofas and chairs were seated groups of people, some deep in conversation, some idly observing, others reading. His presence was quietly acknowledged as he wandered slowly around.

There was the rabbi in one armchair engrossed in his reading. The Catholic priest, Father O'Doyle, was holding sway over a rapt audience in another corner. Everyone he passed seemed friendly but made no inroads on his privacy.

Casually he inspected the framed pictures on the walls.

There were landscapes, Impressionists' prints, some portraiture and some innovative works of the modernists. He stood before a large, heavily-framed oil of attractive geisha girls. It was a Japanese-style painting by E.A. Hornel. This, he guessed, was probably the only original in the collection. He became aware of someone addressing him and turned to face the Englishman in the pinstriped suit.

'They're making quite a statement, don't you think,' the Englishman said, his arm gesture indicating the paintings.

'A very wide-ranging collection, I admit,' replied Steve, 'as wide ranging as the people around here.'

The Englishman offered his hand.

'Fitzgerald - Gerald,' he said. 'Here to offer a short introduction to philosophy.'

'Bruce - Stevenson. Here by accident.'

Gerald Fitzgerald smiled in a relaxed and friendly manner.

'As a philosopher, I might say there is no such thing as an accident.'

Steve wondered how to handle this opening gambit. He veered from getting involved, aware of the fast approaching meeting with Jenny Fraser. On the other hand, he didn't want to miss an opportunity to find out as much as possible about Strathard Castle and its many-hued inhabitants.

'That would make some things difficult to explain,' he ventured.

'Accidents don't just happen,' said the philosopher. 'They are due to cause and effect, an unerring cosmic law from which none of us can escape.'

'You are a determinist?'

'To a degree. I'm what you call a soft determinist.'

'As opposed to?'

'A hard determinist. They believe no one is responsible for their actions. Everything is determined causally.'

'And you?' asked Steve, sneaking a look at the time.

'I believe in free will. You can lose, throw away or be robbed of everything, except the free will to choose your attitude in any set of circumstances. The free will to choose what to do. Do you believe in free will?' he fired at Steve.

Steve felt slightly rattled, then thinking that his impatience might be getting in the way of the right attitude, drew on his limited patience.

'What I've often wondered,' he said, now entrapped in the conversation he'd hoped to avoid, 'is whether or not a person who has inherited bad genes can be held responsible for any actions resulting from these genes.'

The philosopher smiled.

'If I were a hard determinist I'd say, no. If you are already causally determined to act, you cannot be held responsible for your action.'

'People like to believe they are responsible for their decisions and have the freedom to choose,' said Steve. Here the philosopher's smile widened.

'As a soft determinist I agree. If you have alternatives on offer then you have the freedom to choose. You have free will. We soft determinists think that an action is an expression of someone's character and personality, irrespective of antecedents, and that the individual can be held responsible for it.'

'But what about genetic health tendencies? Drink, for instance.'

He could hardly believe he'd said that.

'Difficult to generalise, but I'd say it's still the attitude to what you inherit that counts. As a soft determinist I'd say that it is character which affects attitudes. You don't have to wait until something happens then bear the brunt of the consequences. You can always create a cause and enjoy the fruit of the effect. Free will lets you do this.'

'Too deep for me,' said Steve.

'Look in on one of my lectures while you're here.'

'I'd like that,' said Steve, surprised to realise that he meant it. He excused himself. The hour had passed and it was time for him to find the library and Jenny Fraser. By this action, he decided, he was creating a cause in the hope of an interesting and exciting effect.

He found her in the library alone, except for a shorn-headed Buddhist who sat reading, straight backed, behind a rosewood desk. The Buddhist raised his head as Steve entered, rose to his feet and bowed.

'It's all right, Yeshe. I'll take care of Steve.'

The Buddhist, when introduced, bowed his shorn head, his hands in praying position, his eyes laughing, mouth smiling. Then he sat down and resumed his reading.

'We keep the library manned,' said Jenny. 'Our books are precious to us and we are zealous in our guardianship. They are for borrowing but must be protected, at all times, against the frailties of human nature.'

Jenny explained that the library had originally been the castle ballroom. It was a large room, well proportioned, as were all the rooms in the castle. The high ceiling gave stature, the bay windows with views of herbaceous borders and specimen shrubs decorating expansive, neatly-edged lawns, gave character. A fireplace with smouldering logs scenting the atmosphere lent its own particular graciousness to the scene. Scattered chairs and cushioned beaches offered comfort. The large decorative porcelain vases holding autumn sprays of chrysanthemum and copper beach leaves had been determined by good taste. The highly-polished floor was uncarpeted, enhancing the avenues of mahogany shelving that housed the library of books.

'Most of the books I inherited,' said Jenny, 'but since establishing our community here, they have been enriched by the generosity of others. We are most fortunate.'

Steve was only mildly interested. He wasn't here to talk about books. He wanted to talk about the owner of the books.

'It's always difficult to know where to begin,' said Jenny. 'Perhaps if you would ask questions about anything you'd like to know, we could begin there,' she suggested.

How can I ask her about her husband, flashed Steve's thoughts. Where is he? Who is he? Why isn't he here? Or ask her for her secret of happiness. No one could feign such joie de vivre. Or maybe, his thoughts considered in their lightning track, I could ask her if she has any idea what she is doing to me.

Instead he followed her meekly along the avenues of fossilised thinking, admiring her total perfection of body and mind conveyed by her elegance and erudition. She was offering tempting titbits of information on various volumes as they walked the literary aisles, but he wanted none of them. His hunger was not for this or that author, however erudite or illuminating their works might be. It was for a grasp of understanding of the milieu in which he now found himself. He felt himself caught in a creation of significance, at the heart of which was this woman who had instantaneously captivated him.

'I am humbled,' he now found himself saying like a pathetic Uriah Heap.

She stayed her leisurely progress and turned to him. He forced his eyes to her face and found himself trembling. There was something in the intelligent gaze, the clean lines of her bones and her rich colouring which roused in him an inexplicable need.

'I'm not only humbled,' he told her. 'I'm shattered.'

She stopped at a bench and, seating herself, imperceptibly motioned him beside her. She made no attempt to speak but seemed to be waiting for him to say more.

'My writing is trash,' he blurted.

'That's all right,' she responded.

'How can it be all right?' he asked, momentarily taken aback by her answer.

'I thought you laid great stress on quality.'

'I do because that is how I am at this moment.'

'Meaning I'm not?'

'You would have no problem about it if you were.'

He was confused. He waited for her to elaborate but she said nothing. He knew she had not withdrawn but was leaving the direction to him. He struggled to sound light-hearted.

'I must sound as depressed as a cookie in a crusher.'

She smiled.

'When I am depressed I know it's just that I'm not going where I want to go so if you realise that and know where you want to go, there should be no problem.'

'You make it sound simple.'

'Our thoughts are just little spurts of energy which need direction. Sometimes when worries about the castle and all the organisation it entails grow out of proportion to its worth I take myself off to a rise on the edge of the moors where I can look down on its turrets and tiles. From that distance I can see it in perspective as merely a venue for what is really important. It could just as easily have been a huddle of hamlets or a park full of tents. The edifice with all its heavy maintenance and magnificence isn't the most important thing in my life, after all. It's the powerhouse within that is important. The further away from the problem, the better chance of seeing it for what it really is - a physical arrangement of stone and mortar to house an ideal. Then the castle and all its physical concern soon slips into perspective.'

'Perhaps that's why I have travelled a long way from Canada. I wanted to disentangle myself from my problem and look at it from a distance.'

'And?'

'It travelled with me, I'm afraid.'

She made no comment but did nothing to sever the delicacy of their communications. They sat in a more comfortable silence. There was a whisper of activity from the desk where the Buddhist monk had come to life again. He seemed to be tidying up his papers and books. Jenny broke her silence.

'Our resident Buddhists have enriched Strathard beyond measure.'

'Why are they here?'

'Your English philosopher friend, Gerald, would doubtless say because of cosmic causality. They are Tibetan monks whose monastery, indeed whose country, was violated by Chinese force. Now there was a problem. Some of them made the decision to try to preserve their rich cultural and spiritual heritage. Most of them went to India but there are a few groups who have found refuge in Scotland. Strathard is providing a temporary refuge for some. Sadly they are not going to be with us for much longer. They are needed further south where other Buddhists are building a temple and retreat. Unfortunately their gain will be our loss.'

'What do they actually do here?'

'Their main aim is the preservation of their own timeless culture and in its preservation they are teaching us the secrets of their arts and the vision of their ideals. I shall take you to their small community and you shall see their work. You will see for yourself that it is not just their carvings and paintings that are the inspiration to us here but the manner in which they carve and paint and which is all important to our own spiritual development.'

I wish I could paint you, thought Steve, but I could never do you justice. It would take a Titian to do that.

'They also contribute to our practical needs here,' Jenny was continuing, 'You will find the Buddhists helping in the garden, on the farm, in the kitchen. They do all our printing. Our newsletters are distributed world wide. They will put the same dedication into cleaning toilets as into gilding their little Buddha statues.'

There was a silence. Steve was reluctant to do anything that would bring the conversation to an end. The Buddhist had risen and was bowing to each corner of the room. He seemed to be performing some type of ceremony. Steve watched as he balanced a crescent-shaped bowl in the palm of one hand then began stroking its rim with a wooden stick which he held in the other hand. The resulting vibrations produced an array of rich and powerful overtones, which hung suspended in the air long after the Buddhist had ceased stroking.

Steve was acutely aware of Jenny's hand on his arm as she led him to the Buddhist whose face was lit with laughter and who was happy to explain this delightful phenomenon. At her request Yeshe demonstrated various ways of making the bowl sing. He could strike it or stroke it. His small wooden stick which he had used for stroking was called a wand. He showed Steve another stick which he called a beater and gestured that Steve should strike the bowl. The result was harsh. The Buddhist laughed then explained to the puzzled Steve that, like everything else, to obtain perfection took a long time. He then demonstrated with the beater, producing a breath-catching resonance.

'Very powerful,' said the monk, adding, 'in the spirit. Very psychic.' He smiled broadly. 'Good psychic, good singing. Good for chakras.'

With admirable diplomacy Jenny saved further instruction, promising the Buddhist that Steve and his friends would visit their workshops very soon and learn more of their customs.

'They're rather laid back - the Buddhists,' remarked Steve as they made their way back to the reception lounge.

'On the contrary, they are a very positive people. What I find most positive is their presentation of beliefs. While the Christian is commanded: for example thou shalt not kill; thou shalt not commit adultery; thou shalt not steal; not bear false witness and so on, the Buddhist is advised to have right understanding; right thought; right action; right effort; right awareness; right concentration. Accentuating the positive. It all comes to the same thing in the long run but I know which I prefer. You will find that they are totally absorbed in whatever they are doing. You watch them!'

However, Steve was more favourably disposed to watching Jenny Fraser. They heard music coming from the other wing of the castle where, Jenny informed him, the music room was situated. He recognised Handel's Messiah and when a soprano voice sang 'How Beautiful are the feet of them that preach the gospel of peace, and bring glad tidings of good things', they stopped involuntarily to listen.

'That's Miranda,' said Steve.

To himself he thought how ironic singing of peace, glad tidings and goodwill and secretly plotting to harm this beautiful woman by his side.

It was compulsive listening. Steve, looking at Jenny's face which was expressing surprise and pleasure, again found it difficult to believe that Miranda and she were sisters. For the first time since arriving at the castle he had misgivings about Miranda's deception. Her dislike and distrust of Jenny now seemed indicative of a negative attitude that could only bring trouble in its wake. His discomfort increased when he realised that, willy-nilly, he had been drawn into, and was inevitably implicated, in this deception and the realisation was like discovering a blood stain on pure white raiment. It stank and looked ugly.

Should he tell Jenny now before the situation worsened? But much as he wanted to, he knew his motivation was not for Miranda's sake, not even Jenny's, but for his own. He wanted his own hands clean because he saw in the woman, who was beginning to obsess him, the embodiment of the pure white raiment.

Jenny was speaking as much to herself as to him. He leaned nearer to listen, excited by her scent, a mingling of lavender and woman.

'She is really good.'

'Surprised?' he asked.

'Yes, I am.'

'She's had no training and her repertoire seems to consist of church hymns, folk songs and now, I'm learning, the Messiah which is often sung in churches, I believe.'

'We've been looking for a soprano. Every year at this time, neighbouring church choirs perform the Messiah in our village church. It is billed for Sunday week and our soprano has had to withdraw for health reasons.'

'I'm sure Miranda will be delighted to oblige, if she's good enough to be considered, that is.'

To himself he thought - centre stage! She'll jump.

'Oh she's good enough,' said Jenny. 'No doubt about that. Have you known her long?'

'Buddy and I only met her on the liner. Buddy felt sorry for her, I think. He's soft-centred is Bud!'

'Yes, I've noticed.'

'And, of course, he loves her voice. He's very musical himself. Plays the guitar.'

Jenny sighed, a long audible gasp, as if she were trying to unload then she flicked her wrist to check her watch, a barely perceptible frown denoting concern.

'I have to go.'

Steve began an apology.

'I'm, sorry if.

'Please don't be sorry. I have enjoyed your company. Steve watched her go, thinking she was now on her way to the phantom husband who, without either shape or form, was already threatening his new sense of well-being.

If ever I needed a drink, it is now, he thought. Not to get drunk but just one sip to pay homage to Bacchus and Jove and lovely Venus. The problem was he no longer had a secreted bottle. The night was still young. Buddy and Miranda were, for the time being, out of his hair. The village couldn't be far off. In the village there was bound to be an inn or hotel or somewhere he could buy a bottle of Scotch. He could hardly be expected to be in Scotland and not taste its whisky. My God, that would be throwing their hospitality back in their face. It wasn't as if he was going to get drunk. He had no need for that. He was in control and that was something to celebrate. He'd never have a better chance.

He was on the road into the village. His only light was from a sliver of new moon and the stars. He could smell the sea. He stepped out briskly and as he walked he relived his experiences since Jenny Fraser had spoken in his ear and led him to the dance. Something had happened to him in that dance and this something stayed with him until he reached the brightly welcoming lights of the Strathard Arms.

A friendly landlord, called Jimmy, served him a bottle of his best Scotch. He guessed that Steve was a new resident at the castle, hoped he'd enjoy his visit, and introduced him to his wife who had appeared from behind a beaded curtain. She was a colourful lady like the gypsy girls in illustrated folk lore books. She wore a red bandanna on her black curls and was weighted with sparkling jewellery. Not young, but lively. Not beautiful, but attractive. Her name was Theresa. She wrapped the bottle of whisky in a tartan bag, took his money and gave him his change. As she placed the coins in his hand, she held it open and studied his palm. He might have guessed.

'Ah,' she said.

'Good?'

'Very lucky.'

'You're joking.'

'No. You are going to be lucky,' she said, still studying his palm.

'Lucky in love?'

'I should think a handsome man like you would have no problem where love is concerned.'

'Blonde? Brunette? Or maybe redhead?' he joked.

She looked at him then and he noted the dark intensity of the eyes and the small round ears bedecked by dangling rubies.

'Now that would mean money crossing the palm.'

'I'll take your word for it,' he laughed as he pocketed his change, took a firm grip on his bottle of Scotch and bade the stalwart Scottish landlord and his fiery gypsy lady farewell.

The evening air felt cool after the warmth of the hotel. He'd noted the pleasant arrangement of tables, couples in corners, companions intent on dominoes and a few youngsters letting fly with the darts. Nice place, he thought. Must go back.

His step was light as he set out for the castle. The moon was sulking behind clouds. Even the stars had dimmed.

Lucky, he thought. Two days ago he would have laughed. Tonight he felt it wasn't impossible. Again he had that strange feeling that he was meant to be here in this remote little village in a remote little country at this time. That was his luck. He was meant to be here. The fates had decreed that he should meet Jenny Fraser. Why otherwise could he be so affected by the whole set up which had so impressed itself on his psyche.

He began to sing, "The trumpet shall sound and the dead shall be raised incorruptible, and we shall be changed."

An owl flapped from a tree top. He wanted to laugh. He thought of Jenny as he'd seen her in the library and then, without warning, the balloon of his euphoria burst. His spirit deflated, robbing him of his gusto. What must she think of him? What a fool he was, what a bloody selfish fool! He remembered how proud she had sounded as they had begun the inspection of her library. How happy she had been to share what was obviously of great importance to her. What had he done? He'd shown no interest, made no remark, had failed to honour the occasion or at least respect it. He'd whinged like a spoilt child, gone on about his trashy writing, exchanged her gems of wisdom with a disgusting show of self-pity. He hadn't even thanked her for her time. His feel-good factor was no more.

He had reached the castle gates. He'd go straight to his room and sneak a consolatory drink. He had intended a personal celebration but consolation was more in keeping. One thing was for sure. First thing tomorrow morning he'd seek her out and put matters right.

How fragile is the gift of happiness, he mused.

CHAPTER 11

En route to breakfast Steve found Buddy and Miranda studying the notice board.

'There's a talk on alchemy today,' Buddy pointed out. 'What's that?' asked Miranda.

'A type of medieval chemistry,' replied Buddy, 'when they tried to convert common metals into gold.'

'That would be useful,' she giggled.

'Or, if you prefer, you could listen to a talk about the plight of Tibet,' suggested Buddy but got no response from the other two.

'Papa is lecturing today.'

Beside them stood a young girl, large dark eyes in an oval face framed by raven-black hair. She was olive-skinned, strongly boned and in every way a daughter of Israel. Before they could speak she turned from them and raised her arm.

'There he is. I must go to him.'

Steve recognised the rabbi whom he'd seen on his arrival. He was soberly attired, his cap of identity balanced on top of thick iron-grey hair. His beard was long and thick, his shoulders stooped as if bearing the weight of the world. His sorrowful eyes seemed to mirror all its woes. When they looked upon his daughter's approach they lit up with tenderness. Placing an arm across the young girl's shoulders, they walked off together already deep in conversation.

'There he is,' said Buddy, pointing a finger on the day's itinerary. 'Rabbi Walters, Lecture Room, 2 p.m., speaking on The Mysticism of the West.'

'In the meantime,' said Miranda, 'I suggest we have breakfast?'

'What are your plans for the rest of the day?' Miranda asked Steve when they were seated and Buddy had gone to the counter to give their order.

'Haven't any.'

'In that case will you help me with mine? I want to go into the village. I want to know exactly where I was born.'

'You could ask Jenny Fraser. She could tell you all you want to know,' said Steve, adding, 'Aren't you afraid we might tell her who you really are?'

Miranda looked from one to the other. Steve returned her stare. Buddy poured tea while they waited for their bacon and eggs.

'You might,' she said, 'but somehow I don't think you will. You are both men of honour.'

'I wouldn't count on it.'

'Tell Steve the good news,' said Buddy, passing the tea cups.

'I've been invited to sing soprano at a performance of the Messiah on Sunday week. It's in the village church. It's not the type of venue I'm used to,' she added, 'but they seemed desperate to have me and it seemed churlish to refuse.'

Buddy elaborated on the good news.

'The viola player, who is Italian, is also a trained singer and has offered to give Miranda some master classes.'

'That's great,' said Steve, not wishing to appear churlish either.

Miranda shrugged.

'And,' continued Buddy, as her contribution to the community, she has agreed to be responsible for the music scores.'

'You'll be playing the harp next,' said Steve without a titter.

Miranda glared at him.

'Are you, or are you not, going to help me dig for my roots?'

'I am not. I want to explore. Since I'm neither musician nor gardener I'll have to look around for some way I can make a contribution to the community. You can manage fine without me.'

About to speak, Miranda changed her mind when their cooked breakfast arrived. When they had finished their meal they went their separate ways.

The fine weather was holding. Steve went off to explore the castle grounds. A tempting wooded area turned out to be a miniature forest of a mixed arboreal heritage. Although mainly birches, there were young oaks, rowans, some hazel and ash and on the far fringe, where the moors began, was a belt of Scotch pines. He stopped to watch a squirrel swell her cheeks with the fallen nuts from the hazel trees. Being late autumn the ground was richly carpeted in bracken. Shuffling his way through this he sniffed the rank odour of natural decay and studied the heather shoots creeping out from small boulder cracks. He stood still to watch a thrush picking at the red rowan berries until it was disturbed by the scurry of a squirrel. Was it the same squirrel, racing off with her hoard of nuts? In lighter mood he made his way from patches of shade to dappled sunlight into the low glare of the autumn sun where the forest finally gave way to the moor.

He thought of Sam and how much fun they could have had here together. He imagined Lucky chasing rabbits and Sam chasing Lucky. He visualised them showered with clouds of brown and yellow leaves disturbed by their passage. He heard Lucky's barks and Sam's excited laughter. He realised that he was grinning.

Then he stopped in his tracks. Some yards ahead there was a young girl seated on a stool applying paint to canvas. She was facing him but was so engrossed in her brush strokes that she hadn't seen him. It was the rabbi's daughter.

Politesse required him to retreat. Artists were temperamental people who didn't like to be disturbed when working but he was reluctant to withdraw. Watching a pretty young raven-haired beauty totally absorbed in painting some trees on a fine autumn morning with a wild moorland landscape behind her, cumulus clouds above and birds singing, was yet another tantalising vignette of the happenings in this unusual community in which he now found himself. It seemed a moment to be cherished.

The girl, sensing his presence, raised her head. Seeing him, she smiled, the delight in her large dark eyes clearly visible. Encouraged, he left the cover of the woodland and approached.

'I don't want to disturb you,' he said, keeping a safe distance.

'That's all right,' she assured him. 'I'm almost finished.'

Stretching her arm, she added, 'My name is Rahel, by the way.'

Steve took the small white hand in his and said, 'And I'm Steve. I'm delighted to make your acquaintance. May I see your painting?'

'If you like but I don't think you'll understand it.'

You can say that again, he thought, as he looked in amazement at the canvas. He saw an arrangement of circles, triangles and parallel lines all seemingly interconnected. Inside the circles were finely painted words of some peculiar identity and contained in the connecting paths formed by the parallel lines, were a variety of glyphs and symbols.

'Well?'

She was laughing at his obvious bewilderment.

He was also slightly embarrassed.

'It's quite a surprise,' he managed. 'I was expecting trees.'

'It is a tree.'

Now he was speechless. He hadn't taken her as an oddity. She looked and sounded intelligent. She seemed amused at his dismay but also kindly. He tried a feeble quip. 'A lollipop tree?'

She threw back her head in glorious laughter, startling a rabbit which scuttled off in alarm.

'Don't let my father hear you say that.' She was still chuckling. 'Rabbi Walter,' she explained. 'He's scheduled to give a very deep and learned lecture on this tree this afternoon.'

Steve continued to gape in total ignorance.

'This,' she said, 'is the tree of life. Watch!'

She took a piece of charcoal from her assortment of materials and drew, around the circles, triangles and paths, the outline of a figure sitting in the lotus position. The top circle was now inside the top of the head and where the soles of the feet touched, was the bottom circle with the others geometrically placed between. It still made little sense. Seeing his puzzlement, she painted the title in bold lettering. The Tree of Life. Then above that she painted, even bolder, Kabbalah.

Snippets of memory were surfacing but he still felt inadequate to comment intelligently and he had no desire to give offence. 'I thought it was spelt differently,' he managed to say.

'Like this?' she said, painting Qabalah on a blank piece of canvas.

'Yes, with a Q.'

'That's how it's spelt for the Western versions. And sometimes,' she continued, 'it is like this. Cabala. That's the Christian version. The word itself is derived from the Hebrew, meaning to reveal. It goes back a long time.'

'What does it do exactly?' he asked.

'The Qabalah means to "receive" but it also means to "reveal". As above, so below. This tree is a map. It helps you understand and connect body, personality, soul and spirit.

It shows where you are and where to go to connect. Papa would explain so much better,' she apologised.

'No please,' said Steve, captivated by her wide eyed innocence. 'Go on. You are explaining beautifully.'

'The spheres must balance. In the personality triangle we have opposite spheres of thoughts and feelings. These have to balance and the paths which connect them tell us how to balance. In the higher level of the soul the Will Sphere has to balance with the Love Sphere and higher still, in the spirit, Awareness must balance with Purpose.

'It shows us where we are in life, where we came from and where we can go.'

'Great stuff!' enthused Steve, preparing to join in the joke, but the girl, who casually introduced herself as Rahel, turned serious.

'It is also a map,' she informed him.

'Are these the roads?' he humoured, pointing to the parallel lines.

'Well, yes. You see the top three spheres are for the spirit, the next three for the soul and the bottom three for the body. We can grow from the bottom of the tree, to spirit, at the top, and the many paths along which we must work to get there. You can work upwards in any path from where you are to attain a higher level of consciousness or work in a horizontal path to find balance. You see,' she said, tapping a tidily manicured nail on the canvas, 'in spiritual endeavour one should strive for a balance between spiritual love which you could think of as awareness and spiritual will which is purpose. And see too, Steve,' she said warming to her subject, 'in the spirit section there are the extremities of will and love which need balancing and in the personality level a healthy balance is needed between thoughts and feelings. Understand?'

'Mm. I think so,' not wishing to disappoint.

'The Kabbalah emphasises,' she continued relentlessly, 'balance in all things.'

'I can see that.'

'You are a very good listener, Steve, and especially when I don't believe you understand a word of it.'

Steve grinned.

'I get the drift, but since I've never come across it before I hope I'm excused my lack of enthusiasm. It seems an onerous way of living the daily life.'

'You should come to Papa's lecture.'

'Unfortunately, it is not possible today. Perhaps his next one.'

'We leave tomorrow but we will be back again next year. Papa loves to come to Strathard.'

He decided to return to the castle with her and help carry her load. She talked about her father, the rabbi who admired the ideals of Strathard Castle very much.

'He lectures in many countries,' Rahel said, 'but this is his favourite place. He constantly sings the praises of Jenny Fraser and the imagination she has shown in the use of her inheritance. He was a survivor of the holocaust. All of his family died in a concentration camp. He was twenty when he was released in 1945 and married my mother seven years later. I was born in 1953.'

'So that makes you a mere seventeen years old now,' said Steve.

'And how old do you think my father is?'

A quick calculation told Steve that the rabbi would now be 45 and without the dates he would have guessed he was at least in his late sixties. Rahel read his expression.

'He was already an old man when he left the concentration camp but I suppose you could say he was lucky to have survived at all.'

He looked at her. Such an old mind in a young body, he thought.

Aloud, he said, 'He is lucky to have you.'

'I never really knew my mother. She died when I was born. My father has brought me up alone.'

'He has done a wonderful job.'

To his own ears his words sounded trite in contrast to the way his feelings were being stirred. She is so young to be spending her time balancing thoughts and feelings, treading spiritual paths from one sphere of awareness to another, having the responsibility of an old man's happiness on her shoulders. What should she be doing, an inner voice asked him?

Planning revenge on a sister, discarding an aunt who had brought her up since she was a baby? Was the lovely Rahel so badly off, after all? She had the greatest gift of all. Love. And if she acquired it by studying ancient scripts of the Hebrews that should make no difference. Good was good then as it is now and the sum of human happiness was derived by the same equations.

'My father says that by helping others to understand the great potential of humanity as illustrated in the Kabbalah, he feels he is doing something to balance the extreme powers of evil which he suffered from in the concentration camp.'

They had reached the main driveway. A group of visitors were boarding a bus for departure.

'Many groups come here for the lectures, concerts and exhibitions,' said Rahel. 'They usually come for a good time. Hopefully, some of them might leave, having glimpsed or felt or become aware of other things which start a train of new and exciting thinking.'

'Or they might think it's a crazy mixed up place, neither one thing nor the other but good for a laugh,' replied Steve.

'I hope you don't think like that, Steve,' said Rahel.

'I don't know what I think any more,' was the reply. Steve saw Miranda emerge from the hotel. Seeing him with Rahel she moved towards them.

'I've been looking for you everywhere,' she called before she drew abreast.

'Rahel, this is Miranda. Miranda, Rahel.'

Rahel turned a bright smile on Miranda who barely acknowledged her presence before continuing her attack on Steve.

'You know I wanted you to come to the village with me.'

'I'll be off then,' began Rahel. 'Goodbye. It has been nice meeting you, Steve. I see Papa waiting for me. I must go to him.'

'Let me carry this...'

'No need,' she interrupted. 'I've evolved my own transport system.'

So saying, she skilfully manoeuvred her belongings into a manageable arrangement and left to be joined by her Papa who immediately relieved her of her burden.

'Where on earth did you pick her up?' Miranda asked, making no attempt to hide her annoyance.

'It's your charm and sensitivity I find so delightful,' Steve said, feeling an intense dislike for this woman who brought out the sarcastic boor in him. Was this the woman whose singing could pluck the heart from an audience and who could dignify her body in spontaneous dance?

'You heard what Buddy said,' he now reminded her. 'I've publishers to appease and the sooner I get back to my writing the better.'

'I'll go alone then,' she said peevishly.

'You do that.'

They parted acrimoniously, made no easier for Steve who realised he'd now committed himself to labouring on his book when all he wanted to do was find Jenny Fraser and make things right between them. The longer he carried the guilt of his self-centred behaviour in the library, the heavier became the load.

After a light lunch in the dining room when he sat facing the door and willing her to arrive, he went to his room disappointed, hauled his portable typewriter to a small table and dragged some paper from his luggage, largely still unpacked.

Indulging in the usual reluctance to start writing he wandered to the window and tried to identify Buddy among the workers busy in the gardens. His mind wandered to Rahel and her innocent belief in some outdated doctrine of morality. He remembered the Buddhist monk and his performance on the singing bowl. He recalled the genial philosopher defending man's right to free will, heard again the charmed chuckle of the priestly Father O'Doyle.

He sought solace with thoughts of Buddy's well-intentioned bully tactics and the friendship which was his one lifeline to reality. He felt in no mood to salve his conscience with Miranda. There may be good reasons for her self-centred behaviour which would be better left to Freudian investigation.

Then, like a balm on his own turbulent feelings, he let his mind come to rest on Jenny Fraser. He tried to evoke the feelings she roused in him. He tried to recapture the atom of delight they had experienced on that first momentous meeting. The more he attempted to relive the occasion, the more improbable it seemed. Had it happened? Had he really danced like some animated gnome, hand in hand with a heavenly fairy, in a scene straight from the pages of a book on Woodland Magic?

He turned from the window. His mind was made up. He would write a quality piece which would befit her eyes. He would do it and he would do it well. He hadn't been long here but long enough to find some idea worthy of distilling from its base metal manifestation and transforming it to quality gold. Strathard Castle was like a kaleidoscope which could be patterned and re-patterned in colourful splinters of beauty and wonder. From the array of ideas and identities so far only just touched upon he would create a pattern fit for those wondrously penetrating and evocative eyes. But he wouldn't do it here. Like Rahel, he would carry his tackle to a place more natural to his muse and pen some worthy prose.

He left his room, made his way outside and set off towards the wood where he'd seen the thrush, the squirrel, the rabbit and Rahel with the high ideals. Perhaps some of them would rub off on him.

When he spied Miranda talking to some of the musicians he veered out of her possible view and made quickly for the wood. Having established some affinity with Rahel's spot he headed there, his pen in his pocket and a large notebook in his hand.

There was something about the wide open moorland with the blue hills in the distance and the charms of nature in the wood behind that appealed to him. It was in such contrast to his camping grounds in the Rockies, more intimate and gentle. Emerging from the wood he saw, on the moors, a horse and rider on the point of disappearing from sight. It took him unawares. Sam and he used to ride on camping trips. He felt gutted with longing for his son.

He realised that he had been deliberately pushing Sam out of his conscious mind. It hadn't been too difficult with all that had happened since arriving in Strathard. He'd found plenty here to cushion his pain but now, one unexpected association, had touched him on the raw. Maybe he should get on that plane. He needed Sam. He couldn't just let him slip out of his life without a fight. He'd got his drinking under control now, hadn't he? He was convinced it had never been out of control. Other people had, as near as damn it, tried to convince him otherwise. He no longer believed that he'd lost the will to write again. He just had exhausted his old formulae. He needed new thinking and if he couldn't find it here, in this castle of ideas, he couldn't find it anywhere.

He found a grassy cushion and made himself comfortable, his back supported by a tree trunk, his face towards the moor and distant hills. There was no horse, rider, or any other living thing in sight unless you could count a passing covey of grouse. He relaxed. He'd summon the muse who was invading his psyche. From her he would receive the inspiration to write an article of delight for the goddess who was patterning his emotions into twists and turns he found both exciting and threatening.

As he began to search for his own pattern of prose, his pen, limbering up with doodling seemed to have found a life of its own. It had recreated Rahel's lollipop tree with its connecting paths and overlaid figure sitting in lotus position. Then, apparently undirected as if in the grip of automatic guidance he began labelling the spheres with her name. The earth sphere it named Jenny, the spiritual one in the forehead, also Jenny. The sphere of wisdom and of strength, the spheres of love and beauty were all named Jenny. He began scrolling the connecting paths with the same name then, to give the inspiration real significance he wrote his own name on the two curved legs of the meditating figure. Next, entwining both names, he painstakingly filled the entire picture.

The activity was acting on him like a drug, a form of self-induced euphoria. As his mind busied itself with the pleasantest of images he didn't sense another presence. He did not hear the occasional crunch of dry leaves. His pen had done its job and he felt the better for it. After one admiring glance at his artistic expression he tore the page from the spiral spine and no sooner was it severed when it was torn from his grasp. A fiendish laugh sent his pulse racing and he knew a moment of panic.

Miranda sprang from behind, the paper in her hand. She raced before him, holding it aloft, taunting him with the written revelation of his innermost thoughts. As he sat, near paralysed with shock, she danced before him, singing Jenny's name at the top range of her voice then improvising while torturing him with dawning significance of what this could mean. He sprang to life, empowered by rage.

'You bitch! You bastard! You bloody little fiend!'

'Come and get it,' she mocked.

She was quicker than him and wilier, managing to elude his lunges while continuing her baiting. Pausing for breath he watched her, about six leaps away, crush the paper and push it down her sweater.

'Come on,' she taunted. 'Come and take it. I know you'd like to.'

She threw up her arms and pushed out her chest then ran past him, back on to the edge of the moor, free of the seclusion of trees and shade. The blood pounding in his ears, he renewed chase, gasping for breath while she raised her voice again in a full-throated, top note Jenny which seemed to hang reverberating in the air like the resonance of the Buddhist's singing bowl.

He caught her, trapping her arms in a vice-like grip and shook her in a wild desire to hear the rattle of her bones. She was a fighter. She gasped in pain but remained unnerved, her mockery turned to ridicule.

His back was to the moor, her face lifted to the sky where the bright light showed her eyes ablaze, daring, challenging him. He shook her again, cursing her and demanding the paper.

'Take it,' she urged.

In one movement he had her trapped inside one arm. He ripped her sweater, exposing her breasts, barely protected by a flimsy bra. He plunged his free hand into her cleavage, savagely bruising her breasts in his anxiety to retrieve the incriminating evidence. He felt Miranda's arms round his neck. She did not struggle. As his fingers grasped the paper she let out a yell and waved a hand above her head.

'Hi there!'

Above the hammering of the blood in his ears, Steve became aware of another kind of hammering. It was the pounding of a horse's hooves. He swirled round to confront the horse and its rider about twenty yards distant. At the same time Miranda broke loose, exposing her ripped blouse, her paper-thin bra and bulging breasts. Horrified, Steve looked for one fleeting but significant moment into the eyes of Jenny Fraser before she averted her glance and rode on.

'My! My!' pouted Miranda in obvious glee. 'Too high and mighty to pass the time of day.'

Steve remained rooted, staring into space, making no effort to clear his brain of its clamour.

'Steve?'

Slowly he turned to her and the look in his eyes stopped the words on her tongue.

'I think you'd better leave. Now. Go now because, I tell you, if you don't I won't be responsible for what I might possibly do to you.'

She opened her mouth to speak but no words came.

'Go!' he mouthed.

She turned, walking into the wood, the sound of crunching leaves drowning the sound of his own painful breathing. He stood watching her till she was out of sight, the crushed paper in his clenched hands. Then he turned and walked on the open moor.

CHAPTER 12

Six hours and some dark journeys of the soul later Steve ordered his third whisky in the bar of the Strathard Arms. He had eaten nothing since his scant lunch. Any thought of dinner at the castle had been squashed. He didn't want to see the castle again, or Miranda, or even Jenny Fraser. He gulped his third and ordered his fourth.

He felt okay. Didn't he? He was in control. Things weren't so bad. The thought of Jenny Fraser had touched a raw nerve, that was all. He was only drinking enough to deaden the nerve. It was like a visit to the dentist. The whisky was like the stuff of an injection which cushioned the pain of the drill. He'd stop short of a general anaesthetic. He was still in control. He wouldn't be fit to draw, the comparison if he was drunk, now would he? He lifted his fourth to his mouth in the hope of killing off the one still slightly exposed nerve end called the thinking of Jenny Fraser.

He looked around to confirm his sobriety. Yes. He could see exactly all that was happening. That proved he wasn't drunk, didn't it? There was the barman, a jovial chap called Jimmy. He was talking to his delightfully plump wife, called Theresa. Elbows on the table, he gave them a fingertip wave. Nice people.

Marvelling at his steady hand, Steve raised his glass and, eyes closed, touched it with his lips and sipped. He'd make this one last because he was in control. He lifted his head to the ceiling, eyes closed, lips moving, testing himself. Yes, he could still say the alphabet backwards. He was in control.

When he lowered his head again there was a blockage before his eyes. He blinked and the blockage formed into the black vestment of the priest he'd met at the castle. His delight in remembering the name of the priest added warmth to his greeting.

'Father O'Doyle. Have you come to find me?'

It wasn't what he meant to say but then he wasn't really sure what he had meant to say. He'd do well to concentrate.

'Mr Stevenson Bruce, I'll be bound. Thanks be to St Christopher that I should meet you here.'

'What's St Christopher got to do with it?' asked Steve in genuine amazement.

'He's the blessed saint of travellers.'

'Did he send you?'

'He's always with me on my journeys,' said the priest. 'Now by St Peter and St Paul can I be buying you a drink?'

'Are they with you too?' asked Steve, taking a liking to this saintly person of the church.

'Always. Another whisky, perhaps?'

Steve shook his head slowly, smiling his refusal.

'It's devilish kind of you, Father O'Doyle, but since I have no saints to protect me I must remain in control - understand?'

'There's more than enough saints to go round, my friend. Borrow one of mine. St Amand, perhaps, the saint of the wine trade or St Dympna, the saint of the insane? Now there's a story for you, my son.'

'You are laughing at me, Father O'Doyle,' accused Steve, wagging an admonishing finger.

'Laughing with you, my son. You have the laughter in your eyes, thanks be to the good Saint Aloysius, the saint of youth. You are young and when you are young you can laugh at life and let the world laugh with you.'

'I'd like you to be serious, Father.'

Father O'Doyle drew his hand down his face which emerged like a graven image set in stone. Steve's laughter was like cool water on a parched tongue.

'Do I look serious enough now, my child?'

'You look serious all right, Father, but I think I prefer you as you were.'

The priest smiled.

'Now tell me what troubles you, my friend?'

'I am not a Catholic, Father. I hold no truck with confessions, or saints for that matter.'

'You don't have to be a Catholic to have troubles.' 'I am planning a murder, Father.'

'Ah, for one of your famous stories, is it?'

'No. This one is for real. You are not shocked?'

'Should I be?'

'It is a woman I plan to murder.'

'Women can be difficult. They need a lot of understanding.'

'She has humiliated me.'

'Ah, then it is your pride you should kill, my son. Not the woman. If you kill the woman, you will surely suffer for your sin. If you kill your pride, you will live in the Lord and have the glory of the angels with you always.'

'I want her to suffer.'

'That will make you happy?'

'Very happy.'

'I'd just ask one thing, my child.'

'What's that, Father?'

'Don't leave the dismembered body in Strathard. It's too special a place.'

'What's so special about Strathard, Father?'

'Any place is only as special as the people in it. So many special people seem to have found their way to Strathard, thanks to the sainted lady herself, sweet Jenny.'

Steve wondered if he should perhaps accept that drink after all.

'You think Jenny Fraser is sainted then?'

'Well, that's maybe putting it a bit strong. She'd be the first to admit it. She's only doing what she thinks is sensible, demonstrating how a Jew, a Christian, a Muslim, a Hindu, a Buddhist and a Roman Catholic like myself, can set up their stalls together in the same place without undercutting each other's prices.'

'Is that what she's doing?'

'To put it another way, she hopes to encourage broadening of the mind, to coax people out of their own little refuge and have a look at other places of operation. Not such a bad idea, when you think about it.'

'And do you think an atheist could put up his stall in Strathard?'

'The more, the better, my son. Do you want to rent?'

'I haven't got the down payment.'

'And what might that be?' asked the priest.

'Quality, I'm led to believe.'

'Ah yes, they're sticklers for that here.'

'Tell me something, Father O'Doyle.'

'Gladly, my son.'

'Why are you a Catholic?'

'Now that's a tricky one. I can't say I've ever heard voices or seen visions. It just became a habit, a way of life I've never had reason to question. I'm comfortable with it and it makes me feel good. Everyone's religion should make them feel good.'

'Alcohol makes me feel good,' replied Steve, suspicious that the analgesic was beginning to wear thin. 'Can I call that my religion?'

'Ah, my friend, now we must be philosophical. How does that feeling of goodness connect with the rest of your life? Your feeling good when you drink gives you immediate delight and comfort.'

'And invincibility,' interrupted Steve with a nod.

'And invincibility,' agreed the priest, 'but is it a serviceable delight? Does that good feeling bear good fruits when you are not drinking?'

'I don't mind confessing, Father, that if drink is my religion then it has messed up my life. You see, Father, they don't think I'm in control but I can assure you that I am. Fully in control, Father. Now, look at me. Wouldn't you say I was fully in control?'

'You are indeed, my son. I can see your determination clearly.'

'My father was extraordinarily religious with the drink but he was not in control. It sure messed up his life and my mother's life but he's not going to mess up my life. Is he, Father?'

'No, my son. Not if you don't let him and can find it in your heart to forgive him for messing up his own life and your mother's.'

'He couldn't forgive himself, Father, because he shot himself. Bang!' Steve illustrated with finger to temple. 'A bullet through the brain. That sure messed him up a bit, Father.'

'God rest his soul,' said Father O'Doyle, crossing himself. 'I hope he's in hell,' said Steve.

'Kill your anger, my child. Light a candle for your poor father and mother and pray to the blessed Virgin Mary to bless you and forgive you for your sins.'

'If I were to light a candle I'd want the flame to join all the other flames that are roasting my father in hell.'

The numbness was wearing off, leaving a great discomfort. He was now in little doubt about his sobriety, for which he was grateful when he saw Buddy burst into the bar.

'Thought I might find you here,' he said to Steve then turning to the priest, 'Good evening, Father.'

His eyes turned from one to the other, doing a quick assessment. Looking relieved, he accepted the seat indicated by Father O'Doyle.

'Your friend and I have been having a very interesting conversation. Have you had a good day in the gardens?'

'Incredible,' said Buddy. 'I've never seen anything like it.'

After another searching look at Steve he continued.

'I expected the usual thing, you know, digging, planting, weeding, procreating, repotting, all the usual stuff, even leaf sweeping at this time of the year. When I arrived there wasn't a soul in sight, only row upon faultless row of beans and peas, carrots and beet, onions and miles of potato drills. Everywhere I looked was without blemish. No slug-eaten leaves or wilting flowers. Not even a weed to offend the eye. I waited a while, feeling a bit awkward then I walked through the greenhouses with tiers of staging laden with colourful flowers or berries or the healthiest of foliage with arching or trailing fronds. I peeked into sheds whose walls were accommodating spades, rakes, trowels, shears, each one shinier than the other with not a rusting one among them. I kept hoping to find someone to notice me.'

Buddy paused and seemed to withdraw for a moment.

'Then it happened!'

He paused again, his words hanging in the air. Steve recalled him to their presence.

'Go on then - what happened?'

Buddy shook his head like a dog emerging from a swim. 'I was transported to another world.'

'Oh yeah,' said Steve.

'Go on,' urged the priest with more expectancy in his manner. 'Tell us what happened, my son.'

'I was washed all over in sound.'

'Oh yeah,' repeated Steve.

'My heart palpitated, my whole being throbbed sympathetically to the energy filling the air with a pulsing, resonating, enveloping sound.'

'The singing bowl!' said Steve.

Buddy shook his head.

'No. It wasn't a bowl or any man-made instrument. When I recovered I followed the sound to a nearby building and found a group of people, about a dozen, mostly Buddhists, sitting on the floor, lotus position. I should have known straight away, of course.'

'Amen,' said the priest.

'Om,' said Buddy. 'They were chanting Om.'

'The sound that symbolises all the names and forms of God,' said the priest. "In the beginning was the Word and the Word was with God and the Word was God," he quoted. 'Om.'

'I remember it described as the sound of primal energy,' said Buddy, making no attempt to control his excitement. 'If you hum with lips gently closed, the sound resonates forward in the mouth and buzzes through the head. But the power of their mantra was spine-tingling. There were also a few Westerners and one man who looked sorely, disfigured.'

'That would be Todd,' said the priest.

'You know him. Eh?'

'He's the one who finds all the experts who come from time to time. He brought the wonderful musicians you so much enjoy and made it possible for the Tibetan monks to establish a small community here. His net spreads far and wide. He speaks Spanish, Italian, German and Dutch fluently.'

'Sorry to interrupt,' said Steve, 'but can either of you tell me what this has to do with gardening?'

'Perhaps another wee dram might help,' said Father O'Doyle. 'A thimbleful won't go amiss and the blessed Saint Amand is looking after us.'

He beamed on Steve.

'I'm not sure,' said Buddy so obviously not looking at Steve.

'I want to confess, Father,' said Steve. 'I confess to liking you. You know I'm in control and that is devilish good.'

'Being in control isn't the problem, my son. Staying in control is.' He leaned forward and whispered, 'I know. What do you think my confessions were all about in my heyday?'

Steve sat back in his chair, relaxed. No dram, thimbleful or otherwise, could compare with the feelings this saintly man was bestowing on him. He was conscious of Buddy's contained criticism, conscious of his own misgivings but here was a man who was making him feel good. That was something not to be dismissed lightly.

Father O'Doyle beckoned to the lively Theresa who approached them, smiling.

'Could we be having three of my specials, my lovely one?' asked the priest.

'That you can, Father,' said Theresa, giving Steve a wink which made him feel even better.

The drinks arrived. Father O'Doyle raised his glass. The others followed suit.

'Amen,' said the priest.

'Amen to that,' said Steve.

'Om,' hummed Buddy quietly and his rich tone seemed to wrap them all in its mellowness.

'Now tell us about the gardening,' said the Father, replacing his glass on the table.

Buddy lifted his glass, sniffed the contents, looked at the priest and smiled broadly before tasting.

'One of your specials, Father. Eh?' he asked.

'Never fails,' replied the priest.

Buddy leaned on his elbows, looking at his friends with a great seriousness.

'They rose from their meditation, bowing, beaming and after slipping into their garden shoes which were along one wall went immediately to their various tasks. Everywhere looked so perfect I thought there was nothing that needed doing. I was shown wicker baskets of bulbs to be planted, tubers to be bedded in sand for the winter, tomatoes to be picked, seeds to be enveloped and identified. Plants had to be packed for delivering locally and mailing further afield. This "Todd" chap, the badly disfigured one, was in charge. What was most noticeable was that once each person began a job he gave it his complete undivided attention. They worked with deliberation, never hurried or careless. Plants were neatly boxed, wrapped carefully with string measured to a thou - no wastage. They were all, without exception, totally involved in what they were doing.'

'They call it awareness,' said the priest. 'They are totally alive in each moment. They don't have room for thinking of what went before or what might happen next. They believe that if they leave no gap in the living of each moment, their thoughts can't move in any other direction to play havoc with their equilibrium. They don't spend time in regretting the past or worrying about the future and besides, they've been at it a long time. It certainly didn't happen overnight. Indeed, knowing the blessed souls as I do, they truly believe they are only at the beginning of enlightenment.'

'What did you do, Bud?' asked Steve. 'Just stand and watch them?'

'No way. The man with the disfigured face...'

'Todd,' interrupted the priest.

'Todd,' repeated Buddy. 'He welcomed me and thanked me for my proffered assistance. Their greatest need of the moment, he told me, was help with mail orders. I wasn't told what to do. I was shown and when I was in difficulty I was helped without asking. The funny thing is that I soon found myself becoming totally involved with the moment, giving my job every ounce of care of which I was capable, not because I was forced to, or even asked to, but because I wanted to. I felt included, part of something wonderful. When my job was finished I became conscious of things I'd previously missed.'

'Like what?' asked the grudgingly interested Steve.

'Like the perfume from musk roses, or the heady scents of borage, rosemary, lavender and trellised honeysuckles. My level of concentration had, it seemed, heightened all my senses. I swear I could almost hear the breathing of the ladybirds.'

'Bollocks! Pardon me, Father,' Steve smiled disarmingly.

'Why don't you come with me tomorrow, Steve,' suggested Buddy.

'I don't think so.'

There was no job Steve could imagine that would obliterate the past moment of this day or the dreaded moments of the next, nothing that was likely to mitigate his despair, or even dampen his anger, far less kill it.

'I'll find something,' he said wishing he could find the courage to leave Strathard.

They became aware of the barman's signals. Everyone else had long since left and it was getting late.

'Could I be offering you both a lift to the castle?' asked the priest.

Buddy's response was immediate saying it was such a fine night that the walk would do them both good. Steve didn't argue.

Steve had difficulty matching Buddy's steps. His feet felt twice the weight of his head and seemed determined to wander slightly off course.

Buddy appeared not to notice and the twin pillars of entrance to the castle grounds were visible before he bro silence.

'What, in God's name, did you do to Miranda?' he asked.

'And what, in the name of the blessed St Joseph, did she say I'd done,' returned Steve, striving for a light-heartedness he was far from feeling.

'She said you tried to kill her.'

'I didn't try hard enough.'

'She's in a terrible state.'

'Good.'

'For God's sake, Steve, what was so awful that could bring matters to such a pass?'

'She doesn't like me. I haven't danced to her tune and if she sees any way at all to punish me she'll take it. She's also a selfish bitch, intent on trouble. That's why she's here in the first place, remember.'

'What did you do that was so bad?'

'Forget it, Bud.'

'She's really in a state and when you didn't turn up f or dinner I imagined you'd be in a worse state.'

'Disappointed to find me sober?'

'Only just sober.'

'Well, as I say, forget it. Why should we quarrel because of the multifarious attitudes of mixed-up Miranda?' 'You're right. Let's change the subject. How's the writing?'

'What writing?'

Buddy sighed.

'You're making it difficult for me to placate publishers.'

'They can afford to wait. They've done okay by me. They owe me one. Tell them I'm on safari.'

'Have you written to Sam?'

That was a punch below the belt. Steve quickened steps to get the journey over. His armour was useless against these jolts of memory. Sam. Where was Sam? He seemed to have lost him in the surge of recent events. It was as if he'd been painted into the background of his life, lost in a plethora of warring emotions, buried beneath an avalanche of strange encounters. This land of narrow winding roads and of toy trains and motor cars and a conglomeration of the human race had no connection with Sam and Vancouver. Strathard valley was as far removed from Yellowstone Park as a pea was from a porcupine. Everything was unreal. Susan s far away and unreal. Jenny Fraser was near and necessary. He made up his mind that before he did anything else morrow, he'd find her and put the records straight. He owed it to himself. Like the publishers, Sam and Susan would have to wait.

CHAPTER 13

His determination to confront Jenny had not left him by the morning. Nothing was more important than regaining the woman's respect. He must reassure her that he was not in the habit of sexually assaulting young women.

First he had to find her and that could be difficult. In the vain hope that she might be having breakfast he made his way to the dining room. Where did she eat? Apart from their first evening meal he'd never seen her in the dining room again. Although there was no hangover, his head felt woozy and his common sense told him to have breakfast - coffee, at least.

Few people were breakfasting. Among them were Miranda and Buddy. Steve ignored them and joined Gerald Fitzgerald who was breakfasting alone.

'You couldn't make it to my lecture then,' Fitzgerald was saying without a trace of acrimony or disappointment.

Steve concentrated on the philosopher, trying to recall their last conversation.

'I forgot. Was it about free will?'

'Partly. There was a good attendance from surrounding districts, mostly professional societies. The subject seemed to interest them.'

'Did you talk about those troublesome genes I mentioned?' asked Steve, helping himself to coffee.

Fitzgerald looked at him for a moment before replying.

'Yes. Genes were discussed.'

Steve was interested. He forgot about Miranda and Buddy. He even forgot about Jenny Fraser for a moment. He wasn't interested in anyone else's genes, or any philosophical reflection on genes *per se*. He was interested only in his own genes which still troubled him like hell. He knew he was in control. Okay, but the solemn prognostications of his medical practitioners and their gloomy scientific conclusions still bugged him. Perhaps he was remembering his close shave on the previous evening when he'd been on the verge of another big binge. God bless Father O'Doyle. He cut into his crispy bacon and perfectly cooked egg.

'I seem to remember you saying that you thought a person's character could counteract what might appear to be causal inevitability.'

'Yes.'

'What type of character could do this?'

'What you are really asking is what qualities are needed to effect positive change?'

Steve bit into his toast, chewed reflectively before answering.

'Suppose,' he said, 'someone had an inherited tendency to...' laughing, he held his cup aloft, as if toasting, 'to drink, let us say.'

'I take it you don't mean coffee but serious drink, as in alcohol abuse.'

'Certainly not coffee,' said Steve, replacing his cup carefully on its saucer. 'Actually drink was the first thing to come to mind but it might be an eating disorder or sexual perversion, even smoking,' he said.

'Right!' said the philosopher with another penetrating stare. 'Let's say eating disorder, okay.'

'Sure, or smoking.'

'Right! Well, the first thing he, she, or let's say he for convenience, would have to do is to find out everything that's ever been written or reported about it. That would take some effort so he'd have to feel fairly determined about learning all he could - full scale research, in fact. Then when he does learn of the consequences - like learning smoking bugs the lungs, causes cancer, possibly fatal or, regarding eating, increases fat, hardens arteries, attacks heart, possibly fatal.'

'Or, interrupted Steve, 'drinks to excess, causes dependency, poisons liver, possibly fatal.'

'Right!' said Gerald. 'You'd have to admit just learning that wouldn't be enough. He'd have to do something about it. He'd have to act and if the genes were bad enough he'd have to act quickly, no shilly-shallying.'

'Is that it?' asked Steve, after a silence.

'I'm a philosopher although I seem to be talking more like a psychiatrist but I think that more than anything else he'd have to want to do it. He'd need to be passionate about it and feel it would all be worthwhile. In other words, he'd need to be strongly motivated. It wouldn't be easy and that's where character counts. He'd have to have strength enough to break the chain of causality by creating new causes. He could create more choices in which to exercise his free will. He'd need to be pretty imaginative too.'

Steve, pushing away his crockery, placed his elbows on the table.

'I sure wish I'd attended your lecture - what shall I call you? Dr, Gerald, Gerry?'

'Gerry will do, or just Fitzgerald.'

'Okay, Gerry and I still wish I'd heard your lecture.'

'There will be other opportunities if you hang around long enough. Is that likely?'

'I doubt it but, tell me Gerry, how did you come to be here in the first place?'

'I read about Strathard Castle and what was going on here. It intrigued me. I mean, who would be idealistic enough in this day and age to spend a million on demonstrating the importance of quality living and hoping to influence the mind-sets in society?'

'Do you think it does?'

'Who can say? Drop a pebble in a pool and watch the ripples.'

'Hardly revolutionary.'

'Revolutions aren't the only things that can change the world.'

'You can't tell with pebbles.'

The philosopher wiped a crumb from his lips with his table napkin.

'I've been introduced to ideas that make me think again about my own. I've watched people work with total involvement and seen the results of their work which has made me ashamed of my own backsliding. I suppose I'd go as far as to say I've been inspired yet no one has consciously set out to inspire me. It's just being here that's so good. I like the vibes. I only hope the feeling isn't lost when I'm back in my own life pattern. I expect that's when I'll need the effort and enthusiasm to do something about it.'

'I guess effort and enthusiasm are needed for most things,' agreed Steve.

He'd noticed the exit of Miranda and Buddy, the latter steering his companion skilfully past his table. When they'd disappeared from the dining room, he rose, shook hands with Gerald Fitzgerald and thanked him for his interesting observations on the subject of free will, telling him that he hoped they were predestined to talk further on the subject.

He must find Jenny. The elderly woman, called Aggie, came out of the kitchen. Steve remembered she was one of the two permanent members of kitchen staff. He decided to ask her.

'Jenny. Oh aye. I know where she'll be.'

'I'd really like to find her. It's important.'

'She runs the home farm. You're sure to find her there.'

She volunteered instructions and, lighter of heart, Steve made his way outside into the sunshine. Small groups of people were scattered around the grounds. He saw Miranda and Buddy with the musicians. The rabbi was talking to Father O'Doyle and another cleric who was dressed in sober black, relieved only by his dog collar. Steve couldn't remember having seen him before. He steered clear of everyone as he set forth to find the home farm.

From the full glare of sunlight his journey took him through the filigreed shadows of the wood then past the perimeter of the gardens. Here he saw Buddy assisting in driving stout poles into the ground. Steve halted, watching the two figures dig and hammer, their bodies working in concert to a steady rhythm. They were completing what appeared to be a long avenue of arched trellis work, each pole meticulously spaced. He forced himself to look at Buddy's companion. Poor chap, he thought. Just how did one get through life with a face like that? What chance had he of happiness?

Dismissing the thought, he concentrated on his own problems. Just how was he going to make Jenny Fraser understand that what she had seen on the edge of the wood yesterday was not what she probably was thinking. He realised it would be wrong of him to slate Miranda too much. But he was damned if he was going to take all the blame.

The home farm was separated from the gardens by about half a mile of scrubland beyond which was a sprawling building which could be byre or dairy. Wire netting contained poultry which Steve could see were having free range. When approaching the building he was welcomed by a golden Labrador with threshing tail. By its side was a small cairn pup who was doing all the talking, making occasional scurries from its canine companion to Steve.

'Hi chaps,' said Steve, giving them a minute or two to suss him out.

He continued along the side of the building, the Labrador at his heel, tail whirling, the terrier racing ahead to announce his arrival.

Then he saw her. His anxiety was lost in his pleasure. She wore slacks and sweater, her hair tied back with a bright ribbon. She approached quickly but unhurried. The Labrador had left his side to join the terrier in ecstatic recognition. She stopped to praise them, firmly bade the terrier be quiet then turned the full radiance of her smile on Steve who was wishing he had a tail he could wag. Her welcome took him by surprise.

'Have you come to help?' was her greeting as she smiled brightly.

'I'm here to apologise,' he heard himself say.

She waited for him to continue.

'I'm afraid I was selfish and insensitive in the library. I realise what an invaluable book collection there was and I was so intent on talking about myself I failed to appreciate what you were offering.'

'Apology accepted if it makes you feel better about yourself,' she said. 'We can meet there again some time before you leave and that will make me feel better. I never tire of our library. I like to think it's there for everyone who is interested. Now come and meet the chickens. I'm just about to choose the eggs for breeding purposes. You can help, if you like.'

Temporarily reprieved, Steve followed her alongside a succession of chicken coops with lean-to roofs covered in turf.

She led him into one of the coops explaining how important the housing of the fowl was to good egg production. Remembering what scant attention he'd given to his tour of the library Steve keyed into her every word. He listened to the importance of space for the hens to move around, especially in winter when they are kept inside all day. The cement floors could be cold so it was important to cover with a thick layer of straw, changed daily for cleanliness and to keep them free of disease. The windows should face south for extra warmth. This was all important, she told him because damp and draughty conditions bred disease and for hens of quality any suspicion of disease was to be avoided at all costs.

That word again, thought Steve. Quality! It seemed that for quality results, the list was long.

Steve's interest in chicken housing had been more than satisfied. His mind reverted to why he had come. He had made one apology. There was one other still to make. How should he broach it? He watched the expressions fleeting from eyes and mouth. He was conscious of the scent of her hair, the freckles on her arms, the shapely breast beneath the cotton shirt.

Steve watched the behaviour of a particularly lively hen energetically scratching the earth with both feet. He watched it throw back its head to target the grain with each eye then make a quick grab. Admiring her brilliant red plumage fired by the sun, he listened to her conversations with her sister hens. Into their lively clucking he dropped his own words, ill-thought but which could no longer be contained.

'I fear you may have misjudged my behaviour the other day when you saw me with Miranda.'

There was a long silence. His heart plummeted and his thoughts ran wild. When he felt like dissolving into thin air, she turned to look at him.

'I want to ask you something, Steve.'

'Yes?'

She led him to a nesting box further down the coop. 'Tell me what you see in there,' she asked.

Steve saw a layer of clean straw on top of which was a collection of eggs.

Bemused, he replied, 'Clean straw and a dozen eggs.' 'Are you sure?' she asked with a broad smile. 'Look again.'

He counted the eggs.

'More than a dozen, actually. Fourteen.'

'Fourteen eggs?'

He counted them aloud.

'Yes, I count fourteen.'

'Thirteen,' she said. She reached for one and placed it in his hand. 'Feel that and count again.'

Steve looked at the egg which felt surprisingly heavy and cold. He turned it over in his hands.

'It's china,' she said with a smile, 'placed there initially to encourage laying. She looked steadily. 'Like the fourteen eggs you counted,' she said slowly while holding his gaze, 'I've learned that things are not always what they seem.'

He was not imagining it. Her voice had changed. She was no longer just giving information and he knew that she wasn't just thinking about the chickens. She was, by her illustration, investing deeper significance into her words. Could she be telling him that she had not misjudged his behaviour, that indeed, she had not judged at all?'

'It happens all the time,' she said quietly. 'Things are not always what they seem. It's always better to keep an open mind.'

He didn't know how to respond. He felt relief that she'd spared him the embarrassment of explanation. Sincerity rang in her voice. He saw it in the direct gaze of her eyes, felt it in her touch as she'd placed the china egg in his hands. My God! How easy it was to love this woman. He realised he was half-way there.

'Now you could help by inspecting all the nesting boxes and choosing the best eggs for incubating. They should be not too small, nor too large, clean, of course, no cracks, no ridges or spots. They should be very smooth. I'll show you where to find the nests and give you a box for those of your choice. Quality eggs will incubate quality chicks. All right?'

She was laughing now.

'I should say so,' he almost shouted, wanting to crush her in his arms.

A stalky man in dungarees and wellingtons, wearing a tartan beret, arrived. Jenny introduced him as Jock, her right-hand man, and the husband of Flora, the housekeeper.

'He's the real boss,' she said. 'He just lets me think I am.'

They discussed the farm business at length while Steve began his egg collection. He took his new task very seriously, plundering the nesting boxes for quality eggs, testing carefully for possible cracks, spots or ridges. He found none. The hens knew better than to fail the quality qualifications.

He remembered what Buddy had said about the Buddhists' attitude to activities. They are totally absorbed in the moment because that is reality for them. Thinking back and thinking forward detracts from how things really are. Fine in theory, thought Steve but while I'm supposed to be totally involved in choosing quality eggs for the broodies, I'm remembering the sight of her, the sound of her, the smell of her and her ability to restore my self-esteem and that makes me look forward and hope.

In his next job he swore gently as the chicken wire he was unrolling nipped a finger and drew blood. Now that wouldn't have happened, he thought, if I'd been absorbed in the moment of unwinding the wire instead of fanatisising about Jenny Fraser unwinding my own emotional entanglements. Better concentrate on that clucking broody and in constructing her special run to pander to her maternal anxieties. Oh that Jenny Fraser would construct a special run for him. He was off again, his thoughts racing ahead, his emotions taking precedence over his reason. Frankly, he concluded, it's impossible to stay in the moment when there are strong forces pulling both ways. There was Sam of his past. How he'd love this. I shall write and tell him about poultry keeping. Tonight I shall write him a long and detailed letter.

Someone had arrived with packed lunches. Steve joined the others and listened to their favourable comments on the weather, the scenery, and the lecturers while he watched the woman who was at the centre of it all, wondering who and where the husband was and astonished at how little he cared.

She left mid-afternoon, her parting shot telling him that tomorrow they would look at the ducks. Steve smiled, comfortably warmed by her acceptance of him, reassured by her apparent lack of condemnation which was more than he had any right to expect. He'd show her. He'd show them all.

Returning to the castle, past the scrubland, past the woodland, the glass houses and the profusion of scents and colours, somewhere deep within him a spark was smouldering, a tiny source of energy which, if encouraged, could flare to frightening force. Frightening? What am I afraid of? He saw Buddy and Todd, still together, raking soil already smooth as dust and unaware of everything but their employment of the rake.

'Om,' Steve hummed softly, his spirits rising as he passed them by, his eyes momentarily drawn to the strong physique of the head gardener and his bruised and broken face.

Had Buddy found another lame duck to support?

Still smiling, he continued to the castle, his room, a shower and a quiet contemplation of the day's extraordinary achievement.

CHAPTER 14

He had an hour to spare before dinner. He lit a cigarette. This was as good a time as any to take stock. Placing his cigarette in the ashtray, he crossed to the tallboy and opened one of the drawers, extracting a writing case. Seeing Sam's letter, received on the Empress, gave him a moment's unease but, ignoring the call on his conscience, he took from the case a folded piece of foolscap.

Retrieving the smouldering cigarette he sat down, balanced the ashtray on the arm of his chair, crossed his legs, unfolded the paper and began to read.

It was a letter from his consultant which so far he had managed to ignore. Convinced that the consultant had made a false diagnosis he'd pushed the letter aside in contempt. The venerable Dr Dawson had got it all wrong. He was no more an addict than one of Father O'Doyle's gentle saints. He could go for months without a drink if he had to. The only reason he'd been pushed into the quack's hands had been because he'd lost sight of his common sense when that layabout dragged his wife and son across Canada into America to protest against a stupid war that had nothing to do with either of them. Okay, his drinking had gone over the top. No doubt he'd done some silly things then, so others had said, but what guy wouldn't, under the circumstances? He could leave the damned stuff alone if he chose to. Wasn't he doing that now? He crushed his cigarette butt in the ashtray, rose from his chair, went again to the tallboy and found his bottle of Scotch, still in its tartan bag.

He opened it, sniffed deeply, swore softly and decided to pour it down the drain. Halfway to the bathroom he stopped, deciding that what might appear strength was weakness. 'Things aren't always what they seem' she'd said. If he poured this down the sink now it might appear to be strong-mindedness but actually meant he couldn't trust himself. What about Greenock, a small voice whispered. Did you trust yourself then? Okay, I was in the grip of rage then. I was so angry that even good St Anthony or Joseph or the virgin mother herself would have lost their cool. 'Kill your anger, my child.' The voice of the priest. He had a point.

Steve returned the bottle to the drawer and settled it among his underwear. Returning to the chair, he lit another cigarette. Kill your anger. It would sure save him a lot of trouble, he mused. Wasn't he angry with Miranda? Didn't this anger carry in its wake resentment, confusion, discomfort, the desire for revenge and probably, worst of all, the appearance that she was getting the better of him. She was a stupid mixed-up kid, a liar and a cheat. Was she worth the discomfort of wrath and what that wrath might do to him? Was she worth another Greenock experience? Only luck and the timely appearance of Father O'Doyle had brought him from the edge of another Greenock experience last night.

Kill your anger. God bless Father O'Doyle and all his blessed angels, thought Steve, his face relaxing into a smile. He drew the nicotine into his lungs, narrowing his eyes as the smoke filtered through his nostrils. He inspected an outstretched hand which only a few moments ago had seemed to tremble. Steady as a rock. He looked again at the consultant's letter, forcing himself to take note of the bald facts it proclaimed.

Your sudden departure from our consultation left me no time to ensure that you fully understood the implications of your problem. As already conveyed in our two meetings, my diagnosis was made clear to you. Your problem is not abuse of alcohol but addiction, which is a much more serious matter.

Your sudden termination of our consultation leads me to suspect that you question the veracity of my diagnosis. This is not unusual in patients in your condition. There are many reasons, mainly emotional, that cause denial of the existence of the problem. I fear that you are experiencing such denial and would urge you to consider seriously the full implication of what this means.

As diagnosed, your problem is largely one of predisposition. It makes cure so much more difficult, but not impossible. It is only fair to warn you that even then, the tendency remains. You are faced with a lifelong responsibility to control your unfortunate affliction. It is extremely difficult but it can be done. You are particularly vulnerable under stress. Hence the urgency of this communication.

At present your physical deterioration is in its very early stages but if unchecked, alcohol consumption will eventually destroy every part of you. You will become physically, mentally and emotionally devastated.

Let me assure you that, in your case, there is no cause for shame. You must seek help where you can. Do not let temporary abstinence fool you. It does not take much to trigger an attack but although alcohol addiction is mighty powerful it can be challenged if you have the will.

I hope, while there is still time, that you will take serious thought of this advice. There is help available if you have the courage to accept it.

Steve finished his cigarette. In spite of the letter's gloomy foreboding, he was still convinced that a molehill was being looked at as a mountain. Okay. Suppose I decide to do something about it. What? The only part of the report that bothered him was the genetic tendency part. What could he do about that? According to Gerald Fitzgerald he could exercise his free will. He could side step the causal effects by creating new causes. Hadn't he one on a platter now? Gifted by the Gods. The desire for the approbation of a wonderful woman. He would do a great deal to please her. For her goodwill, Bacchanalia would be for all times a dead duck.

Talking of ducks! 'Tomorrow we will look at the ducks,' she had said. Today had been for the chickens, tomorrow for the ducks. Who could tell what might follow in the days to come?'

He looked again at the letter in his unsteady hand. This was not a prophecy, only a warning of what could happen. But it needn't. He would kill his anger and be stranger to stress. He'd go down to dinner and give Miranda the surprise of her life. He'd be amenable, even charming. He could when he wanted to. She'd be expecting to find his ego in tatters. He'd surprise her. He thrilled again in recollection of his time spent in the company of Jenny. He felt a stirring in his groin and powerful images forming in his mind. He could afford to be generous to Miranda.

He stubbed his half-smoked cigarette, straightened his tie and set out for the dining room.

'Thanks be to sweet Jesus,' said Father O'Doyle who was sitting with Buddy and Miranda when he arrived at their table. 'You are looking happy, my son.'

Steve grinned.

'Good to see you again, Father,' he said as he took his seat at the table.

'As sure as grass is green it is a fine thing to see you all looking so relaxed. Buddy has just been telling me about his gardening and how much he is enjoying it.'

'I'd be happy to spend all my time there,' said Buddy, lifting his fork to attack a dish of risotto. 'The colours, the feel of the soil between my fingers, the smells.' Then rather incongruously he stuck his nose in the steam rising from his plate and sniffed appreciatively. The others laughed and he joined in. 'But seriously,' he continued, 'it is quite humbling to be engrossed in the miracles of growth and especially to be working with Todd.'

'Ah, yes. Todd,' said the priest but before he could say more Buddy continued. 'When you first see Todd you feel pity and astonishment that for someone so disfigured, he can appear to be so apparently happy. After working with him you don't see the malformed features any more. They melt away, leaving only intelligence and kindness and - yes, serenity. I can't put it any better than that.'

The priest smiled a secret smile then turning to Steve asked, 'And what's brought the light into your eyes today, my son?'

'Chickens,' said Steve, grinning, 'and the thought of ducks tomorrow.'

He wanted to laugh aloud at their expressions and at the secret pleasures of his day which, undiminished, were still with him.

'You have the blessing of St Francis,' the priest said. 'Take care of his creatures and he will take care of you.' He turned to Miranda. 'I listen to your sweet singing in praise of Our Lord,' he told her, 'then I light a candle for the blessed St Cecilia for showering her precious gifts on one so young and pretty.'

Miranda was caught between a scowl and a smile. The smile was evoked by the flattery. The scowl, Steve knew, was because he was so cheerful. Obviously she had been expect ing a cowed, revengeful and distinctly unpleasant companion for dinner, that is if he dared to come at all. Instead he had arrived bright, pleasant, even friendly and her face had registered her disappointment. What are you looking so pleased about, her whole demeanour seemed to be asking him? Miranda was looking at the door where Jenny Fraser was framed, standing tall, smiling and scanning the dining room with her usual all-inclusive smile.

Steve was glad to be seated. He caught a look in Miranda's eyes which told him she hadn't failed to notice his reaction. To cover his confusion he let the never-failed yet cliché escape his tongue.

'You're looking lovely tonight Miranda.'

In their short acquaintance he'd learned that Miranda was to compliments as blotting paper was to ink. Jenny stopped at their table.

'Hi there.' The men began struggling to their feet but she stopped them with hand raised. 'No please. I can't stay. Just wanted to say hello. Glad to see you're all settling in.'

Her parting smile included them all.

Miranda was looking at Steve through narrowed eyes. At the end of the meal they dispersed, Father O'Doyle to bestow his saintly blessings on the occupants of another table, Buddy to converse with the musicians who sat together while Miranda clung to Steve's side, out of the dining room, and into reception before he challenged her.

'Is there something you want, Miranda?'

'Yes. I want to know what you told Jenny Fraser today.'

'If you mean about her seeing us together in regrettable behaviour, I told her nothing.'

'Is she blind? She must have seen what you were doing to me. Didn't she want to know what it was all about?'

'These are questions you must ask her.'

'You mean to tell me that she never mentioned that you were sexually attacking me.'

'That's right - she didn't mention it.'

'You agree then that you were sexually attacking me.'

This was Miranda the actress, on stage. She was even, beneath her annoyance, enjoying herself. It would seem that Miranda Morrison thrived on confrontation.

'These are not the words I'd use,' said Steve.

'You must have spun her some yarn.'

'You sound disappointed that she didn't hang, draw and quarter me.'

'It's no more than you deserve.'

'We are attracting attention,' said Steve. 'If you want to talk like this, I suggest we get out of here.'

He led the way to the main door. She followed him. He was glad of the cool evening breeze on his flushed face, glad of a few minutes to decide how to handle this emotional cut and thrust which could so easily get out of hand. Perhaps they needed to face whatever it was they had to face together. He led her to a seat under a trellised bower of honeysuckle serotina whose reddish purple flowers sent out a fragrance almost as disturbing to Steve as Miranda's presence. He had to stop this woman from making a fool of him and herself. It was now time for him to challenge her ridiculous deceit.

'I think it's time you told me what you're up to Miranda.'

'What I'm up to?'

'You never miss a chance to stick the knife in, do you?' 'I've no idea what you're talking about.'

'I think you have. If you're still angry about what happened on board ship I wish you'd get it out of your system. Now! Swear at me. Tell me what a rotter I am. I explained then, and apologised and was led to believe you'd agreed to forgive and forget but I'll apologise again, on my knees if you insist but get the anger out of your system. It's doing neither of us any good.'

'That's easier said than done.' She had dropped her pose and with it her American drawl. 'As you told me - eventually, you are a married man so why are you chasing Jenny Fraser?'

'Don't be ridiculous.'

'Do you deny that you are interested in her?'

Steve sighed.

'Jenny Fraser is an unusual and attractive woman. Any man would find her interesting. There's nothing wrong with that.'

'Do you see any future with her?'

'Get real, Miranda. She's married. I'm married.'

'For how long, I wonder?' she asked with a sigh.

'Steady on. Why should I discuss my marriage with you. You've no claim on my life.'

She leaned close, their faces almost touching as she hissed in his ear.

"Heav'n has no rage, like love to hatred turn'd, Nor Hell a fury, like a woman scorned."

Her delivery was spine-tingling. Miranda, the actress was again on stage.

'You're a witch, Miranda. A superb, beautiful white witch.'

'Beautiful?'

Her eyes shone.

'You could be.'

Her eyes clouded. Her brows rose in question.

'If you were happier and your natural colour restored you would be truly beautiful. You're young, extremely talented - and rich. You've everything to be happy about. Why are you so miserable?'

'You can talk. You're young-ish, handsome, moderately talented - and rich. Why are you so miserable?'

Steve sighed.

'Buddy isn't miserable and he has probably more to complain about than we have.'

'Buddy's looking for happiness. That's the difference,' said Miranda, turned philosopher.

'And we're not?'

'No. I'm looking for revenge and you're looking for escape.'

'From what?'

'From the mess of your marriage and from your addiction to alcohol.'

'Says who?'

'Says me.'

'Buddy?'

'No. He didn't have to. I saw you once or twice on board. And there was the scene in the dining room on our first night on board, remember? And it wasn't difficult to put two and two together when you didn't turn up at Greenock and Buddy knew where to look for you.'

'I'm not addicted. I just like a drink now and then.'

'If you say so.'

'Yes, I say so and I also say that you should count your blessings and be happy.'

'I'm too angry to be happy,' Miranda replied morosely.

'Then you must kill your anger.' Steve could hardly believe what he was saying. Father O'Doyle's seed of wisdom seemed to be germinating. 'Isn't it time you told Jenny Fraser the truth?'

Miranda's temper flared.

'Haven't you been listening?' she accused.

'You can't keep up this deception indefinitely. She's sure to find out.'

'Only if you give me away.'

'You'll give yourself away, sooner or later.'

'Yes, when I'm good and ready. I'm watching her.' 'Watch a little closer and you might learn something to your benefit.'

'You don't know her.'

'Do you?'

'Better than you think.'

'Then who is her husband and where is he?'

Steve regretted the words as soon as they were uttered. 'You don't know?'

She looked long and hard at him.

'You'll find out soon enough,' she replied, 'and you'll also discover that's only the tip of the iceberg.'

'You're paranoid,' said Steve dismissively.

'You fool,' she said. 'My advice is to steer clear of that woman or you're in deep trouble. I could reveal things that would blow the lid off this entire set-up.'

Steve rose, his anger already on the boil. Why did he allow himself to get involved with this woman? Kill your anger, he'd advised her and he couldn't manage his own anger. There seemed nothing more to discuss. Leaving her in the garden, framed by the perfumed lonicera, he returned to his room and reached for the inevitable cigarette. Why is it, he wondered, as he paced restlessly that one moment I can be feeling benevolent and standing on the brink of joy and then the next minute after a battle of egos, my anger erupts? Damn!

He threw himself on the bed and continued poisoning his lungs with nicotine. He realised that his hand was shaking again. Do something, a voice was screaming in his head. If you can't kill your anger, as Father O'Doyle preaches, at least harness its energy into something more productive and exercise your free will, according to the doctrine of Gerald Fitzgerald, Doctor of Philosophy.

More shaken than he cared to admit, he rose, resolutely, stubbed his half-finished cigarette, averted his eyes from the second drawer of the tallboy, fetched his writing case and began a letter to Sam.

Not allowing himself time to consider and maybe change his mind, he set himself to describing life in Strathard, about castles and imaginary knights and moats, drawbridges and white chargers, to Catholic priests, Doctors of Philosophy and lollipop trees. He wove imaginary legends around gentle Buddhist monks and singing bowls, about refugees from beloved countries trying to save their culture, musicians from Europe who had been refugees in the war, that is, if they were lucky. Others who had escaped prison and torture. He wrote about hills and burns, and heather and roaming deer. Then he told of the chickens. And tomorrow, he concluded, I am to meet the ducks. Apart from Buddy he mentioned no names.

When he had finished he realised that what had seemed like a few minutes, was nearly two hours. He sighed in satisfaction. Was this what living in the moment meant? Writing to Sam had filled every part of his mind and feelings leaving no gaps for the past or the future and from frustration and anger he now felt good. No, more than good. He felt right.

Smiling at Sam's photograph which, in its silver frame, he had placed on the mantelpiece, he thought of Sam and Susan and then allowed himself one thought of Jenny Fraser. The gaps had rushed back in again and his thoughts were invaded by the past glories of her smile and the excitement of meeting the ducks in the morning. He slept soundly.

CHAPTER 15

There followed a week of halcyon days. The early mornings were shrouded in seasonal mist till the sun broke through, tinting the loch, evaporating dewdrops on rose petals and highlighting the gossamer beauty of spiders' webs on bush and hedge.

It also warmed the heart of Stevenson Bruce as he set off each morning to tend the ducks, the chickens, the horses and a few highly-privileged cows. The peak of this radiance was, of course, the first glimpse of Jenny Fraser who invariably was pleased to see him.

Among the snowy-white plumaged and pink-billed Aylesburys, the yellowish-tinged Pekins with their extraordinary laying capability, or the claret breasted Rouen - all quality ducks - Steve felt energised and ready for whatever the day might bring. He was happy to fill the barrel troughs with water.

'The bars allow them to drink but not to step into the water', she told him. The food troughs were also barred. 'If food is thrown on the ground the ducklings will tread it dirty,' she said. A little grain given once a day, mixed with a little grit and given in water was her latest instruction. Her motto was A little and often. 'Left to themselves,' she told him, 'they'd eat their heads off.'

God! Doesn't she ever let go of her quality mania? he shocked himself by thinking. Quality control, as he well knew, could mean self-inflicting discomfort, even pain. Did her unremitting dedication to quality operate in the rest of her life outside the farm? Was he criticising? Surely not! He was merely finding Strathard's standards of operation difficult to accommodate to his own less regulated lifestyle.

Buddy was completely off his back now. He must at last have come to realise that his protection was no longer required. Steve noted a subtle change in his friend. His smile, generally heralding a quick fire wit and gentle scathing, had changed. It had become near seraphic. Next to music, Buddhism was becoming Buddy's main interest and topic of conversation. His interest in alcohol addiction had apparently disappeared.

'Om to that!' said Steve.

Miranda had taken to wandering alone and frequently into the village.

'I'm discovering my roots,' she'd tell him when he met her returning from a visit to the village. 'I'd like to show you where I was born. You'll be amazed.'

There had been something unattractive, almost menacing, in the way she spoke. She always managed to make him feel guilty. He was, after all, harbouring her secret and this interfered with his developing feelings for Jenny. More than anything he wanted his relationship with Jenny Fraser to be untarnished. He needed her purity of purpose. He dared not look too closely at his own. In his private moments, he wanted to possess her - mind, body and soul. He'd admitted it at last and couldn't decide whether he felt better or worse for the admission. Tempted as he was to inform on Miranda, caution prevailed. He tried to allay his suspicion that Miranda was up to some mischief, designed, of course, to harm him. She had never recovered from her disappointment that Jenny Fraser had apparently turned a blind eye on the fracas at the edge of the wood. He was prepared for the worst. He would not have long to wait.

It was the last day of August. He had been in Strathard for barely two weeks and already his Canadian life was a universe away. Only a week ago he had been desperate to fly home. Now all he wanted was to stay in Strathard. Something was happening to him. His personality was undergoing some sort of alchemical transformation.

He was being fed a magic brew which was transforming the ordinary to the extraordinary; the stark to the subtle. It was a magic which excited him. It had its castle, its queen, its witch, jester, saint and sage. From that astonishing dance to a Boccherini Quintet to the revelation of quality in action, he felt that his base metals were being refined to something more precious than gold. And, he thought with a secret smile, it was the queen who was weaving the spell. Pity about the witch.

He was sharing an after dinner stroll in the grounds with Fitzgerald. He decided to offer his thoughts to this likeable sage whom he had come to admire and respect.

'What is it about this place that defies description?' he asked the Doctor of Philosophy. 'I know that its raison d'être is supposed to be for the good of humanity and much as I admire the vision and integrity of the people responsible, I just don't get their message - for want of a better word.'

Fitzgerald halted his stride and considered the question.

It was dusk, but light enough to identify fellow guests in huddled groups or in single transit across the lawn

'Its results are not immediate, I admit,' he said. 'Nor can they be quantified.' He resumed his slow stride. 'They remind me of our old pear tree I climbed as a boy. In the spring it was covered in blossom and was a treat to behold. It seemed full of the promise of a bumper harvest but, come autumn, all it produced was a handful of wizened fruit.'

'You don't think that's all Strathard will produce - metaphorically speaking. Eh?'

'No, no. I'm only illustrating the uncertainty of the outcome, in spite of all the present promise.'

'You don't sound very optimistic,' said Steve.

'Nor am I pessimistic. They certainly have quality in their favour.' Fitzgerald smiled. 'Look around you. The splendidly maintained residence and its surroundings; the garden produce and arboreal beauty.'

'The healthy chickens and ducks,' added Steve with a smile.

'Isn't that all quality? And what about that symbolic picture you see before you now?'

On the front lawn, backed by the fountain and hallowed by the strains of a Beethoven sonata spilling from the music room, stood a group of residents deep in conversation. Fitzgerald's voice cut through the music.

'There you see the turban of the Sikh, the crucifix of the Catholic and the saffron robe of the Buddhist monk and here comes the dog collar of the Presbyterian minister. They represent the meeting and fusing of ideas and that's what this place is all about.'

'Who is the dog collar?'

'He is the local preacher, the minister, as they say here. They call him the Rev. Neil.'

Steve looked at the figure of the preacher as he joined the other three men of faith. He was tall and broad, dressed in sober black, hair unruly, good looking in a rugged way but disadvantaged by a staggering limp. He seemed strangely out of keeping with his companions.

'He doesn't visit the castle very often,' said Fitzgerald. 'He was recently honoured for his book on The Struggles of the Scottish Nation for the Freedom of her Faith.'

'What struggles?' queried Steve.

'Struggles against Roman Popes and Stuart Monarchs, such as for instance, when Charles II's "Drunken Parliament" changed Scottish law to Treason.'

Steve cocked his ears. The word 'drunken', even in such impersonal context, could trigger his sensitivity.

'Apart from being the Strathard minister what contribution to this haven of quality does the Rev. Neil make?'

'The Scots are a proud people, rooted in their religion, even if flagrantly discarded today. The Rev. Neil ensures that the Scottish Covenanters are never forgotten. He lectures occasionally but he lectures at length. You have been warned.'

It was a warning he should have heeded, decided Steve as he sat in one of the Rev. Neil's lectures the next afternoon. He listened to a passionate delivery of the minister's aggressive enthusiasm for Women of God. In spite of its length Steve was enthralled by a colourful account of a woman called Mary Slessor who converted blood-streaked savages twice her size by beating them over the head with her umbrella. As if that wasn't enough, she tackled the sex life of cannibals. It was reported that she travelled barefoot among naked men, witnessed sex orgies, and explained to old men just why their young wives ran into the jungle with men of their own age. All of which made Steve wonder what Freudian influence put so much passion into the minister's account of this tale.

Then there was Fair Margaret who lived in the bloodstained eleventh century and who married a Scottish Prince called Malcolm and who founded abbeys and churches. The Rev. Neil recounted with zeal the myriad ways Fair Margaret served Scotland and, more importantly, the Lord. Then he was back in Africa, a country of which the Rev, seemed very fond. Steve held his breath as he watched him lean over his dais, expecting both dais and minister to topple into the front row of the audience when giving a particularly graphic account of life in the jaws of death, as when Livingstone was savaged by a lion.

Watching him, Steve had the feeling that this man was living vicariously for his God. The women he revered had lived and died for God, the men had sacrificed easy living in order to carry the word of God to souls who, without this vital information, would be forever excluded from God's grace.

'Whew!' he breathed as he left the lecture room.

If that's a man of God, give me the devil any day. But if fundamental Christianity was to be included in this circus ground of religious beliefs, the Rev's witness to it had been of the highest quality. Steve wasn't surprised that his books sold. They were blood and thunder at their best. Would he feel like that if he were a full-blooded Scot instead only half-Scottish - and the worst half at that?

God was presented in a more palatable form on Sunday evening when it seemed everyone in Strathard was packed into the small stone church on the edge of the moor to listen to the promised performance of Handel's Messiah. Steve was sandwiched between Buddy and Fitzgerald. His view of Jenny who was sitting side on at the front of the church, near the pulpit, was being constantly obstructed by the fidgeting audience seated between them. They were fidgeting because they had come to hear the music of Handel's Messiah and instead, were being forced to listen to the minister's welcoming remarks which were snowballing into a lengthy interpretation of Handel's work.

'Let me conclude,' the Reverend Neil said, 'with a quotation. "For behold, darkness shall cover the earth and gross darkness the people, but the Lord shall arise upon thee, and His glory shall be seen upon thee." Isaiah, Chapter sixty, verse two.'

He descended from the pulpit with difficulty. Under cover of the opening chord and gentle introduction to the Overture there could be heard faint sighs of relief.

Steve relaxed, positioning himself so that he could see Jenny's profile. When the tenor's first words of comfort filled the building Steve's own comfort was derived more from the presence of Jenny than from the presence of God. A glance at Buddy showed his eyes closed. Fitzgerald's were fixed on the head in front. As the tenor carolled that "Every valley shall be exalted, and every mountain and hill made low," Steve entered the world of dreams with Jenny and Sam and sometimes Susan. Everything crooked he made straight and the rough places he smoothed out. Anything could happen in dreams from the fanciful to the fanatic. He let the music give rein to his fancies and by the end of the first part of the performance with the chorus bellowing about the Everlasting Father, the Prince of Peace, he felt optimistic.

Wanting fresh air and a leg stretch he left his seat during the first break. He wandered idly round the churchyard, content to be alone and let the music's aftermath wash over him.

'Let me show you something,' said a voice in his ear. 'Miranda! Should you be here?' She'd taken him by surprise. 'You sing next, don't you?'

'Yes, but before I do, I want to show you something.'

Reluctantly Steve allowed himself to be led through the graveyard till they reached a granite headstone whose inscription he was instructed to read.

In memory of Fiona McLeod dearly beloved wife of
Angus and mother of Callum, Jenny and Graham
Died aged 42 on 14th April; 1936
Rest in Peace

'Do you see my name there?' asked Miranda.

'No.'

'That was the day I was born and that is the name of my mother who died when I was born. All the others are there - my father and sister and two brothers. I didn't exist as far as they were concerned - still don't, for as much as they care. Isn't that proof of how I was treated?'

'It could also be proof that your story is of your own making and that Jenny is not your sister and indeed, that you were never here at all.'

'I was certainly here. I have my birth certificate to prove it and, hoping I just might be lucky enough to have an opportunity like this, I brought it to show you.'

As she spoke she undid a couple of buttons on her blouse and extracted a folded piece of paper from between her breasts. Alarmed and afraid of another embarrassing encounter, Steve's eyes swept the graveyard. To his relief no one was near. He could see that people were returning to the church entrance for the second part of the performance. Miranda, fortunately had hastily buttoned her blouse and was now pressing the folded paper into his hands.

'Read that. You will see the place, the date, the time and the names of my parents.'

Then she was gone, having succeeded in shattering his calm.

Ruffled, he read what she had predicted. Her story was true in every detail. Place of birth Strathard, date as on gravestone inscription, time 4 p.m. Angus McLeod was recorded as the father and Fiona, the mother. Moira was her registered name. He'd always known that Miranda was not her real name. He had no reason to doubt that the name Moira on the certificate was the Miranda who annoyed, interested, exasperated, amazed and unsettled him.

Someone was waving frantically at him from the church entrance. The congregation had already settled in anticipation and the mellow notes of the Pastoral Symphony lulling the audience when he apologetically squeezed himself along the pew to resume his seat.

Buddy was now alert, his eyes fixed on Miranda, or should he say Moira, while Fitzgerald merely nodded recognition of his return. He glanced at Jenny and saw that she was looking his way. She caught his glance and sent him a radiant smile before returning her gaze to the orchestra. He watched Miranda rise to her feet and step forward for her solo.

Her first notes rekindled the audience's attention and by the time she was singing 'Come unto Him, all ye that labour and are heavily laden, and He shall give you rest,' she had them enthralled. Steve felt Buddy's excitement and he noticed Fitzgerald was at last fully engaged with the performance.

What was Jenny thinking? He had noted, on his return, that the Rev. Neil was now seated on her far side. Alongside his stern and brooding profile Jenny seemed vulnerable. She was absorbed in Miranda's singing. Her almost wistful expression made Steve long to be near her. Thinking that behind that golden voice, singing about the gospel of peace and the glad tidings of good things, was a heart intent on harm made him feel protective. He resented the minister's nearness to this woman who now filled his waking hours. He wanted to push him aside and take his place and put a comforting arm around her. It wasn't right that the woman who, more than anyone, believed in quality living, should herself be so short changed. He was determined to break down Miranda's resistance to reveal her identity. He didn't trust Miranda and her burning resentment should not be left unchecked.

CHAPTER 16

At the end of the performance he left the church with a mixture of feelings - pleasure, resentment, hope, impotence and an inexplicable sadness. He blamed the music for that. He had, like everyone else leaving the church, shaken hands with the Rev, and looking into that grim but honest face he wondered if there was still room in the world for the fundamentalists? He envied them the strength of their convictions. He had no such certainty. One time he'd thought his certainty was Susan. Where had she been when he'd needed her? The strength of his growing belief that in Jenny Fraser he would find the security he craved now threatened his equanimity. What was he thinking of? The trouble was surely that he wasn't thinking. He was feeling. He didn't want to think. His feelings were more compelling than his thoughts. What was it Rahel had said? The Qabalak teaches balance between feelings and thoughts. His scales were heavily tipped towards his feelings.

Now, as he stood outside the emptying church with Buddy on one side and Fitzgerald on the other, he had to stop himself from running in search of Jenny. He looked towards the church porch, hoping to see her emerge but instead, came Miranda, alias Moira.

'Do you mind if I walk back to the castle with you?' She was addressing them all.

Steve glowered. She waited until they turned off the road and into the castle drive before challenging his mood.

'You don't seem to have had much pleasure from the performance,' she said. 'Perhaps you're suffering the after effects of meeting the minister.'

Steve saw the darting look the philosopher gave Miranda. 'Don't worry. He gets up a lot of noses,' she said in mock comfort. 'Even his wife finds him a handful.'

Now the philosopher turned his full gaze upon Miranda. 'I didn't know he had a wife,' said Buddy.

Miranda put on a big act of shocked surprise.

'You didn't know that the Rev. Neil Fraser had a wife! You know his wife!' She spoke directly to Buddy and ignored Steve. 'I believe the natives set the habit of calling him the Rev. Neil to distinguish him from his father, the Rev. Andrew Fraser.'

On the dawning significance of Miranda's words Steve looked stunned.

'Whatever's the matter Steve?' asked Miranda making no attempt to conceal her glee.

'You're lying!' was the most he could manage.

Fitzgerald's face registered undisguised amazement while Buddy had lost his newly-acquired mantle of saintly detachment and became the old Buddy, suspicious, judgmental and concerned.

Jenny Fraser is not that - that person's wife. She can't be,' wailed Steve.

Fitzgerald's amazement was now coloured embarrassment.

'Ah, but she is,' smiled Miranda irritatingly pleased with herself. 'I thought everyone knew. Did you know?' she asked the uncomfortable philosopher.

'Yes,' he replied almost guiltily as he looked at Steve's discomfiture.

Steve rounded on Buddy.

'Did you know?' he shouted.

Buddy's eyes hardened but his voice was quiet when he answered.

'As I've already said, I didn't know but what difference does it make? I don't know Fitzgerald's wife, or even if he has one. He doesn't know yours. It's no big deal that Jenny Fraser is the wife of the Rev. Neil Fraser. What's it to you?'

To Steve these were not questions but accusations. He hadn't known Buddy Regan for as long as he had without learning to interpret his verbal tone and nuances.

'She can't be,' Steve repeated as if in a daze.

Fitzgerald mumbled some excuse and walked ahead. Miranda, having successfully upset Steve as had been her intention, fell in step with the philosopher. Steve and Buddy were left together, the former stunned, the latter perceptive.

'I just don't believe even you can be so foolish,' said Buddy, shaking his head.

'She doesn't love him,' said the dazed Steve.

'How do you know?'

'She has never mentioned his name to me, never even said she was married.'

'Why should she? Did you talk to her about Susan?' Steve shook his head.

'Or tell her that you loved Susan?'

'Of course not.'

'Has anyone else spoken to you about their personal relationships?'

'No.'

He placed a hand on Steve's shoulder as they slowly approached the castle.

'Have you written to Sam?'

'Screeds.'

'Good.'

'But I haven't posted yet.' 'Why ever not?' queried the bemused Buddy.

'Why ever not! Why ever not! I'll tell you why ever not!'

Alarmed, Buddy stretched his arm along Steve's shoulder in an effort to caution but Steve stepped back, rejecting the gesture.

'She's radiant. How could anyone living with that prophet of doom be so radiant?'

'Would you forget Jenny Fraser for a minute,' urged Buddy. 'Let's concentrate on you. You're the important one here.'

'I can't forget her,' sighed Steve.

They'd stopped at the portico. On impulse, Buddy suggested they go to a quiet spot he knew in the garden.

'It's ages since we had a real conversation,' he said.

Steve went with him willingly. The thought of shutting himself in his own room, feeling as he did, was not attractive but although he shied from his own company he was not averse to talking about himself and his feelings for Jenny Fraser which Miranda, by her ill-timed remark, had tipped into total confusion.

'I'm ensnared by her,' he now confessed. 'She's my inspiration. She makes me feel good about myself. When I think of her it never occurs to me to think about alcohol. She's made me feel alive again, free.'

'That's a contradiction for a start,' said Buddy. 'You can't feel ensnared and free at the same time.'

'I was meant to be here - to meet her. From the first time I saw her picture in that magazine I felt the hand of destiny.'

'Get real, mate. You were looking for a Susan substitute. You were also needing a prop for your addiction.'

'Is that what you think?'

'It is. You've had one prop after another, including me and you rejected them all. Know why?'

'Tell me. I know you want to.'

'You bet I do. I've told you before and it made no difference. I'll tell you again but you won't listen.'

'Tell me anyway.'

'You just can't get out of denial. You refuse to admit you are addicted. You know you have a problem. I'll give you that but you look at it the wrong way round. You blame everyone else, your publishers, your father, your mother, Susan, circumstances and me.' As he listed, he ticked off the accused on his fingers. 'We're all wrong. None of us understand. As you keep repeating, we see pygmies as giants.'

His face showed none of its normal geniality. Steve refused to be cowed.

'Is that all?'

'No it isn't bloody all. I could go on and remind you of the time when you turned up drunk at a lunch in your honour. Author of the year - Idiot, more like, and the time Sam missed the finals of his tennis tournament because you were too damned drunk to take him.' About to launch on the third offence, he changed his mind. 'Despite all that,'

he said in a quieter tone, 'I happen to think that you are one lucky bloke.'

'It sure doesn't sound like it.'

Steve's words were barely audible.

'You still have time. Your liver might be tickled but it's still far from being pickled. You sweat a bit but you don't have fits - yet. Your hands shake but only for minutes at a time. You have met with quacks and shrinks but they haven't put you in a straitjacket and institutionalised you - yet. That's all waiting in the wings unless you stop now.'

Steve laughed.

'Shows how much you've been bothering with me since we came here. You've been so busy oming that you haven't noticed that I've stopped.'

'You've said that before. If you'd stopped you'd be back in Vancouver by now, come hell or high water. You're living in cloud-cuckoo-land, fantasising about a woman who's as far removed from you as Mary is from Judas.'

'Will - you - shut - up!'

'No, I won't shut up because I'm too wound up. Since you've got yourself into this mess you taint everything you touch. Just when I've found a glimpse of Shangri-La for myself, your wallowing self delusions make me feel responsible for you again. Get a life, man. Jenny Fraser is a respectable married woman. You're only one of hundreds who spend a few weeks in her castle. She accepts you on trust. You repay her by undermining her principles which you would do well to study. You are a married man with a wife and son who need you even if you've given them hell for the last year or two. You've let drinking rob you of everything that was worth while in your life, not least your self-esteem. You think destiny has thrown you together. Think again. You've sunk so low that you can't see yourself for the selfish, arrogant, uncaring specimen of humanity that you are. Think on, brother, think on.'

He rose and left.

Steve struggled for breath. Buddy had punched like a heavyweight and left him stunned and all but out for the count. He was left feeling paralysed rather than activated. The attack he'd been subjected to was unfounded and totally unjustified. This time Buddy had gone too far. What right did he have to accuse him of selfishness? As for arrogance, no one had ever made him feel as humble as Jenny Fraser did. He'd give much to have a fraction of her outlook on life.

As he sat trying to come to grips with the blows from Buddy's attack, one thing became clearer. Now that he'd absorbed the shock of knowing the identity of Jenny's husband, it made no difference. If anything, it made him feel better. The wonderful woman of quality he'd come to know could not love the dog-collared, boorish individual she couldn't even mention. He clutched on this belief to pull himself back to ground. The more he thought of it the more convinced he was that destiny was playing a strong hand. That dream he'd had of Susan with red hair leaning from the turret window hadn't been Susan at all. It had been Jenny and the turret hadn't been a turret. It was the symbol of her imprisoned spirit and for what he could see from her husband, the Rev. Neil, he was her captor. He convinced himself that Jenny Fraser needed him as much as he needed her.

He rose and walked slowly back to the castle, his mind juggling to balance the weight of Buddy's disapproval with the thoughts of the woman whose approval he needed to win. He was determined that nobody, neither Miranda, nor Buddy, nor the Rev. Neil would rob him of his love for Jenny Fraser. Fate had served him a challenge which he felt more than ready for.

He hadn't seen the reception hall so packed with people since his arrival. In addition to the familiar faces of the current residents, there were the members of the combined choirs who had returned here from the church after their Messiah performance. It had been previously announced that a special dinner was being served in their honour, followed by an entertainment of the arts to which, it was hoped, everyone would feel free to contribute if they so desired.

It was easy for Steve to slip unnoticed through the chattering throngs and make his way, unhindered, to his own quarters.

Feeling that he was still in injury time, he stripped and showered. He took pains with shaving and brushing his hair. He avoided looking at Sam's photograph and the typewriter with a page of his long letter still wrapped round the platen. He became aware that time and again, as his grooming preparations progressed, his eyes kept drifting to the second drawer of the tallboy where lay his Scotch in its tartan bag. He tried to banish the tormenting image which his thoughts created but it consistently teased, titillated and tempted him. When there was nothing more he could do for his physical appearance he settled in the armchair with a cigarette. He tried to brainstorm an idea for a tall story but it was no use. His thoughts were targeted and refused to be deflected. It was time to confront.

He stubbed his cigarette, cleaned his teeth again, examined his perfectly manicured nails, and adjusted the knot in his tie before walking resolutely to the second drawer of the tallboy.

'You are about to enter on the next degree,' he told himself aloud. 'You have proved yourself so far. Now for the next test.'

He opened the drawer, rummaged amongst his underwear and withdrew the tartan-wrapped bottle. What a bloody fool Buddy was, believing all that crap spewed out by the shrinks. I got drunk, thought Steve! So what. You'd think to listen to him he'd never got drunk. Steve remembered more than a handful of times when Buddy had passed out on him. He recalled the bad time when he'd lost his son in Vietnam. Where was I when that happened? Right beside him. Who pulled off his boots and put him to bed? Me! And did I accuse him of alcohol addiction? Not once. Did I drag him to the shrink? I'd have died first.

But when my wife goes off with a man half her age and takes my son with her and I drink myself senseless I'm an alco who is dragged to a shrink and practically condemned to death. Crap! Utter crap and he's the nerve to say I'm in denial in that holier than thou attitude. Sure, I'm in denial. I deny everything I'm accused of.

Steve looked at the bottle in his hands and addressed it. 'Have I abused you? No. Do you tempt me?' He hesitated for a moment. 'No! Am I in control? Yes. What more proof do they want? But we will give them it anyway. They think if I let you touch my lips I won't be able to stop and I'll finish you off in a gulp. Stupid bastards! They think we can't meet without going for the kill. They think I'm no better than a tanked up tramp. Let's show them how dignified we really are. Let's show them the value of true friends. Let's show them who is in control!'

He was now looking at his reflection, noticing the healthy colour, the sparkle in the eye, the steady hand. Any tremor felt was in his thighs, his groin. He opened the bottle then reached for a glass. His eyes closed in secret rapture as the warm liquid trickled down his throat. He knew himself better than anyone. Alcohol was not the enemy they said it was. It was his friend. It made him feel good. He felt better already and there was no danger of abuse. He was totally in control. He spilled another mouthful into his glass but before drinking it he replaced the cap on the bottle and returned it to the drawer. Then he checked his tie at the mirror, drew his palm across his already immaculate hair and smiled at his reflection. Now for the celebration which he was determined to enjoy.

On his way to the door he stopped at Sam's photograph. He pulled the paper from the platen and cast his eyes down the page, feeling a smile twitching at the corners of his mouth. Had he written this? It was good. Pleased with himself he flicked through the pages already piled on his table and his smile widened.

'It's devilish good. Sam, my boy,' he said aloud to the framed picture in his hands. 'This is quality writing, especially for you. I swear I'll finish it tomorrow and mail it without further delay.'

He replaced the picture, gave one more approving glance in the mirror and, determined to enjoy himself, went to join the celebration.

He saw her as soon as he entered the dining room. He looked for her husband but he wasn't there. He saw Miranda who had the audacity to send a bright innocent-looking smile across the room to him. He caught it and returned it with a friendly wave. He laughed to himself when he saw the puzzlement on her face. Buddy was missing and this bothered Steve. It was important that Buddy be there to witness his control. Already his antagonism to his friend had left him. He wanted him to know there was no bad feeling. They had been together a long time now and what did a few hot-tempered words bandied between them matter? Fitzgerald was standing alone surveying the gathering in that kindly detached way of his. Nice chap, Fitzgerald. Steve moved to join him, at the same time watching Jenny as she mingled, bestowing her charm on all she met.

All through supper he watched her. Talking philosophy with Fitzgerald he watched her. Even when bandying jokes with Father O'Doyle he was conscious of her nearness. After the soup and before the fish he saw her husband arrive. Watching them converse for a while he was more convinced than ever that she did not love him. Where was the loving glance, the tactile gesture, shared joke, the togetherness that one would expect to see from a woman like Jenny Fraser and the love of her life? It wasn't there. If anything, her brightness dimmed in her husband's presence. Steve's spirits rose. As course followed course the dynamics of the conversation had reached to near fortissimo and after coffee and the clearing away of the debris Father O'Doyle rose to his feet and called for attention.

'Now you will all be feeling happy and content, my children, after that splendid supper and you will be feeling happy enough to give a hearty round of applause to everyone who had any part at all in the preparation of it. There are too many to mention and all of them too humble to want a special mention. But praise be to God and the Holy Angels for their kind hearts and clever hands nevertheless.' He waited until the applause was spent. 'What a day it has been and it isn't finished yet. I'm sure there's still those among you with a song to sing or a dance or a poem clamouring to be expressed. If you ask me nicely I'll even tell you one of my jokes. Now have you heard the one about the Catholic, the Protestant and the Jew?'

As laughter pealed, Steve saw Buddy enter the room and slip quietly into a chair at the end of the table. He didn't hear the priest's joke for the sudden rush of concern threatening to overwhelm him. He wanted no ill feeling between them. He must make him understand his fears were groundless. As his feelings calmed someone began to sing. It was Miranda's teacher, the handsome Italian. Steve tried to catch Buddy's eye but Buddy gave no sign. His attention was fixed on the Italian tenor. The musicians performed. Someone danced. Someone else read a poem.

Still Steve could not catch Buddy's attention. So intent was he in willing him to look his way that he didn't see Miranda take the floor. There was a burst of spontaneous applause but Miranda, flushed and sparkling with excitement held up her hand for silence.

Steve transferred his attention from Buddy to Jenny who was looking intently at Miranda now addressing the audience. It wasn't until he heard his own name that Steve focused on what she was saying.

'It's unbelievable how shy he is and since I know he'd never dream of reading his work to you, I am more than happy to do it for him. The extract I have chosen is from one of his recent books entitled Bones in the Baggage. This is the passage describing how the bones got into the baggage but, of course, they were at that time covered by flesh and blood.'

Steve listened aghast. His descriptions of killing and disposing of beautiful women were more colourful than exotic flowers in a tropical garden. Miranda, the actress that she was, delivered the detail with relish.

He was too aghast, even to feel angry. She was doing this to humiliate him in Jenny's eyes. It was intended for both of them; for him because he would not dance to her tune; for Jenny because of some long-cherished dream of revenge.

Lowering his gaze he saw that his hands were steady. He felt calm, embarrassed yes, but so what? Did it matter? One thought dominated. If

Miranda's intention was to undermine his writing in Jenny's eyes, he'd already done that for himself. 'My writing's trash,' he'd told her. What had been her response then? 'That's all right,' she'd said.

It didn't matter what others thought. It didn't matter and this realisation was liberating. He looked towards Jenny who was looking intently at Miranda. He looked towards Buddy and caught his eye. His expression was inscrutable. He glanced at Fitzgerald's profile which told him nothing. He saw that Father O'Doyle's eyes were dancing with delight.

'I'll be jiggered, me boy,' he exclaimed when Miranda closed the book and left the stage to a polite ripple of applause. 'By the blessed holy angels methinks you must have been a butcher in a previous existence.'

His cackling relieved any tension Steve might have imagined and it brought forth a sigh of something more than relief. Yes, what did it matter? It was only a story about evil and evil existed everywhere. Did quality mean only writing about good? Had evil no place in quality writing?

There was a final song from the visiting choristers before they left for their coaches to take them to Edinburgh or Inverness or Glasgow. The celebration was over. Steve would have liked to follow Buddy who had quietly left in the general exodus but conscious of Miranda watching him he stayed on, an easy smile on his face. He became aware of Jenny walking his way but pretended not to notice. When she laid a hand on his arm and favoured him with her smile his pulse quickened.

'I understand now what you were trying to tell me,' she began.

'About my writing?' he grinned, matching her mood. 'Trash?'

'Certainly not uplifting,' she said as she grinned back. He saw Miranda's look of puzzlement and began to enjoy himself.

'That's not the worst one,' he said.

'But I recognise good syntax when I hear it and you seem to have a penchant for hyperbole.'

'You mean it was over the top, I guess.'

They looked at each other and laughed heartily. Steve could have hugged her there and then and not just to have sweet revenge on Miranda's treachery but in a rush of gratitude to this woman whose every conversation raised his spirits. She had a way of looking at things like no one he'd ever known. She had perspicacity, generosity and charity. She was a rare one of her breed.

'My husband has gone to Galloway for a few days to hunt down some Covenanters' graves. Why don't we visit the Buddhist centre tomorrow?' Jenny suggested. 'We can spend the whole day there, if you like. Jock will look after the farm.'

What would people think if he lifted this woman and whirled her around? Looking at Jenny she appeared to him more joyful than ever. Could this be because her husband was leaving her for a few days to hunt down ancient graves? Could this possibly be because she found the prospect of spending the day with him exciting? Her face was flushed. Her eyes sparkled and she was waiting for his answer.

'Why don't we?' he replied.

Surely now, Miranda must see that her efforts to destroy were useless.

He underestimated Miranda.

CHAPTER 17

"Oh what a beautiful morning, Oh what a beautiful day I have a beautiful feeling, everything's going my way."

Steve sang at the top of his voice as he towelled himself after his morning's shower. Still singing, he dressed, pausing only to consider whether to wear jeans or jodhpurs. They were to be riding on the moor, so perhaps jodhpurs. Would he need a hat? Probably. He could always leave it at the farm if he changed his mind.

"There's a bright golden haze on the meadow," he sang.

But it won't be a meadow, he thought, as he squeezed paste on his toothbrush. It was a moor. What happened on moors, he wondered, attacking his molars. Eagles? Hawks? He had a vision of a knight astride his charger, hawk on his wrist, jess lead in his expensively suede-gloved hand. Thank God he'd still a clean sports shirt in his luggage.

Then he remembered it was a Buddhist settlement he was visiting.

'Om,' he exploded from his lungs. 'Om, Om.'

He glanced out of the window and saw Buddy make his way to the gardens.

'Om,' he breathed. Buddy, the Buddha, off to his Shangri-La.

Who would have thought it?

After breakfast he whistled his way to the farm and was treated to the Labrador's ecstatic welcome with the yapping terrier at his tail. Steve fussed each dog in turn then went in search of their owner. He saw her coming towards him leading a horse on either side. He gazed in wonder.

'This is Charlie,' said Jenny, indicating the horse on her left, 'and this is Chum. Aren't they handsome?'

Steve ran a practised eye over both animals.

'They're mighty big,' he said, 'Fine heads though. Intelligent eyes. Good movement, considering.'

'What were you expecting?' quizzed Jenny, laughter in her eyes. 'A thoroughbred or maybe one of those American Quarter horses for herding buffalo?'

Steve smiled, circling the stallions.

'Very sturdy.'

'Gentle giants,' she said.

'Strong legs and pretty,' he grinned, referring to their silky-white feathering. 'And mighty powerful.'

He gently stroked the strong sloping shoulders of both horses.

'In other words,' said Jenny, 'they are horses of quality?' 'But of course. How could they be otherwise?' he teased. 'They carry a lot of weight,' she said. 'Knights in full armour once used them. They have a long history.' Her face had settled in mock seriousness. 'They pull well too.' Steve pushed his hat to the back of his head as they grinned at each other.

'Stop pulling my leg,' he said. 'We're not really galloping over the moors on these, are we?'

'You mustn't hurt their feelings,' she said, patting the head of Chum. 'These are Clydesdales and they aren't built for galloping. Nor are we. We have the whole day before us. I had a less strenuous journey in mind. I thought it would be pleasant to take our time and admire the scenery and talk without panting for breath but of course, if you'd rather...'

The twinkle was still in her eyes but Steve was taking no chances.

'No, no,' he interrupted, 'There's nothing I'd like more than a leisurely trot and anyway, I'll feel safer with Charlie - or is it to be Chum?'

'Charlie seems to have taken a fancy to you.'

Charlie tossed his head in agreement.

'Charlie it is then,' smiled Steve, 'all sixteen hands of him.'

She handed him the reins of both horses.

'Take over while I make a final check with Jock,' she said. Steve watched till she disappeared from sight.

'Now Charlie,' he said, his hand caressing the stallion's mane, 'take it as easy as you like and it won't be too slow for me. There's an awful lot of scenery to admire and a lot of talking to do. Understand?'

Nostrils quivering, Charlie tossed his head and raised a feathered leg in reply.

'Good boy. The same goes for you, Chum,' he said, turning to the other Clydesdale who stood motionless, gazing ahead.

'I take it that means No Comment,' said Steve wishing he'd brought along some sugar lumps or carrots or whatever made a Clydesdale bond.

When Jenny rejoined him she wore a haversack on her back containing, she informed him, coffee which they might find welcoming at some stage in the journey. Coffee wouldn't be the only thing he'd find welcoming, thought Steve as they set off.

They left the farm behind them and trotted past the garden acres where volunteers were already at work. Steve saw Buddy and his new friend with the battered face still working together on the construction job. Their heavy hammers were lifting and striking, lifting and striking, in synchronised rhythm as stakes were hammered home and an archway of considerable proportions was beginning to take shape.

'Your friend seems to enjoy his labours,' remarked jenny. 'Can't understand him. I'd have thought he'd be happier with the musicians.'

'Like Miranda,' said jenny.

Steve, like Chum before him, stared straight ahead and made no comment.

'She has a beautiful voice,' said Jenny. 'She should go far.'

Not far enough, thought Steve, conscious of stirrings of guilt at the knowledge he was withholding from Miranda's sister. Quickly he changed the subject.

'Buddy seems to have connected with the Buddhists here,' he remarked.

'It doesn't surprise me,' said Jenny. 'Buddy seems inclined to the contemplative way of life.'

Steve looked at her in surprise.

'It's not a word I'd use about Buddy. Caring yes, optimistic, dependable, demanding - of himself as well as others - but contemplative, no. He's probably just curious and Buddy, being Buddy, is trying to find out what makes them tick.'

'Maybe he's finding out more than he bargained for,' said Jenny.

The gardens were now behind them and they were approaching the main gates.

'I think we'd better keep single file till we reach the village, said Jenny. 'You never can tell on this road what's round the corner.'

With the sound of the horses' hooves on the macadamised road and the glimpses of moor through the berry spattered branches of hawthorn hedge, they headed for the village.

How right you are, thought Steve, manoeuvring Charlie to follow Chum.

'Who'd ever have guessed I'd meet you round the corner of my life?' he mused.

Apart from two women gossiping outside the post office, they saw no one. Only when they reached the edge of the moor did Jenny wait till Steve was alongside.

'It must feel like Tom Thumb country to you after Canada's vast territories,' she commented, turning her head towards him.

'It's sure quaint. I'll give you that, but I'm getting kinda used to it.'

'And enjoying it?' she asked, smiling.

'I guess so,' said Steve, returning her smile.

He held her eyes for a moment before she turned her gaze on the moorland.

'How does Charlie feel?' she asked.

'As solid as a rock - more ways than one.'

Her laugh was hearty and Steve relaxed. This was sure a beautiful morning. Sweet air, the promise of another sunny day, cirrus clouds above, a warm horse beneath and the company of a beautiful woman.

'Did you ride much in Vancouver?'

'A bicycle mostly.' He saw her eyebrows shoot up. 'Most weekends Sam and I - Sam's my son,' he explained, 'cycled in Stanley Park. We're very proud of our Stanley Park, all one thousand acres of it, wild and tamed. The cycle way follows the sea wall for miles.'

'Sounds lovely.'

'We used to hire our cycles for the day and picnic on the beach, sometimes swim or maybe just sit and gaze at the mountains of West Vancouver. At other times we'd visit the zoo then eat in one of the wonderful coffee shops that abound in the park.'

They had been cantering for some time over the open moor, enjoying the autumnal colours, enhanced by the twisting, sparkling ribbon of a creek. Jenny brought Chum to a halt.

'Let's stop here by the burn and have our coffee. This is one of my favourite spots. I can breathe the moors and paddle in the burn if I take the notion.'

As they dismounted the quiet was disturbed by a pair of plump birds with feathered legs flying low above them.

'Grouse,' said Jenny as she dropped the haversack from her shoulders. 'The local game.'

'We have a Grouse mountain in North Vancouver where sometimes we'd go winter skiing. Sam liked that. He was getting pretty good. The views from the top were stunning, as far as the San Juan Islands in Washington State on a good day.'

They dismounted, watched the Clydesdales begin a leisurely forage then, finding a patch of greenery on the bank of the burn, settle themselves comfortably. While Jenny feasted her eyes on the moorland Steve feasted his on Jenny. Afraid of embarrassing, he forced himself to look towards the jagged horizon of mountain peaks.

'Our wee hills hardly compare with the Rocky Mountains, I suppose,' she commented as she unpacked the haversack and began pouring. As she offered him a cup of steaming coffee she gave him a disarming smile. 'Nor, I suppose, can our wee singing burn here match the majestic Rocky Mountain rivers.'

Steve, after a sip of coffee, placed the cup on the grass beside him before dipping a hand in the burn and gently paddling his fingers through the clear, cool water.

'Small is beautiful,' he said. He looked up as more grouse flapped overhead.

'This used to be a grouse moor estate,' said Jenny. 'I remember going with the guns when I was a girl. It's hard to believe that I actually enjoyed seeing my grandfather and the Laird himself shoot these beautiful birds.'

Steve, shaking his hand free of water, took another sip of coffee. 'You wouldn't now. Eh?'

'No. I hate destruction of any kind now.'

'You have always lived here?'

'When the estate was split up and sold I lived with my grandfather in a cottage in the village. It is called Broom Cottage because of its masses of golden broom in the spring. It is perched on a little hill and overlooks both village and the waters of the Firth and has a green field behind. It was one of the old Laird's grace and favour houses which he left to my grandfather for his lifetime. After grandfather died and I moved to Edinburgh to live with my husband it was left untenanted for years. When my husband and I returned here we bought it from my inheritance and for a time it housed bands of workers we had employed for renovating the castle. It's now on the market. So far, no one has shown any interest.'

Steve's interest now quickened. This had been the first mention of her husband. He gently probed.

'I believe your husband writes now.'

'He has completely immersed himself in Scotland's religious history. His books have been widely acclaimed - in Scotland anyway, although there are ongoing negotiations for publishing overseas.'

'Quality writing. Eh?'

She held his gaze.

'He writes from the heart. That, I think, is a quality factor.'

Steve sighed in self-denigration.

'For years I've been writing from the head.'

Cup half-way to her lips, she answered.

'But you have a heart you can work on if you want to.'

'Oh yes. I have a heart - a bit battered and bruised at the moment but still beating.'

His words had floated on the wisp of a sigh and he was immediately appalled. More self pity. What must she think of him?

In a desperate attempt to improve his image he added, 'I'm writing about Strathard at the moment and it's favourable and definitely coming from the heart.'

'You are?'

Beneath her thick lashes her eyes were full of enquiry.

'It's a letter - but a long one - to Sam. I want him to see it through my eyes and maybe he'll feel he's here with me. I think he'd like it.'

She reached for his cup, gesturing a refill.

'Tell me about Sam.'

Steve hesitated. To avoid her eyes he dropped his hand into the burn again, deeper this time, attracted by a pebble lodged on its bed. Sam was a world away, a different world, a laughing, fun-loving world - once.

Snapshots clicked in his mind. Sam cycling, wielding a baseball bat or demonstrating a good backhand. Sam lost in a book, playing with Lucky, his Labrador. Or Sam coaxing some life from a French horn, proud of calloused fingers from stringing a guitar. Sam talking to Buddy, teasing his mother, waving goodbye when his father left for a research trip, as he'd called his many jaunts abroad. Then Sam grinning and back slapping when his father returned home again. Haltingly, he told of all of them.

There were other pictures which Steve decided to keep to himself. Sam unsmiling, eyes averted in disappointment and often, lately, Sam looking lost, confused and hurt.

Steve mentally fended off these last images and returned his attention to the face before him. It was a face he saw as a beacon, able to dispel the shadows lurking in the darker recesses of his mind forever awaiting the opportunity to sneak into an empty space.

'Steve?'

Jenny was recalling him from his inner turmoil. Although he summoned a smile, he was disturbed by his own vulnerability. He realised how much he needed this woman beside him. He knew that if he were ever to get himself on beam again, this was the woman who could help him. A fleeting vision of Susan with her large violet eyes and golden curtain of hair was quickly snatched from his album. He didn't need Susan with her toyboy but if ever he wanted to see Sam again he had to be whole. He was convinced thatJenny could help him. Hadn't she proved that already? Hadn't he, since meeting her, proved himself fit to fight the battle others seemed to think he had to wage? His urge to gather her in his arms was almost irresistible.

He withdrew his hand from the burn and looked at the pebble he had scraped from its bed. It was oval in shape, mottled green like polished marble. It was cool to the touch and fitted comfortably in his palm.

'I shall keep this as a memento of today,' he said.

'It would make a good worry stone,' said Jenny. 'Rubbing it gently calms worries away.'

'I'd wear it down in no time,' Steve sighed.

He'd done it again! Always looking for sympathy. What a wimp he was.

Smiling, she passed him his freshly-filled cup, giving no indication that she'd noticed.

'I love so many of the place names in Canada, like Kicking Horse Pass, Yellowheart Pass, Big Salmon - not to mention,' she added with a smile, 'Lake McLeod and the Fraser River. McLeod was my maiden name,' she explained.

'You are interested in Canada. Eh?'

'My father is there and my brother.'

Steve, although feeling uncomfortable that, unknown to her, he already had this knowledge, couldn't stop himself from prompting further.

'In Vancouver?' he asked, already knowing the answer.

'Just before the war, after my mother died and when Strathard estate was sold and split, my father went to Vancouver to help my uncle in his sweetie factory. Since then he has remarried and now lives with his wife in Toronto.'

'And your brother?'

'He was posted to Canada during the war after some active service in Europe where he was injured. He was transferred to a training unit but is now in civil aviation. He lives in Winnipeg with a Canadian wife and two children, one boy, one girl. They were his wife's from a previous marriage.'

'Were you never tempted to follow them?' he asked, studying his pebble.

'No. I was never tempted.'

'Have you any more family?' He was unable to look at her, uncomfortable with himself for the deliberate intrusion. Her next words shook him.

'Relax, Steve. I know that Miranda is my sister, Moira.' Her voice was matter of fact. She washed both cups in the burn before turning to him. 'I have known since the moment she arrived here.'

Steve's astonishment showed in his face and in his voice as he asked, 'In spite of the disguise?'

'That made no difference. Being forewarned of the possibility of her turning up here helped, I suppose.'

'You were expecting her?'

'She left a very worried family behind. Aunt Sheena was beside herself. She is a hard woman but I believe she cares for Moira in her own way and I understand Moira was not an easy child to rear. She is a real fighter, as my mother told me before she was born. "She's a strong one," my mother said.'

Jenny's gaze had left him, roaming the distance, trapped in some distant memory.

'She also asked me to look after her which I singularly failed to do. I was glad to see the last of my baby sister, Moira. I hated her and blamed her for my mother's death.'

'You must have been very young.'

'And utterly selfish.'

'There were good reasons, I am sure.'

'Yes. We were in no position to look after a baby as well as a handicapped sibling. It was best for everyone - except Moira, perhaps.'

'It was a long time ago.'

'Yes indeed. Thirty years of lost opportunity.'

Steve hated to see the cloud pass across the brightness of her face. He was already gently fingering his polished pebble.

'I've felt guilty knowing about Moira and not saying anything,' he said.

'How could you? I've no doubt Buddy and you had been sworn to silence.'

Steve, still uncomfortable nodded and busied himself with a blade of grass, unable to meet those penetrating eyes.

'She was very lucky to meet you both. You have no reason to feel guilty. You were nothing less than honourable.'

He noticed the Clydesdales were edging away to greener pastures. He pocketed his pebble and half rose to his feet.

'It's different now. I feel no obligation towards her. She spells trouble, Jenny. She's seeking some kind of revenge. I agree she's a fighter but she's a dirty fighter. Shouldn't you tell her that you know she's your sister?'

They were both on their feet now. He handed Jenny the debris for a garbage bag which she produced from the haversack.

'I don't think so,' she said.

'Believe me, I know what damage she can do. She's a mischief-maker and you could get hurt.'

They were now standing close together and it was getting more and more difficult to keep his hands to himself. Fortunately Jenny didn't seem to notice his struggle and continued her tidying. In one quick movement she had slipped her arms under the straps of the haversack and secured it on her shoulders. She moved towards the horses and he could only follow. Before mounting the Clydesdales to continue their journey jenny, who had taken binoculars from her haversack, now handed them to Steve.

'If you set your sights on that white blob in the distance you will see where we're heading.'

Steve, conscious of a lost opportunity, focused the glasses on a long two-storey building nestling beneath a small forest of pines. He saw a car which looked vaguely familiar, arrive and park on the far side of the building. He returned the binoculars.

'It was once a shooting lodge of the estate,' said Jenny, slinging them round her neck. 'The Laird lived out his final years there. It was left untenanted for a long time after and got a bit war o' the weir - worse of the wear,' she added, seeing his puzzled expression.

They mounted and set off at a brisker trot than hitherto. I'm sure there are lighted lamps behind those eyes, thought Steve. How alert, alive and lovely she is.

'We offered the shooting lodge to the Buddhists who set to immediately and restored it. You can't see them from here but there are some neat wooden workshops at the rear. The ground floor has common rooms, library, kitchen and a printing shop. Upstairs is divided into two. One half is for dormitories and the other is a shrine room where they sit.'

'Sit?'

'Just that. Sit.'

About to say more, she changed her mind.

Steve noticed that the nearer they got to the building the more animated she seemed to become. Looking at her he felt almost envious of her radiance. Was it the sun and distant hills, a cloudless sky, birds swooping over the moor? Or, was it maybe his company? Wish on, Stevenson Bruce!

On their arrival at the shooting lodge they were warmly welcomed by the Buddhists. This secluded property, once the shooting lodge of a Scottish Laird, was a world away from the hustle and bustle of life.

Where at one time hunting trophies may have been displayed there were now collections of carved miniature shrines and prayer wheels. Where perhaps the walls had been adorned with tartan hangings there were Thangkas which Steve learned were paintings on silk depicting deities of the Buddhist tradition. With Jenny he toured the workshops behind the main building and saw monks demonstrate to Westerners wood carving in Tibetan design. There were monks making carpets and others gilding scores of eight inch high statues of a one-time famous Buddha. He admired the vivid colours of decorative designs being painted which were intended for a temple shrine which, they told him, was being built somewhere in the south of the country and where they would be moving to very soon. This was the way they were choosing to preserve their cultural heritage which had been violated by the Maoist Red Guards.

Watching the craftsmen at work, Steve was impressed by their total absorption. Every movement was meaningful. Here too, Steve decided, the operative word was quality. Every task was performed with grace and skill. They worked harmoniously with their tools and with each other. Each moment was a joy fulfilled. Steve and Jenny returned to the main building and were ushered into the printing room where even here everything was evidence of organisation and efficiency.

'It is from here that our newsletters and pamphlets are distributed world-wide,' said jenny.

With clasped hands, bowing heads and a smile of serenity, a monk offered them lunch. Steve and Jenny followed him to the kitchens where they were given a bowl of rice. Steve, who hadn't been giving any thought to food all morning, suddenly felt ravenous and looked askance at the rice.

'Not what you're used to?' asked a smiling Jenny.

'Sorry,' he mumbled sheepishly, feeling that if he'd been the blushing type he'd be red-faced with embarrassment.

'That's all right. Only vegan food is served here. It's part of their way of looking at food. Perhaps I should explain,' she added, interpreting his silence. 'To a connoisseur of food a porterhouse steak would be judged by practised eye and nose. To someone accustomed to enjoying good food it would be anticipated with relish. To a penniless beggar it would be looked upon with envy and to a starving man it would be torn apart and shovelled, possibly raw, into a cavernous mouth. Let me finish,' she said gently as Steve prepared to interrupt. 'To a vegetarian it would be the nearest thing to cannibalism but with his reverence for all life and total rejection of greed and envy a Buddhist would simply ignore it. Rice, grains, fruit, vegetables and water are sufficient for healthy living, in his eyes.'

'Am I being humbled?' asked Steve.

'I don't know. Are you? I was merely using it as illustrative of individually perceived reality which is bound to determine individual morality and how our realities and corresponding moralities endlessly change.'

Steve finished his rice before replying.

'What is your perception of reality, Jenny?' he dared to ask, hoping that it might throw light on her perception of morality.

'Ah. I agree with the Buddhists in so far as it is constantly changing.'

Steve, drinking in the colour of her eyes said, 'Surely it must have some permanence?'

Jenny held his gaze.

'Yes, the permanence of change. Would you like more rice?'

Steve shook his head.

'Rice is very satisfying.'

Jenny smiled and said, 'Another point in its favour.' She reached for his empty bowl. 'I'll wash these then we shall go upstairs to the shrine.'

'Are we allowed into their shrine?'

'It is an inclusive society but they do request we remove our shoes. We can sit on the side. The practising monks won't even know we are there. Of course, there is nothing to stop you sitting among them if you wish.'

Steve laughed aloud.

'I wouldn't know what to think if I sat in the lotus position with my eyes closed and my mouth shut.'

'You'd be all right then since you're advised not to think.'

Steve shook his head in mild amazement as he followed her upstairs. Outside the shrine room he unlaced his shoes leaving them beside others which were neatly deposited along the wall and watched Jenny lay her riding boots beside them. Admiring the turn of her ankle - what was there about this woman he didn't admire? - he followed her into the shrine room, having no likely thought of the shock awaiting him.

CHAPTER 18

When Steve stepped inside the blue room he was to have all his previous conceptions knocked into a cocked hat. When he followed Jenny to a wall-side seat he forgot about her well-turned ankles and her lamp-lit eyes because his instant vision had encompassed a scattered group of straight-backed bodies, to all appearance frozen in time. They were sitting in the most uncomfortable position imaginable with eyes and mouths closed. Just sitting! It was when he zoomed in on the sitters that his trouble began.

At the back of the human statuary was his mate, Buddy. Steve's first reaction was to feel betrayed. Being interested in Buddhists was one thing, pretending to be one of them was quite another. What was the dolt thinking of? Here he was, sitting on his arse looking like a dehumanised robot.

Steve glanced at Jenny whose apparent serenity was a match for the best of the Buddhists. She sat motionless, her thickly-fringed eyes fixed on some mid-distance point. Steve's eyes followed her line of vision and came to rest on a figure which jolted him.

So far he'd given little thought to this battered faced gardener who so interested Buddy. Now he forced himself to look closely at the man. He could feel his prejudice against the abnormal asserting itself. He allowed himself the grace to wonder why he was prejudiced. Why should this facially disfigured man, otherwise as good a specimen of macho manhood as any, rouse in him an instinct to abhor? Was it merely distaste? Embarrassment? Was his reaction perhaps tinged with fear, there but for the grace of God stuff? It was certainly uncomfortable. His prejudice was being challenged. If this man had had a hand in bringing Buddy to this sorry pass or if he had the power to hypnotise Jenny, as another glance at his companion seemed to indicate, then he was not to be ignored. The silence in the shrine room was almost tangible. It exerted a power which was only dispelled by the unexpected resonance of a singing bowl.

Steve recognised Yeshi who had so happily introduced him to their powerful beauty on his visit to the library. It had the effect of calming him and distracting Jenny's attention back to himself.

'Do you know much about Buddhism?' she whispered, although the concentration seemed to be lessening and the statues begin to humanise.

'I know nothing about Buddhism.'

'It's most interesting. There are lots of books about it in the library.'

'I'll hunt them out,' he said, not to appear ungrateful.

Steve's eyes were on Buddy who had just become aware of his presence. He's not even embarrassed about being caught red-handed, thought Steve, annoyed.

'I'd like you to meet Todd,' Jenny was saying as Buddy's new mate approached.

He accepted the outstretched hand and forced himself to look the stranger in the face. The first thing he noticed was that the eyes dominated and had the effect of staying his runaway thoughts. Their expression was unfathomable but it drew him like a magnet and as Todd spoke all Steve became aware of were his eyes.

'I trust you're enjoying the Strathard experience. It takes a bit of getting used to.'

'Steve's a writer,' said Jenny. 'He's writing about his Strathard experience at the moment.'

Buddy had joined them and raised his eyebrows when he heard this. Steve got in first.

'Didn't know you were interested in meditation, Bud.'

'I'm not,' said Buddy. 'I just wanted to find out how long I could sit without twitching.'

'And for how long did you?' asked Todd.

'About ten seconds.'

'Good,' said Todd then speaking to Steve added, 'You'll be wondering what's so good about that.'

Steve shrugged.

'I wish you'd tell me.'

'How long do you have?' asked Todd.

'Not long,' said Jenny. 'We're on the slow boat to China today.'

'Charlie and Chum,' said Todd. 'Jenny spoils them rotten.'

'They work hard for their keep,' said Jenny.

Steve noted their relaxed manner with each other. But then Jenny seemed to have the rare gift of a relaxed manner with everyone. He felt chastened.

Jenny was now steering them downstairs, through the printing room where both she and Todd stopped from time to time to have a word with the working monks and with each other, occasionally scrutinising a newsletter or pamphlet from a neatly arranged pile. Jenny, after a quick glance at her watch, ushered them to the kitchen where she proceeded to fill the kettle. Steve followed Todd and Buddy to one of the tables.

Steve found it easier to focus on Buddy than on Todd. 'What on earth were you thinking about sitting on the floor like that?' he asked him, in an attempt to treat the whole matter lightly.

'I was emptying my mind,' said Buddy without as much as a blink.

'Yeah! I guess ten seconds would be just about right,' said Steve.

'Listen to him, Todd,' said Buddy. 'He was born a cynic.' Steve was aware of the penetrating eyes.

'I think you might be giving him the wrong idea about sitting,' Todd said.

'The point is I have no idea about sitting.'

'We sometimes call it practising.'

'You mean you practise just sitting!'

Todd laughed heartily. Jenny beamed. Buddy smirked while Steve felt a bloody fool.

'I'm listening,' he said.

'You tell him, Jenny,' said Todd.

'It's very simple really,' said jenny. 'When we meditate we try to let go of our thoughts - all of them. After all, they are the cause of all our troubles. They're just little blips of energy having a ball. They agitate, deceive, con and upset us. They remind us of what's already happened, worry us about what might possibly happen, excite us about what could happen, or demoralise us about what might never happen. The only thing they don't tell us is what is happening in the here and now and that is the only real happening.'

She was talking fast, eyes flashing, colour heightening, quite breathtaking thought Steve.

'Whoa, whoa!' laughed Todd. 'Give the man a break.'

'That's okay,' said Steve, enjoyingJenny's enthusiasm. He wanted her to go on talking because that way he could legitimately keep looking at her.

Todd had covered her hand with his as he'd cautioned her and this Steve resented. It was an abomination. How could she permit that person to touch her? When she made no attempt to release her hand he had to restrain himself from shouting, hands off, you ugly brute, but all he could muster was to ask another stupid question in the hope that she would look at him and he could go on looking at her.

'What are we supposed to do with all these thoughts if they're such a bother?'

'Let them go,' said Todd. 'Don't grapple with them. They're transitory. Leave them alone and they'll stop bothering.'

'But acknowledge them,' added Jenny, 'just don't give them mind room.'

'You can control them instead of them controlling you,' said Todd.

Again that spurt of resentment, hardly lessened when Buddy offered his pennyworth of advice.

'It leaves room for the state of awareness,' he was smugly saying, or so it seemed to Steve.

He was getting a bit fed up with Buddy's smugness. After all, he was on this trip to look after him. I pay the piper, Steve reminded himself, and I don't like the tune he's playing now.

'When you let your thoughts go, then you can become aware,' said Jenny, 'of the now, each minute lived because that's all you have. You've already left your past and you haven't yet got your future.'

Buddy again chipped in with 'Talking about the future, what will happen when the near future sees the departure of the Buddhists from Strathard?'

'As my grandfather used to say,' said Jenny, 'as one door closes another door opens.'

'No one is indispensable,' said Todd and was it his imagination or did he see Todd's hand give Jenny's a gentle squeeze?

'You will need others to do their jobs,' insisted Buddy. Steve looked at him sharply.

'Are you offering your services?'

'I might be.'

Jenny brought the conversation to an end by suggesting Buddy should ride back with Steve.

'You can tell Steve more about Buddhist sitzen,' she said. 'Todd can drive me home in his car.'

The car he'd seen arriving, thought Steve. He remembered it had looked familiar. Had Jenny known they'd be here, he wondered. Todd nodded. Buddy readily agreed while Steve's heart sank. He felt like a child deprived of his most precious possession and was already in a sulk, blips of energy having invaded his mind to begin agitating, conning and upsetting him. He made no effort to let them go. He couldn't. He was so consumed with childish disappointment that he encouraged them.

By the time Steve and Buddy began their journey across the moor, Steve was locked in the turbulence of his invading thoughts, faintly annoyed by Buddy's continuing humming. That was the exasperating thing about Buddy. He thought everything could be resolved by singing. He had not yet resigned himself to Buddy's enforced company. Next to being with Jenny he would have preferred his own company. Not that it was much comfort at the moment. His introduction to the Buddhist community had upset him. Even if it were an admirable way of life, there was no way it could tell him how to play his duff hand. He might as well stack it now.

"Oh give me a home where the buffalo roam, where the deer and the antelope play," sang Buddy.

'You'll scare the horses,' said Steve.

"Where seldom is heard a discouraging word." 'For. God's sake.'

"And the skies are not cloudy all day."

Steve wondered if he should dig his heels in and hope that Charlie might suffer a gallop but decided against it. 'Let's talk,' said Buddy, suddenly serious.

'Not in front of the horses,' said Steve.

'Okay. We'll talk when we get back to the castle.'

For the rest of the journey, Buddy sang like a roving cowboy. It was only when they were seated in a quiet corner of the lounge that he made his first tackle.

'You're making a fool of yourself.'

'Nothing unusual in that.'

'The woman is married and it will only end in a bloody mess.'

'I'm aware she's married.'

'Then why are you behaving like an undisciplined adolescent?'

'She doesn't love her husband.'

'Has she told you that?'

'It's plain for anyone to see.'

'I don't see it.'

'Have you lost your eyes as well as your mind?'

'Even if she doesn't love her husband that's no excuse for you to walk a minefield. You're married too, remember.' 'I can barely remember.'

'You'd better remember and remember too that you have a son.'

'Leave Sam out of it.'

'Just like you've been doing. Have you phoned him, written to him, thought about him?'

Steve's knuckles were white as he grasped the arm of his chair.

'I thought as much.' Buddy's voice was grim. 'I've had a letter from Sam,' he added, watching Steve closely.

Steve's eyes glazed and it was as much as he could do to stay put.

'It was in answer to one I wrote to him. He is my godchild and that's a privilege I don't take lightly. It's my job to take over when he loses his Dad.'

'He hasn't lost his Dad.'

Buddy leaned forward in his chair, clasped hands dangling between his knees.

'Then how come he has to ask me where you are, what you're doing, when you're coming home - zfyou're coming home?' Ignoring the gathering pain on Steve's face he forced home his argument. 'Jenny says you're writing about Strathard.'

'It's for Sam.'

'The same letter you intended posting days ago?'

'I want it to be good.'

'If it wins a Nobel prize for its goodness it will be a waste of time if Sam doesn't get the chance to read it.'

'What are you trying to say, Bud?'

'I'm saying forget Jenny Fraser. She's no more than an escape route for you - from yourself and your problems. Get yourself sorted out and get back to Susan and for God's sake get in touch with Sam.'

'And how, Buddy the Buddhist, do I sort myself out? 'Empty my mind?'

Buddy leaned closer.

'For a start, you can get rid of that bottle in the second drawer of your tallboy which, incidentally, I see has already been opened.'

'You've been sneaking in my room.'

'That's why I'm with you, remember?' Wasn't that part of the original contract?'

'One small drink,' said Steve, unaware of the hidden plea in his voice.

'Nearer two.'

'Two then. Is that so terrible?'

'In your case, worse than terrible.' 'Don't start that again!'

'Come out of denial, Steve. You know that if it's one small drink today it's likely to be a whole bottle tomorrow. Not until you admit to yourself that you are an addict do you stand a chance of getting your act together again.'

Steve looked disdainfully at his friend which was at odds with his anger. The cheerful, singing cowboy was no more. He could only see a man with a colt 45 willing to shoot at what had been his slowly building self-confidence.

What had begun as a special day had turned sour. He rose and left the room, convincing himself that he'd taken leave with dignity and no offence. Although he knew that Buddy had not said what he had for the fun of it he was nevertheless offended. Buddy was refusing to recognise his new attitude to drinking. Buddy, he thought, had perhaps outgrown his usefulness. What had he done for him since coming here, apart from breaking and entering? He was living in another world now with men in saffron robes intent on emptying their minds. He was showing more allegiance to a malformed stranger than to the man who paid him his salary.

Without intending to, he found himself on the road to the village. The weather had taken a turn for the worse. A chill wind was robbing the trees of the last of their leaves and rippling the surface of roadside puddles. He was reminded of Greenock and that thought added a train of associations in his thought-burbling mind.

This is all wrong, he told himself. No twentieth-century self-respecting adult should be reduced to this mental morass. He felt he'd been carrying it around in his head for years. It had become part of the system and was getting him nowhere. Maybe the Buddhists had it right. If you want to live an uneventful life rid yourself of all thoughts. 'Let them go,' the gardener had said. 'Leave them alone and they'll stop bothering.'

That couldn't be right. Thoughts were necessary to fire action. On the other hand, they could just as easily encourage non-action. It wasn't emptying the mind that was needed, he concluded. It was disciplining it. Like Jenny's chickens, his thoughts were scuffling round his head for pecking order. And as he neared the village and saw the lighted windows of the Strathard Arms ahead, he knew which thought was first in the pecking order. The pub was a picture of cosy welcome. By coming here Buddy would say he was spineless. He knew that by exposing himself to the bar lounge he was demonstrating remarkable strength, that is if he thought that remarkable strength was called for, which he didn't. He still felt he had to prove to Buddy that a drink presented no problem because, thanks to his association with the incredible Jenny Fraser, he was in control. If only to earn her respect he would stay in control. To lose control which, he had to admit, had happened once or twice in the past, he would lose her respect and he would lose Jenny Fraser. He couldn't get that woman out of his skin. These things happened. They were meant to happen. It was written in the stars. He'd be denying his destiny if he let anything or anybody interfere with it. He'd have one drink, possibly two. He'd leave the hotel sober, walk home in a straight line, join the others for dinner and present a steady, forward-looking, confident front.

The hotel lounge welcomed him warmly with its soft lights and dancing flames from a well-banked coal fire. He relaxed his tense muscles as he walked to the bar. A dominoes contest was in progress. Darts were being aimed and fired. Pint glasses were raised and even a few heads were turned in his direction.

'Aye. Fine nicht,' he was greeted by a long-faced local. The greeting was echoed by more voices and a few heads nodded. One glass was even raised in his direction while again in polite, if monotonous tones, the greeting was predictably repeated. 'Fine nicht.'

'Aye, fine nicht.'

After general agreement had been reached, attention returned to dominoes and darts. Steve, after a few polite words with the barman, carried his Scotch to a corner table, partly shielded by a stone pillar with decorative foliage, relieved to have got off so easily. The last thing he wanted was to be trapped in pointless conversation in a tongue he had to struggle to understand at times. Or, even worse, to be invited to join in the dominoes or the darts. He wriggled around in his seat until he had a vantage point where he could see enough without being conspicuous.

He drank slowly, deliberately, and with great pleasure, determined to enjoy his indulgence within clear limits. The door opened and closed against the darkness outside. It must be raining again. People were arriving with damp shoulders and wet hair but the greetings seldom varied.

'Aye, fine nicht.' 'Tis that.'

If the rain was acknowledged at all, it was generally agreed that a wee bit o' rain did nobody any harm.

Rather than leave his corner he caught the barman's eye and ordered another drink. There were still a few niggles that needed his attention. The pecking order of his thoughts was changing. Drink was no problem. He needn't concern himself about that. What niggled him now was Buddy's unjustified accusation that his burgeoning relationship with Jenny would only end in a bloody mess.

Someone had come in bringing cold air with them. Steve finished his drink, this time calling the barman to bring him another. He had to get his thoughts straight before he faced Buddy or Jenny again. As he waited for his third and last drink he injected a little self-criticism into his analysis.

Maybe he was hoping for too much. Maybe, chasing his dream would lead to trouble. He barely looked up as the barman laid his drink on the table because a black shadow of hopelessness all but succeeded in engulfing him. The thought which had now pecked its way to the fore had presented him with a vision of his love undeclared and without the help of another Scotch this was a thought that could not be rebuked.

'She is too pure,' he muttered to himself, unaware of darting glances. 'She's as pure as the Virgin Mary, herself.'

It will never work and I will be condemned to Hades.'

'And what, my son, would the Virgin Mary be doing in Hades?' asked a cheerful voice.

Startled, Steve's head jerked up.

'Are you not content with all the other clever murders in your stories that you've to send the Blessed Virgin to hell?'

Father O'Doyle seated himself opposite, at the same time signalling to Theresa who had stepped through a beaded curtain at the back of the lounge.

'Are you following me, Father?' Steve asked the priest.

'I think it's you that's summoning me, my boy,' said the priest. 'Am I in time?'

'If you mean am I still sober, the answer is yes, Father, and you are in time —just.'

The gypsy woman arrived at their table. The priest beamed at her.

'I'd be wondering, me darlin' Theresa, if you have any of that very special coffee of yours.'

'For you, Father and the lucky one here, of course. I'll be bringing it myself.' She disappeared into the kitchens behind the bar.

'I wish someone had offered to buy me black coffee twenty years ago - and turned up in time,' said the priest. In answer to Steve's long and questioning stare, he added, 'Can you work that one out, my son?'

'Are you telling me, Father that you had a problem twenty years ago?'

'Yes. I had the same problem as you.'

'You were an alcohol abuser. Eh?'

'No. I was an alcohol addict.'

Steve, who had been idly toying with his glass and a couple of tartan coasters, stopped and looking up, caught an uncharacteristic expression in the priest's eyes.

'I know the difference, my son, and that's the hard bit to swallow.'

The coffee arrived and Steve waited impatiently till Theresa left them alone again. He felt like someone stranded on a desert island with no means of escape who had suddenly seen a rescue ship on the horizon. He realised then how alone and helpless he really was and how desperate for that rescue.

'You are cured now. Eh?' asked Steve.

'I'll never be cured,' said the priest quietly, pausing to let his words sink in, 'but there hasn't been a drop pass my lips in fifteen years.'

Steve held the priest's gaze.

'Aren't you forgetting the drinks we had only the other night with Buddy?'

'Theresa and I have an understanding. When she brings me a drink it only looks like a drink.'

'You sly old fox,' laughed Steve. 'You fooled me.'

'Would you rather I'd given a lecture on the evils of alcohol?'

Steve swallowed a mouthful of coffee.

Carefully replacing his tartan mug on the tartan coaster he replied, 'I suppose not but tell me where you found the will to abstain.'

'I didn't.'

'How come?'

'It wasn't will I needed. I had to have the motivation. Will needs motivation. Will is the engine. Motivation is the fuel for the engine. You've got to want something so much you will muster the will to have it.'

'And what did you want so much?' asked Steve then added quickly, 'Perhaps I shouldn't ask you that.'

'You are entitled to ask. I wanted back my faith. With it I always had a lifeline. Drink robbed me of that. Without faith I was in the wilderness. I discovered that the wilderness is a stark and lonely place. I discovered too that the human soul had not been birthed for the wilderness. It was intended to be happy with the smell of roses, taste of honey and sound of music. The wilderness was empty of all these things. Now, symbolically speaking, the smell of roses is not confined to the garden, nor honey to the bees. As for music...'

'Saint Cecilia,' interrupted Steve,

'The blessed Saint Cecilia,' agreed Father O'Doyle.

Steve refilled the mugs. Darts hit the board. Dominoes stacked and fell. The bar door opened and closed causing the flames from the burning coals to jump and jive to the momentary blasts of Highland air. They drank, their faces reflecting the warmth of the congenial atmosphere.

'Remember this, my son,' said the priest. 'I couldn't have done it alone. The blessed saints were on my side. I allowed them to give me the motivation to drive my will. They showed me the way and they are still with me. I shall always need them if I am to stay clear of the wilderness.'

They sat in pregnant silence for some minutes then Steve returned to the conversation.

'The trouble is, Father, I don't have a faith.'

'Faith comes in many guises.'

'I don't think I'm even looking for a faith.'

'No, you're looking for a release from suffering, as are we all. How we find it depends a lot on who we are, where we've been, what we've heard and seen and already weighed in the balance. We are driven by our genes and our environment and they are different for everyone.'

Steve's face was registering a new awareness as if he'd just discovered something.

'Let me tell you, Father, I think I'm winning.'

'You have found the motivation perhaps,' smiled the priest.

'Perhaps,' whispered Steve. 'At least I'd like to think so.' They rose and left the hotel.

As they wound their way to the door someone called, 'A fine nicht.'

'Aye, it is that,' agreed Steve.

CHAPTER 19

Steve awoke next morning feeling that something had changed. At first he couldn't put his finger on it. He had slept well. His body was relaxed; his mind clear; no weight on his chest; no thirst; no shakes. Overriding all was a feeling of expectancy. It was as if warm, milk-frothed waves were washing over him.

The greyness outside his window was relieved by the billing and cooing of doves. He remembered seeing a dovecote in the garden and thinking at the time how appropriate this symbol of peace was to the quiet tenor of the monks' lives, unlike the chattering chickens and quacking ducks of the farm. Everything was going to be all right. Last night he'd made a decision. He thought about it as he swung himself out of bed. He thought about it as he showered and dressed and continued to think about it as he shaved and the more he thought about it the more convinced he was that it was the right decision.

Glancing out of his window he saw Buddy make his way towards the gardens and his day's work. He was going earlier every morning now. Soon he'd be taking root in one of their well-hoed drills, thought Steve, not unkindly. Whatever Buddy said last night must have influenced his thinking or maybe he had Father O'Doyle to thank for slipping him an angel. Whatever the cause, he had seen a great and wonderful light.

This light had illuminated the folly of nourishing any hope that he could win Jenny for himself. He had come to reason that a woman like Jenny Fraser would be appalled if she were ever aware of the thoughts he'd been harbouring. How could he have considered for one moment that she could be persuaded to deceive her husband and sully her reputation? It would destroy the credibility of Strathard with its aims of quality living and working. He must have been crazy ever to have imagined such a possibility.

It did not mean that he loved her any the less or had stopped wanting her. He would think of his decision as poetic justice. 'I could not love thee more, my dear, Loved I not honour more.' What it meant was that he had found within himself a fitting response to his present situation. He could go on loving her without endangering her. She need never know. It would be enough just to be where she was and breathe the same air. Not even Buddy could find fault with that. He would buy Broom Cottage. He would set up his home there, devoting his life to quality writing. He was done with horror stories. He would be happy in the knowledge that he could see Jenny every day, learn from her and help her. His stories would disseminate her core beliefs among a wider public.

Before leaving his room he lifted a package from the top of his tallboy. It was addressed to Sam. It was the finished letter - more a novella - on Strathard. He imagined Sam's face when he received it. Sam would discover that Buddy wasn't the only letter writer in his family circle. After he'd mailed the package he'd find Broom Cottage. Then he would visit the property agents and cast his die.

He'd already decided to forego his hours at the farm this day. He'd have the rest of his future to devote to that and - wonderful thought - to Jenny. So long as he could keep seeing her, everything would be all right. He vowed he'd never hurt a hair on her head or do anything that would put a stain on her principles.

As he walked along the shore road, evidence of last night's rain was on the wet clumps of leaves by the roadside. Above, the clouds were low in the sky. Below, white-combed waves were frolicking with the wind. He felt calm and optimistic. It was all so simple. Some honest thinking had made him realise the impossibility of gratifying his foolish desire. Jenny Fraser was no ordinary woman. She was consciously working for the good of humanity. Her reputation was spreading far. She was the lynch pin of Strathard Castle. Remove that and all her work would be destroyed. He couldn't do that to her. She was strong, honest and aware of the worth of what she was doing. How could he ever have thought for one moment that he could seduce her! After all, to her he owed his new aspiration - to channel his skills into quality writing. It was the answer to his growing dissatisfaction of what writing had been to him for many years now. He still marvelled at the impact of first seeing her face in the magazine article and above all, that surprising, utterly tantalising atom of delight they had experienced when she led him to the dance.

The village post office was a welcome respite from the buffeting wind. A bell tinkled when he opened the door, summoning an elderly woman from the back premises. She was rosy and bonny and had a smudge of flour on her nose. The smell of coffee and ginger and fresh-baked bread took him by surprise but the sight of parcel scales and a Royal Mail poster reassured him that he was in the right shop.

'A fine day,' the postmistress said cheerfully as he wiped his feet on the mat to remove the wet leaves.

'I'm looking for Broom Cottage,' he told her.

'You've come from the castle, I'll be thinkin',' she said. 'That's right.'

'Then you've passed it. It's easily done for it sits on a knoll a wee bittie off the road. Just go back up the hill here and ye'll see a wee turnin' to the left, past Jimmy Broon, the butcher, and follow the track round the corner and you canna miss it.'

He thanked her and left, retracing his steps until he reached Jimmy Broon, the butcher. He was about to turn left off the main road when a voice hailed him from behind.

'I thought it looked like you,' said Miranda, drawing abreast.

Steve was taken aback. He could hardly turn off the road and go to Broom Cottage now. Miranda would demand to know why. The decision was taken out of his hands when she jangled a bunch of keys before him.

'Would you like to come and look at a house with me? It's not far. It won't take long.'

He followed her into the lane which led to Broom Cottage.

'Are you interested in this house?' he asked when they stopped outside the gate and looked at the tiny whitewashed house behind the stone wall. The garden was tidy, the paths clean, the windows shining and the brass knocker on the front door welcoming.

'Very interested,' Miranda replied. Before his heart reached his boots she added, 'This is the house where my grandfather lived after the estate was broken up and my father left for Canada. Needless to say, the wonderful Jenny lived here too until she married Dr Death and went to live in Edinburgh.'

She unlocked the front door and Steve followed her inside, only half-listening to her scathing comments as she explored. Claustrophobic. Ugly. Soul-destroying were her words.

'The view is pretty,' he countered, busy with his own racing excitement.

He'd have the larger bedroom with the view over the village rooftops to the Firth. This must have been Jenny's room. Sam could have the back room looking over a green field. Adjacent to his bedroom he entered a smaller room which, he decided, could serve as his office. As Miranda ranted on, his mind was busy with ideas for plumbing improvement.

'It's primitive,' she wailed.

'It's romantic,' he thought.

'I wouldn't take it in a gift,' she said.

'I'd pay a ransom for it,' he decided.

'Let's get out of here!' said Miranda, slamming a door.

Steve now gave her his full attention noting the scowl, the hunched shoulders then, with a queer twist of dismay, the naked unhappiness in those round, long-lashed nutty-brown eyes.

'Tell you what,' he surprised himself by suggesting, 'Have lunch with me at the Strathard Arms. We can talk and get to know each other.'

She glared at him but seeing the tease in his smile she relaxed.

'I guess,' she shrugged. 'But it will have to be quick. I have a singing lesson with Luciano in an hour's time.'

Strathard Arms offered a warm relief from the cutting wind. A fire roared in the grate. The heavy curtains were protection against the worst of the draughts as they chose a table by the window. Service was quick and the soup, when it arrived, hot and tasty. Miranda's aggravation melted in the rising aromatic steam.

'You enjoy your singing. Eh?' asked Steve when they were half-way through their soup.

'I enjoy Luciano,' she retorted. 'I think he's falling for me. Are you surprised?' she asked in answer to his raised brow.

'Why should I be?' he rushed. 'You are an attractive woman, especially...'

'When I'm not being nasty,' she finished for him.

Steve remembered that this was the woman who was planning something nasty for Jenny. He decided on a direct attack.

'Isn't it time you told Jenny that you are her sister?' He was taken aback by her reply.

'Just what I was thinking,' she said lowering her eyes as she spooned the last of her soup into her mouth.

'I'm glad,' he said. 'You owe her at least the chance to tell her side of the story.'

'I already know her side of the story.'

'Not from how she sees it.'

She raised her eyes to surprise him further.

'You could be right.'

'I know I'm right,' he enthused. Pushing away an intrusive suspicion of Miranda's sudden change of heart and giving her the benefit of the doubt, he continued with rising hope.

'This game you're playing can be doing nothing for you. It isn't fair to either of you, not to mention Buddy and myself.'

'Buddy doesn't complain.'

'I do. I don't like being part of your deceit. I think you should come clean.'

He was careful to keep his voice friendly and persuasive and was pleasantly surprised by her response.

'You're right,' she said.

'After all, you have a lot going for you here,' he pushed. 'You're very lucky to have someone like Luciano to help with your singing. This could be a wonderful opportunity to sing in all the grand opera houses. Doesn't the idea excite you?'

'Not as much as it does you, apparently.'

Steve sighed.

'I know we got off on the wrong foot, Miranda, but I'd really like us to be friends and I particularly would like to see you happy.'

'What's got into you?'

'I just feel life's too short for bad feelings. I want everyone to be happy.'

'Have you been drinking?'

'Me! Drinking! Never touch the stuff.' He could even joke about his drinking. Wasn't that something? 'I'm a reformed character,' he added with exaggerated sobriety. 'I liked you as you were,' she said.

She pushed aside her empty soup bowl, placed her elbows on the table, cupped her chin in her hands and looked at him.

'You know, I really did love you to death that night on board ship when you kissed me.'

Although she spoke lightly he detected a cutting edge of steel in her voice. There was a pause in the conversation while in exchange for the empty soup bowls a plate of sandwiches was placed before them.

'I'm sorry about that night,' he said when they couldn't be overheard. 'I hope you really have forgiven me.'

'Well, you'll never know, will you?' she replied. 'By the way, Buddy tells me you were at the Buddhist shrine with Jenny.'

'That's right.'

'Dr Death wouldn't like that. Where has he disappeared to, by the way?'

'The Rev. Neil is somewhere down south at the moment researching for his book.'

'Why aren't you at the farm today?'

'I felt like a holiday and here we are, talking nicely for a change. Aren't you pleased?'

At that moment the landlord's wife appeared through the bead curtain and moved towards them bearing the coffee pot.

'Hello there,' she said, greeting Steve. 'Nice to see you again.'

Steve smiled at Theresa and began an introduction.

'This must be Miranda,' Theresa interrupted. 'I've heard you sing,' she explained at Miranda's look of surprise.

'Theresa is a soothsayer,' said Steve to Miranda, to which Miranda immediately replied, 'Shall I cross your palm with silver?'

'No need. I can see your future in your face,' Theresa replied. 'You have a beautiful face and it is going to break a thousand hearts.'

'What about her own heart, Theresa?'

'Broken too, but hearts self-regenerate, if allowed to.' The women looked at each other and Miranda was the first to look away.

'I hope to see you again,' smiled Theresa. 'Gold is your colour, Miranda. You wear it well.'

She retreated once more behind the bead curtain.

'Wait, Steve,' Miranda said. 'Before we go I would like you to promise me something.'

Warily Steve searched her expression.

'What?'

'I've found the house where I was born. I want to show it to you.'

'Now?'

'Tonight - after dinner. I'd like to talk to someone about it.'

'You could always talk to Jenny,' he said.

'Jenny! Jenny! Will you forget about Jenny and think of me for once? Will you come with me after dinner tonight? Just the two of us. I don't want Buddy to come.' She leaned across the table and reached for his hand. 'Please, Steve. Will you do this for me? Please.'

He succumbed to her persuasion and, giving her hand a friendly squeeze, replied, 'If you promise to give up this farcical impersonation and own up.'

'I promise.'

'I mean it, Miranda.'

'I mean it too, Steve. I will tell Jenny at the first opportunity, maybe even tonight.'

'You mean that?'

'Yes, I mean that.'

They finished their coffee. Steve offered to return the keys to the property agent, his motive being not entirely altruistic. He could find out more about Broom Cottage at the same time.

On returning to the castle he decided to visit the library and find a book on Buddhism. Apart from furthering his knowledge it would help impress Jenny - maybe even Buddy. His grin widened.

Fitzgerald was on duty behind the desk.

'I like it here,' he said in response to the surprised look on Steve's face. 'Yeshi has gone off somewhere for the day.' 'I'm looking for a book on Buddhism,' said Steve.

'You'll be spoiled for choice. Come, I'll show you their resting places.'

'Why are we whispering?'

Fitzgerald grinned.

'You always whisper in a library. It's a Do-Not-Disturb concession.'

'Who is there to disturb? We're the only ones here.'

'So we are but it does add to the atmosphere, don't you think?'

They grinned at each other.

Steve looked at the array of books on Buddhism.

'It depends what you want to know,' said Fitztgerald. 'Nothing too deep. I just want some broad lines. Something that will tell me why they enjoy sitting, poker-straight, emptying their minds and hoping for enlightenment. Have you ever heard of anything so ridiculous?'

'Maybe this book will explain it,' said Fitzgerald.

Steve accepted the book without a glance, asking if he was allowed to borrow it.

'Sure. I'll make a note of it and its condition.'

'Don't you trust me?'

'I never take anything at face value.'

Now where have I heard that before, thought Steve. They moved back to the desk where Fitzgerald made the necessary recording.

'You're looking remarkably pleased with yourself today,' he said as he returned the book to Steve.

'I'm happy.'

'Aren't you lucky!'

'Are you happy, Mr Philosopher?'

'I'm not unhappy.'

'That isn't the same thing.'

'Playing the balancing trick somewhere in between, I suppose.'

'Do you think these Buddhists are happy?'

'They're always smiling, if that's any indication,' said the philosopher.

'I'm not the religious type myself,' said Steve. 'Am I missing something?'

'Aren't we all?'

Steve took his leave, returned to his room and settled down to read about Buddha.

He discovered sitting - called sitzen - wasn't only a matter of emptying the mind. It was tied up with awareness - a method, conceived by the Buddha, of making ourselves aware of ourselves, our thoughts and emotions. Instead of allowing our thoughts to rampage through our psyche, upsetting us in our constant search for happiness, we could harness them for our own benefit.

How to examine them? We could label them, read the now curiouser than ever Steve. By sitting still and just letting things happen we could discover each thought as it invaded the mind - label it for what it was - not analysing or judging it, certainly not reacting to it -just label it then let it go. That was the important part. After it was recognised, let it go. It could come back, probably would, especially those thoughts which had been embedded over the years. They'll keep coming. Okay - label them then let them go. In time and with practice you'd become aware of the calibre of the mind and what you were up against and if you stuck at it, in due course, the persistent thoughts would become wearier than you. They would become so weary they'd give up and go away and take their resentment, envy, fear, anger or whatever baggage they carried with them and you would be free. Only then did you stand a chance of finding your happiness.

Steve felt the urge to experiment. Not daring even to consider the reaction of anyone who thought they knew him, he seated himself on the floor and tried to position his body as he'd seen the Buddhists do. It was with great difficulty and it sure hurt. Taking a deep breath and assuring himself of readiness, he closed his eyes and waited. In seconds he was suffering discomfort. His predominant thought was the pain in his left leg and the strain on his back muscles. Realising this was part of the exercise he quickly labelled them *Discomfort* then let them go. What would *Susan* think if she saw him now? Quick! Label *Susan*. Then came *Sam* before being ousted by *cramp* in his right calf. He suspended his efforts in order to deal with the cramp then painfully resumed his sitting posture. *Susan* again, bringing kindling resentment. He let it go. Next entered her toyboy - quick *anger*! The toyboy went and *Sam* returned and the pain his image brought was more than physical. His knee was hurting. *Discomfort.* Bring back Sam but no! He wasn't allowed to marshal his thoughts. They had to come of their own accord. Susan again! More anger and building resentment. Nose itching - *Discomfort. Buddy* - more *cramp*!

'To hell with this,' he muttered struggling to rise while slapping his calf. 'It's impossible. No wonder the Zen masters paraded with a stick to wallop the fidgety and those falling asleep. Although how anyone could get comfortable enough to fall asleep is beyond my understanding.'

He had a mental vision of the chief gardener - still, silent and serene, like a frozen image of detachment. How much practice had he endured? And Buddy? How did he label his thoughts? One a prize bloom, one for grafting, another for propagation and ... 'If his thought happened to be me,' said Steve aloud, 'he'd label it a weed for the compost!'

After a total of - a flick of the wrists and a glance at his watch - two hours ten minutes, he knew that Buddhism was not for him.

Still in buoyant mood despite his struggles with sitzen, he changed for dinner. As had become his custom, he joined Fitzgerald at his table. They were at ease with each other, now on first-name terms, their interests forging a mutual respect. Steve felt he was learning a great deal from this man who would profess to teach him nothing, of course. He relayed his experiment in Zen Buddhist sitzen to his receptive ears.

'It's not the road for you, Steve,' he smiled, 'but no doubt your awareness has sharpened because of it and you have learned to respect the beliefs of others and isn't that what this place is all about?'

'I'm certainly aware that there are many strange roads to wherever it is we want to go. I'm just not aware which road I'm supposed to be on and where I'm heading for.'

'Talking of travel, I've just been planning my return route south. Students will be demanding attention.'

'You'll be missed here.'

'I'll be back next year but I still have a little over a week here.'

As friends go, he's pretty good, decided Steve as he drank his after-dinner coffee.

Little did he know then how desperately he was going to need this friend in the hours to come.

CHAPTER 20

Steve wondered if they'd taken leave of their senses. How had it come about that they were lurking in an unlit garage which reeked of petrol and oil and had icy draughts whistling through window frames? The garage housed a van, a car and a bicycle as well as an assortment of tools hanging on wooden beams. Miranda was keeping a watch at the window and he was fingering, almost fondling, a Swiss knife which some careless person had left lying open on the shelf.

After dinner, when they'd left the indoor warmth of the castle, they'd been drenched by rain and buffeted by wind. He'd tried to persuade Miranda to postpone the visit to her birthplace. She would have none of it. 'A wee bit rain never hurt anyone,' she mimicked with perfection. With her arm tucked in his they battled their way down the castle drive. Instead of continuing to the main gates, Miranda pulled him into a tributary path bordered on either side by large bushes which offered a temporary protection from the worst of the storm. On leaving the path and making their way towards a long wall in the middle of which was an arched entry, they were again at the mercy of the storm. Miranda had dragged him across a cobbled yard and practically pulled him into the garage in which he now found himself reacting with heightening irritation. He'd been aware of a building on the edge of the square and this, according to Miranda, was the house in which she'd been born.

From the garage window it was only a grey shape to him. A glance at Miranda convinced him of her excitement. He could feel more than see it. Her breathing was rapid. She seemed poised for some sort of take off.

Her fingers closed on his ann. He tried to capture his earlier good feelings and curb the desire to push her away.

He had begun feeling empathy for her fixation with her childhood. Or so he thought. She had worked herself up to this pitch of excitement for so long now that the sooner matters came to a head the better. Praise be that she'd decided to come clean with Jenny - for both their sakes. He placed his free hand over hers then wished he hadn't. Taking quick advantage, she pushed closer while her lips rubbed against his face as she whispered in barely controlled excitement.

'I was born in the living room in a box bed.'

'What on earth is that?'

'Aunt Sheena described it as a hole in the wall. The wall of the room was on three sides of the bed. A curtain suspended from the ceiling was drawn across the front, ensuring privacy.'

'I see.'

'And my first cot was a dresser drawer.'

Steve's eyes, having become accustomed to the dark, could now make out a solid building of two storeys with central door. Above were small sashed windows. The windows on ground level, flanking the doorway, were much larger and more modern. As he watched, the room on one side of the door was flooded with light.

'Good heavens. There's someone in there. We shouldn't be here.'

'It's all right. We're safe here,' assured Miranda. 'He can't see us and there's no point in standing outside getting soaked.'

'There's no point standing here like a couple of peeping Toms.'

Steve was looking into what he supposed was the living room. The window was large enough to see a fireplace, large bookcases and armchairs. Built into one wall was an office unit. Steve wondered if that had once been the hole in the wall where Miranda had first seen the light of day. He watched as the man entered the room and walked purposefully towards the desk where, seating himself, he slit open an envelope, extracted a letter and began to read. That profile! Steve shook his arm free from Miranda's grasp and turned towards her.

'That's.

'Yes,' she interrupted. 'That's Todd, the chief gardener, your mate Buddy's golden idol. He lives here.'

'We'd better get going,' said Steve.

'No, wait,' said Miranda. 'We're doing no harm. I want to feast my eyes on that room.'

'You're paranoid,' said Steve. 'What good do you think that's likely to do you and besides, you don't think it looked anything like that when you were born, do you?'

'That's not the point. It's still the room, the place. . .'

'We still shouldn't be here,' he interrupted. 'Let's go. It shouldn't be impossible for you to arrange to see it from the inside, especially since you're coming clean tonight. You are coming clean, aren't you?'

'Of course I am - Sh! What's that?'

'What's what?'

'Don't you hear something?' she whispered.

Steve listened.

'I don't hear anything.'

'Footsteps. Listen, and stand back. We mustn't be seen.'

As Miranda spoke she pulled him back from the window. Above the sound of rain hammering on the cobbles and wind tearing dead limbs from trees, Steve heard footsteps, quickly followed by the sight of someone wrapped against the elements in a long cape with hood. The body leaned forward as it battled through the storm. It headed for the door, inserted a key and entered. Seconds later he saw it appear in the doorway of the lighted room.

The gardener rose. The hood fell from the visitor's head revealing the familiar face of Jenny Fraser. She approached, arms wide and face upraised in open invitation for the kiss that was bestowed. The red hair, freed from all restriction, showered over her shoulders before being trapped inside the arms of the man who held her.

Steve was shocked into silence. His eyes glazed at the sight of that battered, now repellent, face kissing the lips of the woman he idolised. He heard Miranda's quiet laugh. He relaxed his fierce grip on the Swiss knife which he didn't remember lifting. He felt the wet trickle of blood where the blade had pierced his skin. His brain hadn't registered the ferocity of his grip. Feeling compelled to gaze once more into the secrets of that room, he saw Todd walk to the window. He took an involuntary step back as the curtains were closed, shutting him out, throwing him into a terrible confusion. Above the drumming of his own heartbeat he heard Miranda's voice. He turned on her.

'You planned this,' he said between his teeth.

He was still holding the Swiss knife, its blade red with his blood. Miranda, on the point of closing up to him, hesitated.

'It was for your own good, Steve. I know you're crazy about her and think her perfect. Everyone thinks she's perfect. The whole world thinks she's perfect. The perfect Jenny Fraser, the woman of quality. Well, now you know just how perfect. Her husband's away for a few days and she's in the arms of another man.'

She gave a little hysterical laugh. 'How can she bear to kiss, even touch him!

'Steve!' she yelled in alarm. 'Steve! Put that knife down. Don't! Please don't!'

Steve's arm was raised, the knife blade glinting in the light filtering across from the house.

'I'll slit your throat, you scheming bitch.'

'Steve!'

'Get out of my sight!'

She screamed at the top of her voice and, scrambling to the door, she tripped over a garden spade and fell full length. Afraid to get up, she crept on her bottom to the back of the building and hunched herself against the wall. Steve threw the knife with giant force. It missed her widely.

Blinded by rage, he reached the door, wrenched it open and, without a backward look, lurched from the garage into the storm. He raced ahead, knowing exactly where he was going. He was going to get drunk. He was already tasting the liquor in the rain streaming down his face.

The bottle of whisky would be waiting for him, tucked among his socks and underwear in the second drawer of the tallboy. He was going to empty that bottle unless, that is, Buddy had confiscated it.

A white heat of resentment against Buddy writhed like a giant maggot in his mind. His resentment was not for his over-protectiveness. It wasn't even against his idiotic conviction that he needed protection. No, it was because he'd brought that treacherous woman into their lives and had consistently refused to hear a word against her. He'd now reached the portico and by the grace of God found a mere trickle of guests in the hail, none of whom seemed to notice the passing flight of a madman.

Inside his room, he went straight for the second drawer of the tallboy. Thank God it was still there. In one continuous movement he unscrewed the cap and raised the bottle to his lip. Gasping for breath, he drew the back of his hand across his mouth, then, filling a glass, he sat down, riveting his mind on what had happened, letting his thoughts have full range until their destructive force threatened his sanity. It was no longer Buddy or Miranda, nor even Jenny or Todd that was driving him to extremes. It was a vision of white raiment, darkly stained. His mind was fixated on the image. It was a raiment whose symbolic perfection had aichemised his baser instincts but whose incorruptibility was no more. The stark revelation of its blemish was an evil destroying all that had been beautiful and good.

He was like an erupting volcano, his destructive lava being forced under pressure from his overheated core.

As the whisky coursed down his gullet, surreal visions came and went.

'I'm not drunk, Father,' he said to the ridiculous spectre of Father O'Doyle, sprouting wings and hovering above his head. 'You can see I'm not drunk. I'm still in control but when I finish this bottle here,' brandishing the bottle in the air, 'I'll buy myself another. It's my religion, you see, Father, and it makes me feel good. It is my friend. It is my only friend.'

Father O'Doyle raised a crucifix above his head and bade him kill his anger.

Steve shook the last of the dregs into his glass, held the bottle high above his head and peered at its emptiness, shook it above his glass again while muttering to himself, 'Kill your anger, kill your anger, kill...'

'Are you all right, Steve?'

He swayed and would have fallen if Miranda hadn't rushed and caught him.

With a lion's strength he threw her off and growled. She landed hard on the floor. His focus on her was absolute and his words surprisingly articulate.

'Come to gloat?'

She looked scared, rising quickly to her feet.

'I only wanted to make sure you were okay. I'm sorry...'

'Sorry! No you're not. You've never been happier. You've meant this to happen all along. Now you've done it. Pleased with yourself. Eh?'

The volcano rumbled dangerously. Miranda sensed the danger, knowing that she stood on its lava-strewn path. Steve hissed as he threw her on the bed. When she opened her mouth to scream he whipped a handkerchief from his pocket and stuffed it inside while, at the same time, with the strength of ten men, pinned her to the bed.

'Is this what you want?' he said in a voice thickened with more than the whisky.

He ripped her blouse in two. He sat on her flailing legs. Terrified, her eyes begged in mute appeal. With one hand he spanned her throat.

Miranda's head was rolling on the pillow, her eyes wide with fear, her face purpling as she struggled like a trapped animal. Steve's hand hovered over her throat lacking the power to grip. The flying priest, with his raised crucifix, distracted him.

'Kill your anger,' the spectre kept repeating.

'Kill, kill,' sobbed Steve in a torment of inaction.

Miranda broke free, pulled the gag from her mouth and screamed. Steve was already powerless. The volcano had spent itself. The door flew open. Powerless to resist, he was hauled to his feet, rotated then given a knockout punch. Before losing consciousness, he heard Buddy's no-nonsense command to Miranda.

'Let's get out of here.'

When he regained consciousness he'd lost himself. He had no idea where he was or what had happened. He couldn't see. He barely heard someone come into the room and approach him. The touch on his body made little impression until it became more insistent and he groaned. The voice became clearer, the concern evident but still he couldn't see.

'You're in a mess,' said Fitzgerald.

'I can't see.'

'I'm not surprised. Someone's just given you a bunch of fives. Let's get you up and sitting.'

Steve didn't, indeed couldn't, resist.

'That's better,' said Fitzgerald when he'd got Steve on to the chair. 'Sit there while I fetch a towel and clean your eyes. You're drowning in blood. Steady on. I won't be a minute.'

Helpless, Steve suffered Fitzgerald's ministrations, trying to get his tongue round some intelligible words of enquiry. He had no control of it and his efforts to speak dissolved into gibberish.

'Let me do the talking,' said Fitzgerald quietly 'while I bathe your eye. I'm afraid you've a beauty of a cut here. It's going to need stitching.'

Steve could feel his senses slipping.

'Try to stay awake,' said Fitzgerald.

The voice seemed to come to Steve from a distance but he was beginning to see again.

'I'll have to get you to hospital and I can't do it if you don't stay awake. I'll help you on to your feet but I can't carry you. I know a quick way out of here where we're not likely to meet anyone. My car's outside. Just stay awake and shuffle as best you can. You can lean on me as much as you like.'

Clinging to Fitzgerald, Steve struggled with nausea. When the outside air hit him he retched on the drive, now beyond the capability of making even a feeble excuse or apology. Fitzgerald persuaded him towards his car, bundled him in and, wasting no time, drove carefully along the narrow drive which led to the main drive and thence to town. Steve slumped in the passenger seat, his senses swimming. He'd lost his vision again and only Fitzgerald's insistence on speaking kept him from sinking once more into unconsciousness. His face hurt. His stomach hurt and he wanted to be sick. He had to struggle to respond to his companion's relentless questions in a voice which had not yet become totally unmanageable.

'Who punched you?'

'Buddy - my good friend, Buddy.'

'I dunno. He tried to help me. He's always trying to help me.'

'Did he help you?'

'I dunno. Father O'Doyle helped me,' Steve added, struggling to sit up before slumping into a helpless bundle again. 'Was Father O'Doyle there?'

'He was flying high above me, waving his crucifix and telling me to kill, to kill, kill. . .'

His voice was fading but Fitzgerald gave him no respite.

'Tell me all about it, from the beginning. Keep talking. We'll soon be at the hospital and you'll feel better then. Keep talking.'

'Did you know Father O'Doyle could fly?'

'You were having an illusion.'

'It was covered in blood.'

'What was covered in blood?'

'The cloth, the pure lily-white cloth. I loved it when it was pure and had qu-qu... Wh's the word?'

'Quality?'

'Yep. That's it. It had quality and was pure and white and beautiful. But it's stained and ugly and has lost its qu...' 'Quality?'

'Yep. It's lost its quality. That's it. It had a big red splatter of blood right in the middle.'

'It was only a dream.'

Fitzgerald was frowning, casting anxious glances at his passenger.

'A pure white cloth with a red stain,' he mumbled. Again he looked at the huddled figure beside him. 'Steve,' he said. 'Don't fall asleep. Listen to me. I want to tell you something. Are you listening?'

'Yep.'

'You've heard of John Ruskin, the famous Victorian writer and art critic?'

'Nope.'

'It doesn't matter. He wrote famous books and painted pictures but one story about him is interesting. He once saw a beautiful white handkerchief with an ugly ink stain. Are you listening, Steve?'

'Yep.'

'Anyone else would have thrown it away as ruined and useless. Don't you agree?'

'Yep.'

'He didn't. Do you know what he did?'

'Nope.'

'He transformed it. Are you listening?'

'Nope.'

'I wish you would.'

'Yep.'

'Ruskin used the ink stain as the centre of a beautiful pattern radiating from the blob. He painted an intricate design, using the ink blob as the centre of radiation. What we would have considered spoiled goods he transformed to a beautiful item. Interesting, don't you think?'

There was no reply. Steve was showing every indication of throwing up.

'Hold on. We're here. I'll help you out of the car but for God's sake hold your drink till you are out.'

Fitzgerald switched off the ignition, pulled hard on the handbrake, jumped out of the car and rushed to haul Steve out before the inevitable happened. On the tarmac Steve spewed out what seemed to be left of his guts.

Leaving him leaning against the bonnet of the car, Fitzgerald ran for help. Half an hour later he looked at the pathetic figure lying on a trolley, diagnosed as unfit to return home and awaiting a porter for transportation to some medical treatment and merciful relief. On the face of it, his condition was pitiable but the doctor needed time and opportunity to make further tests. His eye would be stitched immediately but his deliverer would be better to leave his friend in the doctor's hands and return again in the morning.

Thoughtfully, Gerald Fitzgerald drove carefully back to Strathard Castle, his experience in the upper echelons of thinking about to be put to an unexpected test.

CHAPTER 21

The two women looked at each other. Theresa spoke first. 'I've been expecting a visit from you.'

'I need to talk,' said Jenny.

'Neil's in the south and won't be home until tomorrow. I felt it a good time to call and hope it isn't inconvenient for you.'

'There's never an inconvenient time as far as seeing you is concerned. You know that,' said Theresa, clearing a chair in her kitchen so that jenny could sit down.

She was making soup and continued chopping vegetables while they talked. Jenny sat, trying consciously to relax.

'When I learned that the Buddhists were going to be leaving, I immediately thought of what that would mean to you,' Theresa said, giving her friend a sidelong look.

Jenny's heart sank. Was she going to be made to put into words her secret fears? It was one thing to fear it might happen but desolation to have to admit it would.

'I'm not sure what you mean,' she prevaricated.

She knows, thought Jenny. Dear Theresa, with her psychic insight knows. In their long and close relationship Theresa's psychic powers had been a mixed blessing. When Theresa and her first husband, Guy, had owned Strathard Castle and run it as a hotel, Jenny had been their secretary and friend. Later, when she was married to Neil and Guy was dead, they had both lived in Edinburgh and enjoyed what had been forged over the years as a lasting friendship. Theirs had been a long relationship of strange convolutions but out of which had survived mutual trust and affection.

To Jenny, Theresa was the recipient of her fears and fortunes. She was her source of comfort and support, the one person with whom she enjoyed a full and free relationship. She shouldn't really be surprised to find that Theresa had been expecting her to call.

She braced herself to hear Theresa speak the words she'd dared not speak herself but now she would be forced to declare her worst suspicions.

Keeping her voice light she said, 'Naturally when the Buddhists leave they're going to leave an empty hole in the life of the castle. For a start, who will do our printing?'

She knew and Theresa knew that Jenny's need was not for printer replacements. It was greater than that.

'For a start, yes,' said Theresa continuing to chop, 'but it's only a start, isn't it?'

'I'm not sure what you mean,' Jenny said.

'You know exactly what I mean. I mean Todd! Todd is not just an admirer of the Buddhists, like the rest of us. He is one. Their philosophy suits him. He not only admires it. He lives it. He needs it. The next obvious and necessary step is for him to join the brotherhood and relinquish everything else.'

'Including me,' said Jenny.

'He wouldn't be relinquishing you, only the demands you make on him,' said Theresa, grinding peppercorns into the pot.

The trouble about living the way she did, thought Jenny, was that she was surrounded by sages whose wisdom she didn't always have an appetite for.

'You're right, Theresa. He has outstripped me.'

Theresa waited until she'd towelled her hands before joining Jenny at the table.

'Maybe if you had survived the experience of a concentration camp which maimed you for the ordinary way of life, you would more easily have shed your egocentricity as completely as Todd has.'

'I have to let him go.' There! She'd said it. She'd voiced her worst fears and made them part of her reality. 'Todd wouldn't admit it, probably doesn't realise it, but it is my possessiveness that is holding him back.'

'I think he does realise it,' said Theresa. 'He's just waiting until you're ready.'

'I'll never be ready.'

'Of course, you will. Coffee?'

Jenny nodded and Theresa rose to pour from the already brewing pot.

'Let's face it, Jenny. It's not like an ordinary affair you're having with Todd. As well as the fact that you're a married woman, Todd's hardly the typical other man. No matter how little his disfigurement affects your feelings for Todd... it cannot be ignored. It's time you loosened your grasp and decided what is best for you both.'

Jenny tried not to feel too disconsolate.

'As usual Theresa, you hold up the mirror to my soul and, as usual, I both love and hate you for it.'

'Come on now, Jenny. Look on the bright side. He's not going over Jordan. He will only be moving to the south of Scotland. You can write to each other, even visit and always support your work here.'

'It won't be the same.'

'Of course it won't,' said Theresa, placing two steaming mugs on the table before sitting. 'It will be different but that doesn't mean it will be worse.'

'I shall tell him very soon,' Jenny said, stirring sugar into her cup. 'The sooner I make it easier for him the better. "If it were done when 'tis done, then 'twere well, it were done quickly."'

Theresa roared with laughter.

'You're incorrigible, Jenny, but as long as you can keep pulling those ridiculous quotes of yours out of your memory bank, there's hope for you yet.'

Jenny wrinkled her nose.

'Is that supposed to reassure me? I fear I haven't travelled very far on my own spiritual path.'

'Don't underestimate yourself and don't lose heart. You know perfectly well you'll never leave it.'

'Just make a detour or two,' said Jenny with a wry smile.

'By the way,' said Theresa, as she returned the empty mugs to the sink, 'I was introduced to Moira today. That nice man with a big problem bought her lunch here.'

Jenny's interest quickened.

'And?'

'And she's beautiful but walking with a dagger up her sleeve. You'd better look out. She wanted to cross my hands with silver but I declined.'

'She's another of my worries but I'm leaving the ball in her court for the moment. Her time will come.'

'Perhaps sooner than you think,' remarked Theresa who had lifted Jenny's hand, turning it palm up.

About to withdraw it, Jenny changed her mind and left it there, watching as her friend studied its criss-cross lines and spaces. Theresa could read a palm as easily as a professional musician could read a musical score. She waited, already denying anything she was about to hear, assuming it entirely unfounded. There she was again! Assumptions! Why should I assume Theresa will be talking rubbish? Why not accept whatever she says till proved otherwise?

'More struggles, more victories, more defeats,' said Theresa, 'but you will survive them all.'

Strangely disappointed, Jenny felt her fingers being folded over her palm and returned her friend's cheery smile with a huffy glare. 'I do believe you have lost the power of prophecy,' she accused.

'It's working in this den of iniquity,' Theresa quipped. 'I'm much better with the crystal ball. Would you like to give it a go?'

"I'd have to be desperate for that,' said Jenny, rising to take her leave.

'You'll know what to do,' said Theresa, 'when the time comes.'

These words stayed with Jenny as she cycled home.

She made up her mind that she would visit Todd that night and give him her blessing. In spite of how she might have wanted her life to develop, there were powerful forces afoot taking the matter out of her hands. You will always know what to do when the time comes, Theresa had said.

That remains to be seen, she told herself.

She almost changed her mind when, after her solitary evening meal, she prepared to set out for the castle to visit Todd. She hadn't told him of her impending visit but so great was her resolve to do what had to be done and to do it quickly that she was not to be dissuaded by the storm that was fast gathering momentum. It would be impossible to cycle and Neil had the car. It would have to be Shank's pony.

She dressed in her heavy cloak with hood before setting out. It was hard going and by the time she reached the Stable Square she was never gladder to see the welcoming light from his living room. Thankfully, she inserted the key in the lock and entered, making her way straight to the living room where she'd seen him seated at his desk.

A sudden need to feel his closeness overpowered he and, throwing off her cloak, she fell into his arms. She felt. more than thought that this might be the last time she would ever be able to do this. Never again would she have the freedom to do as she was doing now.

'Come,' said Todd after he'd embraced her. 'Let me close the curtains then we will have some of the hard stuff. Sit by the fire and get yourself warm.'

He walked to the window and pulled the curtains. He poured whisky into two glasses, carried them to the fire, handing one to Jenny who was sitting on the fireside rug, hands outstretched to the flames. He sat on a chair behind her, one hand resting lightly on her head. When she raised her eyes to his, he smoothed her hair from her face and smiled.

'I think you know why I am here.'

'Do I?'

She tried another angle.

'How much do you know regarding what's about to happen?'

'I can tell you what is happening,' he answered.

She should have known he wouldn't choose to speculate on what might happen. He'd shed that anxiety a long time ago. Still keeping her tone light she responded.

'Tell me then what is happening right now.'

'Outside there is a storm. The wind is playing havoc with our trees. The rain is filling our water butts. Inside there is warmth and comfort and a lovely woman who is perturbed.'

'How do you know I'm perturbed?'

'How do I know the sun rises and sets every day?' he replied. 'What's wrong, Jenny? Is it Moira?'

'Partly.'

'If you are perturbed she is near devastated. Remember she doesn't have the advantage of your balanced thinking.'

'My thinking is certainly doing a precarious balancing act at the moment.'

'Do you want to tell me about it?' he asked.

'It is balancing the effects of my wanting you to stay here with me forever and bowing to your need to move on.'

She hadn't meant to say that but once she did she felt relief. She raised her eyes to his and what she saw there was a love that both shamed and humbled.

'Every moment is a balancing act,' he replied. 'At the moment, you are juggling with too many plates and you are afraid of breaking any of them.'

She sighed, comforted by his knowledge, not of the plates she was juggling but about her juggling necessities. He didn't probe. He never did. Looking at him now, holding his gaze in the knowledge that he would be looking at the good in her and not the doubts and fears, she had a lightning insight into the depth of their relationship. He had never failed to understand her and meet her needs. She had always been the one to light the match and feed the fire. He had never failed to warm himself in the flames but, to her sad recollection, he had not been the one to strike the match. With one arm round her shoulder he reached for her hand.

'Our love has no label, Jenny. It has no boundaries. It is a power house. I know that yours shall always generate the best in me but others need it too.'

She knew what he was saying. Boundless love had no need of physical limitation in order to manifest. His experience in the concentration camp had driven him to seek refuge in a Buddhist sitzen where he began his spiritual quest. Todd, her brave Sir Lancelot, who had fought his brother for her honour, her Lochinvar, who had captured her and carried her on his steed to her true and rightful marriage bed. Was he now her Sir Parsifal about to embark on the quest for his Holy Grail? As she turned and laid her head on his lap and felt his hand caressing her hair, knew that there was no standing still or turning back for either of them. What they shared would not cease to manifest but its manifestation would be on a higher level of awareness. They were blessed and as she raised her eyes and met his, each had the certainty they sought.

'Let's be practical,' she suggested.

'Good idea.'

'What shall I do when you leave?'

'I suggest you give Jock complete management of the farm and you train someone in my administrative work.' 'Where shall we find someone suitable?'

'I think we already have or, shall we say, he has found us.'

'Buddy?'

'I think he is waiting to be asked. Strathard has really gripped him by the throat.'

Now to the difficult question.

Bracing herself, she asked it. 'When will you be leaving, Todd?'

His answer was non-committal, but confirmed what still she wished could be denied. He was going and he was going soon.

It was Todd who had first stolen her heart when they were young. Todd who had gone off to war as a freedom fighter when still at school; Todd whom she had mourned when presumed dead. Todd who had returned to Strathard to find her after 30 years. Todd who had never failed her. His had been the inspiration behind the reason for doing what they were doing now. It was at Todd's instigation that the Buddhists had come. The musicians had been his friends. Together, Todd and she had offered inspired service to a just cause. Todd had become so much a part of her that she could not visualise functioning without him. Together they had set their feet on a spiritual path to which they were both dedicated. There was no one way to Nirvana but there came one way which opened its doors to Todd. Slowly, imperceptibly, his spiritual progress outstripped her own.

He had moved so far from material needs. He had long since schooled emotional turmoil. His love was pure, compassionate, caring, unsparing and she still wanted it all for herself. What did Todd want? He had already chosen.

They were alerted by a sound which was more a scream than a sough of wind. They listened and waited but apart from rattling windows and drumming rain, heard nothing. They decided it must have been a freak of the weather after all but the interruption reminded Jenny of other concerns.

'I must go home. Neil will be phoning soon.'

'I'll drive you.'

Jenny sighed.

'Sometimes I.'

Todd stopped her words by covering her lips with his.

'I want this to be our goodbye, Todd.'

She couldn't look at him. She felt his finger on her chin and slowly he raised her face till their eyes met.

'It's all right, Jenny. It's going to be all right. We'll meet in many ways. You'll find we'll never really be apart.'

She wished she had his certainty but all she was certain of now was that this moment was the real goodbye. They moved closer, embracing with that disciplined intensity which was so much a part of their relationship. While it avoided analysis on every passing impulse and restriction of their love, it reassured them of its undiminished strength.

'Come,' said Todd, releasing her gently. 'Let's get you home safely.'

They crossed the cobbled square to the garage. It was still raining but the storm's fury was spent. Todd switched on the light and they entered the garage.

'That's strange,' he said.

Jenny followed the direction of his curiosity and saw the blade of a Swiss knife embedded in a wooden beam.

'That noise we heard earlier,' said Jenny. 'I said it sounded like a scream but we decided it must have bees the wind.'

'Well, whoever the knife was intended for must have escaped,' said Todd. 'There's no sign of a body.'

'I don't like it, Todd.'

'Let's get you home before Neil calls. I'll have a look around outside when I return.'

With the wipers working hard and headlights showing a safe path ahead, Todd drove her to the manse.

Before she left the shelter of the car to make a rush to the manse Todd had one more thing to say.

'I shall write to you.'

'This time make sure you include your address.'

The rain washed the salt from the surging tears as she walked up the path to her front door.

CHAPTER 22

The phone was ringing when Jenny entered the manse. It was Neil. She let him do the talking while she struggled to regain her breath.

'It's been well worth the journey,' he said after initial greetings had been exchanged. 'I think I have some good pictures of the old Covenanters' tombstones.'

As he enthused about his visit she conjured a vision of him as some modern day Old Mortality crouched over the gravestones of the sixteenth-century Covenanters.

Grey recumbent tombs of the dead in desert places. Standing-stones on the vacant wine-red moors,

Hills of sheep, and the howes of the silent vanished races, And winds, austere and pure.

As she fitted Stevenson's words to her image the howling wind outside heightened her imagination.

They exchanged a few more words. He would be staying in Galloway for a day longer than planned since he was anxious to visit the church where Samuel Rutherford, a seventeenth-century Presbyterian and Covenant supporter had preached and from which he had been deposed for refusing to submit to a Bishop of England.

'Safe journey home,' were Jenny's final words before replacing the receiver on its cradle.

She sat on, letting her thoughts linger on her husband and his new literary career. It was quite a change from his years of fire and brimstone preaching to the 'sinners' of his parish. Now he was empathising with rebels of the past and finding a lasting glory in their illegal exploits, something at one time she would never have believed possible.

Jenny liked to think that she had played some considerable part in the transformation of her husband. When she might have abandoned their marriage vows some years ago, she had chosen to stick by him. Even the power of her love for Todd, alive after many years of believing him dead, had not swayed her from her responsibilities. It had taken a lot of heart searching, belief against all odds and a little scheming to bring about a solution.

At the time there had been no question as to where her duty lay and there had been absolute certainty as to where her heart lay. She had found a way where they could coexist and, so far, it had worked to everyone's advantage. She had worked on her duty to her marriage to transform it into love - not 'in love' but a love which would provide for an honourable settlement with her husband and, at the same time, had left her free to love Todd in the fullness of her heart. So far, there had been benefits all round. It had been so simple; a mere matter of mindset; a French form of mindset. She smiled. Both she and Neil had enjoyed the respectability and security of marriage. Todd and she had no need of legalities. Their mutual love was all-encompassing. She had been discreet and had taken no unnecessary risks.

She had been gratified to see Neil gradually relax from a self-imposed martyr of his faith to having a more compassionate interaction with his work and with his flock. He became less demanding as a minister and as a husband and had benefited considerably from the mix of other faiths now an integral part of the castle life.

She involved herself in every interest he demonstrated and it had been a happy day for her when he picked up his pen in pursuit of the tales of the Scottish Covenanters. It was to be expected that the religious zeal of the Covenanters held a special appeal for him. He was deeply stirred by stories of their courage and martyrdom. He wanted to remind his fellow Scots of how much of their religious freedom was due to them.

On Neil's desk was a book, now open at a page earmarking a passage of particular interest. Seeing it, she read again the account of Samuel Rutherford's book, Lex Rex, denouncing the case for absolute monarchy. It had been accepted in Cromwellian times but after the Restoration was ordered to be publicly burnt by the Public Hangman in Edinburgh and St Andrews with a fine of £10,000 levied on anyone who possessed it.

Jenny's smile widened. Changed days, she thought. How well she remembered the day her husband had burned a book she had been reading. It had been a book on astrology which had been anathema to his Christian principles. He had previously forbidden her to read on the subject and had been ruthless in his condemnation when she'd been discovered doing so. How bigoted had been Neil Fraser then. How intolerant of opposing beliefs.

Now, here he was, after years of her careful nurturing, denouncing the monarchists of the seventeenth-century for burning a book because they did not like what it said. Yes, thought Jenny, I'd like to think I've had something to do with that. Her telephone rang, interrupting her reverie.

'Jenny Fraser here. Tonight? Can't it wait till morning? I'll expect you both in ten minutes then.'

She replaced the receiver. What, she wondered, could Fitzgerald and Buddy Regan have to tell her that was so important it couldn't wait until morning? She automatically puffed the scatter cushions, poked the slumbering coals in the fire until the flames leapt, then, lifting the tongs from the companion set on the hearth, dulled their exuberance with a few well-placed larger lumps of coal from the brass scuttle. She was arranging a drinks tray on the side table when the doorbell rang.

Welcoming Fitzgerald and Buddy, she lead them to Neil's study which was the warmest room in the manse at that hour.

'Whisky?'

'I would welcome that,' said Fitzgerald but Buddy declined the offer.

'That should warm you,' she said, offering Gerry a glass. She indicated the fireside chairs and seated herself on a small sofa between them.

'My husband won't mind us using his study. He's in Galloway at the moment, researching Covenanters' gravestones. But I'm stalling, gentlemen,' she confessed. 'Should I be worried about what you are going to tell me?'

'It's bad news, yes - about Steve,' said Gerald. 'I've left him in hospital in a sorry state.'

Jenny waited, her mind riveted on the Swiss knife she'd seen embedded in the wooden beam inside the garage. 'How bad?' she managed.

'He was attacked and wounded.'

'Was it a knife wound?'

'No. It was a hefty upper thrust which knocked him out and bloodied his eye. He tells me his good friend did it.'

'I did it,' said Buddy.

'Why would you want to do that?'

'More a case of needing to do it, I'm afraid,' said Buddy. 'He was on the point of killing Miranda.'

Jenny's eyes rounded in dismay. Fitzgerald took up the tale.

'On returning to my room after dinner, I met Buddy dragging a hysterical Miranda to his room.'

Buddy interrupted him.

'I asked Fitzgerald to check on Steve, knowing I'd aimed to kill.'

'Fortunately, Buddy only wounded him,' said Fitzgerald, 'although that was bad enough. I found Steve on the floor with blood on his face. I could see his eye needed stitching and that he might be suffering from concussion. I thought the best thing to do was to take him straight to hospital.'

'And?' asked Jenny.

And,' said Fiitzgerald, 'his eye has been stitched and luckily there's no concussion. However, worse than that he was stoned rotten and having illusions.'

Fitzgerald told the others of Steve's vision of the winged priest and the even stranger account of the pure white cloth with the ugly stain.

Jenny listened, striving to hide her anxiety.

'Now, Father O'Doyle with angel wings I can understand,' she said when he'd finished. 'He's been keeping a saintly eye on Steve since we guessed his problem but we thought that Steve was doing exceptionally well. I wonder what the ugly stain on the white cloth was about.'

Fitzgerald kept his eyes on Jenny as he spoke.

'I'm a philosopher, not a psychiatrist but now and again the paths converge. I think that the white cloth was, to Steve, a symbol of purity. He spoke of quality so I imagine that the ugly stain was some kind of violation of this purity, some denigration of quality. He could have been devastated by a shock of some kind. Perhaps an idol was found to have clay feet or perhaps it was just the feeling of lost hope.'

Jenny's face drained of colour.

'Where's Miranda?' she asked.

'I've left Miranda with Father O'Doyle.' said Buddy. 'She is a confused and unhappy woman. She needs time and some of the saintliness of Father O'Doyle to begin sorting herself out.' He looked at Jenny whose eyes were reflecting the turbulence of her mind. 'She would like to see you as soon as possible. She has something to tell you.'

His manner was gentle and concerned.

Jenny held Buddy's gaze.

'I think I know what it is. She will tell me she is my sister, Moira.'

'You know?'

'I've known from the beginning. She is so like my mother even if her hair is bleached. Apart from that, my family in Canada guessed she'd come here after disappearing so I was expecting her.'

'I'm sorry to have. . .' began Buddy.

'No need,' said Jenny, interrupting. 'Steve told me you were both sworn to secrecy.'

'So Steve knows that you know.'

'But what has this got to do with Steve wanting to kill Miranda and you wanting to kill Steve?' asked Fitzgerald. Buddy was looking uncomfortable.

'I feel embarrassed to tell you this,' he said, forcing himself to look Jenny straight in the eye. Jenny steeled herself to listen. 'Steve had another illusion,' he began. 'He had convinced himself that he loved you.'

It was worse than she had feared.

Buddy continued.

'I tried to tell him his fixation on you was his need to fill a gap left by Susan, his wife. He denied this vehemently as he has denied and continues to deny his dependence on alcohol. He switched this dependence to you and so long as he felt convinced of his love and nursed a fierce desire to eventually declare it, he didn't need alcohol. You were his motivation for abstaining. You were his salvation and his inspiration was your example of quality living. Before he met you, besides being devastated by his broken marriage, he was questioning the worth of his writing. You inspired him and he convinced himself that you were both destined to come together. I don't think he ever considered the immoral implications. Desperate needs were taking desperate measures.'

'But why,' asked Fitzgerald, hoping to relieve Jenny of her obvious distress, 'did he attack Miranda?'

'Miranda had deceived him,' said Buddy. 'She had played a dirty trick on him which unhinged him. Remember he had a bottle of whisky inside him before he attacked her.'

'She had managed,' said Jenny in a voice both men barely recognised, 'to show him the ugly stain on the pure white cloth.'

She looked distraught.

'That,' said Buddy gently, 'is something she must tell you herself and that is another reason why she wants to see you as soon as possible.'

Jenny, now on her feet, looked from one man to the other.

'Yes,' she said with a sigh. 'Moira and I have a lot to say to each other. I shall meet her tomorrow but first I must speak to Steve. His need is the greater.'

'I despair,' said Buddy. 'I've bullied him, badgered him, cajoled and threatened him but it has made little difference. He can't just ease off. He is an addict and that hardly allows for even a smell of the stuff. He's lost his wife, his son, his friends, his career, and it can only get worse. I care like hell but I'm at a loss to know what to do next.'

'My grandfather used to tell my brother and me that God helps those who help themselves,' said Jenny who was again seated but still wrestling for calm.

'He has to come out of denial,' said Fitzgerald, 'before anything can be done.'

'And how do we get him to do that?' asked the now morose Buddy.

'I have an idea,' said Fitzgerald, 'but I need time to consider it. Leave it with me. We will see how he is in the morning and take it from there.'

'I know exactly how he will be in the morning,' said Buddy. 'I've seen it all before. He will be miserable, repentant but not have a clue as to why he is repentant. He never remembers his behaviour when completely intoxicated. When under the influence he enters another world and when he leaves it, the door closes behind him. He has no memory. All he is left with are the consequences and a sadly-diminishing lifespan.'

'I will accompany you to hospital,' offered Gerry, addressing Jenny.

'I shall want time alone with him.'

'Of course.'

She rose to signify that the meeting was now at an end. The two men took a sombre leave-taking and Jenny returned to her husband's study. She had two important phone calls to make. One to Todd and one to Father O'Doyle.

CHAPTER 23

Gerald Fitzgerald was a careful driver. Jenny looked at his hands on the wheel as he steered the car round a precarious bend on the road. Safe hands, she mused. They could almost be a musician's hands with their long-tapered fingers and perfectly manicured nails. Then again, they were the clean, sensitive and unblemished hands of the surgeon. She thought of one of Father O'Doyle's lectures she had attended when he'd talked about hands reflecting their owners. People, he had said, could lend a hand, be a poor hand, come cap in hand, rule with a heavy hand or come across as high-handed. One thing for sure, thought Jenny, Gerry Fitzgerald, apart from lending a hand, was none of the others. His were the hands of friendship. As his hand moved from wheel to gear lever, she moved her gaze to his finely-chiselled profile.

'You will be leaving us soon,' she said.

He flashed her a smile before returning his grey-speckled eyes to the road.

'Another week.'

'You will be missed. Your lectures are popular.'

'After another year with varsity students I'll have a fresh supply of different ways of viewing life for the entertainment of your visitors.'

'It's more than entertainment,' said Jenny. 'You remind us of the importance of looking at life. So many people never give a thought to the meaning of life. They think that whatever happens that's life. Que sera sera.'

Gerry smiled.

'I think it was Socrates who said that the unconsidered life is not worth living.'

Jenny turned her attention to life on the other side of the windscreen. Winter was drawing close. The trees, encouraged by a fractious wind, were liberally shedding leaves. Clouds bunched together diminishing the warmth of the sun who was already distancing himself from their line of latitude. The stark hills frowned down upon the agitated waters of rivers and lochs.

'I am reassured when our itinerant lecturers keep coming back,' she commented. 'Sometimes my perspective gets clouded, like the sky is now, and my aims for Strathard community are dimmed. That's when the icy blasts of doubts rush in.'

Fitzgerald laughed.

'Don't be hard on yourself, Jenny. Your aims are right on focus.'

'Your lens is clearer than mine. Just how can I be sure that what goes on here is for the good of humanity, which was what my inheritance was purported to achieve?'

'You offer choice. You offer a liberal education in thinking which leads to freedom and that must be good for humanity?'

'Your lectures probably do more."

'My lectures are for the hunger of the mind. I have a cousin who is a chef and owns a famous restaurant. His carefully considered menu is planned for the hunger and nutrition of the body. Strathard Castle is planned for the hunger and nurture of the spirit. So many people today are hungry for spirituality. With your ecumenical gatherings of earnest Jews, Christians and Buddhists widening blinkered visions, you offer something unique in liberal education.'

'The Buddhists are leaving us too.'

Gerry, who had driven into a passing place on the narrow road, acknowledged the salute from the other car and waited until he was on the road again before replying.

'I'm sorry to hear that.'

'They are joining a larger settlement further South where a temple is already under construction and a spiritual retreat is being developed.'

They were nearing the county hospital. No more was said until Gerry drew to a halt on the hospital parking lot.

'Take as long as you need,' he said once he'd directed her to the ward where he'd left Steve on the previous evening. 'I'm expecting Buddy to come but I'll hold him till you return - and Jenny.'

'Yes?'

'Steve needs all the help we can give.'

Jenny nodded and, agreeing on an approximate time for meeting again, they parted company.

Turning from him Jenny looked for a nurse who could take her to Steve, steeling herself to face this man who supposedly had deluded himself into imagining a love they might share but who, in reality, knew her precious secret. She had yet to face the full significance of this. She felt this was an unexpected cause that would have a considerable effect on her life but, not for a moment, did she consider being other than helpful to this man with whom she was about to be face to face. His presence in Strathard had imposed on her a new vulnerability with which she would have to deal but, for the moment, she was compassionately aware of his greater need.

She was hardly prepared for what she found when the nurse led her into a small anteroom. The last time she had seen Stevenson Bruce he had been laughingly enthusiastic about his farm work. He had sent out signals of having the ability to cope with his vicissitudes. In reality he had been deceiving himself and others. He had been living in a fool's paradise and now he was paying for it and, if everything that had been said about him were true, would continue to pay for it.

He was dressed and sitting on a chair by his bed. One eye was masked, giving a threatening belligerence to the other. This wasn't helped by severe swelling and psychedelic bruising. Although his facial expressions were restricted, his body language exposed his resentment at her unannounced entrance. His hands, gripping the wooden arms of his chair, tightened until the knuckles were white. His knees were drawn up to a sharp right angle with his upright body. His voice, when he spoke, was heavy with sarcasm, a protection, Jenny guessed, against his painful embarrassment. She felt that cheerfulness wouldn't be welcome or appropriate. She had trained herself to be sparing in pity and it was too soon for sympathy.

'Come to gloat?'

Taking no offence, she ignored the remark.

'I'm here to see how I can help.'

'I'm surprised you want to.'

Jenny could see how his remarks were clichéd argumentative attack in a vain attempt at self-defence. If she were to tackle the real conflict between them she had to steer them quickly over these puerile preliminaries. The bull had better be grasped by the horn.

'I believe your injuries have something to do with me.' 'Believe what you like. I'm not up to an inquisition.' She saw his pain but persisted. There was much at stake.

'Moira's part in this doesn't need explaining, at least not by you, so we need not talk about her now.'

'She tricked me.'

'She wanted to hurt you - and me.'

'You can say that again.'

'There is no need. What you and I have to do is talk about ourselves. Through fair means or foul you are now privy to personal information of mine which could be open to question.'

'It's your problem.'

'And yours, because however you construe this, it will affect your judgement, not least on yourself. I understand you have been harbouring certain feelings for me.'

Having been deliberate with her choice of words, she was prepared for his reaction. His hands relinquished their vicelike grip on the chair. He jerked to his feet and towered above her.

'I'd rather you left.'

'Not yet.'

'I've nothing to say to you.'

'I have a good deal to say to you and I'm not leaving till I've said it.'

'Bloody Buddy. Bloody, bloody Buddy the Buddhist!' he sneered and the spectacle of the bruised and contorted face touched Jenny in the raw.

'I'll sack him - after I punch him. Why can't he keep his trap shut? I thought he was practising to do just that. You know, sitting like a dummy and emptying his already empty mind and above all, keeping his trap shut. What did he think gave him the right to repeat what was told him in confidence?'

'Especially when it was all an unfortunate self-illusion, pie-in-the-sky idea anyway,' agreed Jenny with a smile meant to disarm him.

Anger suspended, he peered at her from his seeing eye, suspicious of ridicule.

'Events have proved it,' she said, sitting herself on the edge of the bed and forcing him to return to his chair. She wanted this preliminary fencing to be over so that the conversation could begin hitting the right target.

'It's my guess that those feelings you had for me and which you confided to Buddy, have changed. They are different now and you are already wondering how they could ever have been there in the first place. Am I right?'

He didn't reply.

'You don't have to answer that,' she said, 'but I'll take it as agreed anyway. There's nothing earth-shattering in that. The essence of all our feelings is their impermanence. We are driven by our desires but the trouble is they keep changing. You thought you wanted me. You thought I might be the answer to all your problems. In your own need you endowed me with special attributes and when you realised they were not as they seemed they became worthless to you and your feelings changed. You felt as if you'd lost a lifeline. The crux of the matter wasn't me, it was your need of me or what you thought I stood for. You thought I could make you happy, that I could solve all your problems, give you back what you felt you'd lost or probably never had. You built me up in your mind as a paragon of the good and the godly. When you discovered my feet of clay your feelings changed because I could no longer give you what you craved. It happens all the time. We are ruled by our desires and our desires are insatiable and forever on the move. You went into shock when you felt robbed of what you wanted. You did not like the messages you were receiving so you vandalised your reason. You drank yourself insensible and relinquished all sense of responsibility. This vandalising brought you to the brink of murder. You were saved by your friend Buddy, bloody Buddhist Buddy who was supposed to be learning how to sit still and keep his trap shut.'

Jenny stopped. Was she hitting too hard? Having trained herself in the constant awareness of her own feelings she recognised a small burning spot in the depth of her with a compulsion to expand and explode. This man and what he was doing to himself and those around him was managing somehow to revitalise one of her wild horses, called Temper, which she thought she had tamed many years ago.

Elbows on knees, Steve dropped his head to his hands and wept. If she allowed her sudden up-rush of compassion to get out of hand she'd find herself embracing this wretched man and that would solve nothing for either of them. Right now he didn't need to see himself as worthy of pity. He didn't need to look at her or anyone else for understanding. Not now, not yet. What he needed, above all, was to look at himself face to face, to strip himself of all his illusions and habitual excuses and begin to accept his realities. But she doubted his ability to do so. There was something heart-breakingly innocent about Stevenson Bruce which belied his unseemly reputation.

She douched her temper and decided to change tack. He was speaking and she strained to catch his words.

'I can't hear what you're saying. Look at me, Steve. Remember yours is not the only bruised and battered face I have to look at. It does not embarrass me. It needn't embarrass you.'

Steve raised his head and looked at her.

'I've tried it, you know.'

'Tried what?' she asked gently.

'To do what Buddy does - sit still and look at my thoughts. I've tried to put labels on them and let them go but they wouldn't go. They'll never go. I'd had enough after ten minutes. It's a crazy idea. I've got myself into one hell of a mess which I can't seem to get out of. Each time this happens it gets worse.'

'You have a problem. I have a problem. Moira has a problem. Buddy has a problem and Todd has had a problem for most of his life.'

Steve had succeeded in eyeing her squarely.

'You're right about one thing. I do feel differently about you and that bothers me. How is it that one day I am totally convinced that I love you? I even plan to buy your Broom Cottage and settle there for the rest of my life so that I can just breathe the same air as you and see your smile and yet today I am certain that I don't love you. Seeing you with, with...'

'Say it, Steve.'

'With . . .'I'm sorry.'

'Shall I say it for you? Seeing me kissing a man with half a face.'

'No,' he pleaded.

'That's how you see him and it offends your sensibilities. I don't see him like that because I love him.'

'How can you...'

'How can I love him when I'm married to a good-looking man like my husband? I shall tell you why and I think you should listen.'

He made to rise in an instinctive desire to escape hearing what she was going to tell him but Jenny insisted he stay where he was.

'He wasn't always like he is now,' she began. 'He was the handsomest son of the valley at one time. He could climb hills like a deer, row across the loch with the strength of ten galley slaves. He could shoot a covey of grouse with the best of the guns and dance the Highland Fling till the cows come home. He wore the kilt like a prince and could fix anything that was broken. Then he watched his twin brother drop dead at his feet, shot in the chest by a drunken good-for-nothing, a man who sold his soul for the bottle.'

Ignoring Steve's distress, she pressed on.

'His brother's murder changed his thinking. He wanted two things more than anything else - to fly an aeroplane and to go to Spain to fight the fascists. He ran away from home and was smuggled into Spain. He was a freedom fighter.'

She willed him to look at her.

'He was only a lad but old enough to value freedom. How many can you say that for nowadays?' She looked away for a moment before continuing. 'Before he went, he came to see me to say goodbye. I didn't want him to go because to me he was special and I knew that I was special to him. We were young but I adored him and I've adored him ever since.'

She turned to him and this time neither looked away. 'I never saw him again for thirty years. I'd been told he was dead. I thought his plane had been shot down or that he'd been bombed or bayoneted. He'd been helping Jews escape the Nazis in Germany and was betrayed and taken to a concentration camp to be tortured.'

She rose to her feet, relinquishing none of her intensity which underlined every word she continued to utter.

'Now shall I tell you about the face which embarrasses you?' Without waiting for a response, she continued. 'After they'd whipped his back and buttocks and left them like a ploughed field they started on his face. No, hear me out.' She hadn't finished yet. 'They beat him with a manganello. Have you heard of a manganello? It is an instrument made for torture, possibly by the fascists and "borrowed" by the Nazis. It is a kind of blackjack, a flexible, lead-filled truncheon. You can imagine the fun that provided. They did not crack the skull. That would have been letting the prisoner off lightly. Better to break the nose and jaw and the cheek bones until they were beyond repair but, as Father O'Doyle might say, thanks be to God and the Holy Angels, they left him his eyes -. all the better to see himself with, I suppose.'

Wearily she sat down, stretching out to take his hand.

'When Todd left that hell hole he wasn't Todd McGreegor, the handsomest son of the valley any more. You see, Steve, he had a problem. He had to give up or survive.

He spared his family and friends the horror of his fate but it wasn't in his nature to give up. He chose to survive with the help of the bloody Buddhists, and learning to sit still, shut his trap and stick labels on his thoughts - tagging his anger, his hatred, bitterness, and his despair till he could eventually let them go.'

Steve's chin was by now on his chest but he didn't withdraw his hand. 'It took him thirty years before he could do that, thirty years to learn that if you refused those negative thoughts hospitality they eventually did go. Then, after they'd gone he had to learn that there was more than enough room to spare for the invited thoughts of patience, forgiveness, compassion and love. Those "bloody Buddhists" taught him to differentiate between the perishable and imperishable, the things that come and go trailing sorrow, unfulfilled desire and pain in their wake and the things that never die but bring joy, the basic right of every soul born to this world.'

Steve raised his head in time to see the gentle smile playing on her features. 'So after thirty years when Todd had refurbished his mind, Father O'Doyle's saints flew into action. They brought him back home to find, in Todd's words, "the girl who gave me the gumption to survive" and, in my words, the woman who had grieved for him and married another man, not for love, sometimes not even liking, but for the questionable staying power of security.'

Jenny was taken aback by her passion which had been enflamed by the sudden threat to her cherished privacy. Nor was she at ease with the attitudes of this man she hoped to help. She realised, however, that she was in as much need of his help. Her relationship with Todd must be protected. Although Todd's departure meant there was no longer the need to protect the privacy of her ménage a trois, what needed to be protected, at all costs, was Neil's happiness. That's what she was fighting for now.

They were interrupted by the nurse bearing a tray of tea and biscuits. Jenny was thankful, needing a few moments to centre herself. As she sipped the welcome brew, she covertly watched her companion. She noticed the slight tremble in his hand as he accepted his cup of tea from the nurse. She watched him carefully place it on top of the bedside locker and made a point of searching for her handkerchief when the tea over-spilled on to the saucer. He never touched the cup and saucer again. He sat in brooding silence then, just when she was on the point of losing hope, he looked up and spoke.

'I'm glad I do not have to compete with Todd. I'm glad I no longer feel that I love you. After what you've told me I'm not even sure if I know what love is.'

'Real love,' said Jenny, 'is accepting the reality of how things are. Love is freedom from illusion. Love is - but I am sure that in your heart, Steve, you are well aware of what love is. You have a son.'

'Whom I dearly love.'

'Your son is your reality. For thirty years Todd learned to face his reality - his disfigured face and lost hope of ever having an "ordinary" life again. He could no longer afford the false comfort of life's illusions. He had to look at things as they were and learn to accept them and although he didn't know it at the time, he had also to learn to transform them. When he came back into my life I decided that I too, would have to face my reality. My reality was that I had to do my duty by my husband and find a way to express my unbridled love for Todd. I decided that if I went more than the mile with my husband and give him everything he need, I would make him happy and he had to be happy to leave me free to love Todd. After all the years lost, I could not give up Todd. After a serious commitment, I could not give up my husband. So I decided to create a Utopia for us all, a very satisfactory ménage a trois - except for one thing.

Unlike the French arrangement, the husband, in this case, knew nothing about this convenient arrangement. You see, I had never really faced my reality. I was living under the greatest illusion of all. I thought I could control my life and as I grew more self-centred in my needs for physical and emotional satisfaction, Todd's spirituality strengthened in leaps and bounds. He was a true pilgrim, set on a journey from which no one, especially me, could hold him back. He will be leaving soon with the

Buddhists to live their life and seek their Nirvana. I will be left with my husband whose happiness I now value above all else and whose good name must, at all costs, be protected. Do you understand?'

Steve nodded.

'You have nothing to fear from me. I'm beginning to think how lucky I am,' said Steve. 'My reality is nothing compared with Todd's. For him, as you said, it was a case of giving in or surviving. Mine is a choice of giving in or giving up. It's more backbone than Buddhism I need.'

Jenny looked at him, remembering Buddy's concern for his friend. Would Steve ever face his reality? she wondered. He will need more than backbone if he ever does. He will need some honest soul searching and, at the moment, he hasn't even begun.

'How soon before you can be discharged?' she asked.

'Today.'

'That's wonderful. Will you come back with me?'

'I'm not going back to the castle. I intend booking a room in the local hotel.'

'That's silly.'

'No. No, it isn't. I wouldn't feel at all comfortable in the castle.'

'Are you likely to feel more comfortable in Strathard Arms? And anyway, I should think...'

'That it would be too much of a temptation to live in the local pub?' Steve interrupted. 'My mind is made up. It will be difficult enough for you without my unsightly presence.'

'I have a better idea,' said Jenny. 'Spend some time in Broom Cottage. I'm not asking you to buy it. I can withdraw it from the market. I can so easily arrange for a bed to be made up, fires lit and for your larder to be stocked. You can do exactly as you wish there - hold court, go into retreat, read, write. That way you will have a chance for a quick recovery and you can take it from there. I can arrange for someone to work for you and cook, if that's what you'd like. What do you say?'

While Steve hesitated there was a peremptory knock on the door which opened and Father O'Doyle sailed in. On seeing Steve he immediately burst into song.

"Two lovely black eyes, oh-oh-oh, what a surprise." In the name of the good Saint Jude of desperate cases,' he said, 'it must have been some irresistible object you bumped into, my son.' Not waiting for an answer, he turned to Jenny. 'Jenny, my lass, the sight of you cheers an old fool.'

'Good morning, Father. You are just the man I need.'

'Ah, thanks be to Mary. What can I do for you, my dear?'

'You can persuade this man to move into Broom Cottage for a spell and, more than that, you might consider going with him.'

'Well now, that is quite an undertaking and needs much consideration.' He approached the silent Steve in mock seriousness. 'Do you play chess? You do. Good. Now then, do you snore? You don't think so. I could take a chance on that. Will my saints be welcome? Ah, I see that could be a problem.'

At this ridiculous questioning Steve had maintained an amused silence. He had made no instinctive objection and the priest's presence was already working its spell on him.

Jenny waited, knowing the outcome. When agreement was reached, she smiled with evident relief.

'Just give me time to get back and have a word with Flora. She'll soon have Broom Cottage ready for you both.'

She left the two men together and went to look for Gerry. She found him with a rather sombre Buddy, drinking coffee in the hospital refreshment room. They rose in greeting and while Gerry went to fetch another coffee, Buddy told her everything had gone to plan. Father O'Doyle had taken Moira - his so-called parcel of tricks - to Todd, as she had requested by telephone the previous evening.

'She can be in no better hands at the moment,' said Jenny.

Todd will know exactly what to do and say which, she was sure, would make their meeting easier.

'I sure hope so,' said the Canadian. 'The episode has almost unhinged her. She's only just beginning to realise the state she's got herself into. She desperately needs sorting out.'

Gerry rejoined them and the conversation turned to Steve.

'We've been having a powwow with Father O'Doyle,' said Buddy. 'Gerry here had a proposition to put to us about Steve but we need your approval.'

'If it's anything that you think will help him face up to things, approval granted,' she said.

'Our feelings exactly. Here's what we thought.'

CHAPTER 24

Jenny was now on her way to the Castle Square to meet Moira. As she cycled along the shore road she wondered what to expect. The dice were loaded against a harmonious reunion. There had been a long neglect on her part and a deep resentment on Moira's. She could only hope that time already spent with Father O'Doyle and the present company of Todd had prepared Moira for some effort of reconciliation.

She turned into the entrance to the castle, passed the lodge where Flora and Jock now lived. Both would be busy with their respective duties, Jock mucking the byre and Flora carrying the coals.

On reaching Stable Square she propped her bicycle against the wall of the house where both she and Moira had been born and where Todd now lived. The door opened and Todd appeared.

'I saw you coming,' he said, standing aside to let her enter.

Her love for Todd, lived under a veil of enchantment, had always been blind to his disfigurement. She had never considered him other than her valiant knight, her soulmate. He was to her, above and beyond all criticism. Now, looking at him in the wake of her meeting with Steve, she saw him as he had seen him - an object of distaste. She saw him as her husband saw him an object of pity. Now, robbed of her protective veil of enchantment, and meeting, face to face, the starkness of his injuries, thoughts of his incarceration and the cruelty he had been forced to endure, were taking on a new significance. He was different and with each day that passed the difference was growing.

Todd led her from the hall to his living room-cum-dining room-cum-office and library.

'Where's Moira?' she asked.

'Upstairs.'

'How is she?'

'Confused. Angry. Feeling guilty and it's hurting.'

'How am I going to help her, Todd, when I too feel guilty and afraid?'

'That's all being taken care of. You have been helping her all morning. For the last two hours she has been upstairs reading your letters to me.'

'Shall I go to her?' asked jenny.

'Leave her. She'll come down when she's ready,' said Todd. 'Your letters to me will paint a vivid background of Strathard and its people. She will feel part of it. Remember,' taking her hand in both of his, 'I speak from experience. They were food and water to my hungry soul when I came back here. They filled haunting gaps. They will be the same for Moira.'

'I didn't realise how absolutely awful I would feel about this. I'm guilt-ridden and, worse, I feel threatened. Our secret is no longer a secret. My hallowed ground has been defamed. I am a wretched...'

'Sh! Let go these thoughts and tell me how you found Steve.'

It was a welcome, if temporary, relief to talk of her visit to the hospital but when sounds of movement from above were heard, she stopped mid-sentence.

'I'll hear the rest later,' said Todd, seeing her distraction. 'You're not going, surely?'

'It's best that way. Right now it's between you and Moira. I've tried to prepare the ground.'

'Don't go, Todd. Please don't go.'

'It's better that I do.'

He left her standing in the middle of the room, waiting and feeling unprepared. She realised that her fists were clenched. The sounds from above stopped. She uncurled her fingers and let her arms go limp by her sides. She breathed slowly and deeply, feeling her body expand with each inhaled breath and visualising her fears being borne away on each expulsion. She loosened her jaw, letting it slightly drop and relaxed all her facial muscles. By the time she heard footsteps on the stairs she was in control. When Moira entered the room and they stood face to face, she was the picture of serenity, a serenity that cracked when she looked at Moira then splintered to smithereens at her opening remark.

'Where's lover boy?'

'Todd's gone back to work,' she managed to reply calmly. 'Not exactly the glamorous type. Eh?'

Jenny did not respond. She was wrestling with an image of her Aunt. There, before her, was the scowl, the sneer, the cruel derision. She saw her mother's brown eyes but this was no mother's daughter. The imprint of Aunt Sheena was unmistakable.

'I wouldn't have thought he was your type,' sneered Moira.

'And what do you think is my type, Moira?' asked jenny as she studied her sister closely.

With a typical Aunt Sheena smirk, Moira said, 'Oh, someone more like Steve Bruce. Eh? You're sure his type but I expect you know that already. He drools when you're around. He's crazy about you, the fool that he is. No wonder he was cut up when he saw you throw yourself at that freak. Boy, that sure was something.'

Refusing the bait, Jenny tried, but miserably failed, to summon a smile.

'Would you like a cup of tea?' she asked.

'And a cosy sisterly chat?' said Moira. 'No thanks.' 'Won't you at least sit down so that we can talk?'

Moira made an exaggerated curtsey, saying 'Yes ma'am,'

before sitting.

'Would it help if I apologised for my lack of communication?' said Jenny.

'Not much. It's a bit late for that, don't you think?'

'It is never too late to put the records straight and I'd like us to try,' persisted Jenny. 'There was never any love lost between Aunt Sheena and me. She was maybe my mother's sister but she was no more like her...'

'Than I am like you,' interrupted Moira. 'At least she didn't cheat on her husband. She was always morally correct, was Aunt Sheena. She had no time for sinners. A great churchwoman, she was.'

'We're talking as if she's dead,' said Jenny.

'Would be no bad thing,' said Moira.

Jenny sighed. How could she even begin to explain to this woman that her relationship with Todd was something divorced from religious piety.

'Why did you try to disguise yourself, Moira?' was all she could think of saying.

'Not very successfully, it would seem,' said Moira.

'I recognised you immediately. You have my mother's eyes.'

'You mean our mother's eyes, do you not?'

'Of course,' hastened Jenny.

'You seem to have a habit of forgetting that she's my mother too,' Moira accused. 'I noticed I'm not mentioned on her gravestone.'

Jenny's heart sank. This was an omission of which she had long been aware. For years she had intended to do something about it. How could it ever have been forgotten in the first place? At the time she had been the one responsible for the inscription. She liked to think that the family grief had been responsible for the amnesia. She liked to think it had been a Freudian forgetfulness and not a deliberate act of omission on her part. Now, face to face with her sister, she recognised there was no justification for the lack of recognition by any of her family. Her sister had every reason to feel aggrieved.

'Now that you are here I hope you will stay and really get to know Strathard and its people and, dare I say it, get to know me in a more favourable light.' She summoned a smile and hoped it didn't look as crooked as it felt. 'This could be a place of opportunity for you. People of exceptional talent and experience come here. Already you are benefiting from the advice of a one-time famous Italian musician and teacher. He could help you become an opera star, if that's what you would like.'

'What I'd like is to get away from here as soon as possible. I've seen all I want to see and you're welcome to it.'

'Don't be hasty, Moira. We both know Aunt Sheena is no Solomon of wisdom. She excels in mind poisoning and it would seem she's done a very good job on you.' No! No! No! screamed her thoughts as soon as the words left her lips. What had she said? She tried to retract immediately. 'Don't let's quarrel. We've all made our mistakes.'

'You speak for yourself. I'm getting out of here. How you have the nerve to flaunt as Mother Superior when you cheat your husband and sup with the devil, I don't know.'

For the second time that day Jenny's sleeping tiger snarled. It took only one more jibe from Moira before it roared.

'You're right. You don't know. There's a lot you don't know. Why are you so intent on being a troublemaker?'

'I'm not the one cheating on my husband or pretending to be whiter than white.'

'I was prepared to welcome you among us and hope that somehow, between us, we could put things right.'

'Big of you.'

'Don't be ungrateful.'

'Ungrateful for what? There is only one person I'm grateful to and sadly, he's not with me any more. Uncle Peter was the only person who ever really cared for me and I'm mighty grateful that he left me enough money to be quit of the rest of you.'

Already Jenny was feeling scorched by her own fire but the worst was yet to come.

'You know what, sister, I think no one will be happier than you to see the last of me because, right now, you're sitting on a time bomb. Aunt Sheena has done a thorough job with the poisoning of my mind, as you put it. I have already written to your husband - in appropriate funereal stationery found in your quaint little village store - putting him in the picture, telling him what has been going on between Mr Buddha man and yourself while he was away. Aunt Sheena would agree that it was my Christian duty to do so.'

Jenny couldn't hide her dismay. Stunned by Moira's confession she struggled to keep control of her anger. She didn't know which was worse - the horror of what the revelation might do to Neil or the horror of what her anger might do to herself. Already she felt the urge to strike her sister. She was feeling vixen to her threatened cubs who were Neil, Strathard and her own reputation, but especially Neil. She remembered Neil of old and his rigid adherence to principles. She had no reason to believe that he had changed. He would not suffer their abuse kindly.

It seemed that all that was left between her sister and her now was abuse. She was glad when Moira left suddenly.

Alone, she paced the room, one half of her longing for Todd, the other half glad he hadn't witnessed the consequences of her meeting with Moira. He had been so optimistic about the outcome. Had she mishandled it? Had her letters to Todd had an undesirable effect on Moira and instead of giving her the identity she craved, had added fuel to the fire of her hatred?

One thing was certain. She must go home immediately and intercept that letter. With luck she'd get there before Neil's return. If he had to know about Todd and herself it mustn't be this way.

She kept a tight grip on her rising panic as she collected her bicycle and began her journey back to the manse. On her way she saw Buddy and Moira and was thankful they didn't look her way.

Neil was not home. There was no car in the drive. Thankful, she left her bicycle against the wall, unlocked the front door and entered the manse. She went straight to his study where she had left his accumulating mail, which she had bundled together with an elastic band. Slipping this off, she turned over each envelope until she saw it - a small black edged envelope, no doubt containing a black edged sheet of paper - funereal stationery, as Moira had called it. She took it to the sofa, sat down and looked at it.

She decided she would not read it. She would burn it when she lit the fire. Meantime she would put it somewhere safe. Neil must not see it. She studied the writing which was almost calligraphic in its beautiful regularity. She thought of Moira and was unable to stem her rush of bad feeling. Because of Moira she was being forced to steal something of Neil's and burn it. A long time ago, she remembered, Neil had stolen her letters from Theresa and burned them without her knowledge. It was a long time later before his treachery was revealed. Should that be a warning to her. Might it not be better to let her treachery be revealed to him now. No, she couldn't take that risk. She had condemned his action then. She condemned her own now. How had this come to pass? For years she had been disciplining herself in a spiritual path of her own choosing. This was a path which demanded constant self-vigilance in discrimination, desirelessness, good conduct and love, according to the teachings of Krishnamurti and to which she had so enthusiastically aspired. One meeting with Moira had exposed how little she had progressed in her aspirations. She had tried so hard, always keeping herself aware of her acts and their consequences.

She had convinced herself that it would be best for Todd, best for Neil and, of course, best for herself to do what she had done. Hadn't it been? Todd had found a purpose in life by building a community which offered values he had learned the hard way. Neil had been freed from his bigotry and had found fulfilment in writing his books. She had found her joy. The three of them had thrived together.

She had designed their life together like some ancient Arab weaving his genuine Persian carpet with its obligatory flaw. Her design flaw had been cheating on her husband. Imagining that her conscience could be cleared because she had also made him happy, was the greatest illusion of all.

She wondered if she should light the fire now and do the deed quickly. As she hovered uncertainly around the fireplace she looked at Neil's photograph on the mantelpiece. It had been taken recently. He was acquiring a look of distinction. She was surprised at the fondness inherent in that thought. He had changed. She had changed. Their entire relationship had changed. They no longer indulged their differences in games of tug of war.

On the other side of the mantelpiece was a picture of herself, dressed in dungarees and laughingly clutching a protesting chicken. Her father's image was displayed on the wall. Beside him Callum was framed, handsome in his airforce uniform. Her grandfather, sitting on an upturned bucket, pipe in hand, brought a flood of fond memories. What would he think of her situation now? There were formal pictures of Neil's parents and a special framed and mounted one of her brother, Graham. They were all there - except Moira. A number of pictures of Moira had been sent from Canada over the years. They were probably somewhere in the attic. My God! What had she done to her? How great was her sin and how justified was her sister's resentment? If I ever need enlightenment, thought Jenny, I need it now.

She jumped when the telephone rang. It was Neil to say he was extending his visit one more day. Breathing a sigh of relief she laid the letter on his desk.

CHAPTER 25

She was thankful for the reprieve. As she replaced the receiver she saw Neil's manuscript on his desk. Since he'd begun his writing career she had been his typist. She pulled the typewriter towards her now and prepared to work on the loose leafed sheets of manuscript.

Ironically, it was the passage about Lex Rex. She had hoped the mechanical occupation of typing might stem her thoughts of Moira's letter but here she was typing the facts about the burning of a book which told the truth and how those who didn't like the truth it told were hell bent on destroying the evidence. That had been 1644. This was 1967 and nothing had changed.

'You will always know what to do when the time comes,' Theresa had said. Should she leave the letter for Neil to read when she had the opportunity to get rid of it now? To burn or not to burn? Why such a difficult decision? What was more important? Saving her secret and her marriage or her honour?

The doorbell rang and she returned the letter to the desk. It was Buddy, apologising for the intrusion but hoping they could talk.

'I won't beat about the bush, Jenny,' said Buddy as he sat down. 'I've just come from a long session with Moira and I think there's something you should know.'

There's a great deal I'd like to know, thought Jenny but to Buddy she replied, 'I think Moira made herself quite clear.'

'That's just it. She didn't. From what I can gather from her account of meeting you she was confused.'

'She seemed sure minded enough to me.'

'She is distraught,' reminded Buddy, 'and letting her read your letters to Todd was the best thing you could have done for her.'

'That was Todd's idea.'

'She hasn't stopped talking about them,' said Buddy. 'She never mentioned them to me.'

'That proves my point. She is confused. Here are we, two fair-minded people, receiving entirely different messages. Doesn't that spell confusion to you?'

'It spells disaster.'

Jenny persuaded Buddy into a chair and, sitting opposite, looked at him fondly. He made her think of a teddy bear - big and cuddly.

'You seem fond of Moira,' she said, smiling.

'I am fond of Moira. I think I understand her.' He grinned. 'How I feel for Moira is much like how Professor Henry Higgins felt about Eliza Doolittle. I want to prove that I can make something of her. She is exceptionally gifted and her talents should not be allowed to go to waste.

'But, unlike Professor Higgins, you're not doing this for a bet, I take it?'

'I'm doing it because I think she's worth it,' he said. Jenny sighed.

'I think Moira is a lucky girl to have you as a friend.'

'That's as may be,' said Buddy, 'but I'm sure she'll come round to you, Jenny. She has been visualising a confrontation with you for years now and she had to get it out of her system. Now she feels she's done that but she's learning that the results are not what she had expected. She's feeling the pain of remorse. That only confirms my belief that she's a good woman. There's nothing she wants more than reconciliation. I wanted her to come with me now but there seems to be something still holding her back.'

'I think I know what it might be,' said Jenny, conscious of Moira's letter and its, as yet, undecided fate.

'Can I help?'

'It will sort itself out,' she said more confidently than she felt. 'Now what about Steve?'

'I've just left him playing chess with Father O'Doyle. The priest's in control - in more ways than one and that brings us to my other news. Gerry's plans are already rolling into action. Steve's wife and son fly into Inverness tomorrow afternoon. I managed to book them a flight for today.

They dropped everything and I'll be meeting them and bringing them to the castle, as we planned. It's our last shot.'

'Are you going to prepare Steve for this?'

'Fitzgerald thinks it wiser that Steve confronts them unprepared.'

'Poor Steve. I hope we are doing the right thing.'

'We have to play it by ear but both Father O'Doyle and Fitzgerald assure me that group therapy is standard treatment now for alcoholics in denial.'

'It's going to hurt Steve having his family there.'

That's the whole point. They are the people he has hurt most. He would strongly deny this but when they tell him openly and honestly about the hurt they have suffered he will have a chance to come face to face with the reality of his addiction. I've talked long on the phone with Susan and she knows what's entailed and has agreed. She assured me she would prepare Sam. It is the only way Steve can be helped.' '

'It will be harrowing for them all.'

'Providing care is taken not to make the confrontation hostile or judgemental it should be fine. I trust Fitzgerald in his.'

'Fitzgerald is one of the least judgemental people I know,' agreed Jenny.

'He would like you to be there when he broaches Steve.'

'Is that wise?'

'We must trust Fitzgerald's judgement in this too.'

'When is all this going to happen?' asked Jenny.

'The sooner the better. It would be unfair to keep Susan and Sam hanging around too long and worrying. Could you be at Broom Cottage tomorrow morning when Fitzgerald intents telling Steve? I'll be on my way to meet Susan and Sam at the airport.'

Before going to bed Jenny wrote to Canada, a letter to her father and one to her brother Callum. She had already told them of Moira's arrival but now she told them how and why, sparing them nothing. If Moira were to be reconciled to her family they would all have to play their part. Writing to Aunt Sheena was more difficult. She settled on a short note with a few salient facts. She would wait a while before sayng more. It was late when she had finished but, although tired, she was herself again and quite decided on what she would do about the letter.

Next morning she was ready and waiting when she heard Fittzgerald peep his horn. He had telephoned her earlier to say he'd pick her up. She locked the manse door behnd her and joined him in the car.

'Good of you to come,' he said as he slipped into gear. 'I wanted to have a word with you before we see Steve.'

'Buddy tells me that Steve's family arrives today.'

'Yes. That's what I want a word about. I'm hoping we don't have to tell Steve about their arrival but it might be necessary.'

'It does seem a bit hard not to warn him.'

'You may be right. It's no foregone conclusion that he will agree to a group session.'

'All part of his denial, I suppose,' she remarked.

'That and the type of bloke he is. He is both independent and stubborn and I've no doubt he'll tell us to mind our own business – putting it politely. He's probably telling Father O'Doyle that now. He agreed to put the suggestion to him.'

'You're going to need your powers of persuasion, I'm thinking,' said Jenny.

'And yours.'

'I hesitate to interfere.'

'Jenny, your involvement may involve throwing him a lifeline.'

'I'll do what I can, of course.'

'You've already done a lot. Apart from straightening his thinking about yourself, you made him jolly comfortable in the cottage and with Father O'Doyle and his angels in attendance, our way, hopefully, is being paved.'

'It's only a stopgap till we see how things go.'

'We're about to find out.'

An astonishing sight met them as they entered the cottage in answer to Father O'Doyle's call.

'Come in, come in, me darlins. We won't be a minute.'

He was wearing a white coat as worn by hospital doctors. In his hands, in place of stethoscope or syringe, was a pair of scissors and hair clippers. He stood behind Steve, who sat on a chair, with a towel draped round his neck and over his shoulders. Jenny's eyes widened while Fitzgerald couldn't suppress a grin.

Steve's blond hair, which had become rather long and unruly since his arrival in Strathard, was littering the carpet.

'A couple more snips and we've finished,' said the priest cheerfully. 'And I won't be sorry either,' he added in mock seriousness. 'I'll have you know that this customer is a proper fidget. Babies can sit better than he can'

'Babies don't have haircuts,' growled Steve avoiding the visitors' eyes.

The priest had not stinted his labour. Almost all ot Steve's blond locks had been shorn, leaving him with little spikes, like the needles of a startled hedgehog. The line of his stitches above the eye was like a sabre gash. Although his swelling had almost disappeared, his bruises were an unflattering mixture of black, ochre and blue.

'Well, what do you think?' asked Father O'Doyle, indicating his model with a flourish of the towel which he whipped from Steve's shoulders.

Jenny took her lead from Father O'Doyle.

'Convict 99?

Steve glowered.

'Trick or treat?' smiled Fitzgerald but in spite of their light-hearted banter, Jenny could see that Steve was hurting.

She felt a sudden rush of affection for this man whose problems had upset the even tenor of life in Strathard. His cry for help could not go unheard and it seemed that Father O'Doyle had begun preparations for the rescue.

'It's not very flattering, to be sure,' said the priest, 'but I've been telling my friend that looking as frightful as he does, things can only get better.'

'He's also been telling me,' said Steve, that you are planning a little surprise party for me. Am I meant to feel grateful?'

'Some of us want to help you,' said Jenny.

'And how do you propose to do that?'

'By talking out your problems.'

'A dirty linen laundry session?'

'No, of course not.'

Jenny sensed some residual embarrassment at her presence and decided to leave explanations to the others.

'You have a problem' began Fitzgerald.

'If I have than it's my problem and none of your bloody business. Sorry Father, no offence meant.'

'None taken my son. It is a sad business, to be sure, that you are not a Catholic and don't have the comfort of the confessional.'

'It will only be words,' said Fitzgerald 'and you are a man of words. You know how they can help communicate and explain and better understand.'

'Keep your lectures for the lecture hall,' growled Steve. 'They're wasted on me.'

'We all need help from time to time,' said Jenny.

'That doesn't mean we want it. Some of us prefer to fight our own battles and solve our own problems and at the risk of repeating myself, it is nobody's business but mine.'

'I think it is,' said Fitzgerald.

For the first time Steve looked directly at him.'

'How do you make that out?'

'I picked you up from the floor. I stemmed your blood and washed your face. I practically carried you to my car and drove you to hospital. I listened to your hallucinations which did not sound to me like the outpourings of a happy man. I shared your misfortune and your unhappiness because I am your friend. If a friend is in trouble I want to help. If he doesn't know the extent of his trouble I want to tell him. You have other friends who feel as I do, as Jenny does, as Father O'Doyle does by being here and ministering to your needs. And your friend who struck the blow, possibly more than any of us, is concerned for you. We all want to help, if you will let us.'

'And if I don't?'

'We hope you will.'

Steve remained adamant.

'No way! I'll get over this, in my own way and in my own time. It's just a run of bad luck. I've had bad luck before and survived.'

'It's more than that,' said Jenny, deciding to hit hard.

She hadn't bargained for his reaction.

'Thanks to Buddy the Buddhist superior on his moral high ground.'

'He worries about you.'

'To hell with him and the consultant and his prognosis. To hell with the lot of you. I'll be out of here as soon as I can arrange a flight. I'm going back to Canada where I belong. I've a wife and son there. It's with them I want to communicate.'

In spite of the outrageous tone of delivery Jenny was sensitive to a lack of conviction. She saw his hand shake as he reached for his cigarettes. Turning his back on them he walked to the window, lit up with difficulty and stood, gazing at, but as Jenny suspected, not seeing, the distant waters of the Firth.

Father O'Doyle produced a small brandy flask from his pocket and, joining him, made his offering. Steve swore under his breath but did not refuse. They all diverted their eyes as he raised it shakily to his lips. So far, they had been on their feet in varying degrees of agitation. Fitzgerald now requested that they sit down. There was something he had to tell Steve.

'This is not going to be easy, Steve. You are going to have to draw on all your reserves of courage. You are going to have to humble yourself and accept help. Should it not turn out as we all hope, then that's another story that you can write but in the meantime, trust us. If you like, you can think of it as you putting us on trial. Hear what we all have to say before you judge. It's better than doing nothing.'

'I've no intention of doing nothing.'

His voice sounded stronger and he faced them looking from one to the other. 'I've every intention of getting on a plane and going home. Susan and Sam need me. I have to go to them.

Fitzgerald threw the others a quick glance then, without further preamble, told Steve what he had now to know.

'Susan and Sam are not in Canada. They are here. Buddy is meeting them now at Inverness and shall be bringing them to Strathard.'

Steve looked at them, initial shock changing to fury. 'Get rid of them.'

Jenny swallowed hard as she watched his agony. One trembling hand rose to his head and moved over the hairy spikes. His bruises were like an abstract painting on a white canvas. His voice, as he tried to reinforce his objections, scraped like a knife on iron railings. She threw discretion to the wind and went to him.

'Hold on,' she whispered.

Father O'Doyle again offered his flask, relieved when it wasn't swiped out of his hand. The brandy stayed the panic while Fitzgerald's matter of fact voice attempted to discharge the tension.

'They have come a long way to see you,' he said.

'Why?'

His perplexity was revealed in his one word.

Fitzgerald kept his voice even. 'Like us, but more so, they want to help.'

'Are you telling me that they are invited to the party?'

'They will be there.'

'I'm not ready for them. No! I can't let them see me like this.'

He raised a still trembling hand to his bruises.

Jenny signalled to the others to leave her with Steve. They looked from her to Steve then back again. They nodded, quietly departed and left them together.

She waited a few moments, hands firm on his shoulders, looking at his bowed head. Then, after a gentle reassuring pressure, left his side and drew a chair in front of his and sat down facing him.

'Look at me, Steve.'

With difficulty he raised his eyes, revealing a struggle between anger and despair.

'There's nothing I can't handle, Jenny. I only need a little more time.'

She waited, watching his warring before he dropped his eyes from hers.

'Time is a short commodity to do what you need to do, Steve.'

He looked up quickly.

'You actually believe that crap prognosis. Eh?'

'Yes.'

'My God! What do I have to do to convince you that it's one big exaggeration? It isn't drinking that gets me in a mess. It's other people's stupidity. They swallow professional platitudes like they swallow their own spit. It wasn't the drink that gave me this,' lifting his hand to his bruised face, 'it was that bitch's dirty trick.'

'And my fall from grace,' suggested Jenny.

'That was my stupidity,' he mumbled.

'Tell me, Steve. Why are you refusing to meet your wife and son? Is it because of how you feel or how you look?'

He rose abruptly, practically running to a wall mirror on the other side of the room. As he looked at himself his arms rose in a gesture of frustration. He swung round and spat it out.

'That stupid priest! Look what he's done to my hair. I can't - I won't let Susan and Sam see me like this. The stupid, stupid man.'

Jenny restrained her impulse to go to him and kept her voice level.

'How you feel will concern them greatly. How you look will make no difference.'

'How can you be sure?'

'I have told you my own love story and I think you must agree that when you truly love someone looks don't come into the reckoning.'

'I'm not even sure that Susan still loves me.'

'She is here, isn't she?'

'She might be here out of a sense of duty or Buddy's bullying tactics.'

'She is here because she cares and she has brought Sam. She wouldn't do that if she didn't care.'

'If I can only be sure.'

'Don't you think you should find out?'

'Who's going to be there?'

'Father O'Doyle, Fitzgerald, Buddy, Moira, Susan, Sam and me.'

'Why Moira? Why Buddy? Why any of you, for God's sake? What's it all about Jenny and whose idea was it anyway?'

'After Fitzgerald returned from taking you to hospital he told us how troubled you were and was of the opinion that you were much in need of help.'

'I was drunk, for God's sake. That's all.'

'You were hallucinating. You had no recollection of almost killing someone. If you couldn't remember that, what else might you not have remembered? What other acts when under the influence of alcohol might you not have obliterated from your memory? What do you not yet know about yourself? Buddy told us of your spiralling losses and of your doctor's prognosis, especially his belief that you are in denial. You are refusing to face up to your problem. You are denying you even have one.'

Steve uttered a cry between a laugh and a sob.

'I must say it's rich that my family and friends are lining up to spell out my misdeeds.'

'They need to tell you their side of the story and you need to hear it.' She reached for his hand. 'Will you agree to come and listen to them?'

His head bowed. Jenny waited, his hand warm within her own. When he raised his eyes to hers a glimmer of the well-adjusted, charming Stevenson Bruce was trying to assert itself.

'To think I ever thought I fancied you - you bully.' She smiled, squeezing his hand.

'You will come?'

'I seem to have no choice.'

'Then let me rephrase my question. Do you choose to come?'

His other hand lifted and enclosed hers.

'Todd's a lucky man,' he said softly.

'He chose to be,' she said. 'He might just as easily have chosen to let himself go under. Now I'll tell the others.'

Freeing her hand, she turned to leave but at the door she looked over her shoulder receiving from him a reassuring nod.

'Don't be too hard on Father O'Doyle,' she said. 'He's more used to shearing sheep.'

CHAPTER 26

Jenny had decided on one of the smaller rooms in the castle for the venue. She had lit a fire, filled vases with chrysanthemums and made a circle arrangement of chairs. She had included extra chairs in order to widen the circle and reduce any feeling of confrontation. No one would dominate in a circle. That was important. There must be no semblance of the courtroom; no comparison with the classroom; nor indeed any suggestion of authority.

She tried to focus on the pending group session, wishing she need not witness Steve's discomfiture. Had it been wise of them to let his wife and son see him in his present state? Had they, in fact, the right to interfere at all? Wasn't there a chance they could make matters worse?

As she made an adjustment to one of the flower arrangements and straightened a print on the wall, her thoughts returned to Neil. Was he home? Had he found the letter? She mustn't think of that. She must keep her mind on the immediate concern of helping Steve.

The door opened to admit Buddy and his two companions, Steve's wife, Susan, and their young son, Sam. Beside Buddy's bulk they looked frail and vulnerable and Jenny welcomed them warmly. Susan was stunningly beautiful with wide violet eyes and flaxen hair falling in soft waves to her shoulders. Sam was how his father must have looked at his age. He had the same corn-coloured hair, the same stubborn chin, belied by the gentle expression in the same blue eyes.

The introductions were brief. Jenny expressed a hope that their accommodation was satisfactory.

'Everything's splendid,' said Susan, in a soft spoken voice.

'They understand why they're here,' intervened Buddy laying a gentle hand on Sam's head. 'They know what they have to do and why.'

Susan nodded.

'Buddy has explained everything.'

The door opened and Father O'Doyle entered with Moira. Thanks to the priest's easy manner with everyone present, awkwardness was avoided. At Buddy's suggestion they sat down. Moira had avoided Jenny's eyes. Jenny noticed Sam edge his chair closer to his mother. Tension was heightening. Even Father O'Doyle's usual exuberance was dampened.

The relief was almost tangible when the door opened to admit Gerry, followed by Steve. Looking at him, Jenny was glad she was seated. She looked at his family, as Steve, eyes downcast, followed Gerry and sat in the chair indicated. When seated, he looked up and saw his wife and son. Susan had thrown a protective arm across Sam's shoulders. Sam leaned forward, as if about to break free, then slumped back against his mother and hung his head. Jenny grieved to see Steve's naked pain.

Gerry was speaking, thanking everyone for coming, saying that if their meeting had to bear a label, it would be that of Group Therapy.

'What we must remember,' he said, 'is that this therapy could apply to any of us. We each have our individual problem. Some may be more pressing than others but the others are no less significant. We have not come together to cast blame or make judgements. Neither are we here to moralise. We are here to tell our individual story which is, in essence, our individual reality. They are all different and real only to ourselves but sometimes it is necessary for us to share them. This, I believe, is just such a time.'

Gerry was choosing his words with care.

'Our reality,' he continued, 'is how we see things, how situations and events look through our eyes. They will all differ and they will impinge on each other. I hope this increased awareness of the differences can only help us to come to terms with our own reality.'

Gerry finished talking and there was a silence while his words were being absorbed. Jenny saw Father O'Doyle cross himself. Sam edged closer to his mother while stealing a furtive glance at his father. Moira was doing her best to look disdainful. Buddy looked serious. Jenny had lost her own nervousness and wanted to concentrate her mental energy on this circle of individual realities.

'Would you like to begin, Moira?' asked Gerry.

With a little prompting from Buddy, Moira began her story. As she began to speak Jenny saw Steve's anger and resentment.

'If it hadn't been for my friend, Buddy,' Moira told them, 'I'd be dead and that pathetic specimen of humanity over there would have been my murderer.'

'Here we go!' sneered Steve. 'Miranda, the actress, desperate to take centre stage. Did you know guys, that she was a nearly-famous-author except her book was lost in a fire; a nearly-famous-Olympic-swimmer but she fell sick before the trials; a nearly-famous-prima-donna. You name it. She nearly was it. She thrives on drama and she seems to think she's on to a good one now.'

There was no stopping him. His misery was manifesting freely. Miranda was providing an outlet for his own self loathing.

'And I'll tell you this guys,' he shouted. 'If I'd really intended to murder this drama queen I'm certain sure I wouldn't have failed.'

Jenny glanced at Gerry. Was this outburst an expected part of the therapy? Would he try to extricate them, try to stem the tide of ill will between them, for all their sakes, especially young Sam's? She saw that Sam's head was now on his mother's shoulder. His mother's embrace was tightening as if attempting to shield him from the flying insults.

'You tried to kill me,' Moira accused. 'You stuck your filthy handkerchief in my mouth and gagged me then jumped on me and ripped my clothes off.'

'Liar!'

'I thought you were going to rape me. I was terrified.' She began to sob, the tears coursing down her cheeks. She let them roll.

'Raping you would have been the last thing on my mind,' said Steve. 'Not that you haven't asked for it often enough. And all this is because you got nowhere with me. I wasn't interested in you and you didn't like that. You couldn't accept it and you've been doing your damnedest to have your revenge ever since.'

Moira half rose from her chair and raised an arm, gesticulating at Steve.

'He kept saying Kill! Kill! Kill! - on and on. He was mad. He tried to choke me to death.'

'Show us the evidence,' yelled Steve. 'Where are the bruises? I don't see any bruises. You're a liar, an addicted liar.'

He seemed to relish the sound of these words. He repeated them slowly.

'You are an addicted liar. From the moment we were unfortunate enough to set eyes on you, you've lied. You lied about your name, your nationality, your birth, and your family. Why should they believe you now?'

'Because there was a witness,' she yelled. 'Buddy saw you try to kill me. He heard you yelling kill over and over. Why do you think he punched you? It's a pity he didn't kill you.'

'And that would have made you happy. Eh?' yelled Steve. 'Buddy the Buddha become Buddy the murderer. Are you saying that's what you would have liked?'

Jenny looked again at Gerry. Surely, he must stop this. Couldn't he see the effect it was having on Sam? Steve was also noticing Sam.

'Must the boy be here?' he groaned.

'Sam is staying.'

It was Susan squaring on him, still soft-voiced but determined.

'This is no place for him, for any of us.'

Steve made to rise but it was Father O'Doyle who stopped him.

'Sit down, my son,' he advised kindly.

He rounded on the priest. 'It's your fault. You and your Kill your anger. You kept saying it. "Kill - kill. . ."'

His voice tapered to silence.

'It's all right, my son. Sit down now.'

Steve slumped into his chair.

Now Gerry moved on.

'Buddy, will you tell us your story?'

Jenny tried to catch Susan's eye in the hope of signalling some comfort, but Susan remained detached from everyone, except Sam whom she now released and whispered in his ear. Sam straightened himself, pushed his hair off his face and stuck out that determined little chin. Jenny saw him steal a quick glance at his father who, anger spent, had collapsed into utter dejection. She felt his pain.

Buddy was beginning his story.

'I brought it with me,' he was saying as he pulled what looked like a folded newspaper from his inside pocket.

He opened it, and holding it at arm's length, swivelled on his heels that everyone might see. Steve dropped his head in his hands.

'Steve has already seen this,' said Buddy. 'I showed it to him the morning after when I collected him from prison.' He pointed a finger at the picture. 'This is Steve standing beside his trusty steed as he called his imaginary horse. As you can see, it is in actuality, a two-wheeled bicycle with handlebars. You can see he is holding his imaginary shield and sword which were a trash bin lid and fireside poker. Now look carefully. At his feet lies the owner of the bicycle. He is unconscious, made so by a hefty blow from Steve's sword, for which substitute poker. The poor man was attempting to reclaim his bike when he was attacked by this so-called knight who claimed to be Robert the Bruce, king of the Scots.'

There was an audible gasp while everyone's eyes, except Steve's, riveted on the newspaper headlines. Sam's mouth fell open while his eyes widened in amazement and, Jenny sensed, a stealthy excitement.

'By the grace of God and the bike owner's strong constitution,' continued Buddy, 'I am happy to say he survived. King Robert the Bruce was taken to prison, thrown into a cell from which I was the means of freeing him the following morning. But can you imagine what would have happened if that blow had killed.'

Steve's bowed head was rolling in his hands. Jenny noticed that even Moira was transfixed. Had her own powers of imagination met their match? Jenny wondered.

'The police were a decent bunch and didn't prosecute. The victim was more forgiving than Steve deserved and didn't press charges. Some of you may be tempted to seek the humour in this situation, as did the journalist and the bystanders, but I show it to you now as an incident, dramatic as it undoubtedly was, of which Steve was quite ignorant the next day. He could not remember anything about it. He could not remember - and I vouch for this - leaving the hotel, looking for his ridiculous charger, thinking he had found it and the eventual outcome of robbing and attacking an innocent man.'

Steve had kept his bowed head in his hands, only raising it when he heard his wife's voice.

'Why Steve? Why?'

He looked at Susan, his face ravaged with pain and humiliation and tried to speak but nothing came.

'I'd like to answer that, Susan, if I may,' said Buddy.

'There are two reasons why. The first is that he had just drunk a full bottle of whisky, fifty per cent alcohol, one hundred per cent proof, and he'd drunk it neat. After that anything might happen. Good judgement and sense of responsibility fly out of the window and feelings of invincibility take their place. Nothing seems impossible. The tragedy is, that come sobriety, you don't remember what happened when you were drunk.'

Buddy paused for a moment, looking from Susan to Sam then to Steve in his dumb misery.

'Why did he do it, you ask? For six days he had been counting the hours and minutes until he could phone his wife and son. He had vowed six days of abstinence before doing so. He had succeeded and elated, he rang you at home. It was early in the morning when he expected you would be in the kitchen, Susan, preparing Sam's lunchbox for school. Steve's call was answered by a stranger who sounded very much at home in his house where his wife and child were living. His elation fell and it couldn't fall much lower than it did. There was only one escape from his misery. Alcohol would take him to his imaginary world where he was free from the pain of the real world. When he eventually returned to the real world he had no recollection of the imaginary world. In both instances, in Greenock and his attack on Moira, he had lost his judgement and his sense of responsibility. Each incident could have ended in tragedy.'

Gerry interrupted Buddy.

'I think Susan wants to say something.'

Susan, her clasped hands clenched on her lap, gave a nervous little cough before speaking.

'At home when he'd done something awful he always told me the next day that he couldn't remember. I never believed him.'

She lowered her eyes, passing the tip of her tongue over her lips.

'Do you want to tell us some of the awful things he did but never remembered afterwards?'

She nodded but it was a few moments before she found her voice.

'Once we had invited friends for dinner. When they arrived, Steve hadn't returned from wherever he was. I held off the meal as long as I could but after an hour when he still hadn't come home I had to serve. I made excuses but fooled nobody. Getting through the meal was embarrassing enough but when he did turn up as our friends were leaving, he was shamelessly drunk. He made no apology, gave no hint that he'd done anything wrong. He behaved like some moron hustling them to the door even though he could barely stand. Then he left without even a polite goodbye.' Lowering her eyes, she continued. 'He couldn't understand why I didn't fall into his arms. He got nastily rattled when I threw him out of the bedroom and the next morning he denied everything. "Couldn't remember," he said. "You should know that I'd never embarrass you like that," he said. How could I accuse him of such discourtesy, he wondered. I called him a liar.'

She looked across at her husband who was shaking his head in denial.

'I didn't remember, Susan. I still don't.'

'Did you remember taking me to a thanksgiving ball, having one dance, meeting a mate then disappearing for the rest of the evening, leaving me on my own? Utterly humiliated, I had to search for you but you'd gone off on a pub crawl. I had to phone a taxi to get home. The next day you hadn't a clue of what you'd done. I called you a liar.'

'Susan.'

It was a cry of anguish but Susan continued to relate an increasing number of incidents to every one of which Steve insisted he had no memory.

'When you weren't drunk and insensible I couldn't have wished for a better husband. That's what made it so hard. You sure were really a wonderful guy most of the time. Foolishly I thought each humiliation would be the last one. I stuck it as long as I could until, until...'

She looked around, faltered and stopped.

'Go on Susan,' said Gerry quietly.

She took a deep breath.

'On my last birthday he had planned a special celebration. I was excited. He made me excited because of his own enthusiasm. Things had been fine for some time and I really thought he'd stopped heavy drinking. When he was an hour late, I feared the worst. After two hours I'd had enough. Friends I knew were leaving the next day for America to join the Civil Rights march to Montgomery. I rang them and asked if Sam and I could join them. They said okay so I packed the minimum of what I thought we'd need. I wrote a note to the principal of Sam's school and went to bed. I couldn't sleep and I heard a car come up the drive. I looked out the window. It was Buddy bringing my husband home. He'd found him on the sidewalk outside a club. He carried him into the house and, being the considerate person he is, he did what he had to do quietly so as not to disturb Sam and me. Steve was as good as unconscious. Buddy took off his shoes and settled him on the lounge sofa and then went quietly away. I stayed in my room. I dressed for the trip and lay on top of my bed till I felt I could waken Sam.'

She swallowed hard, reached out for Sam's hand and continued.

'Sam was wonderful. He got himself ready while I slipped into the kitchen to make us some breakfast. I guessed Steve would be senseless for hours yet. We were opening the front door to leave when Steve appeared unexpectedly. He was in a bad way and short tempered.'

She stopped for a few moments while everyone seemed to be holding their breath. Her voice was unsteady when she continued.

'I want you all to know that Steve has never once laid a finger on me or Sam and I know that that morning he had no intention of hurting us but he was so angry at me for leaving. He had no idea what had happened to him and why he had wakened up on the sofa. He'd also completely forgotten about the birthday celebration. He forbade me to leave the house. I told Sam to go ahead and I made to follow. Steve grabbed me. His strength was uncanny. I panicked. I kneed him where I knew it would hurt most and, in his pain, he released me. He doesn't know it but in the struggle he'd broken a bone in my wrist.'

Steve's mouth moved but no words came.

'I decided that was it,' said Susan. 'I was finished with him.'

Jenny's heart bled for Steve. It all sounded so final and she could see that all his defences were down. Then into the silence Sam spoke.

'He didn't mean to hurt Mummy. He would never hurt her or me.'

Gerry's voice cut in quickly.

'We know your Dad would never hurt you, Sam, but did he ever make you sad?'

Sam's mouth closed tight while his chin thrust further forward.

'Remember what Uncle Buddy told you, Sam.'

It was Susan speaking gently but firmly, reminding her son what they'd come for.

It was then Jenny knew that the real point of the therapy was about to begin. She looked at Gerry. His eyes were on Sam. They were kind and with a few encouraging words he prompted.

'Tell us your story, Sam. When did your Dad disappoint you?'

Jenny could see that Steve had reached his nadir of desolation. His facial bruises and Father O'Doyle's ridiculous haircut added pathos to his pain. The priest had edged closer to him. Buddy's eyes never left him. Susan had lost what little colour she'd had. Even Moira looked concerned. Gerry remained resolute.

'Go on, Sam,' he urged.

After another look at his mother, who nodded, Sam spoke.

'You didn't come to hear me play solo horn at the concert. You said you would. I played swell and everyone clapped but you weren't there. All the other Dads were there. When Mummy and I got home you were drunk and dancing in the hall with a skeleton. You said you wanted to get to know its bones.'

Jenny looked fearfully at the others but only pity registered on the faces.

'The first time I played in the baseball team you weren't there. You promised. I played swell. The coach said he'd keep me in the team. He said he'd expected to see you. I told a lie and said you were abroad on a project.' Sam hesitated then, his voice rising a tone, continued. 'But the worst thing of all was when you made Mummy cry and when you'd say it wasn't your fault. It made us feel it must be our fault and I know it wasn't Mummy's fault.'

His face began to crumple. Steve, at breaking point, was already in tears. He rose from his chair making a blind move to escape.

'Don't go, Daddy,' sobbed Sam. 'Please don't leave us.' He ran to Steve. 'I love you, Daddy. Please come home. Mummy loves you too. She told me. We both love you and that's why we've said all these things.'

They were in each other's arms, locked in love. Susan joined them, her tears mingled with theirs. Buddy looked relieved but was already on his way to the weeping Moira. Gerry sat back on his chair and, for the first time, relaxed. Father O'Doyle's face was alight with the radiance from his entourage of angels. Empowered from the energy of their flapping wings, he took centre stage and crossed himself before asking the group to please sit. Everyone did. The family sat united. Buddy held Moira's hand while Jenny exchanged a tentative smile with Gerry.

Father O'Doyle made the sign of the cross.

'God bless you all,' he began. 'When Saint Paul spoke to the good people of Corinth he talked about the power of love. He proclaimed that it was greater than prophecy and the understanding of mysteries; greater than knowledge; greater than faith itself. Without love the ability to move mountains is as nothing, he told them. Without love it was like looking through a glass darkly but with love we see God face to face and we are to know Him as we are known by Him. We pass from darkness to light and from clouds to clear sunshine. With love, my friends, we can do whatever we set our minds to do.'

Father O'Doyle crossed himself, blessed them and left the stage. The show was over. The therapy had begun. He made his way straight to Jenny.

'I'll take the little family to Broom Cottage, Jenny, me darlin',' he said. 'I'll come back to my room here. I'll leave Saint Valentine, the blessed saint of lovers and Saint Monica, blessed saint of mothers, looking over them. I hope you agree.'

Jenny smiled fondly on the saintly priest. In spite of his evident relief and joy, she saw his weariness. The good man that he was, he had shouldered much of the pain of this difficult session.

'Tell them I shall see them tomorrow,' she asked the priest. 'It is best that we all go home now.'

She saw that Moira, quietly weeping, had left with Buddy. Only Gerry and herself remained.

'If it had been anything other than the type of meeting it was, I would suggest buying you a stiff drink,' Gerry said. Jenny smiled ruefully.

'Strange, isn't it. We know that alcohol would do us no harm, indeed give us comfort appropriate to the occasion, whereas it would be Steve's undoing.'

'It would seem that the real problem doesn't lie with alcohol per se but with our use of it.'

'What happens now?' asked Jenny.

'It's only the beginning for Steve but it is a good beginning. He's out of denial and has found his motivation. As long as he has Sam he'll be fine. That young lad is the best motivation he could have.'

Sighing, he made to take his leave. Jenny, deliberately detained him, knowing that her greatest problem was going to be the journey home and fearing what she would find when she arrived there. She was in no hurry.

'Do you think he will be all right?' she persisted. Gerry looked at her.

'He is always going to be vulnerable,' he said. He has a life's struggle ahead but with courage and luck he should be all right. He'll need professional help for a while, continued counselling, group support and, of course, he's lucky to have his writing. I think we'll find a difference there.'

'Quality writing,' mused Jenny. 'I know that's what he'd like.'

'Quality of the individual,' said Gerry. 'I know that's what the world needs.'

It was Jenny's time to sigh now. Already her fears were heightening and she wished she were going anywhere but back home to Neil. He would be there now and waiting for her. He would have read Moira's letter. What was she going to find?'

Gerry had gone. She should be going too but her footsteps dragged. About to enter the reception lounge she changed her mind and backtracked to the library. Just for a few moments, she promised herself.

The casserole won't waste and I'll still be in good time for dinner.

It wasn't dinner or the casserole she was worried about. It was her marriage.

CHAPTER 27

When she entered the library the air was vibrating with the resonance from Yeshi's singing bowl. Although no one else appeared to be present Yeshi was performing his closing ritual.

Most of the lights were switched off. Only the lamp on his desk and one table lamp at the far end of the room were diffusing a soft luminance.

'It's all right, Yeshi. You can go now. I'll lock up tonight,' said Jenny.

When Yeshi had gone, Jenny switched off the desk lamp and walked slowly between the rows of shelves, occasionally pausing to touch a leather-bound volume, remembering with a rush of emotion her first encounter with the wonderful collection. She could almost convince herself that the professor's spirit walked by her side and that his voice spoke in her ear. She remembered his words.

'You have so many friends around you now,' he'd told her, indicating his book-lined walls, 'Get to know them. Listen to what they have to say. They will all say something different. Some may be wrong for you but, then again, some may be right. It will be for you to choose.'

Little did she know then that all these 'friends' would be hers for life, standing there on their mahogany shelves, offering her all the wisdom of the ages. She had grown to love them and they never failed her.

As she wound her way round the various shelves, she read the names on the neatly printed labels: Essays, Poetry, Occultism, Philosophy, Homeopathy, Meditation, Theosophy, Eastern Religions, Buddhism, Zen, Occult, Islam, Legends, Rosicrucian, Rosh Hashana, Confucianism, Christianity. She halted there and reached for the Holy Bible. Father O'Doyle had pointed the way. She carried it to her favourite seat, softly lit by an arc of light from the nearby lamp. She turned the pages carefully till she'd found Saint Paul's message to the Corinthians. There was something she had to understand before she journeyed home.

For now we see through a glass, darkly; but then face to face; now I know in part; but then shall I know even as also I am known.

She returned to the beginning of the chapter and read all of the passage, heightening her awareness of each word, savouring their beauty and inspiration.

Paul was telling me, she thought, that with love God is to be seen face to face and we are to know Him as we are known by Him. We pass from darkness to light, from clouds to clear sunshine. There is faith. There is hope. There is love but the greatest of these is love.

It is the same for us, she thought. Tonight Steve had been forced to see himself face to face; to see himself as others saw him, to face his reality and shoulder the blame and have the courage to change.

And what about herself? Hadn't the events of the last few days forced her to look at herself face to face? What had she seen? Oh yes. She had loved. That was the good part. What of the bad? Hypocrisy? She had flaunted her ideals of quality. She had suffered pride in her self-image and the image presented to others. What effect had her quality image had on Steve and Moira? They had both seen what she herself had not dared to see. They had seen hypocrisy, the stain on the white cloth as visualised by Steve, the cheating on her husband as condemned by Moira. She had justified her cheating in the name of love. Love for Todd, a kind of love for Neil. Face to face she now saw it for what it was. Love of Self. All these years she had travelled with her high ideals and holier-than-thou attitude and she was worse off than ever. She hadn't begun to know the true meaning of love, as Todd knew. If she had, she would still be with him in his spiritual quest. Now she was back in the foothills and he had moved on. What was she to do? All of Neil's principles she had constantly scoffed but, in the end, his strength was the greater and now, she thought disconsolately, she had lost him. His enduring principles would not suffer her betrayal and he would be right.

Why was she so anguished? Face to face with herself she had to admit it. She didn't want to lose him. It wasn't just a kind of love she felt. It was love. It bore no comparison with her love for Todd. That had now entered a new and higher dimension. But it did bear comparison with what she had offered Neil before. This was different.

She was jolted out of her thoughts by the sound of the door opening. She hoped whoever had entered would turn and go away. She didn't want company right now.

She sat quietly, the Bible on her lap. The footsteps were slow and hesitant. They were coming near along an aisle not open to her vision. Perhaps if she did nothing they'd turn and go away. That was not to be. Whoever it was must soon come into view. She gazed in amazement. The figure stopped and they looked at each other.

'Moira,' was all she managed to say.

'I saw you come here,' said Moira.

'Are you all right?' asked Jenny, noting her sister's discomfiture. 'Come and sit down,' she offered and was surprised when Moira accepted the invitation. She decided to wait and follow Moira's lead.

'Is that the Bible you're reading?'

'I was thinking of what Father O'Doyle said about Paul's letter to the Corinthians and wanted to read it for myself.' When Moira remained silent, she began to read. "Now I see through a glass darkly but then face to face. Now I know in part but then shall I know even as also I am known."

Moira seemed to be listening but still said nothing so she carried on talking.

'I was thinking how applicable this passage was for us all tonight, especially Steve. He was forced to listen to the awful things he did when he'd been drinking. For the first time he saw himself face to face.'

She glanced again at her sister and saw her tears. Curbing her instinct to comfort, she kept her silence.

'It was awful,' said Moira. 'I felt so sorry for him. He really suffered.'

'It was all for the best,' said Jenny gently. 'Everyone was trying to help.'

'I wasn't,' said Moira. 'I was beastly. I've always been beastly to him.'

'You had your own problems,' said Jenny.

'That's no excuse. He saw through me very quickly and I hated him for that. Come to think of it I hated everybody. Steve wasn't the only one who saw things face to face tonight.'

Jenny watched as Moira abstractedly fingered a tendril of hair.

'I'm not just unpleasant. I'm nasty. It all started with Aunt Sheena. She was such a nasty person you had to be nasty to survive. You've no idea what it was like.'

She was sitting up now, looking directly at Jenny.

'I think I have,' said Jenny. 'There was no love lost between Aunt Sheena and me. She was very good at bringing out the worst in people.'

'Father couldn't stand her,' said Moira. 'I think that's why he went to Toronto and I think that's probably why he didn't visit much. It got that I was as nasty as Aunt Sheena to him, especially when he kept singing your praises.'

'Don't be too hard on yourself, Moira.'

'I hate myself. I know people think I love nobody but myself but I really hate myself.'

'Buddy doesn't think the worst of you.'

'Buddy's a swell guy.'

'Do you know he might be staying on here?'

'He hinted as much. I've come to depend on him a lot. I don't think he hates me.'

'He's very fond of you and he is enthusiastic about your singing. He is a good friend to have around.'

Jenny thought she'd better leave it at that. She mustn't be too persuasive in wanting Moira to stay in Strathard. A strong-willed person, especially one like Moira, didn't change overnight.

Reluctant as she was to confide in Moira, she just couldn't leave it there. She owed her sister something and hoped that it wasn't too late.

'You and Steve are not the only ones looking at themselves face to face,' Jenny said. 'I've been doing the same. Neil is a good man and a good husband,' she began. 'I know you find it difficult to understand my relationship with Todd.'

Moira interrupted.

'Todd came to see me today.'

'He did!'

'Just before Father O'Doyle arrived to take me to the meeting.'

'He told me he was leaving and we had a long talk.' Jenny was afraid to interrupt.

'He helped me to understand things, especially you and what it had been like for you when your mother died.'

'Our mother,' said Jenny.

They looked at each other and Jenny felt that perhaps, after all, there was much to hope for.

'He made me feel differently about a lot of things and I began to feel panicky when I thought of the letter I'd sent to your husband.'

'Did you tell Todd about that?'

'Yes.'

Please don't make me ask, Jenny silently pleaded.

'I said I'd written to Neil and told him about your affair. Todd wasn't angry. He didn't even look worried. Do you know what he said?'

Jenny shook her head. She couldn't have spoken if she'd wanted to.

'He said, "Jenny will know what to do. Jenny is a wise woman." Are you wise, Jenny?'

'Not as I'd wish to be. I'm just like any other ordinary woman, Moira - full of feelings and wishes and dreams. Like most ordinary women I try to do what's right. I try not to hurt anyone. I do the best I can in this difficult business of getting along in life.'

'I told Todd I had a terrible temper,' added Moira. Jenny smiled.

'And he probably told you it couldn't be worse than mine.'

'He told me you had trained yours until you could manage to control it.'

'He told you a lot, it seems,' smiled Jenny. Just thinking of Todd had calmed and comforted and she knew it would always be like that. 'Just before you were born,' she said to Moira, 'mother asked me to put my hand on her stomach and feel how strong my wee sister was. "She's a real fighter," mother said. 'And I told her,' Jenny said with a smile, 'that you weren't as strong as me. You know, Moira, I think that between us we could kick up quite a stoor if we wanted to. Do you know what that means?'

Moira nodded.

'Kick up the dust?'

'We could make our presence felt - in important things. We shouldn't fight each other. We should fight together for all the things that are important.'

Moira's eyes were shining, her body erect in her chair, her words rushed in the air with released energy.

'Do you think we can?'

'I know we can.'

'And what shall we fight together?' wondered the new Moira.

'We could fight Aunt Sheena and Father and Callum.'

Moira's jaw dropped until she managed to say, 'How?'

'The Buddhists will be leaving. That means extra accommodation at the shooting lodge. We could invite all the family over for a holiday. Father and his wife. Callum and his wife and two children and, of course, Aunt Sheena.'

The idea had been voiced before considered. She had yet to weigh the pros and cons. It seemed Moira had already done this.

'I don't think that's a good idea.'

'Are you afraid of them?' asked Jenny, already tuned to Moira's moods.

She was realising that her young sister wasn't all that different from herself, after all. Had she ever refused a challenge?

Moira tossed her head - another characteristic Jenny was learning.

'Of course not.'

'It's quite a challenge, I agree,' said Jenny, quick to notice the gleam the word produced in Moira's eyes.

'They may not come,' said Moira. 'We'll have to make the invitation irresistible.'

'How can we do that?'

'That's something we can plan - together.'

'You know, sister,' said Moira. 'I think I might stay around here after all - for a bit anyway,' she quickly added, as a possible let out clause.

Rising, Jenny curbed the impulse to embrace her sister. Anyone, brought up by Aunt Sheena, wouldn't be the tactile type. It was enough that the air had been cleared between them and they both had something to fight for, together.

'The first thing I'll do is have your name inscribed on the tombstone,' she said.

A wide grin lit up Moira's hitherto solemn face.

'I'll bet that isn't everyone's idea of a favour,' she said.

Her grin broke into a laugh and the next moment they were both laughing. Her next words stopped Jenny's laughter.

'I'm sorry about the letter I wrote to Neil. Very, very sorry. It was a mean thing to do and I hope I haven't caused trouble between Neil and you. Was he very angry?'

'I don't know, Moira. Neil wasn't at home when it was delivered. In fact, he will just have arrived home some time this afternoon.'

'So you have destroyed the letter. Eh?'

'No.'

'You left it for him to read?'

Yes.'

'Was that wise?'

Jenny smiled.

'Todd would think so.'

'I'll see him, Jenny. I'll tell him it isn't true. I'll tell him I just wanted to cause trouble which is true.'

'The matter's out of both our hands now, Moira. It's up to Neil. He is the one who will choose what to do.'

'But suppose...'

'Don't let's worry about what hasn't yet happened.' 'I don't know how you can be so calm.'

On her way home, Jenny felt far from calm. Talking about Neil had brought the situation very close indeed. In less than an hour she would know the outcome of Moira's letter and she feared the worst. The choice she had made when Todd came back into her life had been no choice. She had done exactly what she wanted. She had kept one bird in her hand and fed the other in the bush.

CHAPTER 28

As Jenny opened the front door of the manse she found the air rich with the smell of venison cooking in red wine which served to kill rather than kindle her appetite.

'Jenny! Come in here! I want to show you something.'

Feeling that she was being called to the witness stand, she entered Neil's study. He was seated at his desk in undisguised excitement.

'Look at this.'

Bracing herself, she looked then she stared uncomprehendingly. Where she had expected to see Moira's calligraphic hand in black-bordered writing paper, she was looking at a photograph of a gravestone. It was no ordinary gravestone but a large and elaborate monument.

'There's the real stone,' said Neil pointing a finger at an older stone embedded in the monument.

'Read that,' he said, referring to a written inscription on the headstone.

> Here lies Gilbert McAdam who was shot in this parish
> By the Laird of Coizean and Baliochmil
> For his adherence to the Word of God and
> Scotland's Covenanted work of Reformation

'Use the glass.' He passed her a magnifying glass. 'Do you notice anything about the second line?'

He waited while she carefully scrutinised the second line. She shook her head.

'Only that Culzean and Ballochmyle are spelt differently.'

'That was 17th century spelling,' he said. 'If you look again you'll see that the second line has been tampered with then later reset. Do you know why?'

'I think you'd better tell me,' she said, her earlier fears for the moment in abeyance.

She was glad to sit down.

This was the Neil she knew at his best. He was the antithesis of the sombre, Sabbath preacher. He was the exuberant child inside the dour and cautious man and this side was not the one she had geared herself up to expect tonight.

'The negroes weren't the first slaves in America,' he said. Gilbert McAdam was transported from Scotland to the plantation of America and sold into slavery. When his father had scraped enough money to buy his son's freedom, Gilbert came home but was later shot by the two gentlemen named in the epitaph. And do you know what his crime was?'

Jenny shook her head.

'Attending an illegal prayer meeting!'

While Neil elaborated on his story, Jenny's eyes searched his desk for the bundle of letters. It was no longer there. She saw the elastic band which meant he had handled his mail. Some of the envelopes were slit but nowhere could she see one bordered in black.

'After the Reformation, when Presbyterianism was once again legal, the Laird of Ballochmil changed sides. The damage to the stone was made when he chipped away the incriminating evidence.'

She looked at him, suspicious of a double entendre. Her only concern was for the incriminating evidence of her own deceit. Where was it? Why didn't he mention it? What game was Neil playing?

'It was later restored,' he said, smiling into her puzzled eyes. 'Just think, Jenny. The poor man sold into slavery because he refused to go to church which had a foreign preacher forced on the Presbyterians and, what was worse, a preacher of a different faith.'

She gave what she hoped was a sympathetic grunt and said she'd cook the potatoes and let him know when dinner was on the table.

She was at the door when his next words stopped her on her track.

'That's not all I've discovered.'

She turned her head slowly fearing the worst.

'I can't wait to put pen to paper,' he told her. 'I must record my findings when they're fresh in my mind.'

He joined her at the dining table when she called, sniffing in anticipation of his favourite meal. Still waiting for the death knell, she watched him furtively, totally at a loss to understand his attitude.

'Tell me about the meeting,' he said. 'Do you think it helped Steve?'

She grasped the lifeline and gave a full and vivid account of what had happened, playing down Moira's involvement. The less said about her sister, the better. It was the only subject of conversation throughout the meal.

'You're exhausted,' he said as she began to clear the table. 'Leave this and have an early night.'

He brushed aside her objections.

'Off you go. A good night's sleep will do you the world of good. I'll probably be burning the midnight oil.'

She couldn't sleep. Why hadn't he said anything? She couldn't believe he was being deliberately cruel. That wasn't Neil's style. For one crazy moment she wondered if she had burned the letter after all. She'd sat by the fire long enough with it in her hands. No, she hadn't burned, it she assured herself. She'd left it quite deliberately for him to find.

She heard the grandfather clock strike the hours and by four o'clock Neil had not come to bed. Ashamed of her timidity, whe threw back the blankets to go downstairs and confront him but realised that, as far as Neil was concerned, she would have no knowledge of the letter. There was nothing for it but to endure the agony of waiting for him to speak.

She got out of bed to straighten the sheets. She'd tossed and turned to such an extent that they had more wrinkles than the skin of a wizened apple. She was barely between them again when she heard Neil come upstairs and by the time he slipped into bed beside her she was feigning sleep. She lay, muscles tensed, as she felt him settle. She listened to his steady breathing not daring to move until it deepened enough to convince her that he was asleep. She felt hot, had a headache and began to count sheep. It was useless. Neither sheep, deep breathing nor mentally reciting Words-worth's ode Intimations of Immortality did the trick. She saw the first faint streak of dawn and the familiar objects in the room begin to take shape before sleep claimed her.

When she woke she was alone. She had overslept. She stood for a moment under a cold shower, hoping it would vitalise her, dressed quickly and went downstairs. Neil was not there. He had left a note on the kitchen table. It did not say where he had gone or why he had gone but just that he would be back some time in the afternoon. He wished her a good day at the farm. He left her the car. Walking would do him good.

Jenny made up her mind. She must see Theresa. First, she phoned Jock to make sure everything was okay at the farm. Next, she phoned Flora to ensure no problems had arisen in the household. Then she drove to the village and parked at the back of the Strathard Arms.

She entered by the back door. Jimmy, after his usual hearty greeting, called Theresa who took one look at Jenny then led her behind the beaded curtain, along a narrow lobby and into a room which had Theresa's stamp everywhere. The centre lamp was a model of planet Earth. The walls were covered by posters of the solar system and Theresa's attendant astrological litter was liberally strewn on furniture and floor.

'Something's happened,' she said as she cleared a chair for Jenny to sit. 'I haven't seen you so worried since our Edinburgh days.'

'Something's happening,' said Jenny, 'and I don't know what.'

'Tell me about it,' said Theresa.

'No. You tell me,' said jenny.

A slow smile lit up Theresa's face.

'Are you asking Theresa, the friend or Theresa, the prophetess?'

'Theresa, the prophetess and I did say that I'd only ask if I were desperate. Well, I am. Desperate! I'd like you to polish your crystal ball and take a peep. You don't need to travel far. Today, tomorrow or next week will be far enough.'

The smile broadened and Theresa's chuckle raised a glimmer of response in Jenny's eyes.

'Don't you think that a heart-to-heart would be just as good?' asked her friend.

'The crystal ball,' insisted jenny.

'Help me clear the table.'

Books, papers, pens and a coffee-stained recipe for bigarade sauce were transferred from table to dresser top, a duster whipped across the ancient oak and a black velvet cloth placed in position to receive a sphere of misty natural quartz crystal.

Almost reverently, Theresa cupped the ball in her hands before placing it on the cloth.

'First, I shall prepare myself.'

She went to the mirror and arranged a red kerchief on her head. Next, she painted her lips and bedecked ears, neck, and hands with many jewels then reseated herself at the table opposite Jenny.

'Next, I must focus.'

She closed her eyes, breathed deeply and spread her hands on the table top. After a few moments of concentrated breathing, she began a ritual of delicate hand movement above the glacial sphere which was now reflecting the fire of her jewels.

As she inclined her head to gaze into the crystal galaxies, Jenny committed the sin of interrupting.

'Get on with it, Theresa.'

Theresa threw her a rapier-edged look and returned to the breathing ritual and Jenny had to put the lid on her impatience until Theresa's expression changed from mystique to one of genuine interest.

'How strange,' she said.

'What a landscape! I see a field of breast-high corn. It is ripe and golden. I see the protective earth maple with its glistening bark and running sap. The sky is cloudless and peace is everywhere.'

There was a long pause while Theresa gazed soulfully into her misty mystic ball. Jenny released the faintest of sighs, looking affectionately at her friend but feeling none the wiser for what she had heard. Theresa raised her eyes.

'It is a harvest rich for the reaping,' she concluded.

She waited for Jenny's reaction.

'Is that the best you can do?' was what she heard.

'I think, Jenny,' she said, beginning to wrap her crystal in its velvet shroud, 'we should have that heart to heart all. Now tell me,' she said after she'd removed both headscarf and jewels, is it Todd?

'No,' said Jenny. 'I have said my goodbyes to Todd. I can bear that.'

'It was inevitable,' said Theresa. 'It was all so wonderfully right and natural and noble to begin with but it never stood a chance against the harsh reality of life.'

'It was the reality of Buddhism that it didn't stand chance against,' said Jenny. 'There is no place in this materially-driven Western society for Todd. He left behind its five poisons long ago. I think he has only remained in Strathard as long as he has for my sake.'

'I need an explanation of the five poisons,' said the down-to-earth, up-in-the-sky Theresa.

'To Tibetans the Five Poisons are delusion, fear, pride, craving and envy. They are the ego's weapons of defence. Since Todd has already purged himself of illusion and fanaticism, there is only one way for him to go and that is the Middle Way of Buddhism.'

'Well then,' said Theresa, 'if it isn't Todd, is it Moira?'

'Moira has made the move towards reconciliation. It won't happen completely overnight but I am hopeful of a closer relationship in the future.'

While the September sun invaded the small room circulating dust particles in the air and distributing them on the few surfaces still left uncluttered, Jenny filled Theresa in about the group session and why it had been necessary.

'Whew!' said Theresa when she'd finished. 'The little vixen.'

'Moira is fierce and over protective, like the vixen, but unlike the vixen she is protective of all the wrong things.'

'You'll soon teach her, Jenny.'

'We'll learn from each other.'

Theresa looked duly humbled.

'It's Neil,' said Jenny. 'He must have read Moira's letter. Why has he not confronted me? What is he feeling? What am I to do, Theresa?'

Her friend looked at her kindly.

'Reap your fields of corn. It is your harvest I saw.'

'Riddles!' scoffed Jenny.

'At least think on it,' advised Theresa.

'And in the meantime?'

'God be with you, my child, as Father O'Doyle would say. And all the saints preserve you.'

'Amen.' said Jenny, gently exasperated.

She rose, bade her friend a fond farewell and drove to the farm. At least, for a few moments, she'd shared her worry and that had helped. She must be satisfied with that.

Her lack of sleep was beginning to tell on her. She might have been tempted to have a power nap but events awaiting her at the farm incited an adrenaline rush.

The first person she saw, after she'd disengaged herself from the welcoming dogs was Father O'Doyle. Susan followed in his wake. Jenny looked at this vision of loveliness with the violet eyes, who approached her smiling from their depths.

'We've been looking at the ducks,' she said. 'I was so afraid we would miss seeing you. Jock has taken my two boys to see the horses. Sam could wait no longer.'

'I'll just tell them you're here,' said the priest, fluttering off.

'I want to thank you, Jenny.'

Jenny made an attempt to stave off the thanks but Susan ignored her and expressed her gratitude simply and sincerely.

'You have transformed my husband.'

'Not me,' protested Jenny. 'Strathard.'

'You *are* Strathard,' Susan said.

This unexpected remark caught Jenny off guard. She had a sudden vision of herself as a young girl, loving her family, her home, her valley, her school, her friends and the gentle Laird who at that time, and still, epitomised all that was best in the community of Strathard. She warmed to think she might have helped to keep his spirit alive.

'I hope things go well for you all,' she said to Susan. 'We're going to be all right,' said Susan again smiling. The priest returned with Susan's two boys in his wake and Jock bringing up the rear.

What a portrait, thought Jenny with a rush of pleasure. An angel-faced and portly priest, a beautiful wife and mother, handsome rejuvenated husband and father and trusty Highlandman, Jock. As for Sam! Before her was a young replica of Steve and Father O'Doyle's handiwork was patently obvious. Sam's head had been closely cropped and spiked.

'Like father, like son. Eh?' said Steve, giving Jenny a wink. 'A model customer he was,' said Father O'Doyle proudly. 'Much better behaved than his father.'

'You look wonderful,' Jenny told Sam.

Sam had his father's haircut but he had his mother's shy smile.

Jock took us to see Charlie and Chum. I love them,' he said with a rush.

'Then you must ride them,' said Jenny.

'I'm afraid it won't be this time, Jenny,' said Steve. 'We leave tomorrow.'

'And today I take them to my chapel on the coast where there is a leaking roof that Steve insists on inspecting and it is the pity that we must go soon if we are to arrive before the roof falls in. Saint Vincent of the Builders will not wait forever.'

'Dad's going to hire workers to repair the roof,' explained Sam seriously, 'and he's going to buy Broom Cottage so that we can come whenever we want.'

'Now that was to have been my surprise,' said Steve. 'Why don't you take your mother to see the horses while I speak to Jenny.'

Sam grinned.

'Come on, Mum. You'll love them.'

Susan smiled as she followed Sam and Jock. Father O'Doyle after a glance at Steve's face, followed them. 'What's this about Broom Cottage?'

'Susan fell in love with it and Sam thinks he's found heaven. It's only by promising we'll come back that he's agreeing to go home.'

'You don't have to buy it.'

'Oh yes we do,' laughed Steve, 'but you can use it for others when we're not in residence. And jenny.' She raised her brows in query. 'I've left a cheque in the office. It's a mere token of thanks. You can buy all the books I'm going to write and put them in your library. I promise you that they will be quality books which many people will read. I shall tell all my friends about Strathard and what you are trying to do here. They will visit in droves. Now don't look so worried. I'm by no means out of the wood yet, I know. I will have my battles to fight but this time they will be real battles and I shall know what I am fighting for. Sam says he's going to keep his eye on me. He's grown up these last few days. I'll be in good hands and I know I will win in the end because, as our friend and Doctor of Philosophy might say, I have found my motivation.'

'I'm glad,' said jenny, 'and good luck.'

The others returned and with excitement and good humour they squeezed into Father O'Doyle's little mini and, arms waving from all windows, set off to his chapel on the coast with the leaking roof and the waiting Saint Vincent of the Builders.

Jenny watched them go but, despite the happy interlude, she knew that's all it had been - an interlude. Her worry and concern had been merely suspended.

With the speed at which things were happening, it hardly surprised her when Moira turned up at the farm.

'I've come to save your marriage and my own skin,' she said. 'I must be sure that Neil isn't here.'

'He isn't here,' confirmed Jenny.

'I've been trying to get in touch with you all morning. Where have you been?'

'Why are you here?' countered jenny.

'It's vital I speak to you before you see Neil.'

'Then speak.'

'He came to see me earlier about the letter I sent him. Don't look so worried. It's all right. At least, it will be if you can keep your mouth shut.'

With mixed feelings jenny listened to an account of Neil's meeting with Moira. He had assumed that Jenny knew nothing about the letter and, according to Moira, had threatened her within an inch of her life if she breathed a word to her sister.

'Didn't you tell him that I knew you had sent the letter?' Of course not. You don't argue with Neil Fraser when he's angry.'

Jenny smiled inwardly. How well she knew.

'He doesn't want you threatened in any way. Not a hair on your head has to be harmed, not a word of gossip - as he called it - must reach your delicate ears.'

'Moira!' Jenny cut in, 'Why? Did he say why?'

'Did he have to? Do you have to ask? He loves you - unconditionally it would seem. How do you do it, sister? Steve, Todd, Neil all ready to die for you.'

'Don't exaggerate,' said Jenny firmly but inside she was wobbling like a half-set jelly.

Moira, afraid of Neil turning up and finding her with Jenny, made a hasty retreat. Long after she had gone Jenny brooded on her visit. So he knew. What a clever actor her husband had become. She should be feeling reassured. She was to be spared the great denouement. Neil loved her *unconditionally*. The word troubled her. She remembered a time when she had pitied him because he did not know the meaning of that concept. She had been so quick to claim its significance for herself.

When Todd had returned to Strathard so bruised and battle-scarred it had evoked a mixed response in her husband. He had instinctively felt threatened by the love he knew she felt for Todd. He had also felt reassured that Todd's disfigurement would destroy this love. It had been impossible for him to imagine that she could continue to love a man so physically disfigured and that her passion for Todd could ever survive his shattered good looks. She had despised him for this and considered him incapable of understanding the meaning of unconditional love.

'Love is not love which alters when it alteration finds,' one of her 'friends' had written and Jenny had proved that so. Now she must go home and find out if Neil's love for her was unaltered or, what was more likely, he was just going to do the noble thing.

However, if what Moira had said were true, her marriage was secure and her life was not going to be turned on its head. Neil wasn't going to make an issue out of her deceit. The old Neil would have waved his bannered principles before her eyes.

Had he changed so much that he was prepared to protect her in spite of his rigid rules of morality? Why? Was it his unconditional love for her or was it his own need of security?

We've all changed, she decided. My dashing Lochinvar has changed to Parsifal and he has already left me and embarked on a quest for his Holy Grail.

A terrible sadness dropped on her like a deathly shroud. Where is my Holy Grail? Where are all those high ideals? Compromised! They were buried in the dregs of her five poisons. She searched her soul for comfort. She could not follow Todd but she had Neil. They had each other. She clung to this thought as she entered her car for the journey home.

Then it happened! Her intuition which had served her so well in the past sprang unannounced into her consciousness, by-passing logic and intellect and going directly to her heart. And she understood.

As her hands rested lightly on the wheel, she gazed through the window of her car. The half mile of scrubland between the farm and the gardens with the silhouetted castle turrets beyond had disappeared. She was gazing into Theresa's crystal ball. She saw the golden corn, with the protective trees and nurturing sun. It was all there, ripe and ready for reaping. Then it faded out and in its place was barren land. As she looked she saw a few blades push through the hard and crusted soil in their instinctive efforts to reach the sun. The few became more, then many, pushing, multiplying, enriching until breast-high and golden, just ripe enough for reaping.

She sat looking through her windscreen until the vision dissolved and the scrubland and gardens beyond with their protecting castle turrets returned. Dropping her head on her hands which had never left the steering wheel, she unashamedly shed a tear. She understood now why both she and her husband had changed. Had the vision in the quartz crystal come from Theresa's subconscious? she wondered. Would Theresa remember from the Edinburgh days when her friend Jenny had been so aware of the challenges life offered and when her ideals for living had shone like beacons on a hilltop? Those beacons were going to light up her life, she had told Theresa. What matter that her husband and she had differences, that their love had many loopholes and that their marriage was struggling on hard ground, leaving much to be desired? She was developing her 'God within' and Neil was working hard for his 'God out there'. With a surfeit of faith in her own ability she had told Theresa that she would sow seeds of kindness in every crevice she could find. She would drop them in the cracks where they would germinate and eventually push their way to the sun. She would work hard to make their marriage more fertile, especially for the sprouting of ideas.

She had worked hard. Neil had worked hard. The cracks had widened. The seeds had multiplied. The crop of kindness had grown. Now it was breast-high and golden and ready for reaping. Did it matter that her spur to effort had been to salve her conscience? She had not starved her husband of affection. She had enough love for Todd and him, or so she had thought. Had Todd known better? Had Neil known better? Had any of them been able to do other than they had done? Were all three of them working through their karma? Had they transformed themselves and each other? There were so many questions but only one to which she now had the answer. She loved her husband. She turned on the ignition and let in the clutch. The question now, she asked herself, is how does Neil feel? How does he really feel? Very soon now, she would find out.

She stepped back from the window as her husband arrived home. She did not want him to know that he was being observed. He made the unusual decision of closing the gate, generally left open for the convenience of cars. To Jenny, it seemed symbolic of shutting out the world. But he still seemed to carry the world's cares on his slightly stooping shoulders, in the awkwardness of his gait and the downcast eyes as if in search of something lost.

She watched him pause for a moment before raising his eyes to the church spire. Next they swept the landscape of the adjoining moors. What was he thinking? Taking time to stand and stare? Or did he too have a crystal ball vision? Instead of a field of ripe corn was he seeing, like the self-deluded Stevenson Bruce, a blemished vestment symbolising betrayal.

As she watched him turn towards the house and saw his shoulders square, a rush of feeling threatened to overwhelm her. They had come through so much together, starting their relationship from opposite ends of the love spectrum. Now they were meeting where it mattered most - face to face with their realities to themselves and to each other. What were they discovering? The beauty and truth of a Song of Solomon perhaps. "Many waters cannot quench love, neither can the floods drown it." Her heart now burst in full flood of her own emotions. She was waiting for him in the hall as he let himself in.

'Hello,' he said, trying to instil lightness in the somber salutation.

'Let me help you,' she said as he struggled with his jacket. She slipped it gently down his extended arms and turned to hang it on the hall stand. His expression was nfathomable when she turned to face him.

'Now *you* look exhausted,' she said. 'You've been working hard. You need to rest.'

Quieting her desire to hold him, she made to pass when he stopped her.

'It isn't rest I need, Jenny.'

She had never seen him look so vulnerable and in need of protection.

'I need you.' It came as a whisper hoarse with emotion. Their eyes met and neither could look away. 'I need you so much. I love you so much. I want you so much.'

They clung together, in individual need and interdependency. His lips sought hers while his arms tightened round her body. As her fingers crept through his hair and his lips now travelled her face, she understood what it meant to hear the voice of an angel.

'Thou are blessed among women,' it was saying.

Gently he disentangled his body, walked to the door and turned the key in the lock. Leaning against the banister and already tingling with expectancy, she watched him take the telephone off the hook. She held out her hand as he returned to her.

'Come,' he said, leading her to the stairs.

Gladly she went, knowing it was now the time to reap her harvest.